A WARRIOR'S CURSE

SAGA OF THE KNOWN LANDS

BOOK THREE

By

JACOB PEPPERS

This book is a work of fiction. Names, characters, places and incidents are either the product of the author's imagination or are used fictitiously. Any resemblance to actual persons, living or dead, or to actual events or locales is entirely coincidental.

A Warrior's Curse: Saga of the Known Lands Book 3
This book is licensed for your personal enjoyment only. This book may not be re-sold or given away to other people. If you would like to share this book with another person, please purchase an additional copy for each person you share it with. If you're reading this book and did not purchase it, or it was not purchased for your use only, then you should return to the retailer and purchase your own copy. Thank you for respecting the hard work of the author.

Copyright © 2022 Jacob Nathaniel Peppers. All rights reserved, including the right to reproduce this book, or portions thereof, in any form. No part of this text may be reproduced, transmitted, downloaded, decompiled, reverse engineered, or stored in or introduced into any information storage and retrieval system, in any form or by any means, whether electronic or mechanical without the express written permission of the author. The scanning, uploading, and distribution of this book via the Internet or via any other means without the permission of the publisher is illegal and punishable by law. Please purchase only authorized electronic editions, and do not participate in or encourage electronic piracy of copyrighted materials.

The publisher does not have any control over and does not assume any responsibility for author or third-party websites or their content.

Visit the author's website:
www.JacobPeppersAuthor.com

This book is dedicated to child number three,

He or she who is currently residing in my wife's belly.

Sorry for not knowing your gender—your mom wanted us to be surprised.

What can I say? She's a glutton for punishment.

Which, of course, goes a long way to explaining why she married me.

Anyway, I can't wait to meet you.

And hey, if you could come out with a name-tag, that'd really speed things along.

Sign up for the author's mailing list and for a limited time receive a FREE copy of *The Silent Blade*, prequel to the bestselling fantasy series *The Seven Virtues*.
Head to JacobPeppersAuthor.com and get your free book now!

CHAPTER ONE

Men like to believe their dreams, their nightmares, no more than figments of weary minds, errant phantoms which signify nothing. But dreams are not figments—they are mirrors. Mirrors which, free of our waking designs, free of the lies we tell ourselves, reflect one thing and one thing only—
The truth.
—Excerpt from "Between Light and Shadow" by Philosopher Hiladrian Elrest

He dreamed of her again that night.

Perhaps it was being back in the castle, where he had first seen her, where they had first met. Perhaps it was the newfound knowledge that Matt was his son. Or perhaps it was simply because sometimes he dreamed, and often, when he dreamed, he dreamed of her.

He dreamt of that night, the night when stolen glances and whispered words became something more, when he became a traitor to his brother not just in thought but in deed.

After days and weeks of lust, of *need*, a need more powerful than any he had ever felt, a letter had come, slid quietly beneath the door to his quarters. He remembered that he had been holding his axe at the time, the Destroyer of Pacts, the one gifted him by the Fey king Yeladrian. He did not remember why.

He had set the axe down, had, in that moment, laid down one sin for another. He walked to the door, knelt, and retrieved the letter.

Come to me.

Three words and three words only. It was all it had taken. Three words to destroy a relationship between two brothers, one that had been a lifetime in the building. Three words to destroy a kingdom.

Cutter liked to believe, remembering that night, that he had hesitated, that, having some inkling of what might be lost, he had paused to consider. But the truth was that he did not pause. He laid his axe down, for he would not need it, not that night. The greatest sunderings of the world, after all, happen not with a sword or axe, but with a word, with a gesture.

The guards normally posted at the hallway to her quarters were nowhere in evidence, and he grinned as he walked to her door, as perverse an expression, recalling it now, as it might be on the face of a headsman about his task.

He knocked. The door eased open of its own accord, and *she* was there. Waiting for him. Naked and pale in the moonlight. Naked and pale and beautiful. And he did what the man he had been always did—he saw what he wanted, and he took it. He took it because some part of him, a very large part, believed that he was owed it, that he *deserved* it, even while another part screamed that he did not.

Even now, looking back, he could not say that they made love, though he wished he could. He wished that his greatest crime could at least have had something of love in it. But no. She had offered, and he had done what he always did. He took.

In time it was over and they lay in her bed, the light of the stars pouring in through her balcony window, spilling across the floor like a doorway to another world. She said nothing, but her eyes, as dark and deep and mysterious as the night itself, spoke volumes.

"What's wrong?" he asked.

"Much," she said quietly, almost too quiet to hear. "Too much." She turned to him then, and in her gaze he thought he saw some of the truth of his crime, some knowledge of what the days to follow would bring, all of his own doing. "Do you not understand that? Do you not understand what we have done?"

"We've done what we wanted," he said, "what *both* of us wanted. It's not like we committed a crime, hurt anybody. We didn't do anything wrong." But even as he said the words, he felt the lie in them.

She smiled then, but it was a smile sadder than any frown he had ever seen. "Oh, Prince, but you are wrong. The worst of the world's tragedies are not born from hate but from love. Often it is love for one's self, but it is love just the same. And what we have done here...it is a great tragedy."

He grunted, saying nothing, for he knew that she wanted something from him, something he could not give.

In time, she spoke again. "Deeds done in the darkness bear fruit in the day."

He frowned. "What's that supposed to mean?" he asked, though he knew well enough. Even then, he knew.

"Nothing," she said sadly, giving her head a shake as if to shrug off some errant thought. "It is only something my mother used to say to me. My real mother, long ago."

He thought to ask her, then, what she meant by that, for he had met her mother, her father, too, and they *were* her real ones. Her identity would have been verified early on in her and Feledias's courting, that much was sure. Which meant that there was something buried within her words, some truth, one that puzzled him even now, so many years later. But the man who lay in the bed was angry; he always was, but angrier now that she had shown him the blemish upon what they had done. Had shown him that the flower he had grasped had wilted in his hands as it must and never mind that it was he who had done the wilting. In that moment, he hated her for that. Hated her for the truth, and so he scowled, leaving the question unasked.

The dream shifted, the world blurring, taking with it her room, her bed, her face, blank with grief, her eyes filled to brimming with unshed tears. It took her, too, in time. In time, it took even him.

But he did not wake, not then, for the dream was not finished with him, nor he it. He was standing before her again, only this time he did not relive his crime itself but the product of it as she lay in the bed, exhausted and covered in sweat, the sheets stained from the difficult birth.

"I...have something I would ask of you," she said.

"Anything."

"If something should happen to me—"

"Nothing's going to happen to you."

"But if it does...will you watch out for him?"

"Of course." Two words, and though he did not know it at the time, they would change the course of his life forever.

Come to me, she had said, and with three words a life had been destroyed.

Of course, he had said, and with two words, a new one had begun.

There was a loud knock, and he started, sure that it was his brother, Feledias, come to see his bride, sure that he would find him here, would find her, and would know the truth. He looked back at her, expecting to see the fear of that knowledge on her own features, but she did not react. In fact, she looked frozen, impossibly still, looking at him as she had been.

The knock came again, louder this time, so loud that it seemed to reverberate inside his head, so loud that it shook the floor beneath his feet, the bed upon which she lay, the entire room...yet still she did not move.

A third knock and the scene before him shattered, and he jerked up.

He was not in the dream any longer but in his quarters in the castle once more. He was breathing hard, his body covered in sweat, and he rubbed a hand across his face, across his weary eyes.

He glanced at the window. It was still in the deep of night which meant he had only lain down a few hours ago. He frowned. Had the knock been real or had he only imagined it? And what felt far more pressing—what had she meant by her *real* mother?

He told himself it was probably nothing, no more than a false memory, his mind adding things that weren't there as men's minds often did when looking at the past, making the light brighter, the shadows lighter, smoothing the edges away. The problem, though, was that it did not *feel* like a false memory. It felt true.

He was still puzzling over that when another knock came on the door, answering one question at least, and he rose, wondering who might be calling on him in the middle of the night. He walked to the door barefoot and opened it to find two castle guards standing outside. He did not recognize them, but then that was no great surprise. Fifteen years was a long time, and even back then he had rarely spent time getting to know the guards. He did note, however, that both men looked winded, and there was a wildness in their eyes.

"Yes?" he asked. "What is it?"

"Prince Bernard," one panted, "i-it's King Matthias, sir. He's in trouble."

Cutter frowned, his heart beginning to race. "Trouble? What kind of trouble?"

"Assassins, sir," the man said, "they've broken into the castle."

Assassins. A shock of cold fear ran through him as if he had just leapt into a frozen winter lake. "Show me," he growled, not stopping to get his boots, not stopping, in fact, even to get his axe.

The guards jogged down the hallway, and he followed them, his hands knotting into fists as he recalled the promise he'd made, one he'd so recently been reminded of in his dream. He had promised to protect him. "Where is he?" he demanded.

"This way, sir," one of the guards said, still jogging, "it's not far now."

Cutter had a thousand questions, not the least of which was why these men were coming to get him instead of doing their job and defending their sovereign king against assassins. He was just about to ask them when the two guards stopped in front of a door. "The king's through here, sir."

Cutter frowned. He might not have paid much attention to the guards in the castle, but he had lived years in the castle itself and he knew every nook and cranny, every room, every hidden alcove. Or, at least, he had fifteen years ago, and the door at which they stood had once led to a large storeroom for ale and other goods. "Are you sure?"

"Yes, sir," the guard said, "the king told us to get you and bring you here as quickly as we could."

"Alright. Let's go then."

He moved past the guards, opening the door and stepping through. He paused inside the room, frowning. The room was completely dark. "Matt?" he asked, walking further in, his hands out in front of him. "Where are you, lad?"

A moment later, he heard the footsteps of the guards as they followed behind him, heard, too, as they closed the door. And as it closed, a thought struck him, one that he would have had earlier had he not allowed his fear for Matt's safety to override his reason. A foolish mistake, but it was too late now, so he asked the obvious question. "Where is he then? Where's Matt?"

"Don't you mean *King* Matthias?" someone said from the darkness, and it was not one of the guards who had spoken but someone standing ahead of him.

Cutter narrowed his eyes, peering into the darkness. "Who are you? What's the meaning of this?"

Suddenly, ruddy orange light bloomed in the darkness, revealing three men. All had swords bared, and the one in the center was the one that held the lantern. Beyond the three men, as Bernard remembered, were rows after rows of stacked barrels on shelves. Still a storeroom then but, at that moment, what caught his attention was the man holding the lantern, for his was a face he recognized. "You're the escort," he said. "The man who works for Belle."

The man grinned, displaying his teeth. "I would worry less about others and more about myself, were I you, Prince. What is the meaning of this, you asked. Well, that is easily answered—the meaning, Prince, is your death."

Cutter frowned. "With me," he said to the guards behind him, but when they did not move he glanced back and saw that while they had drawn their swords, their blades were not pointed at the three men waiting in ambush but instead at him.

"That's the way of it, then," he growled.

"Aye, Prince," his once escort said, grinning widely once more, "that is the way of it. You see, there is someone out there who is willing to pay a pretty penny for that head of yours, and they're not all particular on whether or not the rest of you is attached to it, if you catch my meaning."

"I think I do," Cutter said, doing his best to keep track of the men ahead and behind with his gaze. "But how did you get into the castle?"

The man laughed. "The same way that you got into the dungeons to rescue that historian of yours, Prince." He shrugged. "Suffice to say, we got in because we wanted to. Do you know," he went on, cocking his head, "I have thought of this moment often. Wondered what it would be like to kill not just some guardsman or rival crime boss, but to feel my sword take the life of what the fools believe to be the world's greatest warrior."

"Well," Cutter said. "We all have our dreams."

The man sneered. "So we do, though in my dreams I must admit that you always carried your axe. A foolish mistake, and one you will pay for. You should have brought your axe, Prince."

"And you should have brought more men," Cutter growled. Then, before the man could say anything more, Cutter spun on the two guards behind him. One lunged forward, meaning to impale him on his blade, but Cutter caught his wrist, changing the sword's course so that it drove deep into the stomach of his attacker's companion instead.

The companion in question screamed in surprised pain as the blade sank in, but Cutter paid him no mind. Instead, he gave the wrist he held a savage twist, until he heard, until he *felt* the thin bones of the man's wrist *snap*. Then the guard was screaming along with his companion, at least, that was, until Cutter grabbed him by the face and slammed the back of his head into the stone wall.

There was a sickening, meaty, *squishing* sound, and the man's eyes rolled back into his head. Cutter released the body to collapse at his feet. He reached down to retrieve the sword, but a metallic blur flashed toward him, and he stumbled away, though not quick enough to avoid a shallow but painful cut along his arm before the metal struck the stone wall in a shower of sparks.

Hissing, his hand clamped over the bleeding wound, Cutter backed away as the three men eased toward him, and he saw that the one who'd scored him was the assassin who worked for Belle.

"Two...down," Cutter said as the men slowly followed him.

The man grinned. "It matters not. You only saved me the trouble of killing them myself—I *abhor* loose ends, you see. And now my blade has tasted a prince's blood." His smile widened. "And it will taste more before I'm through."

Cutter allowed them to force him back in the direction of the rows of barrels, barrels heavy with ale, allowed them to think they had him cornered. Which was no difficult matter as, of course, they did.

"Who hired you?" he asked.

"Oh no," the man said, "no, Prince, I believe I will keep that bit of information to myself, and you will go to your death knowing that all of those you call friends will soon meet you in the afterlife."

Cutter continued to back up, into an aisle surrounded by barrels sitting on shelves. Here, the men would not be able to surround him and would be forced to come at him one at a time. They followed him, as he'd known they would, and he allowed himself to stumble on the cobbled stone, catching himself on the shelf just in time to keep from falling over. Which made it easier, as one of the assassins rushed forward, intent on taking advantage of the opportunity, to lever one of the barrels out.

It was heavy, that barrel, and Cutter grunted with effort as he pulled it free then stepped to the side, avoiding the man's darting sword before bringing the barrel and its contents crashing down on his head.

The barrel had been made with thick, heavy, wood, built to withstand time and any accidental knocks it received, but what Cutter did was no accident. He brought it down with all the force he could muster, the staves of the barrel shattering on the man's head. Ale spewed out, showering the floor and shelves, Cutter himself, and the man collapsed, his head and face covered in blood and ale.

"Die, you bastard!" someone shouted, and Cutter looked up in time to see another of the men charging toward him, bringing his sword down in a two-handed grip. Cutter leapt to the side, slamming hard into the shelves and narrowly avoiding the sharp steel. The man struck the puddle of beer and stumbled, losing his balance. Before he could recover Cutter promptly kicked his shin, and the man screamed as it broke.

He fell at his feet, and Cutter stomped on him again, only this time his foot landed not on the man's leg but his face, and he felt his attacker's nose shatter beneath his heel, felt a sharp pain as something—perhaps one of the man's teeth—dug into the bottom of his foot.

The only sound to alert him to the last assassin's approach was the soft padding of his footfalls in the spilled ale, and Cutter looked up in time to see Belle's man bearing down on him, his sword flashing in a blur. With no weapon to defend himself, he was forced back under the assault, doing his best to keep out of the way of the darting blade but receiving several cuts along his arms and chest for those times when he inevitably failed.

Cutter stumbled out of the aisle, bleeding from a dozen shallow cuts, and the man followed, taking his time now, in no hurry. "Time to die, Prince."

Exhausted, hurting, without so much as a knife to defend himself, Cutter was in no position to argue, and as the man darted forward again, his blade lashing out, all he could do was try to dodge.

The man made a game of it, his blade licking this way and that, leaving lines of fire along Cutter's flesh where it scored him. The man continued, enjoying himself, confident, as he should have been. But too confident. When he lunged forward, meaning to impale Cutter, Cutter, lacking the energy to jump out of the way, turned so that the blade cut a thin, crimson line across his stomach and caught the man's wrist.

The assassin had time for his eyes to go wide in realization of his mistake, but that realization came too late, and with a growl, Cutter picked him up in both hands and hurled him at the shelves. He struck hard, wood splintering as he did, and the sword he'd held was sent flying off into the darkness.

The man lay gasping, moaning on the floor, and Cutter watched him, his chest heaving, his body smarting with the many cuts he'd received. Then he shambled forward until he stood over his would-be assassin. He knelt with an effort, jerking the man up by the front of his shirt and slamming his back against the shelves again. "Who sent you?" Cutter growled. "Who's after Matt?"

The man showed a bloody grin. "Stones and starlight, but you have no idea what's going on, do you?"

"So why don't you tell me?" Cutter growled, giving the man a shake. He was thinking only of Matt, of his safety, and was intent on the man, on getting an answer out of him. It was for this reason, then, that he did not notice the man's hand dart to his belt where a dagger was sheathed, was not aware of it at all until he felt the blade plunge into his thigh.

Cutter roared in pain and surprise. He grabbed the man's head in both hands and, before he could think better of it, gave it a hard *jerk*, and was rewarded with the sound of his neck snapping.

Cutter blinked, staring at what he'd done, cursing himself for a fool as he let the body slump to the ground. He was tired. Exhausted really, and he wanted nothing more than to lie down and rest for a while.

But Matt could be in danger of being attacked, might, for all he knew, be being attacked already, so Cutter grabbed hold of the shelves and with a feral growl levered himself to his feet. He made his way slowly, painfully, back through the aisle, hissing in agony as he knelt to retrieve one of the assassins' swords from where it had fallen during the fight. That done, he rose, wincing at his many wounds. He left then, leaving the storeroom and the dead to care for themselves.

In the castle hallway, he glanced around, his vision blurring, trying to decide where Matt would be. It should have been an easy enough thing, but he'd lost a lot of blood, and his thoughts felt as if they were swimming. He was having difficulty concentrating on anything, and it took all of his willpower, all of his attention just to keep his feet beneath him.

Matt, he suspected, would be in his quarters, but they were all the way across the castle, and he knew he would not make it that far. He hesitated, unsure of what to do, scared that, whatever he did, he would be too late, when suddenly he had an idea.

Challadius.

The mage's quarters were near this area of the castle. At least, he thought they were. With one hand on the wall to support himself, Cutter began lumbering down the hall in the direction he believed them to be.

It could have taken him no more than a few minutes to reach the man's room, but it felt as if he walked for a lifetime, his body on fire with pain, leaving a bloody trail behind him to mark his path. Finally, though, he made it to the door and, using one hand on the frame to prop himself up, banged on it with his other fist.

He waited a moment, but there was no response, and he began to think that he had been wrong. It was a big castle after all and in his current state, with his vision blurring and his thoughts scattering like leaves in a high wind, it was no surprise that he had gotten turned around. Still, he knew that he would not make it much farther, had only minutes at most before the loss of blood robbed him of consciousness, so hoping against hope, he knocked again.

"*Just hold on a damned minute!*"

Cutter blinked, wavering drunkenly, as a great feeling of relief washed over him, for the voice was one he recognized.

Moments later, the door swung open, revealing the mage. "Just what in the name of the gods are you doing waking a man u—" The man cut off, staring at him with wide eyes. "P-Prince Bernard?" he asked. "I-is that you?"

"C-call me Cutter," he said, with no idea of why he said it.

"More like Cut, if you ask me," Chall said in shock. "Fire and salt, Prince, is that blood on your...everything?"

"Yes," Cutter said, feeling his speech slurring. "Not all of it's mine...some is."

"And is...is there a *knife* sticking out of your leg?"

"Last...I checked," Cutter said, holding onto consciousness like a man hanging from a great drop and scrabbling at the cliff face, knowing, even as he did, that it was not a question of *if* he would fall, only *when.* "Assassins," he croaked. "In...the castle. Have to find...Matt. Keep him...safe."

"What we have to do is get you to a healer," Chall said "if you're even half as bad off as you look then there isn't much time."

"*No,*" Cutter growled, grabbing the man by the front of his nightshirt. "Matt...first."

"Okay, Prince," the mage said, his face pale with fright. "Okay."

"Okay," Cutter agreed.

Then he passed out.

CHAPTER TWO

I met a man today,
Walking down the street
He stood to bar my way
He said it's time we meet
Not now, I said, there are those who for me wait,
He laughed then, and told me I should stay
For the dead do not hurry—and they are never late.
—Avaress the Bard, known as "The Drunken Poet"

He drifted in a great black ocean, a black sky overhead. He could not move, could not swim, could only lie there as the water buoyed him up one moment and dragged him down the next, going from breathing to drowning, from living to dying and back again on the current's whim.

Then, suddenly, he was drifting no longer. There was a break in the dark clouds overhead, a peek of sunlight, and within that sunlight, a face, one he knew.

"M-Maeve?" he croaked, his throat as dry as if someone had been at it with sandpaper.

"It's me, Prince," she said, her features twisted with concern. "Thank the gods, you're awake. The healer...he said...he didn't know..." She cut off then, turning away, but not so quickly that he did not see the tears in her eyes.

"She said..." Cutter hesitated, clearing his throat. "She said...her real mother."

Maeve turned back to him then and, if anything, she looked even more worried than before. "Wait here, Prince," she said, wiping at her eyes, "I'll go get the healer and—"

He reached out, weakly grabbing her wrist as she rose from the bed. "W-wait, Maeve," he said. "Wait. Matt...is...is he..."

"Matt is fine, Prince," she said, the tears spilling freely down her face now. "The men, whoever they were...they didn't come for him or, it seems anyone else in the castle. They came for you."

"For...me," Cutter said, blinking, feeling great relief that Matt was safe, feeling as if some crushing weight had been lifted from him.

"Yes," she said. "To kill you, and they damn near succeeded. Maybe next time you'll think twice before following men you don't know into a castle storeroom."

She must have seen some of his confusion in his face, for she gave an angry laugh. "Oh yes, Prince, we found the storeroom. It wasn't all that hard—all we had to do was follow the trail of blood. What were you *thinking* following them in there? And without your axe? What were you—" She shook her head angrily. "No, never mind. It doesn't matter. All that matters is that you're okay, that you're alive. Now, I'm going to go get the healer—you stay here. You're alive and by the gods I intend for you to stay that way."

Cutter wanted to stop her, but he did not have the strength, barely had the strength left to speak. She wondered what he had been thinking, but he realized the truth was that he hadn't been. The men had told him Matt was in trouble, and that had been all he needed to know. He had not thought, after that, had only reacted.

A warrior without reason, without logic, is only a corpse. His father's words, told to him long ago after one training session with his master-at-arms when Cutter had grown angry, when he had allowed his emotions to get the better of him and so had lost.

Words from long ago, yes, but true words just the same, and they were the words that accompanied him as he drifted back into the darkness, without Maeve to anchor him to the world.

The next time he came to he saw another figure sitting beside his bed. It was not Maeve, not this time, but was still someone he recognized. "Hello...brother," he managed.

Feledias had been busy studying his hands, looking at them as if they belonged to someone else, and he glanced up with an almost guilty expression on his face, his eyes widening. "You're awake. The healer said that he believed you had made it past the worst, said that he thought you would recover, but I confess I had my doubts."

"What...what are you doing here?" Cutter managed.

Feledias cocked his head at him, studying him with a strange expression. Slowly, his eyes widened, and he nodded in realization. "Ah. You are wondering if I came to finish the assassins' job for them, is that it?"

"Have you?"

His brother seemed to think that over then finally shook his head. "No. I will admit that I considered it. After all, though you helped to save the city, that does not change what you...what you did."

"No."

"I tell you that I considered killing you while you lay unconscious from your wounds and that's all you have to say?" Feledias said, anger flashing in his eyes.

"What...would you have me say?"

His brother shook his head in a mixture of anger and amazement. "My brother, the hero, the legendary warrior. Too brave to feel fear, too stubborn to die, even when five assassins set their minds to it, and he is weaponless."

"Not...too brave," Cutter said. "I feel...fear, Fel," he managed in a croaking whisper. "The truth...the truth is...I feel little else."

His brother watched him in silence for several moments. "Well. At any rate, you'll be happy to know that I've decided not to kill you—not yet at least."

"Thanks."

"Don't mention it. Anyway, in all my imaginings of your death—and there were a lot, I won't deny it—I never pictured stabbing you in your sleep or suffocating you while you were too weak to fight me." His brother made a face as if he had just eaten something sour. "The thought didn't sit well with me."

"Fel...the assassins...do we know who they were?"

His brother shook his head. "Not yet. I've got my captain of the guard—or, I suppose I should say *Matthias's* captain of the guard looking into their identities, though. It's only a matter of time before we know everything there is to know about them from the names of their favorite pets to the names of their mothers and fathers."

"Their *real* mothers," Cutter said.

Feledias frowned. "What's that?"

Cutter winced. "Tell me...Fel. About Layna—"

"No, brother," Feledias interrupted in a growl. "No. I will not kill you, but neither can I forgive you, and I will not speak to you of her. Do you understand?"

Cutter nodded, his breath catching at the pain even so small a movement caused. "I understand."

His brother sat back at that, nodding. "Only what, five, six men? And look at you," his brother said, glancing over Bernard, his eyes taking in his naked chest—naked, at least, save the bandages wrapped around him almost anywhere visible. "There was a time when I would have given you odds against twice as many. So what's changed? Is it age finally catching up with you, brother, or is it something else?"

Cutter recounted the way he had charged after men, giving no thought to why the guards would have come to him instead of rousing the entire castle, no thought to why Matthias himself might not have come if he wanted him and there were assassins pursuing him. "I acted like a fool," he said, "and while a man might act a fool for free—"

"There is always a cost," Feledias finished, giving him a wry smile. "One of Father's favorite sayings."

"He had many favorites," Cutter agreed, giving a smile of his own.

"Yes, yes he did."

The two sat in silence then and for a few brief moments Bernard felt that they were closer than they had been in many years, closer than they had been even before his betrayal, since before the Skaalden had invaded their homeland.

"Bernard—" Feledias began, and then, suddenly, there was a knock on the door. His brother cut off. "Don't get up," he said with a smile as he examined Cutter's bandaged form. "I'll get it." He moved to the door then paused with his hand on the handle, glancing back. "If it's assassins should I just let them in, or would you prefer them to lead you to an area of their choosing? Maybe a dark storeroom or some back alley?"

"Not going to live that down, am I?"

"Make many more such senseless decisions, Bernard," Feledias said, "and you won't live at all."

"Which, of course, would get you all choked up."

"Positively bereft," his brother answered. He opened the door then, and Cutter saw that Maeve and Chall stood on the other side.

"Eh...Prince," Chall said uncertainly.

"Mage," Feledias said dryly.

They stood in uncomfortable silence for a few seconds until Maeve and Chall looked past Feledias to Cutter lying in the bed. "You're awake!" Chall said, rushing forward and burying Cutter in a massive hug which made him let out an involuntary groan.

"Sorry," the mage said, quickly pulling away. "Too tight?"

"Only...when I need to breathe," Cutter said, giving him a grin to show that it was a joke—which, of course, it wasn't.

He glanced at Maeve and saw her looking at the mage's back with a rare, unguarded expression of love. "Maeve," he said.

The woman started then flushed, lifting something which he realized, in another moment, was his axe. "I got this for you. Thought maybe if you meant to be getting in many more life or death fights you'd best keep it on you—you know, like someone who isn't a complete fool."

Cutter winced at that. "Thanks," he said as she propped it against the wall.

Maeve raised an eyebrow at him. "Don't mention it."

"So, how do you feel?" Chall asked, then winced. "Sorry, stupid question. I guess you probably feel like a man who got stabbed—like, a lot."

"Just a sec," Cutter said, then glanced past them at Feledias who still stood by the door, watching them with an unreadable expression on his face. "Hey, Fel. Thanks...for coming, I mean. And for not killing me. If you stick around, maybe we can talk more about—"

"No, no, that won't be necessary," his brother answered quickly. "We will talk later."

And with that, he retreated out of the room at a quicker pace than was strictly necessary.

Maeve and Chall watched him go then turned back. "And what was all that about?" Chall asked. "He come to finish what the assassins started?"

Cutter grunted a laugh and immediately regretted it as a fresh spasm of pain ran through him. "I hear he considered it."

"Oh, I wouldn't be overly worried about that, Prince," Maeve said, smiling, "I'm fairly sure we all have."

Cutter smiled. "It is good to see you both."

"It's good to be seen," Maeve said, putting a gentle hand on his shoulder. "Now all you've got to do is to avoid following assassins into shadowy alcoves for a little while and we can do a bit more seeing."

Cutter grunted. "So I've been told. Anyway, what news of the castle?"

"Well," Chall said, "they're considering remodeling some of the bedrooms, but to be honest, I don't really care for the proposed look, seems a bit too…you meant about the assassins."

Maeve rolled her eyes. "It's only been a few hours since last you and I spoke," she said to him. "Not much has changed since then. Despite Feledias's confidence in his guards' investigations, they haven't found out anything of note about the assassins so far except that they were alive and now they are dead."

"Very, very dead," Chall said, his face paling. "Gods, Prince, but if you are nothing else, you *are* thorough."

"And what was he *supposed* to do?" Maeve snapped. "*Not* kill them? Just let them go on about their bloody work?"

"Of course not," Chall said. "He had to kill them, I understand that. Only…" He glanced at Cutter. "Did you have to kill them so *much?*"

"Sorry, Chall," Cutter said, "I was a bit busy to take time to clean up after myself. I'll try to do better next time."

"Thank you," the mage said with relief, "that's all I'm saying."

Cutter shared a glance with Maeve. "Anyway, what of Priest? I would have thought to see him."

Maeve grunted. "He hasn't left Matt's side, not since the attack on you. He knew that you'd want someone to protect the boy—sorry, the *king*—and he insisted on taking the duty himself, won't even dream of letting me or Chall spot him for a while so he can take a break. I think he's scared he'll fail you again."

"He didn't fail me the first time."

"Maybe not," Maeve said, "but that's not the way he sees it."

"Anyway," Chall said, "he sent his regards but..." He paused, making a show of patting at his nightshirt. "Wouldn't you know it, I must have misplaced them."

Maeve rolled her eyes again. "Well, keep checking. I'm sure you're bound to find them in that tent you call a nightshirt sooner or later.

"And...Matt? How...how is he?"

The two shared a look at that. "He's fine, of course," Maeve said. "Maybe those assassins meant to come for him after they dealt with you, but thanks to you I'd say their assassinating days are well and truly over."

Cutter nodded. "Good. That's...good."

The two shared another troubled look, and this time it was Chall who spoke. "Prince, Matt—that is, the king—wants to come by. Only, with the assassination attempt and everything, he's been busy. I'm sure that as soon as things calm down, he'll—"

Cutter held up a hand, surprised by how much effort it took, how much pain it caused. "It's...fine, Chall. Really. He's busy—I understand that."

The two nodded in unison. "So," Maeve said. "What do we do now? Cutter?"

He realized that he'd allowed himself to become distracted thinking of the boy and grunted, meeting their eyes. "I've got some ideas about that. The man who led the assassins—he was the same man who worked for Belle, the one that got us into the dungeons."

They both looked shocked at that, Chall letting out a low whistle, and Cutter frowned. "Surely you knew that. After all, you would have recognized him."

Chall gave him a sickly smile. "You were...quite thorough, Prince. I'm fairly certain that, after what you did to those men, their own mothers wouldn't recognize them." He frowned. "Anyway, if that's true, and the men really were led by Belle's assassin then...what does it mean? That is, Belle's in prison, isn't she? Do you think that she's, what, somehow managed to talk to her men? And that she's ordered those men to assassinate us? Not liking a job left unfinished?"

Cutter gave a slight shake of his head. "I don't know. Maybe. Either way, I mean to find out."

He moved to get out of the bed, and Maeve put a hand on his chest. "No, sir. The healer said you need a week of rest, a week *at least,* I believe were his exact words. You tell us what you want to ask the woman, and I'll go myself."

Cutter grunted. "Don't you get it, Maeve? Those men who attacked me—at least some of them—they were *guards.*"

Maeve frowned. "I don't know what that's got to do with you getting better. I told you, Prince, Matt's taken care of—Priest is looking out for him, and we'll keep an eye on him too, just as often as we have them to spare."

Cutter sighed, shaking his head. "You're all talented, Maeve, I know that and there isn't anyone I'd rather have beside me in a scrap than the three of you. But there's no knowing how many of the guards are corrupted. Whether by Belle or by the Fey, it makes little difference. The three of you, however skilled, wouldn't stand a chance against so many."

"I'd like to see them try," she hissed angrily.

Cutter rubbed wearily at his eyes. "You're assuming you'll see them coming."

Chall frowned. "What do you mean?"

Cutter shrugged. "Only that if I were a corrupt guardsman looking to kill a famous assassin and an equally famous mage, I wouldn't bother doing it while they were awake. I'd wait until they'd gone to bed for the night then let myself in their rooms and slit their throats." He met the woman's eyes. "Everyone has to sleep, Maeve."

Both of their faces grew pale at that. "You mean..." Maeve said, "that you don't think the guards you fought were the only ones who were corrupt?"

Cutter met her eyes. "Do you?"

The woman winced, clearly not pleased by the thought. "No," she said finally, "no, I don't. Which, I suppose, means that you can't stay here."

Cutter shook his head. "I don't look forward to a knife in the throat any more than you do."

She sighed. "I still don't like it."

"What's to like?" Chall asked. "Fire and salt, but I would have thought things would have got less complicated after Matt became king, not more."

Maeve grunted. "Why in the name of the gods would you think that?"

Chall sighed. "I don't know. Just a fool, I guess."

"You'll get no argument here," Maeve said. "Anyway, if you can't stay here, and we can't trust the guards...what are we supposed to do?" she asked Cutter.

"I've got an idea about that," Cutter said. "But you're not going to like it."

"Well sure," Chall said. "I haven't liked pretty much anything up to this point and that's led us to exile, a price on our heads, and nearly being killed by...well, to be honest I've lost count. Anyway, why change now?"

"What do you intend?" Maeve asked.

"We've got a lot of questions that need answering," Cutter said, "and as far as I can tell, there's only one person that can give us answers."

She blinked. "You mean to go see Belle."

He nodded. "I do."

"The same Belle who, if you're right, ordered your assassination?"

"The same Belle who, thanks to Feledias, spent a full day and night being tortured before Matt took over and ordered it stopped. I doubt she's in any shape to threaten me, Maeve."

Maeve hissed. "She's not the problem, and you know it. A woman like that, she doesn't bother getting her own knife bloody—she's got plenty of hirelings to do it for her. And for all you know those same hirelings are working in the dungeons."

Cutter grunted. "If that were the case, I doubt she'd still be wasting away in some cell, don't you?"

She frowned. "Still, you don't *know*."

"No, I don't know, Maeve," he said. "What I *do* know is that I'm not in any more danger here than I will be there."

"Which is to say mortal peril," Chall grumbled.

Maeve shook her head, heaving a heavy sigh. "Fine. When should we visit this Belle?"

"I'm going alone."

"*What?*" Maeve snapped.

"You heard me, Maeve. I'm going alone."

"Fire and salt I bet you *aren't*," she growled.

"It's the way it has to be, Maeve."

"But *why?*" she demanded.

"For one, I don't think Belle would be as willing to talk to me if I showed up with a small army." She opened her mouth as if she would say something, and he held up a hand. "Let me say my piece, Maeve. I know Belle—or, at least, I know her type—and she'll be a lot more likely to talk to me if I'm alone, if she thinks she can work some sort of deal to her favor."

Maeve frowned. "What sort of deal?"

He shrugged. "A deal like letting her loose."

Maeve snorted then blinked, her eyes going wide. "Wait. You're serious."

"I promised her a boon, Maeve."

"Yeah," she snapped, "but I think that sort of ran out the same time she ordered assassins to come into the castle and kill you."

"We don't know that she was behind that."

"But we *do* know that she was behind telling Feledias where we were and trying to get us all killed. Or have you forgotten that little tidbit?"

He sighed. "You know I haven't."

"Then *why?*" she demanded. "Why put yourself at risk and walk there by yourself? By the gods, Prince, are you even sure you *can* walk?"

He gave her a small smile. "I think I remember how."

"That's not what I mean and you know it."

"I'll be fine, Mae," he said softly. "And it isn't as if we have any choice. Besides, I can't have you there—I need you and Chall to look after Matt. If things really are as bad as they seem, he'll need you more than me."

She glanced at the mage. "Well?" she demanded. "Aren't you going to say something?"

Chall winced. "I...I think he's right, Maeve." She made an angry sound at that, but he spoke over her. "Look, you've dealt with people like this, you know how they are. Criminals, all sneaky and shady. Anyway, he's right—she's locked in a cell, Maeve. She can't be too much danger there."

She hissed, rubbing at her temples as if a headache were beginning to form there before glancing back at Cutter. "I don't like this, Prince. Not any of it."

"I know," Cutter said quietly. "But what choice do we have?"

She sighed. "Seems I've been asking myself that my entire life. Fled Daltenia, left the bodies of my husband and child behind for those frost demons, the Skaalden, to do with what they would. Told myself I had no choice. Killed countless people over the years, countless creatures, and always I told myself I had no choice. That, deep down, I was a good person, just a person without any *choice*. But did you ever wonder, Prince, if maybe it just *seems* like we don't have a choice? That in fact there is another option, another way, but maybe our souls are just too stained to see it? Did you ever wonder if maybe we're not the bad guys after all, and all that telling ourselves there isn't a choice wasn't anything more than an excuse so that we could sleep when our heads hit the pillows at night?"

"Yes," Cutter said. "I've wondered."

She sighed again, seeming to somehow shrink. "That's it then."

"That's it."

She nodded. "Suppose you'll be careful?"

"As careful as I can be."

She met his eyes and for several seconds neither of them said anything, each of them thinking their own thoughts.

"Don't worry," Chall offered, "I'll be careful too."

"Oh don't you worry your pretty little head none, Chall," Maeve said. "You'll be with me, and I'll be careful enough for the two of us. Now, come on. Let's go find the king."

***

Chall waited until they'd stepped outside of the room and closed the door, until they had walked down the hallway, away from the prince's quarters, before he turned and glanced at Maeve. The woman looked troubled—but then, she always did. He wondered what she would think if he ever told her the truth, if he ever told her that so much of his jokes, his mocking demeanor was just because he wanted to see her smile.

It was a fine smile, the best he'd ever seen, at least he remembered it as such. It had been so long since he'd seen it last—sometimes it seemed to have been a lifetime—that it wasn't easy to know for sure. Probably, if he told her the truth, she'd laugh at him, and sometimes he thought maybe that would be okay. Better laughter, after all, than that terrible expression of worry and fear, and more than that, too. Pain, pain of the heart, as if she were grieving for some terrible tragedy, one that had yet to occur.

But then, they had both had more than their share of tragedy in their lifetime, and who was to say that she wasn't grieving for one that had already come to pass? "Maeve?" he asked softly, thinking that maybe he would tell her how he felt after all, that maybe he would tell her that he loved her, that he had always loved her.

"What is it, Chall?" she asked, turning to him with a weary expression on her face, weary and grieving all at once.

Probably she thought of her late husband, her daughter. *No, he decided. Now is not the time.* But then, that was the most damning part of it. He'd been waiting to tell her the truth for years, had mulled over what he might do, how he might say it, always waiting for the perfect time. Turned out, though, that there never was a good time to tell someone you loved them. Maybe there never was a good time for the truth at all. "Do you think..." he said, then seeing the grief on her face, the pain, decided he could not say it, not now, and changed what he'd been saying. "Do you think that we should have told him?"

"Told him what?" she asked, as if she had no idea what he was talking about.

"You know *what,*" he said. "I mean...Maeve, the gods know I've told my share of lies, mostly to farmers' daughters or farmers daughters' fathers, but not to the prince. He...doesn't he deserve to know the truth?"

"What *truth?*" she spat. "The truth that his *son,* the one who he has saved from so many terrible deaths over the last fifteen years that I've lost count, acts as if he doesn't even care that he nearly died? Do you mean that his son who he would do anything for—the one he *has* done everything for—can't even find it in his busy schedule to come visit him? That when we ask him about it he acts annoyed and tells us to leave his presence? Is that the truth you mean?"

Chall winced. "That's the one."

She shook her head. "No. The prince has enough trouble on his plate already without us adding to it, Chall. Better if we wait to tell him later." She sighed. "Assuming any of us survives the night."

And with that grim pronouncement, she quickened her pace. Chall watched her go, feeling pretty damned grim himself. At least, that was, until he noticed the way her hips swayed slightly as she walked, the way her hair swayed with her steps. Beautiful, the most beautiful woman he'd ever seen and time had done nothing to change that.

And what do you imagine she might say? he asked himself. *What do you imagine she might do? Declare her own undying love for you, and the two of you might run off into the sunset, leaving the kingdom and the corpses behind?*

He gave a soft, derisory snort. He'd always told himself that he'd only been pretending the fool in order to make her laugh, to see her smile, for it was a smile that was well worth the effort. Now, he decided that, having played the fool for so long, he'd quite gotten the hang of it. With a sigh, he followed her.

CHAPTER THREE

To fight the shadows, a man must first step into the darkness.
And sometimes, if he is not wary, he will get lost there.
  —An ex-communicated priest of Raveza

Cutter watched the mage and assassin leave, frowning as the door closed behind them. He'd known the pair for a long time. Sometimes, it seemed since birth. Not true, of course, but in many ways, it was. After all, he, they, *everyone* had been changed when they had been forced to flee their kingdom to make it away from the Skaalden. They had all been forced to come here, to this place of strangeness, of Fey creatures and the Black Wood, and find new lives for themselves.

It had been a grim trip over the great seas, one during which more than one ship and its inhabitants had been lost to the sea's terrible storms. Some others had simply vanished during the night, as if the vessels, and their grieving inhabitants—for all grieved in those days—simply sank beneath the water's surface, not even bothering to raise so much as a shout or a creaking timber in protest.

Yes, the people of Daltenia had been born again among the ocean's wind-tossed waves, birthed out of their grief. And if they were born again, then they had been born in the mist, in the cold that the frost demons brought with them, had been born and borne to a land that hated them. And since that day, he had known Maeve and Chall and Priest. He knew them better than anyone, knew them better, perhaps, than he knew himself.

It was for this reason that he knew they were keeping something from him. What that something was, he did not know and did not now have the time to think of it. Whatever it was would keep—it *must* keep, for there was much to be done.

He had to deal with the problems they faced, the corrupt guards, the Fey, or else Matt would never be safe. And so he rose from his bed. Or, at least, he tried to.

In actuality, he managed only to make it to where he was propped up on his elbows before his forehead was bathed in a cold sweat, and he collapsed, shaking and gasping with exhaustion and pain.

The greatest warrior in the world, his brother had said. Likely, he had been mocking when he said it, and he had been right to. Cutter never made any claims to being the greatest warrior in the world—not in fifteen years, at least—and no one would have claimed as much now, that was sure.

Besides, Cutter had seen many warriors in his time, and he knew well that he was not the most talented. He had not been the most skillful under the tutelage of his father's master-at-arms, had never been the fastest or the strongest. But after his near-death experience at the hands of the mugger in a shadowed alleyway of Daltenia's poor district, what he *had* been was willing to work harder than everyone else. He had *wanted* to be the best, but it had been more than even that. He had *needed* to be. It was the only way to quiet the voices, the voices that always told him he wasn't good enough, that he was useless and always would be.

And in time he had managed to quiet those voices to no more than a whisper—they never left completely. But as they grew quieter, his own had grown louder and louder still until it wasn't a voice anymore but a scream, a war cry of rage and hate and bloodthirst.

He was not that man, not any longer, but part of that man was left in him. And so, though he had failed once, though it hurt to fail, he gave himself only a few moments, no more than that, and then he tried again. And again. And again.

It took him five tries before he managed to lever himself up enough so that he was sitting in the bed. By the time he was finished his chest heaved, and his entire body was bathed in a cold sweat.

It took another fifteen minutes of recovering—fifteen minutes where he felt as if his heart would explode in his chest, where his entire body shook with exhaustion and pain—and three more tries before he made it to his feet.

But he *did* make it, and then he stood, one hand on the bed's headboard for support, regarding the room's door the way a man might regard an enemy commander across a battlefield before the bloodshed began.

Only feet away, that door, certainly no more than ten, but it felt as if it might as well have been in another world. Still, when a man had a long journey ahead, the way he did it, the only way he *could* do it was one step at a time. That was another of his father's favorites and it, like those other bits of wisdom he'd given Bernard over the years, was a true one.

But while his father had been right, he had never claimed the "one step" would be easy, and it was not. In fact, the movement shot agony through him, and he wasn't sure he'd be able to finish it until he did. The second hurt, too, but this time he knew what to expect at least. And then he was moving.

He used the wall for support as he made his way across the room. He retrieved his axe with a grunt of effort, securing it at his back, then moved to the door. He hesitated, staring at the handle. He had told Maeve he was fine, but that couldn't have been further from the truth. The truth was that he wasn't sure he could even *make* it to the dungeons and, if he did and any of the guards there proved to have mixed allegiances, they could take care of him with little more effort than a harsh word or a heavy breath, axe or no axe.

But then, the rest of what he had told Maeve *was* true. Namely the fact that if they didn't do something—and soon—then there was no telling what might happen. They had to secure the capital, had to secure it *now*. After all, if things were as bad with the Fey as they seemed then the last thing they needed was to have unrest and insurrection in the capital.

In the end, Cutter reached out and turned the handle, slowly easing the door open before stepping outside into the hallway.

One step at a time, he told himself as he began shambling down the hallway, his legs shaking with effort, *it's the only way to get it done.*

***

The dungeons were much as he remembered them only this time there were two men on duty instead of one. Cutter spoke briefly to them, the two eyeing his bandages questioningly but saying nothing. In time, one began leading him down the staircase into the dungeons.

Down in the dank, dimly-lit corridor, Cutter tensed and prepared for the man to try to kill him now that they were alone, though what he hoped to do if the man did, he had no idea. Die probably.

The guard, though, didn't seem to take any more notice of him, turning and peering into the shadows. "This way, Prince," he said.

Cutter grunted—it was either that or gasp for breath in the man's face—then followed as the guard started forward into the dungeons.

Some prisoners cried out for release, others in anger, shouting perverse curses at them and some few regarding them with silent, angry expressions. In time the guard brought them to a cell. "This is it, Prince. The one they call Aunt Belle. Though, I warn you," he said quietly, turning to look at Cutter, "the torturers have been at her, askin' their questions, you know and...based on the look of things....seems to me the woman wasn't all that helpful, if you know what I mean."

"I think I do," Cutter said. "Thanks."

The man nodded then winced, leaning forward. "I hope you don't take this the wrong way, Prince, but...well, that is...you don't look so good either, you don't mind my sayin'."

Nor do I feel so good, Cutter thought. "I'm fine."

The man nodded. "Of course, Prince. As you say. And can *I* just say—it's good to have a king in New Daltenia again."

Cutter watched the man carefully. A true guard making small talk, expressing his gratitude, or some corrupted soul looking for an opportunity? No way to know for sure. "Yes," Cutter said, thinking of Matt, "it is."

"Only...and I don't mean no offense, sir," the guard said, "but King Matthias...well, he's a bit of a cold one, ain't he?"

Cutter frowned. "Cold? Let me tell you something, guardsman, I have known many people in my time, and King Matthias is the kindest, most honorable person I have ever met."

"O-of course," the man said, obviously put-off by Cutter's growled response. "I-I'm sure it is, of course, as you say, Prince."

"Yes."

The man nodded, swallowing hard, no doubt well aware of the stories regarding Cutter and his temper. "Well, Prince," he said, "if there's nothing else?"

"No."

The man gave him a sickly smile, inclining his head in a bow then turned and hurried down the poorly-lit hallway of the dungeons, leaving the lantern sitting on the ground beside Cutter.

Once the man was gone, Cutter scolded himself. The guard had told him his opinion, that was all. There was no reason to snap at him over it. Anyway, the man was wrong, and he would learn just *how* wrong soon enough. After all, Matt had only been king for less than a week. Soon, the guard would realize that there could be no better person in all the realm, in all the *world* to lead the people of the Known Lands.

Cutter glanced at the lantern and cursed himself again for losing his temper with the guard. It was for that reason that the man had hurried away, setting the lantern down on the dungeon floor instead of handing it to him as he likely might have. Normally, reaching down and snatching it up would have been an easy enough thing but then Bernard hadn't had a particularly normal night—after all, it wasn't every day that assassins woke a man from his sleep to make an attempt on his life.

Gritting his teeth, he held onto the cell bars with one hand and then knelt, reaching out and grabbing the lantern with the other. He hissed in pain at the sudden movement of standing up then hoisted the lantern, peering inside the cell.

He had expected her to be far back, curled into a ball the way the historian, Petran Quinn, had been, and he let out a grunt of surprise when the lantern light illuminated Belle, the crime boss, standing at the cell bars, gripping them with one hand and staring at him. The woman's face was lined and stained with dried blood and it looked to Cutter as if she had aged a decade in the couple of days it had been since last he'd seen her, and these were far from the only changes time had wrought.

The woman's head was shaved, at least mostly so, with patches of hair still clinging on. He frowned. The torturers' work, no doubt, the men meaning to embarrass her, to steal her dignity and make of her little more than an animal. After all, men, women, *people* were notoriously difficult, possessed as they were of their own opinions, their own imperatives. Animals, though, were different. Animals might be taught, might be *trained.*

"*Prince Bernard,*" the woman hissed in a dry, rasping croak. "*So you've come to kill me then.*"

Bernard sighed. It wasn't the first time he'd heard as much when visiting someone in the dungeons—Petran Quinn came to mind—but then such was his reputation, a reputation he had worked hard to create during the Fey Wars. "No, Belle," he said. "I have not come to kill you. I've come to ask you some questions."

"More questions, is it?" the woman asked, baring her teeth in a sharp, humorless smile and displaying several gaps that he had not noticed before. Likely because they had not been there. Not at least, until the torturers began their work on her. "The torturers have questions too, thousands of them it seems, and no matter how many I answer, no matter how *fast* I answer, they are never satisfied. No matter what I say or don't say, no matter what I do or don't do, they are never satisfied, and they make their dissatisfaction known with the instruments of their trade. That is my reward for answering their questions, but it is worse if I do not. Tell me, Prince, what is it you offer?"

"You know what I offer," Cutter said. "We had a deal. A prince's boon. Just so long as it does not endanger the lives of any of my companions or any of the people of Two Rivers."

The woman snorted, a sneer coming to her face. "You have come to mock me then, is that it? Like some child visiting a traveling menagerie, you come to poke the lion in its cage, with its teeth safely behind iron bars. But I warn you, Prince, that the lion does not forget its tormenter, and so, too, will I never forget those who have wronged me."

Cutter grunted, shaking his head. "You're wrong, Belle. I've not come to taunt you. I've come with questions. As for the boon, it is true that you betrayed us to Feledias, but the boon still stands. Or, at least, it will if you answer some questions."

"*Questions,*" she sneered. "Gods, but I am sick of men with their questions."

"First..." Cutter hesitated. Belle had tried to have him and the others killed, it was true, or at the very least had betrayed them to Feledias without any major concern over the fact that it would almost certainly end in their deaths. And yet...looking at her...at her filthy clothes, her lined features and shaved head, he felt pity stirring in his chest. "Is there anything you need?" he asked. "Anything I can get you?"

The woman stared at him, blinking in the dim light, then, finally, she leaned back and let out a sharp, cackling laugh, sharp enough to cut. She leaned forward again, eyeing Cutter. "My hero, come to rescue me, is that it?" she asked.

"Say that it is."

"And this hero wants to know if he can get me anything," she hissed, and Cutter was surprised by the hate in her voice. "Very well, Prince." She leaned forward and suddenly thrust her other hand at him. Or, at least, she thrust what was left of it forward, in between the cell bars. The hand was wrapped in bloody bandages, but it took Cutter only a moment to see that there were no fingers left. "What about my hand, Prince?" she hissed. "Can you get my hand back for me?"

He stared at the mangled hand, abruptly at a loss for words.

"Yes," she said, grinning sharply, the expression reminding him of a vulture. "You see, those men, those torturers, they had their promises too. Promises of leniency, promises that they would stop, that the *pain* would stop, just as soon as I complied. Just as soon as I answered their questions to their satisfaction. The problem, you see, is that those men, they are never satisfied, and try as I might, I could never answer the questions as well as they wished."

Cutter looked at the woman's mutilated hand, and he felt a great surge of pity but not just that—anger. It was true that there was no knowing how much misery the woman had caused. After all, the first time he'd met her she had tried to convince Priest to kill a guardsman and his wife. There was no knowing how many people had died or suffered at her command...and yet that did nothing to change the fact that he felt sorry for her.

She must have seen something of that pity in his face, for she sneered, snatching her mangled hand back. "And what of you, *Prince?* You don't look so good yourself. Looks to me like somebody did a number on you." She grinned, displaying her gapped teeth again. "Maybe quite a few somebodies."

Cutter nodded, hesitating, wondering if it was wise to share what had happened with the crime boss. He told himself that it didn't matter—after all, Belle was in a cage, and she could do little enough harm here. Besides, if he wanted to have any chance of her telling him what he wanted to know he needed to build a little trust. "Some of the castle guards came into my room last night, led me into an ambush. There were five of them in all. They tried to kill me."

She nodded slowly. "And by the looks of things, they failed, eh? Though, it appears it was a near thing. Still...assassins making it into the castle itself...why, that's interesting, don't you think?"

"That's not all," Cutter said. "I knew one of them."

The woman grunted. "That's not so surprising a thing, is it, Prince? I knew you only for a few minutes before I decided I wanted to see you dead."

Cutter shook his head. "That's not what I mean. He was the man—the one who worked for you. The same one who got us into the dungeons."

She raised an eyebrow. "Ah. Now, that *is* interesting. Seems that Balk has not spent the time of my absence in mourning as I might have hoped." She shrugged one shoulder. "Still. He always was a man who enjoyed his trade. Though..." She paused, glancing meaningfully at Cutter's hands where they held the torch. More specifically at the cuts and scrapes on them. "If I'm any judge, something tells me he won't be enjoying that trade any longer. Am I right?"

Cutter shrugged. "Hard to say. Who knows what a man does in the afterlife?"

She snorted, then winced, cradling her bandaged hand against her chest. "Don't make me laugh, Prince. It makes it hurt. Of course, it *always* hurts, but laughing makes it hurt worse.

Anyway, if you're looking for sympathy, you're not likely to get it here."

"I didn't come looking for sympathy."

"Just as well," she said. "So...why did you come?"

"I think you know why. The man who tried to kill me worked for *you*. I came to see what you know of it."

She snorted. "What I *know* of it? In case it somehow escaped your damned attention, *Prince Bernard*, I have been stuck in this cell for what feels like an eternity now."

"Someone like you, she probably has people, contacts, who can make it to her, even here. I don't think something so small as being locked in a cage would keep you from giving orders."

"Do you think if I had contacts, Prince, that I'd still be here, enjoying your brother's...*hospitality*, as it were?"

"Maybe you don't have someone in a position to effect your escape, but there's a big difference between opening a cell door and sharing a quiet whisper between bars."

The woman shrugged. "What difference does it make? You will either believe me or you will not, but I tell you this, Prince. I knew nothing of the attempt on your life—I was not behind it. If I had been, I can assure you, we would not be having this conversation right now."

"If you weren't behind it then who was?"

She raised an eyebrow. "That's the question, isn't it? Seems to me that there's no shortage of people—and Fey—who'd be willing to pay quite a bit to see you put in the ground. Might be they held a raffle to figure out who got the honor."

Cutter frowned. "That's it, then? That's all you can tell me? All you know?"

"Of course not, Prince," she said. "But anything more than that'll cost you."

"I already told you—there is still the boon to speak of. I promised you one and I'm still willing to offer it to you. In exchange for what you know."

"Oh, Prince, you wouldn't want to fill that pretty little head of yours with all the things I know. Why, the nightmares you'd have! Still..." She made a show of considering it. "Can't say as getting out of this dungeon doesn't offer some appeal." She nodded. "Fine. What is it you'd like to know?"

"For starters, I'd like to know who hired Balk."

She sighed, shaking her head. "I can't help you there, I'm afraid. A man like Balk, he enjoys his work, you see. When I was captured...well, it wouldn't have taken him long to find someone who'd pay him for his favorite pastime. As for who that someone is..." She shrugged. "I can't say for sure."

"But you have a theory."

"Oh, I have plenty of theories, Prince. There's little else to do, sitting in this cell, besides mourn the loss of my fingers and come up with theories."

Cutter sighed. "I'm not liking these answers, Belle. Seems to me that they're not worth the price of your freedom."

"If you aren't liking the answers, Prince, then perhaps you aren't asking the right questions."

He frowned at that, thinking maybe he should have brought Chall and Maeve after all. Both would have been far better at knowing the right questions to ask than he was himself, for his strengths had always lain in different areas. Usually bloody ones.

Suddenly, a thought struck him, and he met the crime boss's eyes. "When Priest and I first visited you in the poor district, you asked him to kill a man—a guardsman, I believe."

Her eyes flashed, and she gave a small, humorless smile. "Better, Prince. Yes, I did. So go on—ask your question."

"This guardsman," Cutter said. "What's his name?"

"Ah," she said, nodding slowly. "That *is* the right question—at least, one of them. You'll be looking for Guardsman Nigel. He's stationed at the southern gate of the city, last I checked. But I'd hurry, if I were you, Prince. I'm not the only one who knows the danger Guardsman Nigel represents, not the only one who has been...*inconvenienced* by his investigations. If there really is a conspiracy in the city, they'll be looking to silence anyone who might out them, and I do not doubt that Guardsman Nigel will be high on that list."

Cutter nodded, thinking. The guardsman was obviously honest enough and persistent enough to warrant Belle's attention. If there was anyone who might be able to tell him which of the city's guards were honest and which weren't it was this Nigel.

"Very well," he said. "Thank you, Belle. I'll go and see about the guardsman now."

He started away, pausing as the woman spoke. "And what of my boon, Prince? What of my freedom?"

She was making an effort to sound casual, but he could hear the desperation in her voice. He turned back. "As soon as I get back from checking on this guardsman Nigel. If your information is good, I'll see you released. Until then, I'll make sure there's no more..." He paused, glancing at her ruined hand where it hung at her side. "That is, I'll make sure that no one bothers you. You'll have your release tomorrow at the latest."

She nodded. "I thank you, Prince. I don't know if you really were the man that the stories said, but if so, then it seems you have proved me wrong. Maybe people really do change after all."

Cutter met her eyes, nodding slowly. "Maybe."

He turned to go again at that, and she stopped him by speaking once more. "Prince?"

"Yes?"

"I won't tell you all that I know—I believe you when you say that you'll free me from this...this place, but I've long since learned that leverage works far better than trust when it comes to not being disappointed by people. But I will tell you this much, at least. Whoever was behind the attempt on your life, they had to have intimate knowledge of the castle, likely access to it. And whoever they are, they are dangerous."

"Why do you say that?"

"Despite how it may appear, it's not easy to buy guards, and it is certainly not easy to sneak assassins into the castle. To do something like that, a person would have to have a lot of guards on their side and not all of those guards can be bought no matter the price—believe me, I've tried. I may not know who it is that hired the men to kill you, but I can tell you that, whoever he is—or she—they are powerful."

Cutter considered that. It wasn't exactly comforting to know that whoever had sought his life was powerful in his or her own right, but it made sense. "Thanks, Belle."

She gave him a small, fragile smile. "You're welcome. My Prince."

Cutter gave her a nod, and then he was moving again, hurrying down the dungeon hallway as much as his wounds and his exhaustion would allow. He felt as if he were running out of time—could only hope that he wasn't out already.

CHAPTER FOUR

In battle, as in life, things are never as they seem.
They are always, without fail, considerably worse.
    —General Ichavian, famed military strategist

Cutter shambled out of the dungeon as quickly as his weary legs could carry him. He emerged into the entryway where, what felt like only yesterday, he saw the man who had escorted him and the others here to free the historian kill the guard on duty, stabbing him in the neck and taking his life with no more thought than another man might give to squishing a bug.

"Did you get what you needed, Prince?" one of the two guards stationed at the entryway asked as he emerged from the dungeons.

"Maybe," Cutter said. "Thanks." He started past them then paused, glancing back at the man who'd spoken, the older of the two. "Guardsman?"

"Yes, Prince?"

"What's your name?"

"It's Trevor, Prince, if it pleases you."

Cutter nodded. "Alright, Guardsman Trevor, I have a favor to ask."

"Name it, Highness."

Cutter watched the man, searching for any sign of devious intent, but if it was there, he did not see it. Finally, he grunted. "My request is two-fold. First, I would like to ensure that the woman inside, Belle by name, remains unharmed, by my order. She is cooperating with the crown and therefore is to be treated fairly—

no more visits from the torturers and please make her as comfortable as possible."

"As you say, sir," the guardsman nodded. "And...the other?"

"I want you to find a woman named Maeve. She should be near the king. She's about a foot shorter than me and—"

"Forgive me, Highness," Guardsman Trevor said, "but I am familiar with Maeve the Marvelous." He smiled. "I think all the lads are. A formidable woman, that one."

"Yes, she is," Cutter agreed. "Anyway, you're to find her and tell her that I need her help. Tell her I've gone to the southern gate in search of a Guardsman Nigel. Tell her to bring Chall and Priest and any guardsmen she can round up but tell her not to take too long."

The man blinked. "Forgive me, Prince, but are you expecting trouble, sir?"

"I find that it's best, Guardsman Trevor, to always expect trouble. That way, a man isn't surprised when it shows up at his door."

"B-but, sir," the guardsman said, "if it's trouble, I'd just as soon come with you—that is, if it's alright with you."

"It's not," Cutter said, more abruptly than he'd intended. After all, he had no way of knowing if the guardsman was crooked or not, and the last thing he needed in his current, wounded state was to invite along a man who might stab him in the back the first chance he got. The man looked crestfallen, and Cutter sighed. "Sorry, I wasn't trying to be rude, and I appreciate the offer—truly. But the best way you can help me is to hurry and take the message to Maeve—just make sure that Belle isn't harmed any more, do you understand?"

"Of course, Highness."

Cutter nodded. "Thank you." He started away and had his hand on the door leading out of the dungeons and into the castle courtyard when the man spoke again.

"Highness?"

Cutter turned to regard him.

"Good luck," the man said.

Two simple words, but Cutter was surprised by how much they meant, for the man seemed to be sincere. If he was a conspirator, he was a damned good one. "Thanks," Cutter said, meaning it. "And good luck to you as well."

Then he turned, rushing through the door and starting across the castle courtyard as quick as he could without collapsing. *Good luck to us all.*

***

The guards at the gate looked at him strangely as he shuffled past, and Cutter couldn't blame them. He'd grabbed a black cloak when leaving the castle in the hopes of hiding most of his bandages, but he could not hide them all, particularly the one covering a gash on his forehead or the one wrapped tightly around the palm of his left hand where he had received a cut he did not even remember.

No doubt to the guards he looked like a man destined either for a healer's bed or the grave, but he raised a hand in acknowledgment of them as he moved out and into the street.

"P-Prince," one of them said, "is…is everything alright?"

Cutter studied the man, wondering if he was loyal or if he was not. He had never been good with understanding people or their motivations, had always left such things to wiser, better men, but now, when anyone might be an enemy, he found that he wished he had given himself a chance to practice.

He hesitated, trying to decide how much to tell the man. If he were indeed a corrupt guard, then it would be best if he didn't know Cutter was hunting down the one person who might be able to expose him as such. On the other hand, if he were loyal, then according to Belle, the less he knew the safer he and his family would be.

In the end, Cutter nodded. "Everything's fine. How's the gate?"

"Quiet, Highness," the guard said, glancing at the bandages wrapped around Cutter's midsection and arms—some of which had begun to bleed anew from his exertions. "Forgive me for asking, Highness, but…are you sure you're—"

"Fine," Cutter interrupted, pulling the cloak tighter around himself.

The man glanced at the other guardsman uncertainly then bowed. "As you say, Prince. If I might ask you where you're going, I can summon a carriage to get you there faster and with less...effort."

An innocent offer of aid or a ploy to get him into a carriage, one he would never leave alive? The simple fact was there was no way to tell, so even though speed was of the essence and the thought of walking one step further, let alone through the entire city, sounded like its own brand of torture, Cutter shook his head. "That won't be necessary. I think I'll walk."

"As you say, Prince," the guard nodded. "Then, if you'll give me but a few minutes, I'll summon an escort to ensure your safety—"

"That's quite alright," Cutter interrupted. "I won't be gone long."

And then, before the man could say anything more, he turned and headed into the city, doing his best to walk as if his wounds did not pain him, as if his legs didn't feel like they might give way beneath him with each step he took.

The early morning sun was peeking over the horizon, bathing the city in pale, weak light, and as he struggled on, Cutter took a moment to look at it and appreciate it. Had the assassins had their way—and they very nearly *had*—it was a sunrise he never would have seen. He continued thinking on that—better than concentrating on the exhaustion and pain suffusing his body—as he moved further into the city.

He waited until he rounded the corner of a building, out of sight of the guards, before he came to a shaky stop, propping his back against the side of a tailor's shop and resting with his hands on his knees, wheezing and covered in sweat.

This early in the morning, the streets of the capital were, if not deserted, then as close as they ever got. Not many people were out, which was good, for those who were could not help but mark the bandaged, bloody man leaned against the side of a building as if it was the only thing holding him up—which, of course, it was.

As he caught his breath, Cutter considered his options. He knew that he could not travel all the way across the city to the southern gate, not as he was, just as he knew that, even if he could, he dared not take so long. Sitting on a horse was largely out of the question, even if he didn't mind the thought of crossing by the guards once more to reach the royal stables and giving anyone with a mind to a chance to catch him unawares. The simple fact was that he doubted he'd be able to remain on his mount for long before the pain or exhaustion got the better of him.

That left only one option, then. A carriage. It had been fifteen years and more since Cutter had set foot in the city of New Daltenia, and he racked his brain trying to remember if there was a livery stable nearby.

Finally, it came to him that there was one only a street away, the same one that generally provided carriages for the castle. Or at least there had been, once. Much had changed in New Daltenia, and little for the better. He could only hope that this much, at least, had remained the same.

Taking a deep, steadying breath, he started off again. The closer he grew to the livery stables, the more certain he became that it would be gone, that of course it *must* be gone. After all, little had worked out in his and the others' favors so far, and so he should not be surprised to find that in this, too, he was bound to be disappointed.

But when he exited a side street a wash of heady relief came over him as he saw that, despite his worries, the stables remained, looking much as he remembered them.

Cutter took in the stable yard, the mews, and was unable to keep the grin from spreading across his face as he started forward. Apparently, he had some luck left after all, which was a good thing. If things were as bad as he thought—and, generally, he'd found that things had a way of always being considerably *worse*—then he was going to need all the luck he could get.

He stepped into the main office of the livery stables, sure that he would find it abandoned or that, perhaps, there would be no drivers ready for work this early in the morning. And yet, for all his worries, his luck held. A middle-aged woman, her dark hair streaked with silver, sat behind the counter, and several men who could only be carriage drivers sat at a table, drinking and talking in quiet conversation.

Cutter wrapped his cloak tightly about him and moved toward the counter, doing his best to walk normally. "Good morning, madam."

The woman behind the counter glanced up from some ledgers she'd been studying and raised an eyebrow at him. "Is it?" she asked. "I hadn't noticed."

Cutter tried a smile. "Yes. Well. I come looking to hire a carriage."

"What'ya know?" the woman said. "Same reason most folks come here." She retrieved a quill and a parchment looking up at him.

Cutter stood there uncertainly, not sure what was expected of him, until the woman sighed. "First time, is it?"

In fact, it was. During his stay in the castle, Cutter had never had to hire his carriages himself—there had always been someone around to do it for him. Not that he'd ridden in them often, always eschewing what he considered a needless luxury. "Well...yes. Yes, it is."

She gave a sour grunt at that. "Well, you see, generally speaking it's easier to hire a carriage if one has a destination in mind."

Cutter winced. "Right. The southern gate—as quickly as possible."

She raised another eyebrow at that. "I see. And when will you be wanting the carriage then?"

"Um...now would be good."

The woman rolled her eyes. "Of course it would be. Very well. A trip to the southern gate," she said, hastily writing something on the parchment. "And a return trip as well?"

"One hopes," Cutter said.

The woman frowned at that, eyeing him again. "A jester, are you?"

"No."

She sniffed. "Didn't think so." She went on, scribbling something else on her parchment. "Fine. A trip and a return to the southern gate. And you are?"

He opened his mouth to say Cutter or Prince Bernard then hesitated realizing that neither of the two would work. "I...I would rather remain anonymous, if it's all the same to you."

"Is that right?" she asked. "Well, I'd rather my teats didn't sag and I woke up in bed with a prince every morning, but here we both are."

Not likely, Cutter thought. "I...that is..."

She frowned, motioning to a big man who'd been standing at the side of the wall. "We don't much care for people wasting our time here, sir, and we don't care for shady men with blood-stained bandages who show up asking for a carriage and refuse to give their name. Now, are you going to turn around and go, or am I going to have to get Clem here to show you the way out?"

The big man, Clem presumably, grinned wide displaying several gaps in his teeth as if he was hoping Cutter would choose the second option. Cutter hesitated, unsure of what to do, knowing that he needed a carriage but knowing also that he could not give the woman his real name. It would raise too many questions and if someone *was* marking his progress, he'd rather it not be so easy for them to track him down.

He was still hesitating, Clem's grin widening, when he felt a hand on his shoulder. "Ah, Cend, it's good to see you!"

Cutter turned and was surprised to find that the man who stood beside him was one he recognized. It was the driver who'd taken them away from the castle when they'd escaped the dungeons with Petran Quinn.

It took his pain-addled, exhausted mind a moment, and then he grunted. "Ned?"

"Why, of course—you know your own cousin, don't you?" the man exclaimed.

"C-cousin?" Cutter asked, feeling even more confused if anything.

The man sighed, shaking his head and turning back to the woman at the counter. "You'll have to forgive Cend here, Delilah. A big bastard he is, but not all that bright."

The woman glanced between the two of them frowning. "This is your cousin?" she asked.

"That's right," the small man said, puffing out his chest. "I know, I know, the resemblance is uncanny, isn't it?"

"Not quite the word I would use," the woman said.

Ned laughed as if she had told some hilarious joke. "Just so!" He leaned forward with one arm on the counter. "And can I just tell you, Delilah, that you look particularly radiant today? Why, the sunrise itself does not compare to your beauty."

The woman's scowl was belied by the flush that came to her cheeks at that, and she ran an unconscious hand through her hair. "Well, cousin or not, he still needs to register. And there's the matter of payment, of course."

"Oh come now, Delilah," Ned said, still smiling, "you and I both know the boss doesn't bother reading the ledgers anymore'n he bothers getting out of bed to show up. Anyhow, I already told you, this man here is my cousin, Cend...Cend Aberdeen."

"Aberdeen," she said. "A strange name."

"Indeed," the driver said, grinning, "a strange name for a strange fellow. As for the coin, well, how about we take it out of my wages, eh?"

"You want to pay for his trip yourself?" the woman asked.

"Well, of course!" Ned said. "After all, in my experience that's what family is—costly with little pay off." He nudged Cutter with his elbow as if it were a joke, and Cutter did his best to smile, focused as he was on keeping his feet beneath him.

The woman's eyebrows drew down thoughtfully, and she glanced between the two of them. Then, finally, she sighed. "Very well, but it will come out of your own wages—I will not forget."

"Oh, that I don't doubt!" the driver said, smiling. "Besides, if you did, well, you'd always have your ledger there to remind you, wouldn't you?"

The woman frowned but before she could say anything more, Ned clapped a hand on Cutter's shoulder. "Well, come on then, cousin. Best we get you to the gate—you've left Auntie waiting on you, and we both know she ain't a patient woman."

Then he was guiding Cutter to the exit of the office and out into the daylight.

"Thanks, Ned," Cutter said once the door was closed behind them, "I wasn't sure—"

"Not here," the driver said, the wide smile he'd worn nowhere in evidence as he glanced around. "Come on, Prince," he said quietly. "Best we get you in a carriage and quick—there's folks around the city who would see you in such a state and take it as an opportunity to...well, let's say voice their complaints about the way things have been runnin' lately. Stables are this way."

The man started away and Cutter was left with nothing to do but to follow. Not that he was too worried. There were very few people in the city he could trust, but he thought that the driver was one of them. After all, the man had had the opportunity, not long ago, to turn Cutter and his companions into his brother, Feledias, and instead he had helped them.

Ned led him into the stables where he began hitching two horses up to a carriage, whistling all the while. "So tell me, cousin," the man said after a minute, "how is Auntie anyway?"

Cutter glanced around the stables. Stalls lined either side where the horses were kept, a wide avenue in the center where several carriages waited. He did not see anyone who might overhear, save beasts, but he chose to follow the man's lead. "Oh, you know Mother," he said, peering into each stall.

"Ha, that's right I do, gods help me!" Ned said, then he rose from cinching several straps and nodded. "Well. Ready to go if you are—best we not be late, not where Auntie's involved."

"Yes," Cutter said, "best not." He moved to the carriage and climbed inside, doing his best not to groan with the pain the movement caused and noting the tacky feel of blood where it was seeping through several of the bandages.

By the time he managed to get himself into the carriage seat, he was sweating again, his hands shaking.

Ned glanced back at him through the opening in the covered carriage, a frown on his face, then he turned and clucked at the horses and they were moving again.

For a time, neither of them spoke but once they had left the stable yard and were navigating their way through the street, Ned turned and glanced back once more. "Sorry for all the play-acting, Prince, but it seemed to me you were in a bit of a hurry and didn't want folks knowing who you were."

"You were right," Cutter said, "and thank you...again. For your help."

The man grinned. "Nothing to it. If a man ain't willing to help his prince, what sort of a man is he?"

Cutter grunted, though the truth was that he thought, just then, most folks in the city would have been willing to help him only so far as putting a knife into his back, and the *absolute* truth was that he didn't blame them for it. The princes of the Known Lands had not been kind to their people, and so it was no surprise that their people, in turn, did not mean to be kind to them.

"Anyway," the driver said, "you don't mind my sayin' so, Prince, but you look just about done in. How's about we stop by a healer first before we get on with your business?"

Cutter winced at that.

"Weren't so hard to tell, Prince," Ned said, "not with anyone for eyes to see the blood comin' through those wraps, nor ears to hear the way you were wheezin' when you climbed your way into the carriage there. Tell me, there anything I can do to help?"

"You're doing it," Cutter said, allowing himself to lay his head back or a moment, to close his eyes as his breathing slowly began to slow. "But no to the healer's. I just came from there."

Ned grunted. "Seems to me the fella left a bit of work unfinished."

"Not his fault," Cutter said. "It's hard to work on a man who isn't there to work on."

The driver nodded, glancing back at the road before looking back at him once more. "And this trip to the southern gate, I take it it's an important one, then?"

"Yes," Cutter said, then frowned. "Maybe."

The man nodded again. "Well. I don't know what it's all about, but we'll get you to the southern gate just as quick as we can. Ought not take too long, and I expect the southern gate'll still be there when we arrive."

"I hope so," Cutter said, and he saw the man frown at that. "Sorry, Ned. I fear I am poor company just now."

"Oh, don't you worry on that score, Prince. I think I told you before, when we spoke, that I'm married. I know all about poor company. I don't show up to the livery before the sun's up on account of I got such a wonderful home life, I can tell you that much."

Cutter nodded, finding himself grinning despite everything. He liked the man. He couldn't say that about many people he'd met in his life, but Ned seemed a genuine sort, funny, too, though Cutter thought the driver's sense of humor was likely wasted on him. He'd always been a lot better at roaring a battle cry than roaring with laughter. "Ned?"

"Yes, Prince?"

"Aberdeen?"

The man glanced back from the road, grinning. "Caught that, did you?"

"Yes."

The driver grunted. "Well. Had a dog named Aberdeen once. A mut really, but he was a fine beast."

"What happened to him?"

The driver sighed, shrugging. "The same thing happens to all flesh, sooner or later, Prince. Just the same."

And with that grim statement, they rode on in silence, Ned clucking at the horses, Cutter wincing with each bouncing jostle of the carriage beneath him.

***

Maeve stood beside Chall at the side of the audience room as the two guards stationed there swung wide the doors and in walked a man in fine vermillion robes.

"*Your Majesty,*" the crier intoned, "*I present Merchant Guild Head Frederick Itannen.*"

The man might as well not have bothered with the announcement as far as Maeve was concerned, for one need only glance at the heavy-set man in his fine robes with rings bedecking his fingers to know that he was part of the Merchant's Guild. Of course, Maeve remembered the man from years ago before her exile. He had only been a merchant at that time, but even then Maeve had thought the man possessed the necessary cleverness and, perhaps, more importantly, greed, to rise highly in the ranks of the guild. Apparently, she had not been wrong, though she couldn't help but notice that the man had gained at least an extra hundred and fifty pounds since last she'd seen him.

"Fire and salt but I hate merchants," Chall muttered.

"Yeah?" Maeve asked quietly. "Well, there's a lot there to hate, isn't there?" And that was nothing short of the truth. She watched the merchant saunter in, puffing out a chest any noblewoman would have been proud of, then glanced at Matt. When first he'd sat on the throne after his coronation, the youth hadn't seemed to sit on it so much as he had seemed to be swallowed by it but that had changed.

Now, Matt reclined in the throne, one leg dangled over the side, nibbling at an apple. He looked far removed from the scared youth she had first seen in the Black Woods, and she did not think the change a good one.

"He should be resting," Chall muttered, "not taking audiences. Stones and starlight, Maeve, we should *all* be resting. It's been a long few days and that doesn't look to be letting up anytime soon."

That, too, was true, and Maeve found herself frowning at Matt—*King Matthias,* she corrected herself. For all the arrogance on his features, the youth looked exhausted, with great purple circles under his eyes, his face lined with his weariness. And yet, he had insisted on taking audiences instead of getting some much-needed rest.

Priest stood beside him, his hands behind his back, looking every bit the favored guard of the king, his expression unreadable. She wondered if he felt the same anxiety she did, wondered if he also thought he could almost hear the premonitory sounding of the horns which signaled doom's approach. Dramatic, perhaps, but she did not like the look of Matt, did not like the way he sat so casually, almost disrespectfully on a throne which had been hard-earned.

"Head merchant, is it?" Matt asked as the man stopped the expected twenty feet away from the throne, kneeling. "And what a head it is!" he exclaimed, laughing at his own joke. "Why, it looks like a great melon, doesn't it? One waiting to be squished!"

The merchant's head was bowed, but even still Maeve could see the way his face flushed with embarrassment. She frowned, glancing over at Chall, and saw a troubled expression on the mage's face as he peered at Matt like the boy was some puzzle he was trying to figure out.

"Oh, do stand!" Matt said, grinning and pausing to take a bite of his apple. "Your king greets you, head merchant. Now, how may the crown help the Merchant's Guild?"

The man did stand, heaving his bulk up with obvious effort which elicited a giggle from the youth on the throne, reddening the merchant's face further. "Your Majesty," the man said, his head bobbing in a bow. "I am honored that you would see me so soon after your coronation."

Matt shrugged. "I had little else to do. Now, on with it, man. What is it I can do for you?"

The merchant winced. "Of course, sire. I come to speak to you about a particularly important matter, one regarding—"

"I should hope so," Matt interrupted. "I'd hate to think that I was roused from my bed for an *unimportant* one."

Maeve's frown deepened. In point of fact, the boy had not slept at all the night past, at least not since the prince had sent her and Chall to look after him. Perhaps that went some way toward explaining his arrogant, rude behavior. At least, she hoped it did. She loved Prince Bernard dearly, but the Known Lands had had enough poor leaders. She had hoped, *still* hoped that Matt would change that.

"As you say, sir," the merchant said, giving a small, uncertain laugh. "Anyway, as Prince Feledias, your uncle, appointed us the custodians of the kingdom's tariffs, I thought it my responsibility to inform you that several of those from the outlying regions are...late."

Matt raised an eyebrow. "Late, is it?"

The man bowed his head. "Just so, Highness. Some nearly as much as a year."

Matt frowned. "And this is the first the crown is hearing of this?" he demanded.

The merchant paled. "Forgive me, sire, but I tried to speak with your uncle about it, only...he was unavailable. I told the regent, of course, many times, and he promised to get back with me about it, only...only, I have heard nothing."

"Am I to understand, Merchant Itannen, that you are calling the crown incompetent?"

The merchant blanched, his face, so recently flushed crimson, going a sickly pale. "O-of course not, Majesty. I...that is, I would never think to say such a thing. Only...the tariffs have still not been paid."

"It's true what they say, isn't it?" Matt said. "Merchants care only about their coin and nothing else. I'd heard tale men such as you would bed it, if they could, and it seems that those who told me were not wrong to say as much. But very well, I see you will not let it go. Tell me, have you ever considered that the tax collectors you sent chose to keep the coin for themselves and make off with it?"

"I would like to say, Majesty, that members of the Merchants' Guild would never do as you describe, only..." He sighed, hanging his head low. "It has happened before. It is for this reason that more men were sent."

"*And?*" Matt demanded.

The merchant winced. "And they, too, have not returned."

"So send more!" Matt roared, and Maeve found herself recoiling in shock, feeling as if she was meeting the lad for the first time, for surely this could not be the same shy, kind youth who she had first met in the Black Woods. "What would you have me do?" Matt continued, leaping up from his chair as if he meant to rush forward and throttle the fat merchant and, indeed, Maeve did not appear to be the only person who thought as much, for the merchant tensed as if terrified.

Matt did not rush forward though. Instead, he paced angrily back and forth before his throne. "What do you think, Itannen? Do you believe that I will send what little of an army we have traipsing across the countryside to each hamlet or hovel so that you can buy a new ring to bedeck your *fingers?*"

"Th-that is unfair, Majesty," the guild head said, "I only sought to—"

"Never mind what you *sought*," Matt yelled. "*I* sought to live a peaceful life with my people in the wood—we do not always get what we seek, merchant."

Maeve frowned at that, glancing at Chall. The mage turned and stared at her a moment later.

"I thought Matt grew up in Brighton," he whispered.

"He did," Maeve said, then turned back to the king, still pacing angrily back and forth before his throne, flexing his fists as if it were all he could do to keep from charging the merchant in a rage. "Or so I thought."

"Then...I don't understand," Chall said.

"Something strange is going on here, Chall," Maeve said. "Something...something is wrong."

The mage opened his mouth to respond, but before he got a chance Matt spoke again. Or more accurately, he yelled. "I will hear no more of it! If the collectors you have sent have not returned, then send more, and if *those* do not return, then send more yet, but do not bother the crown with this, this *nonsense* anymore!"

"B-but, Majesty—" the merchant began.

"*Be gone!*" Matt roared. "Leave us at once!"

The head of the Merchant Guild's face turned crimson, and he bowed before hastily retreating to the door which the guards opened, then vanishing beyond it.

Maeve waited until the man was gone, until the doors were once more closed behind him, then she glanced at Chall and started toward the throne. Matt had sat once more by the time they arrived, but he was leaning forward in his chair, his hands knotted into angry fists.

"That was ill done, lad," Maeve said quietly. "Itannen may be a greedy fool, but he is a clever one. If he says that the collectors have not returned then we cannot so easily dismiss—"

"What do *you* know of it?" Matt demanded. "And I am not your *lad*—I am your *king*. Or have you so soon forgotten?"

Maeve recoiled, taken aback, at a loss for words by the anger on the youth's face. She tried to speak, to say something, but the words would not come past her shock, and it was Chall who spoke.

"That is unfair, Matt—Majesty," the mage said. "Maeve is one of the reasons, after all, that you *are* king instead of just another corpse in a world full of them. And more than that, she's right. I have little love for Itannen, but the man knows his business. If he says there's a problem, I believe him."

Matt seemed to shrink at this, collapsing heavily back into his throne and running a weary, shaky hand across his face. "I am sorry, Chall. Maeve. I...I am sorry."

Maeve breathed a heavy sigh of relief. Perhaps the youth was just tired, that was all. Surely, that must be—

"Sorry that you both think to question my reign as king, so soon at its beginning," Matt said.

His hand came away from his face, and it was not regret that twisted his features but anger, a strange, alien anger. "Matt," Maeve began, "we do not mean to question you. We only want to help, that's all."

"Is that so?" the youth asked. "And how would you do that, I wonder? How would you help me? How would *any of you?*" he finished, roaring the last. "You cannot! That is the truth of it, for I am beyond all help!"

Again, Maeve found herself recoiling at the youth's unexpected outburst. But Maeve had seen much in her life, and she refused to be so easily cowed. She forced herself to straighten her shoulders. "How would I help you? Very well, *Majesty*, since you ask, I will tell you. First, I would tell you that you do Cutter, Prince Bernard, your *father* a great cruelty for having not gone to see him. A great cruelty and one he does not deserve. Secondly, I would tell you to summon back the head of the Merchant's Guild, to question him further about the issue with the tariffs instead of acting like a spoiled child who has gotten his first sip of power and finds he has far too much of a taste for it."

Matt stared at her in shock, as if he could not believe her words, and she could feel Chall doing the same beside her. Even Priest's eyes widened slightly, an expression on the man that, on another, might have been a shout of surprise. "You...you cannot talk to me that way," Matt said. "I am your king," he whined.

"Then *act* like a king," Maeve snapped. "Instead of some coddled child throwing a temper tantrum."

The boy's face twisted in a storm of emotion and, for a moment, Maeve thought that she had finally gotten through to him, but then his eyes hardened, his jaw clenched, and he let out an angry growl. "What would you have me do, *Maeve the Marvelous?*" he demanded. "Would you have me summon back the fat merchant? Perhaps I should send my dog to do it," he finished, glancing at Priest to show who he meant.

Priest's face paled at that, but he said nothing.

"That is what she called you, isn't it, the crime boss?" Matt needled. "Her dog? Like a pet that might be led around? That might be trained?"

Priest's mouth worked for several seconds, but finally he nodded. "Yes, Majesty. It is what Belle called me."

"What has happened to you, lad?" Maeve said, wanting to scream it, to grab the youth and shake him. "You have changed. You are not the same youth I met in the Black Woods. You...you have changed. And not for the better."

Matt glanced at her, met her eyes. "I have changed, have I?" He laughed, then but it was not a laugh of humor. Instead, it was one that sounded very close to a scream. "Oh gods, Maeve, but you have no idea how right you are. I am *not* the same boy you met in the Black Woods. Not at all." A look of what might have been grief passed over his features then, and he sat heavily back in his throne once more, bringing a hand to his face. "Go," he said quietly in a voice that sounded almost apologetic. "Go, both of you. Get out of my sight. Speak to your merchant friend, if you wish, for I will have no part of it."

"Matt," Maeve said softly, stepping forward and extending a hand to the youth, for she could see that he was hurting, hurting terribly. "What is it? What's the—"

"*Go!*" he suddenly roared, swiping her questing hand away, a look of insane fury on his face. "*Go before it becomes worse, before I become worse!*"

"Matt?" Chall asked. "I...I do not understand. What do you mean become worse?"

The youth shook his head. "Leave now. Both of you. I will summon you when I want you. *If* I want you."

Maeve glanced at the mage, and they both shared a troubled look. She turned to Valden and the man only gave the slightest of nods, as if to say that he would keep an eye on the youth. Left with no other options, Maeve turned back to the mage. "Come, Challadius," she said softly. "The king needs his rest."

"But, Maeve," Chall said, "surely you can't be—"

"Now, Chall," she said, then she grabbed the mage's shoulder, and led him out the doors.

They made it to the hallway outside the audience chamber in time to see the back of the departing merchant. "*Headsman Itannen!*" Maeve shouted.

The man turned, and she hurried forward, Chall in tow.

"What do you want?" the merchant demanded. "Have you come to mock me some more?"

"No, sir," Maeve said, "I have not. We wanted to talk with you more about the towns that haven't paid their tariffs."

The man frowned, looking over both of them then finally sighed. "What's the point? The king has already shown no interest in it."

"I will speak to him," Maeve said, "but first I need to know—how many such towns are there?"

The merchant sighed, clearly making a show of it, enjoying being waited on. He really was a bastard, but then Maeve had known that already and just because a man was a bastard didn't mean he was wrong. "Very well," the man said. "How many towns, you ask?" He leaned forward, his words coming out in a grim pronouncement. *"Four."*

But for all the man's theatrics, Maeve found herself glancing at Chall.

"That's…that's it?" Chall asked.

The merchant rounded on him. "I'm sorry is that not good enough for you?"

The mage winced. "No, it's not that. Only, the way you spoke of it, I thought that there'd…well, I thought that there'd be more."

The headsman shook his head. "A year and a half ago, there were none. Then, shortly after the regent took over, the first tax collector did not return. I knew the man. He had a wife, a family."

Listening to the man, Maeve began to think that perhaps she had misjudged the merchant after all.

"Nearly a dozen collectors have been sent in all between the four towns and none have returned. And even worse, you cannot imagine the amount of money the guild has lost."

Or maybe not, Maeve corrected. "You mean the kingdom, of course," she said.

"Y-yes, of course," the man said. "All are suffering from it."

Some more than others, Maeve thought, considering the many rings bedecking the man's fingers and the ostentatious robe he wore, but she kept the thought to herself. "And the na—" Maeve began then cut off at the sound of heavy approaching footfalls.

She turned, suddenly sure that she would see an assassin running at her, and as she saw the man round the corner at a run, she was not comforted by the fact that he wore a guard's uniform. After all, those who had attacked Cutter had worn guard uniforms also. "Get behind me," she hissed at the merchant, drawing her blades.

The approaching guard, though, stopped several feet away, coming to a panting halt with both of his hands on his knees. "F-forgive me, my lady," he panted, "but I did not mean to startle you. Or you, my lord," he said, glancing at Chall.

"Easy enough to avoid if you don't go charging at us like a madman," Chall snapped.

"I apologize for my haste, Sir Challadius," the guard said. "My name is Guardsman Trevor. I am normally stationed at the dungeons, and I have come on orders from Prince Bernard."

Maeve glanced at the merchant headsman. "Forgive me, guildhead Itannen, but I will catch up with you soon about what we discussed. You may leave now."

The merchant frowned, clearly wanting to stick around and hear what all the fuss was about. Maeve only stared at him, waiting until he turned and walked away in a huff before she looked back to the guard. "What is your message, Guardsman Trevor?"

"The prince..." the guard said, still struggling to get his breath back, "he said to tell you that he has gone to the southern gate of the city, that he needs your help as soon as you are able. He says its urgent."

Maeve frowned at that. Cutter was many things but the man was no alarmist. Indeed, the man could do with being a far bit more anxious about life or death situations as far as she was concerned. If he'd told the guard it was urgent then something serious must be happening, particularly if he found it important enough to call them away from defending Matt. "The southern gate, you say?" she asked.

"Yes ma'am."

Chall frowned. "What could be at the southern gate?"

"Does it matter?" Maeve asked. "The prince needs us."

"No," Chall sighed, "no, I suppose not. But Maeve...should we tell Priest?"

Maeve considered for a moment then shook her head. "No. Cutter did not ask for him—likely he wants him to stay with Matt, make sure the boy is kept safe."

"Of course," Chall muttered, "otherwise who would be around to harass merchants and call their friends dogs?"

Maeve winced at that. "That's a problem for later, Chall. Right now, we need to go."

The mage sighed again. "I suppose you're wanting to run."

"I think that would be appropriate."

***

Cutter knew that Ned was hurrying as fast as he could, expertly weaving in and out of those in the street, yet as each minute slipped away the sense of urgency in Cutter grew so that, by the time they finally arrived at the southern gate, his shoulders ached from being tense so long.

"Here we are, Prince," Ned said, jerking the carriage to a stop. "You want me to wait or...?"

"Would you mind?"

"'Course not," the man said. "You go ahead and take care of whatever business you need, and I'll be here when you're ready." He eyed Cutter up and down. "Unless, of course, you'd rather I came with you. Can't say I'm a good hand with a sword, but then I don't look a couple inches from the grave, neither."

Cutter considered that then finally shook his head. "Best not, but Ned I do have a favor to ask."

"Name it."

"If...if anything should happen, I need you to go find Maeve, Challadius, or Valden at the castle—the companions who were with me last time. Tell them to find a Guardsman Nigel."

The man nodded. "I'll do it, Prince. But try not to let anythin' happen, will ya? I'd rather not be the one to tell Maeve the Marvelous, the world's most famous assassin, that I took my ease in a carriage while you breathed your last."

Cutter grunted. "I'll do my best."

It was difficult work, making his way out of the carriage. He promised himself that, when he healed—if he ever got a *chance* to heal—he would never again take for granted the simple things, like moving without pain. Yet, even as he had the thought, he knew that it was a lie. He would forget the same way that man with a headache tells himself that, when the headache departs, he will appreciate with each moment that follows, how wonderful it is to feel fine. But he, like that man, would forget. Forgetting life's small aches and pains was, after all, one of the things men were best at. It was the only reason, he suspected, that they were able to get on living at all.

He was panting heavily by the time he was out in the street, and he was forced to hold onto the carriage for a moment as he waited for the worst of the dizziness to pass. Then he glanced at Ned, gave the driver a nod, and started toward the guards stationed at the gate, using his cloak to hide the worst of his wounds.

He might as well not have bothered, for the men both watched him approach warily. "Who goes there and what do you want?" one demanded.

Cutter raised his head—which had hung wearily to that point as he shuffled toward the gate—and one of the men, the older of the two, grunted in surprise.

"Prince Bernard?" he asked, recognizing him immediately, unlike the woman at the livery stables.

The other guard grunted, spitting. "If he's a prince then I'm the king. Gods' sake look at him, Vince. You ever seen a prince look half beaten to death like that?"

"You'd be surprised," Cutter answered.

"Look, stranger," the younger guard said, "I don't know who you are, but why don't you tell us what you want before—"

"*Shut your damned gob, Clint,*" the older guard hissed. "That's Prince Bernard you're talkin' to."

The younger guard recoiled as if he'd been slapped then stared wide-eyed at the man. "You...you mean it, Vince? Is this really him? The Crimson Prince?" His eyes went wider still as if he'd just realized he'd used a not particularly flattering nickname for a prince who was known for his willingness to court bloodshed, and his face paled. "F-forgive me, Prince," he stammered. "I-that is, I didn't mean—"

"You'll have to excuse him, Highness," the older guard, Vince, said. "He's a fool, but a harmless one." He eyed Cutter up and down. "Is there something you need help with, sir? Something we can do or—"

"As a matter of fact, there is. I'm looking for a man—Guardsman Nigel by name."

The younger of the two snorted. "You and us both."

Cutter frowned at that. "What do you mean?"

The older guard stared at the younger, shaking his head in exasperation before turning back to the prince. "What my fool companion means, Prince, is that Nigel ought to have been here more'n an hour gone. Him and his partner. We're havin' to stay over on account of they never showed up for their shift."

Cutter's frown deepened. "Is that normal? For him to be late, I mean."

The older guard scratched at his chin thoughtfully. "Can't say as I remember Nigel ever bein' late before. His layabout partner, sure, that Willem is a piece of shit." He grunted. "Excuse my language."

Cutter bit back a curse. The man was late—that didn't bode well for his chances of finding him, not alive at least. "Does either of you know where Nigel lives?"

The guard scratched his chin again, thinking it over. Cutter wanted to scream at him to hurry up, but knew that doing so would do no good, so he waited impatiently. "Seems I recall Nigel had a place over on Crafter's Row. Right beside the blacksmith's, if I recollect." He glanced at the guard house. "I can check the ledgers, if you want, get you a—"

"That's alright," Cutter said, a sinking certainty in his gut that he was running out of time, that he might be out already. "I'll find it."

He shambled back to the carriage as fast as his weary legs could carry him, climbing inside. "Crafter's Row," he said to the driver, "quick as you can."

"As you say, Prince." Then they were moving, Ned driving the horses at a rapid pace down the street.

They arrived on Crafter's Row a short time later. No mob of assassins rushed through the streets, nor did he hear any screams. At first, Cutter took this as a good sign, but his relief faded quickly. The street was quiet, yes, but it was almost *too* quiet. Not the normal quiet of a street little-traveled but instead the hushed, dread silence of a child hiding beneath the covers as the monster prowls about his room, terrified of making a sound lest it notice him.

Indeed, they were alone on the street. Was it some dark knowledge which had caused the people of the city to avoid this street at this time, or was it only happenstance? Cutter frowned, wanting to believe the latter but finding it to be a difficult task.

Ned slowed as they approached the house the gate guard had indicated, pulling the carriage to a stop across the street.

Cutter climbed out, examining the place. It was a simple house, small but clearly well-maintained. In the early morning hours, the front was cast in dappled pale light mixed with obscuring shadows, the door itself a dark void.

Ned glanced uncertainly at the home, frowning. "Sure you don't want me to go in with you, Prince?" he asked.

"I'm sure," Cutter said. "But remember, Ned, if I don't come back, I need you to find Maeve and the others. Tell them to speak with Belle and, if I don't manage it, find Guardsman Nigel. If he's still alive."

The man sighed. "I hear you, Prince, though I still think you ought to let me come in with you. Likely you'll find this Guardsman Nigel abed with his lady wife, but if not...well, the state you're in—"

"I'll be okay," Cutter said. "Just remember what I said, alright?"

"Aye," the carriage driver said, heaving a heavy breath. "I'll remember. Good luck, Prince."

"Thanks," Cutter said, and with that he started toward the house.

He walked up to the door, raising his hand to knock and then noted something that dispelled any hope that the guardsman's tardiness might be innocent. The door sat open several inches, the latch dangling, clearly broken by a powerful blow.

He looked back at the driver, Ned, saw the man watching him from his carriage across the street, a worried expression on his face. Then, with nothing left to do, Cutter drew his axe as quietly as he could and eased the door open with his foot. It creaked as he did and though the sound was light, it rang like an alarm bell in his mind, and he was sure that anyone within the house must have heard it. So he stood in the darkness of the doorway, breathing quietly, listening for the sounds of someone charging at him.

He stood that way for several seconds, his eyes scanning the gloom of the entry way. A small dining room sat to his right. On his left was a stairway leading up and disappearing into the shadows. Cutter waited, unmoving, his ears perked for any furtive sound that might betray someone sharing the darkness with him.

For several seconds he heard nothing but his own quiet breaths. Then the silence was suddenly split by a woman's terrified scream.

"*Found the bitch!*" a voice shouted in the darkness. Cutter started toward the stairs, for the woman's scream, and the man's yell had come from somewhere above him. He had just reached the stairs' base when his foot struck something he hadn't been able to make out in the near darkness.

Cutter frowned, kneeling down, all too sure of what he would find and, indeed, as his eyes began to adjust to the gloom he saw that it was a dead man. The man had suffered a terrible cut from what looked like a sword across his face. For a moment, Cutter thought that this must be Guardsman Nigel and that, for all his effort, he had come too late after all.

A closer inspection, though, showed that the corpse was of an elderly man in his fifties at the least, and not a man wearing a guard uniform but instead one dressed in the garb of a household servant. One of the man's hands clutched what appeared to be a fire poker.

Cutter glanced back at the doorway, his mind working rapidly. He could see easily enough how the thing had happened. The men—how many of them he wasn't sure—had come through the doorway, catching the family by surprise. Based on the food that lay half-eaten on the dining room table, they had been caught off-guard and had been forced to flee up the stairs. The men had given chase and the servant, in an effort to buy his masters time, had armed himself with a poker from the nearby fireplace and stood against the ambushers.

Cutter knew hardly anything about the man by the name of Guardsman Nigel, only what he had heard from Belle, a crime boss who was just about the last person he'd trust if given a choice. But seeing that the elderly servant had been willing to give his life for him was all he needed to know.

He rose, taking the stairs two at a time, abandoning stealth in favor of speed. The woman's scream moments ago was proof that she, at least, was alive, but that would not remain the case for long if he tarried. So, gritting his teeth against the pain of his wounds and, with one hand on the wall to keep him steady, he continued forward.

A Warrior's Curse

A loud *crack* split the silence as he was halfway up the stairs, and the woman screamed again. Moments later he reached the landing and was greeted by the sight of two men in front of a door. One held an axe and was cursing as he worked it out of the doorway where it had smashed a great rent into the wood. Another hit, maybe two, and he would have it open and would be at the woman who Cutter could hear still screaming on the other side.

The second man stood behind his companion, a sword in his hand, waiting for the door to be breached. Cutter didn't hesitate. He moved forward as quick as he was able, counting on the sound of the splintering wood to cover his approach.

The man in the back spun just as Cutter reached him, he gave a startled cry of surprise but no more than that before Cutter buried his axe in his chest. The man screamed, collapsing, and Cutter, knowing he didn't have time to retrieve his axe before the second man was on him, allowed it to be pulled out of his hands to go down with the corpse. The second man had just managed to turn when Cutter charged him, lifting him with a growl of anger and pain and pushing him over the banister.

He saw the man's eyes open wide with shock and then he fell, hitting the floor below head first and crumpling into a broken pile. Panting heavily, his entire body throbbing with pain, Cutter turned back to the body of the first man and reached down to retrieve his axe. No sooner had he reached, however, than the strength suddenly vanished from his legs, and he fell to his knees, wavering drunkenly.

He would have fallen then had he not reached out a hand and caught himself on the floor. The world blurred around him, the landing on which he knelt seemed to spin, and he gave his head a shake in an effort to clear it.

He remained there for several seconds, one hand on his axe, the other on the floor to steady him, his breath wheezing in and out of his chest like a blacksmith's bellows. *Get up, damn you*, he told himself. *Get up.*

It took a monumental effort to move, but he grabbed hold of the railing and with a hiss of effort levered his way to his feet, leaving his axe to dangle in his other hand. Movement at the door caught his eye, and he glanced over to see the woman who must be the guardsman's wife staring through the great rents the attacker's axe had left.

"Your husband," he croaked. "Where is he?"

"W-who are you?" the woman asked.

"A friend," he said. "Now where is he?"

"I-I don't know," the woman said. "He led them away or tried to. These two must have seen me come in here but...please. Can you help him?"

"I'll try," Cutter said, thinking it was just about all he could manage to remain standing. "Is there somewhere you can hide?"

"Th-there's a closet."

He nodded. "Get in it. I'll go and see about your husband."

Cutter waited until the woman disappeared into the room then heaved a heavy breath and began shuffling his way down the walkway.

He didn't have to go far before he caught sight of light from somewhere up ahead, the flickering glow of a lantern or candle, splashing the wall in erratic orange light. He heard voices raised in anger and knew that he must be on the right track.

He followed the light, coming around a corner in the walkway and seeing an open door at the end of the hall. He moved to the doorway and was greeted with the sight of a large study.

Bookshelves lined the walls, and at the back of the study sat a large desk. Several chairs had been knocked over, scattered across the floor, but what drew Cutter's attention were the six men all armed with swords. Their backs were currently to him, for their attention was focused on another man who stood behind the desk. The man clenched the handle of his sword in both hands and was bleeding from a head wound. Corpses lay on either side of the desk where the men had tried to rush him.

This then, he decided, must be guardsman Nigel. It seemed that at least what Belle had said about the man being a capable swordsman was true. Otherwise, he'd already be dead. Instead, having seen two of their number go down, the assassins were hesitating despite the fact that they outnumbered their target six to one.

"Look, you bastard," one of the six hissed, "you're going to die either way, alright? Nothin' you can do to change that. But the harder you make it on us, the more I swear we'll make your woman suffer once you're gone. Pretty thing from what I saw of her, nice backside. Now, how about you put that blade down and let us get on with it, eh? You do, I promise we'll make your woman's death quick."

The man seemed to hesitate, considering it, and Cutter wondered, not for the first time, whether it was hate, as many thought, or love that caused the majority of the world's grief. After all, it had been love—or at least as close to it as the man he'd been was capable of—that had caused the rent between him and his brother, that had brought an entire kingdom to the brink of destruction.

"Doesn't sound like a great deal," Cutter said loudly. "What else do you have to offer?"

The men in the room had all been so focused on their quarry that they had not noticed his approach, and several let out shouts of surprise as they spun. "Who the fuck are you?" one demanded.

Cutter shrugged, seeing no reason to lie. "I'm Prince Bernard. Any chance you've got enough loyalty to your kingdom left to leave for my asking?"

"*The Crimson Prince,*" one of the men whispered.

"*Maybe we oughtta get out of here,*" another whispered to the speaker of the group, his voice uncertain. "*They say he's the greatest warrior of—*"

"*Shut your fucking mouths,*" the leader hissed.

He eyed Cutter, and slowly a grin spread across his face. "Greatest warrior of our time?" he grunted. "Looks to me like our prince here's seen better days. Why, you ask me, given time enough he'll fall over dead on his own."

Cutter gave a nod. "Guess we'd better get on with it then." He looked up at the swordsman, Guardsman Nigel. The man met his eyes, and Cutter gave a nod. Then, with a shout, he charged forward. His wounds slowed him, and so the first man he came upon had time to get his sword up for a parry as the axe swept toward him. Not that it did him any good. Cutter was wielding the weapon two-handed, putting all his weight behind the blow, and it swept the man's blade aside as if it didn't exist at all, cleaving deeply into the man's chest and making of it a bloody ruin.

The man screamed, stumbling away. Cutter started to pursue, to make sure the man was out of it, but a sound beside him alerted him to another attacker, and he spun in time to see a sword flashing at him. He started to bring his axe up in time to parry, knowing he would be too slow even as he did, then suddenly there was a metallic flash as another sword interposed itself between him and his opponent's killing thrust.

He grunted, looking up to see that the swordsman, Guardsman Nigel, had left the relative safety of the desk and that it was his sword which had halted the killing thrust. With a growl, the guardsman knocked the blade away and before his opponent could recover, he lunged forward, impaling the assassin on his sword.

The assassin screamed in pain, dropping his own blade, and the guardsman planted his boot in his midsection, sending him sprawling on the ground. The four remaining assassins charged them then, and Cutter and the swordsman were forced to fight back-to-back.

Two came at Cutter, and it was all he could do to keep his axe in front of their strikes, parrying them and having no opportunity to counter. And with each parry, he felt himself growing weaker, felt what little bit of strength his body had left leaving him, oozing out with the blood now soaking his bandages.

He knew that there was not much time left, knew that in a minute, maybe two, he wouldn't have even the strength necessary to raise his axe, so when he parried one of the mens' strikes, instead of moving his axe to block the second man's blow, he gave a roar, charging forward with all the speed he could muster.

It wasn't much, and although he avoided the worst of the man's strike, he felt the blade slice across his arm a second before he bowled into the man. He kept going, knowing he had to put some distance between him in the second man lest he finish him while he was distracted with the first. With a growl, Cutter lifted the man up with his free hand and continued forward until he reached the bookcase at the far wall, then he slammed the man into it with all his strength.

Something *snapped,* and the assassin screamed in pain. Whether the sound had come from the man's back or the bookshelf, Cutter didn't know and didn't care. He let the man drop, satisfied that he was out of it, at least for the moment, then turned to see that the second man had taken advantage of his absence to close on the guardsman and was raising his blade for a strike that the guardsman, focused on the two at his front, would have no way of avoiding.

There was no time to make it back, so Cutter did the only thing he could think to do, he lifted his axe and with a grunt of effort, hurled it at the man coming up behind the swordsman. It was a heavy weapon, not made to be thrown, and that, coupled with an exhausted stumble at the last moment meant that it did not fly true. Instead of embedding itself, blade first, in the man's back as Cutter had intended, the haft struck the man in the chest. Not a killing blow but hard enough to make him stumble, fouling his own strike.

Then Cutter was running, a shambling, dragging run that sent a fire of pain roaring through him with each step. By the time he reached the man his axe had struck, his vision was blurred, but the man, thankfully, had only just righted himself, and so did not see Cutter coming before Cutter's fist lashed out, striking him in the face. The man fell then, and Cutter, unable to stop his forward momentum, stumbled and came down on top of him.

The assassin struggled beneath him. Barely able to see anything more than a vague blur, Cutter brought his fists down again and again. He missed the first, hitting the floor instead, but after the second hit the man's struggles weakened. By the fourth, they had stopped altogether.

He was just starting to climb to his feet when something struck him in the side and sent him tumbling over to land on his back. A blur stood above him, and though he could not tell for sure he thought he saw a grin on the man's face as he raised his sword.

"Time to die, Prince," the blurred figure said, and Cutter watched the sword, his end, waiting for it to come.

But just then, another figure rose up behind the first, its features too blurred by Cutter's failing vision for him to make out. The figure behind the first moved, and the next thing Cutter knew, his would-be killer collapsed on top of him. Either the man was dead or he was working on it, nothing more than limp weight on Cutter's chest. He was still struggling to roll the body off him—

feeling just about as strong as a newborn kitten—when a blurred face appeared, peeking over the body.

"Hi there, Prince."

Cutter blinked. He still could not recognize the figure's features, but he recognized his voice clearly enough. "Ned?" he wheezed.

The driver grunted. "'Fraid so, sire. And, if I might say, your reaction is eerily close to that of my lovin' wife when she sees that I've made it home safe and sound after another day of potentially dying at the hands—or feet, I suppose—of runaway horses or cruel muggers."

"She also...have...a body...lying on her chest, keeping her from being able to breathe?" Cutter managed in a croak.

The driver shook his head. "No...no, she just hates me, but then I catch your point, Highness. Just a moment."

The man knelt and after a lot of hissing and straining and cursing—some particularly *inventive* cursing, Cutter had to admit—the pressing weight was levered off his body, and he let out a great sigh of relief.

"Ned..." Cutter said, offering the man a weak smile. "I thought I...told you...not to come in."

"That so?" the driver asked in an innocent tone. "Well, can't say as I remember that, Prince. Seems to me I recall you sayin' to come on in, if I had a mind."

"That right?" Cutter asked, giving the man a smile.

"Just so," Ned agreed.

"I begin to understand your wife a little more."

The man's grin was wide enough that even through his failing sight, he could see it. Cutter returned the smile until a panicked thought made its way into his clouded mind, and he grunted. "Ned, Guardsman Nigel, we have to...have to find him, he—"

"He's fine, Prince," the driver said. "Though, you ask me, the man's picked a pretty terrible time to go takin' a nap."

Cutter had used up the last bit of his strength in his fight with the assassins, the last bit and then some, and so it took an almost monumental effort to turn his head in the direction the driver indicated. He recognized the guardsman's form a short distance away by the uniform he wore. The man lay on his side, his back to Cutter, but Cutter could see enough of him to note his back rising and falling with his even breaths.

"And...the assassins?" Cutter asked, figuring he knew the truth, since if any of the men were still alive he wouldn't be, but he thought he should probably ask just the same.

Ned grunted. "Well and truly assassinated. Might be they got their jobs confused a bit."

Cutter gave a soft laugh at that—the best of which he was capable just then—and they were silent for a moment. That was when he smelled something and frowned.

"Ned, that smell..."

"Smoke," the driver said grimly, then coughed. "And a lot of it." Indeed, Cutter's own throat was beginning to grow scratchy.

He hissed with the effort of turning to look at the study door, the one through which he'd entered only minutes ago, and saw an unsettling image. Smoke, great, black smoke, was rising up from somewhere below the second story landing, moving into the room. Slowly now, but where there was smoke there was fire. And if any of that fire should make it here, to the study, then the entire room, stacked as it was with books and tomes, would become an inferno.

And the fire *was* spreading, of that there was no doubt, for the amount of smoke rising into the study was growing by the moment. Cutter's eyes were already beginning to water, and his throat was growing increasingly scratchier. Soon, it would be near impossible to breathe, and the only real question would be whether anyone left in the study would succumb to the smoke or the flame first.

"Ned—" he began then cut off, coughing. "Ned, you need to get out of here. As quick as you can."

"Sure," the driver said, kneeling, and the next thing Cutter knew the man's hands were snaking underneath his arms. "But not without you, Prince."

The man hissed and grunted with the effort of trying to lift him, and Cutter shook his head. "No, Ned, listen—"

"Don't you worry, Prince," the man grunted, "I'll get you out of here." There followed some more hissing and grunting, but very little movement. *"Just...gods be good what do you eat rocks?"* the driver groaned.

"Ned, there isn't enough—"

"Just...hold on...Prince," the man said, but despite his best efforts the man couldn't budge Cutter and despite Cutter's own best efforts, he was exhausted, his body without any strength left, and so he could do nothing to help.

"*Ned,*" he snapped. "Listen to me."

The driver halted in his useless efforts at that. "I've got it," he said. "I'll go to the street, find help. It'll be daylight now, and the fire will have drawn a crowd anyway, like flies to shit. One or two more people and we ought—"

"There isn't *time*," Cutter growled, and the man cut off. "You and I both know it, Ned," he continued, softer now that he'd finally got the man's attention. "By the time you get someone to help everyone in this house is going to be dead already."

"But Prince—"

"If I am your prince," Cutter demanded in a pained hiss, "will you not now *listen?*"

"V-very well, Prince," the man said, and Cutter was immediately sorry for raising his voice, but he found some consolation in that while the man might think him an ass, he would at least be alive to think it. At least, that was, if Cutter had anything to say about it.

"Listen, Ned," he said. "I need...one more favor. I need you to get the guardsman out of here. And...down the hall, there's a woman, hiding in a room with a broken door. Get them out."

"But what about you?" the driver asked.

Cutter grunted. "I'll...be along directly."

The man hesitated, and though his face was little more than a blur, Cutter thought he saw enough to see the knowledge of the truth in the man's eyes. "Prince..." he said, "I'm sorry. I wish—"

"You've nothing to apologize for, Ned," Cutter wheezed, finding it difficult to breathe now. "Th-thank you. For all your help."

"You...you saved me, Prince, me and the others of my village. It don't seem right...me not bein' able to save you."

"A lot doesn't seem right," Cutter said, "that's the world. Now...will you do it?"

The man's shoulders slumped, his head hung, but he gave a single nod. "I will, Prince. Since you ask it of me. And...probably it doesn't mean anything, comin' from a nobody carriage driver, but I just want you to know...it was an honor, Highness, havin' you as my prince."

"It...means more than you know," Cutter said, and no sooner were the words out of his mouth then there was a loud *crack* of wood splintering somewhere outside the room. "You have to go, Ned. Now...and...thank you."

The man nodded again. "Good luck, Prince," he said.

"And...to you," Cutter managed.

Then the man was gone, turning away, and Cutter listened to the sounds of the world burning around him, listened to Ned's groans as he levered the swordsman off the ground and began dragging him toward the study's exit.

Unable to do anything else, Cutter watched them go, watched the driver disappear around the corner, his burden in tow.

And then he was alone with the dead and soon to be one of them. The smoke was thick now, and his skin felt warm as the raging fire began to draw closer. It wouldn't be long now. His death was coming, and it was only a question of which would take him first, the darkness which was even now creeping into his vision, shadows spreading across his world, or the fire. One or the other would take him. Soon.

Cutter had courted death often in his life, had spat in its face and laughed as the Crimson Prince, reaping a bloody harvest with his axe and confident that he was invincible, immune to death's chilling touch. And after that, during his days spent in the village of Brighton, his guilt had weighed heavily upon him, and the answer had seemed to lie in the knife he had kept sheathed at his side, the knife that was still sheathed there.

He had courted death, had yearned for it. But now, now that the moment was upon him, he found that he did not feel relief that it was all over. Instead, he felt only regret. Regret that he would not be able to help Matt, regret that he would not be able to help the kingdom, that he would not be able to attempt to atone for all the terrible things he had done, the terrible things he had *caused.*

He lay there, wishing things were different, searching for strength and finding none, and waited for his death to come. And in the end, it was not the fire that took him. Instead, it was the darkness. A darkness that, as he fell completely into it, he realized had been waiting to take him for all his life.

CHAPTER FIVE

No, I ain't scared of death.
Shit, dyin's easy.
We been doin' it for thousands of years, and I reckon we've pretty well got it down.
Living, though...well, that's another story.
—Soldier crippled during the Fey War

Maeve and Chall, mounted on horses they'd borrowed from the royal stables, galloped through the streets of New Daltenia, forcing shouting townspeople out of their way as they followed the directions the guards at the southern gate had given them to the guardsman's house.

Maeve didn't know what had brought Cutter out into the city, particularly in his wounded state and with no idea how many others were part of the conspiracy which had very nearly seen him dead, but she hoped that it was a good reason. Hoped, too, that the man was okay.

They rounded a corner onto the street the guard had indicated, and Maeve pulled her horse up in shock. A moment later, a gasping, groaning Chall—who hadn't been riding his horse so much as barely staying on it—pulled up beside her.

"*Fire and salt,*" the mage breathed. "Maeve, you don't think—"

"I do think," Maeve said grimly as she stared at the raging inferno in the distance.

"Gotta give it to the prince," Chall said, "the man knows how to have a good time."

Despite the flippancy of his remark, Maeve could hear the concern in the mage's voice, and she gave her horse's sides a kick. "Come on," she said.

They galloped down the street until, in time, they were forced to slow as a crowd of several hundred had gathered outside the home, staring at the blaze in amazement. All standing there, watching, but none helping. Maeve wanted to scream at them, to call them all fools, but she simply didn't have the time.

"Come on," she said to Chall, "we'll have to go on foot—there's no room for the horses."

"Thank the gods for that at least," the mage said, not dismounting so much as falling off his agitated horse and just managing to keep his feet by grasping desperately at one of the saddle straps. His horse snorted in obvious annoyance and Chall grunted. "The feeling's mutual, you bastard," the mage said.

Maeve paid him no mind, dismounting her own frightened horse and starting forward into the crowd.

"What about the horses?" Chall said.

"They'll be here when we get back or they won't—we've no time to worry about them in either case. Bernard needs us." At least, she hoped that he still needed them. The dead, after all, were beyond any need, just as they were beyond any help.

Cursing and growling, Maeve pushed her way through the crowd, shoving the onlookers out of her way and ignoring their offended cries. By the time they made it to the front facing the house she was covered in sweat and angry enough to kill someone—maybe quite a few someones.

No sooner had they arrived than a man staggered out of the home, the smoke parting like a curtain before him. He was covered in soot and ash, which was bad, but Maeve saw other stains among his clothing, stains that could only be blood. Which was worse.

As the man staggered, hacking and coughing, out of the smoke, Maeve saw that he was dragging a man's limp form behind him. And after them came a woman, struggling to hold the unconscious man's feet, her eyes wild with terror.

None of those in the crowd moved to help, and Maeve growled angrily. *"Out of the way, you bastards,"* she said, shoving them away as she hurried forward.

Just as she reached them the man at the front stumbled and would have fallen if she hadn't reached out to steady him. "What is it?" she demanded. "What's happened?"

The man looked up, his head swaying drunkenly. "Miss...Miss Maeve?"

She frowned, shocked to be so easily recognized particularly by a man who looked barely conscious, then something clicked into place, and she blinked. "Ned? You're...the carriage driver, aren't you?"

"I—" The man cut off into a hacking fit of coughs, then nodded. "I am, my lady."

"But...why are you here?" she asked. "I don't—"

"Prince Bernard," Chall said, coming up to stand beside her, gasping for breath. "Where is he?"

The man began coughing again, but he did not need to answer, at least not with words, for the shamed look he shot back at the blazing inferno that was the house was answer enough.

"He's...you mean he's in there?" Maeve asked, shocked.

"I...I tried to save him, my lady," the driver said, "but...he was too heavy. He ordered me to get the guardsman and his wife out...I'm...I'm sorr—"

"It's not your fault," Maeve said, putting a hand on the man's shoulder. "I'm sure you did what you could. Where is he? Where *exactly*?"

"Top of the...stairs," the man wheezed, "first hallway on...on your left. There's a study."

Chall hissed. "Of course the man'd choose now to become interested in books."

"Come on," Maeve said, "there might still be time."

"Sure," the mage said, staring at the burning house. "Time to burn to death."

Maeve glanced at him, and he grunted. "Of course I'm coming but...well, ladies first."

And with that, Maeve started forward at a jog. Several feet from the doorway the heat hit her in a wave, and she staggered, suddenly feeling as if she couldn't catch a breath. She looked back at Chall and saw that the mage had raised a hand against the heat, was looking at her, his face pale, a strained expression on it.

"Try not to breathe," Maeve hissed, and then she took a deep breath and stepped through the doorway, Chall following her a moment later.

She had thought that the heat was bad outside the home, but inside it was almost unbearable. She stared around at the smoke-filled, burning home, feeling as if she had been dropped into some terrible afterlife for the damned. The world seemed to burn around her, and she could hardly make out anything for the dark smoke billowing everywhere.

She narrowed her burning eyes, peering into the gloom and finally caught sight of the stairs on her left. She didn't bother speaking—wasn't sure if she could even if she wanted to. Instead, she moved toward the stairs as fast as she could, picking her way among the burning debris, trusting that Chall would follow.

By the time she reached the base of the stairs her chest burned from holding her breath, and hot tears were leaking from her eyes from the smoke. She grabbed hold of the stair railing, meaning to steady herself then jerked her hand away at the heat, cursing herself for a fool. She started up the stairs, her arm held in front of her in a vain effort to keep the worst of the heat from her face.

The stairs seemed to stretch on forever into the smoky gloom, and Maeve grew more and more certain with each step that she was indeed in some terrible, cursed afterlife where she would travel up the stairs for eternity. Or, at least, until the fire raging all around her caught up to her. But despite her fears, she finally reached the top. The visibility was so poor that she stepped up, thinking there would be another stair. There wasn't. She stumbled and would have fallen had Chall not reached out, steadying her.

She turned back to the mage and nodded her head in thanks. Despite the fact that the man made her life difficult seemingly every chance he got, she was glad to have him with her. Her lungs burned in earnest now, as if they had somehow caught flame, and she staggered blindly onward until she came to the hallway the driver had told them about, then she moved into the room.

The fire had not yet come to the study which was just as well for, based on the number of books and scrolls scattered about the place, if it had their rescue effort would have failed even before it had begun. She scanned the smoky room, rubbing at her burning eyes as she did. She saw several figures lying unmoving on the floor, their identities impossible to define for the smoke. She was beginning to despair when suddenly her gaze alighted on a figure, far bigger than the rest, lying on its back and surrounded by several others.

Bernard, she thought desperately, *it has to be.*

She moved to the man's side, not kneeling so much as falling to her knees. The prince's eyes were closed, and he did not stir. *Unconscious,* she thought desperately. *Please gods just unconscious.* "Get his feet," she wheezed, and Chall moved to comply.

Maeve moved Cutter's head, and she was forced to take a breath now, one that burned like fire, and she immediately began to hack and cough. She put her hands underneath the man's arms and with a desperate growl, strained to lift him. With Chall's help, they just managed it, though it was no easy thing.

And then they were shuffling toward the door, Chall leading. Each step was an effort she wasn't sure she was capable of making until she did and as they staggered down the hallway through the clouds of smoke, Maeve did not focus on the flames around her. She did not focus on the smoke filling her lungs, her eyes, her throat. Instead, she focused only on taking one step and then another, then another.

She thought it a miracle when they finally reached the stairs, and it was hard going then, Chall's face red with heat and effort as he backed carefully down the stairs as fast as he was able, losing his hold and dropping the prince's legs several times only to have to grab them again.

The house was coming apart around them, pieces of ceiling and wall falling off in burning rubble, raining everywhere, and Maeve was sure that they would never make it, that it was impossible. Her legs burned, her arms burned, her *lungs* burned, but eventually they *did* reach the door, and then they were staggering through.

She and Chall made it as far away from the house as they could—not far—before their strength gave out, and they both collapsed to the ground beside the prince's unconscious form. Gasping in air that felt finer than anything in her life, Maeve crawled to Cutter and held a shaky, soot-stained hand in front of his face, her own heart seeming to stop as she waited.

At first, she felt nothing and then the slightest bit of air against her hand, so small that she thought she must have imagined it, but then another came, and another, and she sat back, heaving a great, shaky sigh of relief, the tears streaming down her face now not only ones caused by the smoke and heat.

"He's...he's okay?" Chall offered, his voice sounding like that of a small child looking for comfort.

"Alive," Maeve managed. "At least...for now."

She saw a figure approaching and turned to see that it was the driver, Ned. "He...he alright?"

"So far," Maeve answered.

The man nodded, and Maeve was surprised to see what looked like tears in his eyes. "Thank the gods for that, at least."

"*Hey,*" someone in the crowd said, "*isn't that Prince Bernard?*"

Maeve looked up, realizing that she'd forgotten all about the gathered people in her exhaustion and fear for Bernard's life. They were all peering at the unconscious prince now.

"*Fire and salt it is!*" another said. "*That's the Crimson Prince sure as anything!*"

She looked at Chall. "We have to get out of here. Now. Berna—that is, Cutter, isn't much loved in the city, and that's before you consider the conspiracy."

Chall winced. "But how, Maeve? I got to be honest, I don't think I can carry him another foot, let alone all the way to the castle. And even if we did...who's to say it's safe there?"

Maeve grunted. The man was right, damn him. "I don't know," she said. "I just know we have to get off this street and soon. We're easy targets here and—"

"I can help."

She turned to look at the man, Ned. "You mean...your carriage? It's nearby?"

The man glanced at the people in the crowd whose muttered conversations were beginning to grow louder as they started to agree on the prince's identity. "Can't see it for that crowd—if you can still call it a crowd, seems to me it's growin' into a mob—but it's just there, at the edge of the street."

Maeve nodded, struggling to her feet then hesitating, meeting the man's eyes. "Are you sure, Ned? Likely there's people—probably some in that crowd—who are looking to kill the prince and wouldn't be all that put-out by killing anyone that gets in their way."

Ned frowned, glancing at Cutter's unconscious form. "He's a good man, the prince," he said softly. "Most folks might not know it—I'd say it's a safe bet he doesn't know it himself, but he is. A good man."

"A dead one soon, if we don't get movin'," Chall said, grunting as he climbed to his feet. "And that's something that goes for all of us. Except you, Maeve. You know, you being a woman and all."

"Come on," the driver said. "This way."

"But...what about the others in the house?" Chall asked with obvious reluctance.

Ned hocked and spat again. "Assassins. Ones who meant to kill Guardsman Nigel, the man the prince came to talk to."

"Let them burn," Maeve said. "Now lead the way, Ned. We haven't much time."

Maeve took up the prince's heavy burden again, Chall the other side, and they followed as the driver moved toward the street. He growled and hissed, knocking people out of the way until they finally dispersed enough for Maeve to catch sight of the carriage. Moments later, they were loading the prince's form inside, and she could not help but notice the mutters—growing increasingly angry—as they did.

"Best get out of here, Ned," Maeve said.

The man nodded. "But...beggin' your pardon, my lady, what about the guardsman and his wife?" Maeve followed his pointing finger to where the woman crouched, weeping, over her husband's unconscious form a short distance away.

She took a moment to consider. She didn't know what had prompted Cutter to come here, to risk his life, not anymore than she understood what had prompted the assassins to come to the guardsman's house. What she did know, though, was that, according to Ned, Cutter had been willing to sacrifice himself to save the guardsman. *The damned fool,* Maeve thought.

"Come on, Chall," she said, "help me get him."

"Much...more lifting," the mage said, grunting with the effort of stuffing Cutter's legs into the carriage, "and I'm going to expect to be paid for it."

"Oh come now, Chall," she said, "you lift that belly every morning when you get out of bed—how much trouble can a person really be? Now, let's hurry up—I don't like the look of some of these people in the crowd."

Chall said nothing to that, and in another moment they were kneeling down before the guardsman. Maeve grabbed his legs, Chall underneath his arms, and they both grunted as they began to lift him.

"Don't touch him!" a voice shrieked.

Chall grunted with surprise at that, nearly fumbling his grip on the unconscious man, and Maeve hissed as she was forced to take the brunt of the weight herself. The mage gave a sharp intake of breath that sounded as if he were in pain—likely he'd pulled something, just as likely Maeve had herself, though she probably wouldn't know it until the morning—but she didn't' have time to look. Instead, she was turning to the woman who'd risen from where she'd knelt beside her husband's unconscious form and was brandishing what looked like a knitting needle.

"Y-you, you put him down," she said, her voice and, more importantly, the hand holding the long, sharp needle, shaking terribly.

"Listen, miss," Maeve said, making an effort to keep her voice calm so as to hopefully not stress the woman out further, "we haven't come to—"

"Maeve."

Chall's voice, strained and why not? The bastard was heavier than he had a right to be, though that might have only been because they were both exhausted from lifting the prince.

"Not now, Chall," she said, still watching the woman. "Look, we're here to help, alright?"

"And how would I know that?" she demanded. "Or were those men who came into our-our *home* with swords and fire, were they here to help too?"

Maeve took a slow, deep breath struggling to keep her patience as she glanced back at the crowd—though, at this point, "burgeoning mob" would have been closer to the truth.

"Look, we're not with them, alright? We're with the prince and—"

"What *prince?*" the woman demanded.

Maeve pinched her nose between her thumb and forefinger, telling herself to be calm. The woman was hysterical that was all, and she had a right to be, didn't she? After all, men had broken into her home and tried to kill her and her husba—

"Maeve," Chall hissed again. "We really need to—"

"*Not now, Chall!*" she snapped, finally turning on the mage in anger. But as she did her eyes alighted on something sticking out of his arm, the one still wrapped around the unconscious guardsman. At first, her brain couldn't seem to make sense of what she was seeing then, finally, it did, and her breath caught in her throat. "Chall?" she asked. "Is...is that—"

"Crossbow bolt," the mage grunted, his teeth gritted together in obvious pain.

"But...what is it doing—" Maeve started, still confused.

"In my arm?" the mage asked. "Oh, I don't know, just thought I'd try it out, a new style maybe—because someone *shot me in the damned arm, Maeve,*" he hissed. "Now can we get out of here before they try again? In case you haven't noticed, I'm not exactly a small target."

Maeve frowned at the crowd surrounding them. No madman with a crossbow showed himself, and so there was no telling from where the bolt had come. Only...there was. It had struck the mage in the meat of his forearm where it had been wrapped around the guardsman's chest. Maeve suddenly went cold. "They weren't aiming for you," she said.

"Damn shitty time to miss," the mage said.

"They were aiming for him," Maeve finished, looking down at the unconscious guardsman. She spun to look at the woman. "Listen," she said, "I know you've had a pretty shitty night so far, and it isn't looking at getting any better. I know, too, that you've got no reason to trust us and plenty of reasons not to. But I need you to get in that carriage—now. Do you understand?"

The woman glanced between Chall and Maeve, her eyes wide with fear. "P-put him down," she demanded. "O-or I'll call the guards."

Shit, Maeve thought. *The guards.* There was pretty much zero chance that someone hadn't called them already. Worse, from what she'd seen so far, it seemed all too likely that at least one of those who answered the call would be looking to stick a knife in the guardsman and would be more than willing to do the same to anyone who got in their way. A new danger, then, to add to the growing list.

"*You listen to me,*" Maeve growled, shifting the guardsman's weight so that she could get one hand free then jabbing her finger at the bolt in Chall's arm, at the blood slowly leaking from the wound. "That bolt was not meant for Chall," she said. "So who do you think it was for?"

The woman stared wide-eyed at the crossbow bolt, her mouth opened in a silent "O" as she began to slowly shake her head, hoping to deny it the same way a child, closing her eyes and hiding under her coverlet hopes to deny the monsters she imagines underneath her bed.

"Your *husband,*" Maeve said. "Now listen—we can stand around here arguing, you not trusting us, but we won't be standing for long. Someone, lady—a lot of someones in fact—wants your husband dead, and, him being unconscious and all, I doubt he'll be able to put up much of an argument. My prince—the greatest warrior of the age—has already nearly died saving him. How about you, lass? You a great warrior?"

The woman swallowed. "Um...no...but..."

"So how about you let us get him into the carriage?" Maeve asked, talking softer now. "Take it from a widow who's lost far more than her share lass, we're the only chance the two of you have of making it out of this alive." *And not a very good one, truth be told.*

The woman met her eyes for several seconds, then, finally, she nodded. "Okay."

"Good. Let's go Chall, and best hurry unless you want another arrow sticking out of you."

That got the mage moving quickly enough, shoving their way through some of those in the crowd who had drifted over in a not-so-subtle attempt to listen in on their conversation.

As they walked, Maeve got a distinct, unpleasant itch between her shoulder blades, wondered if someone was lining up a shot to put a bolt between them. She and Chall walked as fast as they could, hauling the unconscious guardsman between them, and to her great surprise they reached the carriage without any fresh steel-tipped accessories sticking out of them in some grisly fashion statement.

Ned was there in a moment, helping them to load the unconscious man in beside Cutter, the guardsman's wife hurrying into the carriage after him. "You're next, Chall," Maeve said as the driver turned and climbed into his seat at the front of the carriage.

The mage nodded, hissing and cursing with effort as he heaved his bulk inside. Maeve followed after, and no sooner had she closed the door to the carriage than she heard a *thunk* in the wood of the door. Frowning she stuck her head out of the slitted window and her eyes went wide as she took in a second crossbow bolt, this one not sticking out of her or the mage, thankfully, but out of the carriage wall. "Best be going, Ned," she said, jerking away from the window. "Now."

The driver needed no more motivation than that. He gave a shout to the horses and with a snap of the reins they were off, knocking aside a small crowd that had gathered at the front.

"*Excuse me, ma'am, but where are we headed?*" the driver called back.

"Let's start with 'away,'" Maeve called back, "see how we get on!"

"You got it."

The driver went fast, and Maeve hissed in pain as the carriage bumped and rocked beneath her. She glanced at Chall and saw the mage cradling his arm—with a crossbow bolt still protruding out of it—against his chest, his eyes closed, his face pale with pain.

"How bad is it?" she asked.

The magician opened one eye, frowning. "Well, I'm no healer, Maeve," he said in a pained voice, "but it isn't good, I can tell you that much. We'd best get back to the castle, see if the fella saw to Cutter has any more potions lying around."

Maeve considered that, thinking. Chall was right—the castle healer would be able to set them all back to right. Only…"We can't go back to the castle, Chall," she said.

The mage frowned. "Sure we can. Anyway, if it's all the same to you, Maeve, I've done enough sight-seeing for one day. I'd just as soon be safe and secure in my own bed at the castle."

"But that's the problem, Chall," she said. "You *wouldn't* be safe, none of us would. After all, the castle is where the prince was attacked. And whoever poked a hole in your arm, I suspect there's more of them, the gods alone know how many. If *I* were out to kill a prince and those with him, well, where better to wait than on the roads leading to the castle where they might mean to take refuge?"

Chall groaned. "I hadn't thought of that. So...if we're not heading back to the castle...where are we going?"

Maeve glanced at the unconscious prince, the unconscious guardsman laid out beside him, his wife knelt over him, his face buried in his chest sobbing. Maeve gave her head a frustrated shake. "I don't know. We don't know how deep the conspiracy goes. We need a safe place with a healer, somewhere we can go where no one would expect."

"Sure," Chall agreed, his eyes closed against the pain, "and while we're at it, why don't we wish for a flying horse—crossbowmen would have a hard time shooting us if we were up in the clouds."

"I might know a place."

They both turned to look at the front of the carriage to see the driver, Ned, with his head poked through the opening.

"Where?" Maeve asked.

The man grunted, giving a small smile. "Well. My home. My wife knows quite a bit of healing. Not a healer exactly, but she used to be the herbwoman of a small village, if you can believe it. Why folks used to come to her for all manner of illnesses and ailments. What's more, nobody would think to look for you all there." He grinned wider. "My wife keeps a clean house, understand—despite my best efforts—but I wouldn't say it's exactly fit for a king..." He paused, glancing at Cutter. "Or a prince." He looked at Chall and gave a small apologetic shrug of his shoulders. "Can't say I can help with the flying horses though."

Maeve and Chall shared a look and the mage gave a small shrug of his own. She nodded. "Are you sure, Ned?" she asked, turning back to the driver. "That you want to do this, I mean? I don't want you and your wife getting wrapped up in…well, in whatever's going on."

"My wife and I live in New Daltenia," the man said, his expression serious, "it's our home, and Prince Bernard there, our prince. No offense, ma'am, but it seems to me we're already wrapped up in it."

Maeve couldn't argue with that, so she nodded reluctantly. "Very well only…if you're sure."

The driver gave her a wink. "Alright then. I can't wait to see the look on my wife's face when I tell her I brought Prince Bernard, Maeve the Marvelous, and Challadius the Charmer home for dinner!"

With that, he turned back to the road, and Maeve shook her head in wonder, only grateful that the man had offered. If he hadn't, she had no idea what they would have done. Or, perhaps, the truth was that she had too much of an idea, and despite her sometimes grim thoughts, she didn't fancy dying. Not yet at least.

CHAPTER SIX

If the puppet, pulled by its master's strings, had a mind of its own,
Would we know?
And if we did...would we care?
—Famed troupe leader Arl Belanin

His exhaustion and lack of sleep finally caught up to Matt, and only an hour or two after sunset, he shuffled wearily to his quarters, the *king's* quarters, crawled into his bed and fell asleep.

He did not sleep peacefully.

But then, since the events of Two Rivers, since he had killed the Feyling creature called Emma, since she had *touched* him, he never did. He did not sink into the waiting, blissful oblivion of unconsciousness. Instead, he was transported back to Two Rivers, back to the stage where he and the others had been held prisoner, where they had been meant to be executed.

But he did not stand at the front of the stage as he did in many of his dreaded recollections of that moment, when the creature posing as the mayor intended to devour him. Instead, he was shocked and unnerved to find himself in a cage, the one with iron bars had held even against Cutter's prodigious strength.

The cage door was closed, but unlike how it had been in reality, there was no clasp nor lock to keep it closed. Instead, it was as if whoever had fashioned the cage had done so with the intent that it never be opened, as if it had somehow been crafted *around* him. Matt stared at that, confused, his mind trying to understand what was happening, and was still staring when he heard a woman's familiar voice.

"Do you like it?"

He looked up from the cage and saw Emma standing a short distance away, a small smile on her face.

"Emma? I...I don't understand," he said. "What...what's happening?"

She shrugged. "What *must* happen, of course, Matthias. You see, we have both been crowned king, haven't we? And that is a problem, for you must understand that a kingdom cannot have two kings. Else, the two will argue and in their strife they will destroy the kingdom they are meant to protect. After all," she said, giving him a small smile, "much the same happened with the kingdom's two princes, did it not?"

"But...but you *weren't* crowned king," Matt said. "*I* was."

"Wasn't I?" the woman asked, smiling wider, her completely black eyes seeming to dance with mirth. "After all, I am you, Matt, and you are me. We are the same and yet...we are not."

"But...why am I here? Why am I in a cage?"

"As I believe I said," Emma answered, "a kingdom cannot have two kings, Matthias. And so I have taken...measures to rectify that."

"M-measures?" Matt asked.

She shrugged. "Hard to start a war from within a cage, isn't it? Hard to do anything, really."

"Y-you promised to protect me," Matt said, "to keep me safe. But you haven't. You're trying to, to take over. It's you who's behind the...the way I've been treating my friends, isn't it?"

She smiled. "So it is."

"This...this is wrong. You have to let me out."

She sighed with feigned regret. "Forgive me, Matthias, but I'm afraid I cannot. You would only get in my way, and I cannot have that. There is a reckoning coming to the Known Lands, to this city of New Daltenia." She paused, her eyes flashing again, only not with mirth this time but with an insane fury. "There are consequences for what your people have done, Matthias. Consequences they cannot even imagine. But soon...soon, they will not have to."

"Y-you can't do this," Matt said, anger making its way past his confusion and fear. "Y-you can't keep me prisoner in my own mind."

The woman gave a soft giggle, the same giggle that had so entranced him with her when he'd first met her and one which he was growing to hate. "Can't I? Oh, do not worry yourself so much, Matthias. I promised to keep you safe, and here, imprisoned in your own mind, you *will* be safe." She smiled wider. "At least for a while."

"B-but...you can't—"

She sighed, shaking her head like a mother weary of a child's questions. "Relax, Matthias. This is for the best, believe me. You mortals, you are always so proud of your ability to choose the courses of your lives for yourselves, and why? When left to your own devices, you most always choose hate over love, fear over understanding, and cruelty over compassion. I have given you a great gift, then. The gift of no longer being able to choose when the choice you would make could only be the wrong one. The gift of having another to choose your path for you, and not *just* for you but for all your people."

"You're...you're wrong," Matt said. "You're *evil*."

She sighed again. "Evil. Good. They are just words, Matthias. Mortal constructs used to justify the most heinous of crimes, the most terrible of tragedies. Thousands of your own people have died in the pursuit of what they believe to be 'good.'" She leaned forward then, and her face twisted with uncontrolled fury. "Thousands of *my* people have died in your search for it. But no more. Now, *you* will be the ones made to suffer. *You* will be the ones made to *die!*"

She screamed the last, and Matt stared at her in shock. "You're...you're insane."

She stood there for several seconds, her chest heaving with great, angry breaths, then, slowly, her lips curled into a humorless smile. "No, Matthias. I am not insane. I am *king*."

Matt watched her walk away, disappearing into the shadows of his mind—*her* mind, now. He could not stop her. He could not break free of the cage, the cage which had never meant to be opened. He could do nothing. Nothing but scream.

And so he did.

***

Matt woke with a gasp, jerking up in bed, his skin and bedclothes soaked in sweat. Moonlight splashed through the windows of his castle room, puddling on the floor, but otherwise the room was dark, cloaked in shadow.

He scanned the room, seeing nothing, and yet he did not feel that he was alone. Felt that someone was there with him. "Emma?" he asked, his voice a harsh croak in the stillness.

The woman did not answer, and he felt a little better. Had it just been a dream, after all? But no—he was past such empty comforts. It was real. She was there, somewhere, lurking in the corners of his mind. And somewhere, within that mind, he sat caged, screaming. Was he even now in control of himself, or did he only feel as if he were?

Sudden movement in the shadows caught his attention, and he gasped as a figure stepped forward. He thought it was her at first, thought he could see her black eyes shining in the darkness, but a moment later the figure stepped into the moonlight and he saw that it was not Emma after all but another familiar figure. "P-Priest?" he said.

"I am here, King."

Matt licked his lips, his throat suddenly unaccountably dry. "Have...have you come to kill me then?"

The man cocked his head. "Kill you, Highness? I would never do such a thing."

"Why not?" Matt asked, and then before he knew it he was burying his face in his hands, tears, hot and wet, streaking down his face.

He continued that way until he felt a hand on his shoulder and looked up to see the man standing over him. "What is wrong, King? Tell me, and I will do what I can to help. I swear it."

Matt watched the man for a second, wondering if he were telling the truth. Emma said that men lied, that they couldn't help it, for it was in their nature. And yet...the man *seemed* sincere. Still, Matt's eyes caught on the sheaths at the man's waist where the knives Matt had seen him use to great effect sat waiting to be drawn. How many had they been used against? "You cannot help me, Priest," he said softly. "No one can." The man opened his mouth to speak, but Matt forestalled him with a shaky hand. He could not tell the man. Perhaps it would be best if he did, best if

Priest drew the blades at his side and killed him, but he found that he was too afraid. "Why *are* you here, Priest?"

The man frowned, as if he knew that Matt had been about to say something else. "You cried out in your sleep, Majesty."

"Cried out?" Matt asked.

"Yes, Highness."

Matt licked his lips, suddenly nervous again, all too aware of the man's hands hanging only inches from where his blades were sheathed. "Did...did I say anything? In my sleep, I mean?"

The man watched him for several seconds, Matt waiting, tensed, sure that now would be the time he drew his blades. In the end, though, the older man only shook his head. "No, my lord. Your words were...incoherent."

Matt nodded, breathing a heavy sigh of relief. "That...that is good, at least."

"Are you sure, my King?" the man pressed. "Sure that there is nothing you would like to tell me? Perhaps I could help."

"*Help,*" Matt snarled, an alien anger rising in him. "And what help would you offer, *Priest?* Would you take my crown and set it atop your own head? Would you make of yourself a king and I no more than your puppet?"

The man recoiled as if he'd been slapped. "O-of course not. I would never do anything like that. I want...I want only to help."

Matt sneered. "Very well. If you want to help then I will tell you how—you can leave me to my sleep. And do not disturb me again. *Matthias,* not Valden, is king in New Daltenia." Then, with that, he turned over, putting his back to the man, to the world, and closing his eyes. He slept then.

But he did not sleep well.

***

Priest stood in the pale moonlight filtering through the window, staring at Matt's recumbent form, frowning. Something was wrong with the boy. Maybe badly. He wished that the others were here, Chall and Maeve and Prince Bernard. Perhaps they would have some idea of what might be bothering the youth.

True, it was a big change, starting as a villager in an out of the way place like Brighton to being king of the realm, and perhaps it was no more than that. Only...Priest did not think so. It seemed to him that there was something truly wrong with the lad, something plaguing his thoughts, his dreams.

"Watch over him, Raveza, Goddess of Temperance," Priest whispered. *"As you watch over all your children."*

He felt a little better after that, but not completely, for there was something else troubling him. When the boy had first woken from whatever nightmare had tormented him, he had said a name. "Emma." It was the same name the Fey creature in Two Rivers had used. Did he still dream of her, the first life he had ever taken? Was it only natural remorse which troubled him so...or was it something more?

He didn't know, but he determined that, next he saw Chall, he would ask the mage to examine the youth. The Fey were creatures of magic. Perhaps there was some taint left over from their encounter, and it was that which so troubled the youth. Priest knew nothing of magic, but he was confident that if there were such a taint, Challadius would be able to find it. The man was powerful, far more powerful in the gift than he liked to pretend. If anyone could discover what was bothering Matthias, it would be him.

"Watch over him, Goddess," he whispered again. And so he believed she would. Yet he did not leave the room but instead moved to the corner, propping his back against the wall and preparing for a long few hours. He believed that the goddess would do what she could, but in a world full of war and hate, she would no doubt be busy. He would remain, then, to watch when she could not.

After all, had it not been for his failure, Emma would have never taken Matt in the first place.

CHAPTER SEVEN

Am I a hero?
You're damned right I am.
I got out of bed this morning, didn't I?
The world being what it is, what could be more heroic than that?
—Challadius the Charmer

He felt her hands on him, so gentle and soft. How long had it been since he'd felt such a touch? A touch not of hostility or hate, not of violence, but of kindness?

"I missed you," he whispered, feeling tears gather in his eyes. "Fire and salt, how I missed you, Layna."

She stood over him, smiling, but when she spoke it was not to return his sentiment. Instead, her eyes pierced him, and she opened her mouth. "My *real* mother," she said. She smiled then, and the touch was gentle no longer, harder and harder by the moment, and then suddenly pain, terrible, hot pain flashed through him, and he arched his back, crying out.

His eyes snapped open, and he saw that it was not Layna who stood over him but instead another woman, one he did not recognize. She appeared to be in her mid-forties, and her hand was on Cutter's chest in an attempt to hold him still. And either she was the strongest person Cutter had ever met, or—and this was more likely—his wounds had been bad indeed and had stolen his strength.

"Easy," the woman said, using the sort of voice a person might use with a frightened horse. "Just take it easy."

Slowly, the worst of the pain began to fade, and Cutter was left breathing heavily, his body covered in sweat. "W-who are you?" he croaked.

The woman snorted. "Who am I? Just the person that saved your life, that's all. Not that you seem to ready to be thankin' me for it and I'm doubting anyone else will either. Still, I did, and it was no small task, that much I can assure you. Why, when they dragged you in here you were bloody from your feet to your withers."

Cutter frowned. "Withers? You...you know I'm not an animal, right? Like a horse."

"Better if you were," the woman said. "Horses, after all, tend not to get so torn up that it's like solvin' a puzzle trying to put them back to rights. Besides, animals rarely hurt out of cruelty. *Unlike some people*," she finished, muttering the last in a quiet voice as she turned away, grabbing several bloody rags sat on a small table beside the bed on which he lay and tossing them into a bucket on the floor.

"Well," Cutter said. "How uh...how is it?"

She glanced back at him, raising an eyebrow. "How is it? Your body, I suppose you mean? Well—it's put back together anyway, or as near as I can get it. I'm no healer, and my fool of a husband ought to have known better than to bring you here in the first place." She shrugged, wiping her hands on a rag. "Still. Done is done, I say, but I won't lie to you, Princeling. I've seen dead men and animals that looked a pretty fine improvement over you."

But Cutter was not so focused on that last bit. Instead, he found his attention going to something else the woman had said. "Your...husband?"

"That's right," she said, "though my trial might be more to the point, one set to me by the gods themselves and likely to earn me sainthood, if I make it out alive. Which likely I will. Him, though...well now that's hard to say." She glanced at him, giving a soft, humorless laugh. "My but you look confused, don't you? Well, let me go ahead and put your mind at ease. My husband is Ned. He brought you and your friends here not a couple of hours gone now."

"And...where...are they now?"

"Your friends are all resting, as you should be," the woman said. "You very nearly made a long trip tonight, Prince, all the way to the land of the dead."

"You...know?"

"That you're a prince? Of course I do," she said. "I'm not so old I can't recognize the Crimson Prince when he's lying on a bed in front of me. Anyway, all your friends are sleeping. As for Ned, he's gone off to return the carriage, though the gods alone know what he'll say to explain all the blood you and that guardsman left in there—I've seen slaughterhouses that weren't so messy. But then, my husband, while he has many faults, also has some few talents, among which is a way with words that's nothing short of extraordinary. You can thank that particular talent for being the only reason I haven't dumped you and your friends out in the street."

Cutter was just trying to catch up, as the last thing he remembered, he'd been lying in the floor of the guardsman's study, bleeding out and looking to be burning up soon enough. If what the woman was saying were true—and he had no reason to doubt it—then apparently Ned had made it out with the guardsman after all and, unsure of where to go, had brought them here. Still, that didn't explain everything the woman had said. "My...friends, you said?"

She shook her head, a disapproving scowl on her face. "My but you really were out of it, weren't you? Your *friends*, you know, the fat mage Challadius, and Maeve the Marvelous, of course." She shook her head. "That woman's as pretty as a king's dagger and, you ask me, likely just as sharp."

"Ah," Cutter said, nodding, or at least, doing the closest approximation to a nod that he was capable of just then. Maeve and Chall had come then, which of course went a long way toward explaining how he'd made it out of that burning house alive in the first place. After all Ned couldn't have carried both him and the guardsman out alone.

That brought a fresh moment of panic as a thought occurred, and he looked at the woman once more. "The guardsman, the one that came here with us, is he—"

"He's fine," she said, then made a sour face. "Or, at least, he's a damned sight closer to it than you are, and a lot closer than my fool of a husband and I will be if folks in the city find out I'm harboring the Crimson Prince."

Cutter winced. "Listen, miss—"

"My friends call me Emille. Not that I'll have any if anyone figures out I've had you as a visitor."

"Right. Look, Emi—"

"Said my friends call me Emille," she said, frowning and crossing her arms across her chest. "Them and the man I was fool enough to marry. For you, 'miss' will do fine."

"Very well," Cutter said. "All I mean, miss, is that if I've done something to offend you, it wasn't intentional."

The woman snorted at that. "Go around choppin' folks's heads off on accident a lot, do ya?"

It was Cutter's turn to frown then. "I don't understand."

"Don't you?" she asked. "You say you don't know what you've done to offend me—you who have done enough in your time to offend any right thinking man or woman in the Known Lands?"

"You mean the Fey King Yeladrian," Cutter said quietly, watching her closely now. After all, the Fey had infiltrated the capital, that much he knew, and there was no telling how many had been corrupted by their influence. Ned had proved himself loyal to the kingdom and that more than once, but just because the man was loyal, didn't mean his wife was. Suddenly, Cutter was very aware of how weak he was, aware, too, of the sharp instruments the woman had laid out on a nearby table. Some of those instruments were stained with his blood already, and it didn't seem crazy to think that they might be stained with more before the day was done.

She must have seen him taking in the instruments, for she followed his gaze, grunting. "What? You're thinking that instruments that might be used to heal might as easily be used to hurt? As if I'd have spent the last hours sweating and struggling to keep you alive just to kill you in the end?" She shook her head. "Leave it to a killer to see killers everywhere he looks." She sighed, a sigh that was angry and weary all at once. "No, Crimson Prince, the answer is not always blood, no matter how much you might think otherwise, and the gods know there's been more than enough killing in these last years. Too much. But then, you ought to know something about that, considering you're the one behind it."

"I don't understand."

"That right?" the woman asked. "Somehow while you were off marching to war, slaughtering and warring, did you miss the fact that there were plenty of good men died because you couldn't keep your axe in its sheath where it belonged? *Good* men," she snapped. "Men like my brother."

"Your brother...he died during the war?"

"Sure," she said, "him along with plenty of others. Why, you can't hardly find a man or woman in the city didn't lose someone to that damned war of yours."

Cutter could explain to the woman that there was more to it than that, that he had only killed Yeladrian because the Fey king had attacked him when he'd refused to sacrifice his own brother for peace, but he didn't. Likely she wouldn't believe him anyway and, besides, there was a better way. "Listen," he said, "despite what you think, I don't mean you or your family any harm."

She snorted. "That's what most folks say before the harm comes though, isn't it?"

He nodded. "Yes. Anyway, I thank you and your husband for all that you've done. Really. But as you say, I'd best be going. The last thing I want is to repay your kindness by getting you in trouble with anyone."

He started to rise, or at least started to *try* to rise, but she put a hand on his chest, forcing him down again. "No you don't," she snapped. "My mother, gods keep her, always said that there's plenty enough hurt in the world to go around, that a body ought to do what good she could *when* she could, try to balance the scales a bit. And I won't have you wastin' all my work getting yourself killed by running around like a fool before the stitches set. No, you'll stay right here until you're well enough to move and that's final."

Cutter frowned. "Look, I appreciate everything you've done, really, but I don't want to put you or your husband in any danger. My friends and I will leave, and you need not worry anymore over the matter."

She stared at him for several seconds, as if he were a puzzle she was trying to figure out. "You aren't the way I imagined you would be."

He gave a small, humorless smile. "Imagined I'd be drooling like a mad dog, growling and hissing, swinging my axe at anything that moved?"

She snorted. "Something like that."

He nodded. "There was a time when you wouldn't have been far wrong."

"You'd have me believe you've changed, that it?"

Cutter considered that for a minute then shrugged. "I think I have. Anyway, as for the rest, in my experience people are always different than we imagine."

"I think you may be right," she said, giving a small smile, the first sign of anything other than outright contempt since he'd woken.

"Look, miss—" he began.

"Emille," she said. "You're my prince, like it or not. I suppose you may as well call me Emille."

"Very well. Emille, there are things going on—"

"There always are," she said. He opened his mouth, meaning to respond, but she held up a hand, a gentleness to the movement he wouldn't have expected. "You just relax, Prince," she said softly, her voice not unkind, "and listen to me for a moment, how would that be?"

"Alright."

She nodded, gazing away, and her eyes took on a strange cast, as if she were staring at something far away. "You have to understand, Prince, when my brother, Elliot, was killed in the war, I was distraught, upset. I needed something, some*one* to blame, something to *hate*. Do you know what I mean?"

Cutter, who had spent the majority of his life doing the things he did for hate, nodded. "I understand."

She watched him for a few seconds then grunted. "I think maybe you do. Anyway, we were close, Elliot and me. When he was killed…well, I thought I'd never love anyone as much as I loved him ever again. But I was wrong. I came to the capital then and…I had a bad time of it. Won't waste time telling you how bad as there doesn't seem much point. Anyway, I guess I was here a year or two when I met Ned." She gave a slight sniff, running a finger along her eyes. "He was the driver of the carriage I took from my brother's funeral, as a matter of fact, though we didn't realize that 'til much later. Me and Ned got to talking and...well, you know how these things go. One thing led to another, and I realized that I'd been wrong, that, as it turned out, I could love again after all."

She sighed. "Ned was funny, you understand, but he's more than that. He's...he's a good man, a kind one. One of the few walking the face of the world, you ask me. Kind to a fault, I sometimes think. Still, it was his kindness, his willingness to do what was right no matter the consequences that made me love him so. Made me love him so much that I wanted nothing more than to have kids with him. Only...after we tried for a time, we went to see a healer and she told us that we couldn't. That *I* couldn't."

She cut off for a moment at that, her head hung in what might have been shame. "I'm...I'm sorry," Cutter said.

She looked at him, gave him a small, pained smile. "Me too, Prince. Me too. Anyway, I felt so ashamed at the time, so...useless. But Ned..." She shook her head, the pain, the sadness in her face replaced with a deep love. "Well, Ned was how he always is. Funny. And kind. That most of all. And I thought maybe it would be alright. That if the gods saw fit to keep us from having children then that was alright, just so long as I had him. Have you...have you ever felt something like that?"

Cutter considered the brief time he'd spent with Layna. He had thought, at the time, that he loved her, but he knew now, looking back, that the man he'd been had not been capable of love, not really. To love, a person has to be willing to put something or someone before themselves, and that man had not been capable of that. Not love, then. Lust, perhaps, not just for her body but for *her*, lust to have something that was coveted by others, his brother included.

My real mother.

Cutter shook his head, banishing the thought. Later, perhaps, he would seek out Petran Quinn in the castle, would ask him if he knew anything about Layna. For now, though, Emille was watching him. "No," he said finally. "No, I don't think I've ever felt something like that."

She nodded. "Not many have, I think, and the world would be a far finer place if that weren't true. Anyway, I loved him then, and I love him now. And miracle of miracles and for reasons I cannot begin to understand, he loves me back. And so, now, as then, I count myself the luckiest person in the world, possessed of something fine that I did not earn, that I could *never* earn. And so when Ned showed up, a bloody guardsman and half-dead prince in his carriage...well, perhaps you can understand some of the fear I felt. Or not fear, so much, as it was a certainty that the world had finally realized I had been given something I did not deserve and had come to even things out. To take it, to take *him* away from me. And that...that I would not allow," she said. "I would rather *die* first, for without him I'd be worse than dead. I'd be some walking corpse with nothing and no one in all the world. Do you...do you understand?"

I begin to, Cutter thought, watching her, noting the conviction in her face. He wondered what it must be like to love someone like that, to *be* loved like that. Terrifying, yes, but also amazing. "I have done a lot of bad things in my life, Emille," he said. "A lot of things I'm not proud of. But I promise you this—whatever I can do to keep your family safe, I'll do it."

Her eyes widened at that. "It almost seems like you mean that."

"I do," Cutter said, meeting her eyes.

"But...why?" she asked.

Cutter shrugged. "Because you're right. Ned is a good man, and in a world full of evil, that which is good has to be protected. Otherwise, what's the point of anything?"

She let out a heavy, shaky sigh and nodded, wiping a hand across her eyes. "Seems...seems we understand each other then."

Cutter inclined his head. "It seems we do."

She smiled then, and it was a beautiful smile, transforming her stern face, and he saw why Ned had fallen in love with her. "You know what I think? I think maybe the stories I heard about you weren't true after all."

"No," Cutter said, wincing. "They were likely true, Emille. I would not lie to you about that."

She nodded slowly. "Well. True or not, they don't fit you. Maybe they once did, but they don't now. Time to make some new stories, I guess."

He gave her a small, grateful smile. "I'm trying."

Just then, the door burst open, and Chall stepped inside, followed closely by Maeve. "Everything okay, Emille?" the mage said. "We thought we heard voices—" He cut off, his eyes widening as he saw Cutter. "Prince!" he exclaimed, grinning wide. "You're alive!"

"Mostly anyway," Cutter said, "and that thanks to Emille."

"Gods be good," Maeve said, and then she and the mage were rushing forward, embracing him so tightly that it hurt. Still, Cutter said nothing, for while it might have hurt, it was exactly what he needed.

"Alright, alright, that's enough," Emille's voice came, amused and stern all at once, "you keep goin' at him like that you're liable to undo all my hard work."

Cutter felt at once disappointed and relieved when the two pulled away, both of them grinning widely.

"We weren't...weren't sure you were going to make it," Maeve said.

Cutter gave them a smile, doing his best to hide the pain the embrace had caused. "Oh, you know. It'll take a little more than assassins, more assassins, a burning building and a suffocating bearhug to kill me."

Chall laughed at that. "Well, Prince, I don't mind telling you it's good to see you up and about."

The woman, Emille, snorted. "Not 'about', not if I can help it."

Chall winced. "Well, up anyway." He leaned forward. "She's terrifying," he whispered to Cutter.

Cutter laughed. He couldn't help it. They were still in danger, true, and not just them but the kingdom itself. And yet, they were alive and as long as there was life, there was hope.

Maeve opened her mouth to speak but, just then, there was the sound of a door opening, and she froze, her face going pale.

"Stones and starlight they've found us," Chall whispered, "we have to—"

"*Hello, the wench!*" a familiar voice called from the other room, and Cutter glanced at the woman, Emille.

She rolled her eyes, but he saw that she was grinning. "*Hello, the arse!*" she shouted back.

In another moment, Ned appeared at the doorway, the driver smiling from ear to ear as if he'd just found a fortune instead of becoming embroiled in something that could have easily ended in his death. "Hello all," he said, stepping into the room. He glanced at Cutter and grinned wider before turning to his wife. "Well. Seems you didn't kill him after all."

She sighed. "Not for lack of trying."

"Gods, but you're a terrible healer."

"And you a terrible husband."

They both grinned then, and in another moment they were embracing tightly.

Chall frowned, glancing at Cutter. "Did I miss something?"

"Oh, Challadius," Maeve said, smiling, "I think maybe we all have."

"So, how'd it go at the livery stables?" Emille asked.

"Oh, you know how it is," Ned said, giving her cheek a kiss before pulling away. "Had to battle a few assassins, save a few princes, but all in all it went off without an issue."

Emille, still grinning, rolled her eyes. "My husband, the hero."

He winked. "Don't tell anyone, eh? Wouldn't want to spoil my reputation."

"As a wife-hating lech?"

"Exactly." He sobered then, turning to look at Cutter. "So, Prince, how are you feeling?"

Cutter grunted. "Like you ran me over in your carriage."

The driver grinned. "And here I thought you were unconscious for that part. I been meanin' to get straps in the carriage, you know, specially designed for securing unconscious princes, but more's the pity I've been puttin' it off."

Cutter laughed, shaking his head. "Thank you, Ned. For everything." He turned and looked at Emille. "Thank you both."

The driver fidgeted, the praise making him uncomfortable where a dozen assassins could not. "Ah it weren't nothin' anyone else wouldn't have done in my stead," he said, avoiding Cutter's gaze. "Anyway, the she-wench here is the one to thank. Like most fools I've got fair enough practice at takin' stuff apart. She's the one knows how to put it back together again."

He gave her a fond look at that, one she returned, and Cutter and his companions only watched them in silence. Then, Ned seemed to become aware of their gazes and cleared his throat. "So what have you got fixed for dinner, woman? Gruel, I shouldn't wonder."

"That's right," she said dryly, "and yours with extra spit."

He laughed. "Just the way I like it." He turned to Cutter. "Think you could stomach some food, Highness? Or you just going to lie around all day?"

Cutter glanced at Emille, not prepared to be scolded by the woman again quite yet, and she smiled, inclining her head.

"I suppose you can move as far as the table, but take it slow, mind. You've got enough holes in you that if you were a water skin you'd have been tossed out. Why, I imagine there's more thread keepin' you together than bones and tendons just now."

Cutter nodded preparing to perform the unenviable task of sitting up, but before he could start Maeve and Chall each grabbed one of his hands, grunting with the effort of pulling him to a sitting position.

"Gods, but you're heavy one, Prince. Might want to think about going on a diet."

Cutter raised an eyebrow at Chall. "I'll...give it some thought," he panted, weary even from that small exertion. "Here, help me stand."

They did, draping his arms over their shoulders, and Cutter made it to his feet. Each step was a trial, but in time they made it through the door and into the small dining room where Cutter breathed a heavy sigh of relief as he took a chair. A moment later, the others were sitting save Ned and his wife. Emille began laying out plates and bowls of a rich-smelling soup. Cutter winced.

"Here," he said, "I can help—"

"You can help by staying right where you are," the woman said, not unkindly. "I normally work on animals, not people, Prince. Anyway, if you test those stitches enough I can't guarantee they'll hold. Besides, you look like you're about to pass out."

Cutter didn't argue with that, mostly because he *felt* like he was about to pass out, and so he remained seated as Maeve and Chall helped set the table.

"What did I tell you, Prince?" Ned asked, grinning at his wife and staring at her with what could only be deep affection. "A real ball-buster, this one."

Emille snorted. "Why don't you make yourself useful, and go and get our other guests? Before you end up wearing this stew."

"Better than eating it, I imagine," Ned quipped, but he left quickly enough through another door.

A moment later, he reappeared and, behind him, the frightened woman Cutter had briefly spoken to in the burning house, and then after her shuffled the swordsman, Guardsman Nigel. The man looked exhausted, and there was a bandage wrapped around his stomach, as well as another on his head, but his eyes were alert, his gaze clear, as he started toward the table, his wife busily fussing over him as he did.

The man's eyes alighted on Cutter, and his gaze went wide. "Prince," he said, then he started to one knee, meaning to bow.

"Relax," Cutter said, "there's no need for that, really."

The man nodded, settling for bending at the waist in a deep bow. "As you say, Highness. Only…I would like to thank you. For saving my wife and me. It…" He glanced at her, smiling. "I do not know what I would have done had I lost her."

"And thankfully you don't have to," Chall said. "Now, can we eat? The food smells delicious."

Maeve rolled her eyes. "Fire and salt, Chall, do you ever think about anything besides food?"

"Well," the mage said, making a show of thinking it over, "there's ale. You know, to wash the food down."

"Anyway," Cutter interrupted before the two devolved into an argument, "you really shouldn't be thanking me."

"Right," Chall said, "anyone can lie down in a burning building and take a nap. It was Ned who pulled you out of that inferno."

Emille frowned, glancing at her husband who began to whistle in mock innocence. "You didn't mention traipsing around in a burning building."

"Wouldn't really call it *traipsing*," Ned said. "Traipsing implies without purpose."

"And the gods know you've got a purpose—scaring your wife half to death."

"On account of you love me so much and you can't imagine your life without me?" he asked, grinning.

She scowled. "On account of it'd be a shame to lose my poison-tester before I've perfected my recipe."

The driver tipped his head back and roared with laughter at that, then started toward a chair.

"Prince," Guardsman Nigel began, "not that I don't appreciate your saving me and all, but might I ask why—"

"No, no you may not, Guardsman," Emille said. "Not during dinner. No doubt whatever matters you might have to discuss will keep for an hour, at least. After all, even conspirators and murderers have to eat, don't they?"

Cutter wasn't so sure that she was right on that, but he saw by the expression on her face that she would not be deterred, and he thought he understood. She was scared, terrified, maybe. The danger she had feared for so long had seemingly found her and her husband at last. She had spent the night patching up a bloody prince, one known for attracting violence—or perhaps for running to it. As far as she knew, she was watching her world fall apart, and in the midst of that collapse she was searching, desperately, for something normal, something familiar, some way of reassuring herself, *convincing* herself that life would go on.

The guardsman and the others were glancing at Cutter, and he gave them a nod. "Of course," he said, "we will do as the lady of the house demands."

"I'd be careful with that," Ned said, leaning back in his chair with a grin, "she comes to expect it."

They all laughed at that, Emille as well, and Cutter noted her shooting her husband a grateful look. Glad, he suspected, to have the man bring some levity to their situation.

Soon, they were all eating, helping themselves to a meal of beef and potatoes, the best meal Cutter could ever remember having. And, based on the amount of appreciative noises coming from the others—Chall in particular—he didn't think he was the only one who was impressed. There was more than enough to go around and save for the compliments tossed in Emille's direction—some words, some only noises—they ate in appreciative silence.

Finally, seeing that everyone appeared to be finished with their meal, Cutter leaned back in his chair. "Well. Best we discuss our options."

"A-are you sure?" Emille said, glancing nervously at her husband. "I mean, that is, does anyone want seconds?"

Ned gave her a small, sad smile. "Everyone's had seconds, dear. It's time."

"B-but what about dessert?" Emille said, a quiet desperation in her tone. "Surely everyone would want some dessert. I have a pie made and—"

"Later, dear," Ned said softly, putting a hand on hers. "Later, okay?"

She took a slow, shuddering breath then nodded, rising and beginning to pick up the plates from around the table.

"Oh, we can help—" Maeve said, starting to stand, but the woman waved her down.

"No, no," Emille said, "you have your talk. Assassins and conspiracies, that's your business—cleaning the table, that'll be mine." And with that, she scooped up an armful of plates and retreated into another room.

"Is...is she okay?" Nigel's wife asked.

"Oh, don't mind her," Ned said, though it was clear by the troubled look he gave the door through which she walked that he was minding her well enough, "my wife worries, that's all."

Cutter figured that if now wasn't the time to start worrying there never was one, but there was much to discuss, to decide, and little time in which to do it, so he let it go. "Well, Guardsman Nigel, I guess you're probably wondering why I came to visit you."

"Begging your pardon, Highness," the man said, inclining his head in a bow, "but...well, the thought had crossed my mind."

Cutter nodded, opening his mouth to speak, then hesitated. He didn't know how many people knew about the conspiracy, and it wouldn't do much for the city's morale if they knew assassins had made it—seemingly with little difficulty—into the castle itself. But he needed the guardsman's help, assuming he *could* help, and a quick glance at Maeve and Chall, where they inclined their heads in reluctant nods, showed that they agreed.

Cutter took a slow, deep breath. "Very well, Nigel. Best settle in—there's a bit of a story to tell."

Cutter spent the next half hour—with regular interruptions from Chall, mostly curses—recounting the events in Two Rivers and then the events which had led them to discovering the regent's true identity and him and the others confronting the Feyling within the castle and, past that, to the assassins making an attempt—very nearly a successful one—on his life. He also told the man about their encounter with Belle and his conversation with her in the dungeon.

When he was finished, he sat back in his chair, the guardsman and all those others present staring at him with wide eyes.

"*That's* why you left the castle," Maeve said.

Cutter nodded. "Yes."

She shook her head angrily. "You could have been killed, Prince, going out on your own like that, wounded as you were. You should have come and got me and Chall. If you had—"

"If he had, then the assassins would have taken my wife and I," Guardsman Nigel said. "Forgive me, my lady, for interrupting, but...thank you, Prince. I do not know what help you wish from me but..." He reached over, holding his wife's hand, the woman pale with fright. "But...thank you. For saving us."

Despite everything, despite the many dangers they faced, Cutter felt a satisfied warmth suffuse him at that. Years ago, before his exile, he had saved people before, of course, but he had never really cared. The man he had been had enjoyed only the killing, only the fighting, and had given little thought to those who happened, by coincidence, to be helped by it. He nodded. "You're welcome."

"Still," the man said, fidgeting, "forgive me, Prince, but while I'm very grateful for what you did, I'm afraid I'm not sure how I can help."

"You can help by telling me what you know of the other guards in the city," Cutter said. "There's a reason, Nigel, that those assassins were sent to your house. We killed the regent, yes, chopped the head off the snake, but even in its death throes a serpent's teeth are still sharp, might still hurt the unwary. And there is no way for us to know how many more people might be involved. No way, at least, except you."

"Me?" the guardsman asked, surprised. "But...why me?"

Cutter shrugged. "Because—"

"Isn't it obvious, man?" Chall said. "You're honest. If a crime boss like Belle wants you dead then that's about as good a vote of confidence as we're likely to get."

Cutter nodded. "We'll need to get you to the castle. We'll want you to go over all the guardsmen you know...Belle said that you had been investigating the corruption in the city. Is that right?"

The guardsman nodded. "Yes, Prince, I have, but most of my theories are only that—theories. I am afraid I do not have as much proof as I might like."

"You heard what's happened," Chall said. "Theories, guardsman, are as good as we're likely to get."

The man nodded, glancing at his wife and taking a deep breath. "I will do what I can to help, of course."

Cutter inclined his head. "Thank you," he said. "I know what we ask is no small thing."

Chall snorted. "Not small? That's a bit of an understatement isn't it, Prince? Anyway, how do we even start going about it?'

Cutter winced. "I've been thinking about that. And first we need to go back to the castle."

The mage grunted. "You mean the same castle where a group of assassins tried to kill you? *That* castle?"

"That's the one."

"The same castle," Chall went on, "that lies across the city? A city full of the gods alone know how many men and women who would like nothing more than to see us dead?"

"Well," Maeve said, "you're the one that's been complaining about being bored."

The mage frowned. "Pretty sure I never said that, Maeve."

"No?" the woman asked, then shrugged. "Sorry. You complain so much, sometimes it's hard to remember it all."

Chall scowled, but it was Cutter who spoke. "Still, Chall's right. We'll have to be careful. There's no way of knowing how many people are out looking for us now."

Chall sighed. "Suppose it'd be too much to hope they all got tired and went home."

"Yes," Cutter said, "I believe it would."

"Fine," the mage said, "so we have to make it back to the castle. That still doesn't explain *how* we'll do it. I mean, do you not think it would be better to stay here for a while, Prince? I mean, stones and starlight, you can barely walk and the guardsman here isn't much better off."

"I don't see that we have a choice," Cutter said. "We can't stay here. Sooner or later, the men looking for us will find us and when they do, they'll no doubt mean to punish Ned and his wife for giving us shelter." He shook his head grimly. "And I won't have them getting hurt because of us."

Chall frowned. "Well, she is a damned fine cook." The mage pointedly avoided looking at Maeve who was scowling at him. "Anyway, do we have any idea of how we might *make* it back to the castle? You know, with all our parts in their proper places?"

Cutter glanced around at the others but no one seemed to have any answer for the mage's query, so he sighed. "Not ye—"

"Might be I can help you with that," Ned said, walking back into the room. "Sorry," he said, smiling and not looking sorry at all, "couldn't help but overhear—mostly because I had my ear pressed to the door. Anyway, if it's the castle you need to make it to, there might be a way we can do that. After all, I'm a carriage driver, ain't I?"

Chall snorted. "Unless you're a carriage driver whose carriage is maybe made of iron, impervious to arrows or assassins trying to break their way in, then I don't think that'll help much."

"Iron?" Ned asked, frowning, then shaking his head. "No, no just a regular carriage. You see—" he paused, leaning in and speaking in a conspiratorial whisper as if divulging some great secret—"were it to be made of iron, the horses wouldn't be able to bear the load."

Chall sighed, rubbing a weary hand across his eyes. "You know, people hate jokes made in poor taste."

"Do they, Chall?" Maeve said. "Do they?"

The mage frowned. "Fine, fine, but my point still stands. In a carriage, why we'd be sitting ducks for anybody who took it in mind to put a few arrows in us. We only made it away from Nigel here's house because they expected us all to be too busy being dead to think much on escaping."

Cutter grunted. "Chall's right, Ned. I appreciate the offer, but a carriage won't work."

"Not a normal carriage, maybe," Ned admitted, "but what about one running a plague banner?"

Chall let out a snort. "Look, Ned, I don't want to get hacked to pieces by angry assassins, but I don't much care for the idea of catching the plague either."

Ned laughed. "Well, we wouldn't *actually* be transporting plague victims, would we? Instead we'd just be carrying a prince and his...housekeeper?"

"*Mage,*" Chall growled.

"Huh," Ned said. "Alright, mage, then...they don't have any physical requirements for that sort of thing?"

Cutter laughed at that—he couldn't help it. Soon, the others joined in, and Chall was left scowling until, finally, he too grinned. "Fine, fine, I deserve that," he said. "But do you really think it'd work?"

Ned shrugged. "Well, it ain't a perfect plan, maybe, but I figure it's better than the others on offer. Mostly because, well, you know...there *aren't* any others."

They all turned to Cutter then, and he frowned, thinking it through. He remembered the plague banners, of course, for they had been used only shortly after he and the rest of the people who'd fled their homeland arrived. Their time on the ships had not been easy. Poor, overcrowded conditions, not enough food to go around, it was no wonder that a sickness had begun to transfer among the people. When they arrived in the city, the banners had been one way they'd undertaken to fight the plague and thankfully they, combined with the other measures, had worked, finally getting the sickness under control.

"Are any of those banners still around?"

Ned grunted. "I'll admit it's been a bit since they were used, but I imagine I could scrounge one up. Delilah—the sour-faced woman you met—might not be a sweetheart, but she's nothing if not organized. A proper place for everything and everything in its proper place, or so she loves to tell me. Anyway, I figure if anyone in this city knows what became of those old banners, it'll be her."

Cutter nodded, thinking it through. It would be dangerous, of course, but then, unlike the other ideas that had flitted through his mind, it, at least, had the added benefit of *possibly* working. "And these banners...won't someone know you shouldn't be running them, or..."

"Well," the driver said, "there's just one thing, of course. The banners can't be run except for on express permission from one of the royal line. Luckily..." he paused, grinning—"we've got us a prince handy."

Cutter scratched at his chin, examining it further, looking for holes. He found plenty, of course, but then when a man only had one option it was, by default, the best one. He looked back up at Ned and then saw, beyond him, the man's wife, Emille.

She stood in the doorway, staring at her husband's back, an unmistakable expression of concern on her face.

Cutter watched her for a moment, wondering again what it might be like to love and be loved in that way. Thinking, too, that such a love ought to be protected. Otherwise, what was the point of anything? Finally, he shook his head. "No."

The carriage driver raised an eyebrow. "Sorry, Prince, but...why?"

Cutter glanced at Emille, and the woman met his eyes for a moment, then he turned back to her husband. "It's too dangerous, Ned. You and your wife, you have done enough for us—*more* than enough. I can't ask anymore of you. It wouldn't be right. Besides, we have no idea how bad it is in the city. Already the two of you might be in danger."

"Excuse me, Prince, if I'm out of line," the driver said, "but every man or woman walkin' this earth with breath in their lungs is in danger. That's sort of the deal with life. You can't have it without the danger that comes along with it. And, beggin' your pardon, Highness, but New Daltenia ain't just your city. It's *our* city. Our *home*. And if a man won't risk himself to protect his home..." He paused, glancing back at his wife. "To protect his family...well, then he ain't no man at all, least so far as I'm concerned."

Cutter grunted. "I understand, Ned, really I do. But it's out of the question. We'll find another wa—"

"No, you won't."

He cut off, and they all turned to regard Emille who had come to stand beside her husband, one of her hands, seemingly of its own will, coming to rest on his shoulder. The woman gazed at her husband for a second and give a heavy sigh. "You won't find another way, Prince, because there isn't one. You know it, my Ned knows it, and gods forgive me but I know it too. The plague banners aren't the right choice—they're the only one."

Cutter shared a glance with Maeve and Chall then turned back to the woman. "Are you sure? Because we can find another way, there's still time."

"Forgive me, Prince, but no, there isn't. If things are as bad as you say, then every moment that passes puts everyone in the city at risk. The king himself is at risk, and though I don't know much about this King Matthias, what I've heard is good. Besides, we've tried princes—I think it's high time we tried a king." She gave him a small smile to take the worst of the bite away, and Cutter sighed.

"You're sure?"

Emille and Ned met each other's eyes for a moment and, finally, the woman nodded. "I'm sure."

Cutter gave her a moment, gave them both a moment, to change their mind, but they only turned to him, and finally he nodded. "Alright," he said. "Then that's what we'll do."

He started to his feet, then a wave of dizziness overcame him, and he was forced to catch himself on the table.

"You need to take it easy," Emille said. "You're alive—though the gods know how—but if you keep overdoing it...well, I think there's even a limit to what the great Crimson Prince can endure."

Cutter grunted. "Right."

"Well," Ned said, "if I'm not going to have to hold you down lest you go tryin' to do cartwheels, Prince, then I'd best be off."

"Off?" Emille said, spinning to look at him.

The driver gave her a smile. "Well, sure, wife of mine. All well and good outfitting the carriage with plague banners, a damned fine plan if I do say so myself, but it'll prove a bit tricky if we don't have the banners. Or...well, you know, the carriage to put them on, seein's as I left the other with Delilah back at the stables."

Cutter could see the worry in the woman's face, and he nodded. "Fine," he said. "I'll go with you."

Ned winced. "Prince, I don't mean to argue—the gods know I've no wish to see the angry end of that axe of yours, but it seems to me that…begging your pardon, in your current state, well, you'd prove more of a burden than a boon, if you understand my meaning."

"It's out of the question," Emille said. "What you need, Prince, is rest. A good month of it, if I had my way, but since you all seem intent on getting your fool selves killed, you'll at least take a few hours, the time it takes Ned to get the carriage and come back." She turned on Ned, her expression dangerous, challenging. "And you *will* come back. Won't you, husband?"

He cleared his throat. "Of course, dear."

"As for you," Emille said, turning to gaze at Guardsman's Nigel's wife then frowning. "I'm sorry, I didn't get your name."

The woman shifted in her chair, clearly uncomfortable being the center of attention. "It…it's Paula, ma'am."

"Paula then," Emille said, smiling. "Now, tell me, Paula, are you as set on getting yourself killed as these damned fool men are?'

Paula hesitated, clearly unsure of what to say, glancing at her husband for support. "I…that is—"

"Good," Emille said. "That settles it. You'll be staying with me until the prince and the rest of this lot deal with the…well, the vermin infestation they seem to have acquired back at the castle."

"Thank you, ma'am," Guardsman Nigel said, "but are you sure she…that is we don't want to be a burden—"

"I'll hear no more of it," Emille said. "It's decided. Besides, what burden? It'll be good to have someone to talk about my wayward husband to."

"Complain, you mean," Ned grumbled.

"Oh, sweet one," Emille said in mock affection, running a hand along his face, "as it comes to husbands, don't you know that they are one in the same?"

The man winced but nodded. "Very well," he said, "seeing as it all seems settled, I suppose I'd best be off. If I'm lucky, I can catch Delilah before she goes off shift—you know, have a nice chat. Or, well, I'll chat. Mostly, she'll scowl and scold, but then that's life, isn't it?" He turned to his wife. "A kiss before I go, my dear?"

"I think not," Emille said, pulling her face away.

Ned watched her for a moment, an almost pained look on his normally amiable, jolly face. "Very well then. I'll return shortly."

He walked toward the door and paused as Emille called out. "The kiss—it'll be waiting for you. When you get back."

Ned grinned at that, giving her a wink, and then he was gone. Cutter watched him go. No soldier or warrior this, and certainly he had not been in as many battles as Cutter himself had. And yet...in many ways, at least in all the ways that counted, Cutter thought the man was far braver than he was. And not just braver—better.

"Alright you lot," Emille said, a strained sound to her voice that made it apparent she was struggling to hold back tears, "well, let's not just sit around idly, eh? There's empty plates and dishes need cleaning. You lot get to work—if you ate, you clean."

They all rose to follow her orders. Cutter rose, too, but Emille hurried forward, putting a hand on him before he could rise. "Not you, Prince," she said. "You come with me."

"But I can—"

"What you can do is follow me, Prince. You need to lie down before you fall down."

"It's fine, Cutter," Maeve said. "We'll keep watch. You get some rest—I imagine you'll need it."

Cutter put up no more argument than that, for he didn't have the energy. "Very well, Emille," he said. "Lead the way."

But as it turned out, Cutter was barely able to stand under his own power, exhausted from his wounds and lack of sleep, and the woman snorted, draping one of his arms over her shoulders before starting to guide him back to the room in which he'd awoken.

"Cutter, huh?" the woman asked in a strained voice as she helped him into the room. "Well, can't say it doesn't fit. Bit on the nose though, isn't it?"

Cutter grunted. "I didn't choose it."

She sighed. "Well, no I suppose not." She led him to the small cot he'd woken on and after considerable effort on both their parts, he was laying down. "Hold for a moment—I've got something that will help you sleep."

"I really don't—"

"I'll hear no more argument out of you, *Cutter*, prince or not," the woman snapped.

He watched as she moved to a side of the room, opening a cupboard and retrieving a glass and a flask containing an amber-colored liquid. She poured some of the liquid into the glass, replaced the flask, then moved toward him.

He frowned, looking at it. "What is it?"

"Does it matter?" she asked, arching an eyebrow.

Cutter gave her a small smile. "I suppose it doesn't." He took the glass, drinking it, and no sooner had the liquid gone down his throat than a pleasant numbness began to spread through his body, taking away the worst of the pain, the worst of the exhaustion.

"Better?" she asked, her voice seeming to come from very far away.

"Better," he said, blinking eyelids that felt impossibly heavy.

The world began to slowly blur then, and the blur that was Emille nodded, glancing around. "Not much of a room, is it?"

"It's…fine," Cutter said muzzily.

"No, it's not," she countered. "Still…it might have been. You see, before…before we knew that I couldn't have children…this was going to be the baby's room."

Cutter didn't know what to say to that, thought that whatever he said could only be the wrong thing, and so he said nothing.

"I love that man, Prince," she said. "I love him more than all the world. Love him more than all the princes and all the kingdoms in it. Do you understand that?"

"I…I think I do."

"Then understand this," she said, leaning in close, and though her face was only inches from his own, it, like the room behind it, was still little more than a blur. "I would do anything to keep him safe," she hissed, "*anything*. And gods help the person who brings him to harm. I am a healer, Prince, it is true, but remember, I am not *only* that."

"I promise you, Emille," Cutter said, having to force the words out past a tongue that felt numb, "I don't mean Ned any harm."

"I believe you," she said. "But the truth of this cruel world, Prince, is that in our lives—and in our deaths—intent has very little to do with it."

"I'll keep him safe, Emille," Cutter said, his own voice sounding as if it came from very far away as he slowly sank further toward unconsciousness. "You have my word."

She might have said something then or perhaps she did not. Either way, Cutter was beyond it, beyond the sights and sounds of the mortal world, and whatever words she might have spoken did not follow him into the darkness. The only thing that did was a memory of another promise he had made to another woman, long ago, a promise to protect her child, to protect *his* child, though at the time he knew it not.

The same child who had grown to the age of fifteen before he'd lost his entire village and everything he called home, before he was forced to flee into the Black Woods, the heart of the Fey power. There to be attacked by a gretchling only to flee to the burned-out shell of another village, to be forced to kill to protect himself and then, after all of it, to be made king of a kingdom so very close to the brink of destruction.

He had promised to keep the baby safe, and by any accounting, he had done a poor job.

His last thought, then, before the darkness took him, his last hope, was that this time perhaps his promise might mean something.

CHAPTER EIGHT

There are always two faces to any man—
The face he shows the world...
And the real one.
—Murderer interviewed in his cell in New Daltenia's dungeons an hour before his execution

"Look at them down there, *Priest,*" Matt sneered, staring out the window of the castle's high tower. "Scurrying about like insects."

Priest watched the youth's back, tensed with some emotion. He sounded angry. But then, he always sounded angry now. "They are your people, Highness."

"My people," Matt said with disgust. "And I their lucky king. Do you see, Priest, the way they scuttle here and there? Do you see that great line going into and out of the castle gate?"

"I see them, Highness," Priest answered, wishing more than anything that Chall and the others would return. He wanted to talk to the mage about Matt's condition, *needed* to talk to him, but so far there had been no sign of them. Another thing to worry over then and with plenty of company.

"Like rats," Matt said. "Or...no. Ants. That's what they are. Ants. I have studied ants before, you know, as a boy. Me and some of the other boys from Brighton used to watch them, to wonder at their complex anthills. Before invariably kicking them down, of course."

"Most children do as much," Priest said, unsure of how to answer.

"So they do," Matt nodded, still not turning away from the window. "So they do. They're funny things, ants. Always walking in their orderly rows, going out into the world in a line empty-handed and returning with food and whatever else the little bastards might want for their hives. Just like those people down below, Priest. They come here, leaving their homes, their *hives,* empty-handed, and yet when they leave, they carry nothing that I can see. So tell me then, Priest, what is it that they take with them? What is it that they carry away from here, from me?" He gave a ragged, humorless laugh. "Besides my patience, of course."

"Isn't it obvious, Highness?" Priest asked. "They carry hope."

"Hope," Matt repeated, and he did turn away from the window then, studying Priest from eyes surrounded by dark, ugly purple bruises which spoke of a desperate need for sleep.

"That's right, sire," Priest said. "Hope."

"Hope," Matt said again, making a sour face as if even the word tasted bad. "For what?"

"I imagine they hope for what all men and women hope for, Highness. That today will be good, that tomorrow will be better. For themselves, yes, but for their families also. They hope, too, that their king cares for them, that he will protect them."

Matt snorted, but he said nothing, turning back to the window once more. "That is what I'm supposed to be then?" he said finally in a weary voice, so quiet that Priest could barely make it out. "A source of hope?" He gave another soft, humorless laugh as if even the very idea was ridiculous.

"A good king, Highness," Priest said, "is, like a good mother or father, whatever those he watches over needs him to be."

Matt grunted. "Where are Cutter and the others?"

Priest blinked, surprised by the sudden change of topic. "Sire?"

Matt turned to look at him then, his eyes narrowing as if in suspicion. "You heard me—where are they, *Priest?* It is they, after all, who put me here on this throne. Have they so soon abandoned me to rot on it alone? Or is it worse than that? Do they plot against me, somehow?"

"Majesty, I don't understand what you mean. Cutter and the others, they would never plot against you—they are your friends."

"Are they?" Matt asked. "Then where *are* my friends, Priest?" the king shouted. "Where have they gone? Oh, sure, you would have me believe that they care only for my welfare, but if that were true then why are they not here to see to it themselves? What's more, I am not so sure—for all I know, they do indeed plot. For all *I* know, you might well plot with them. After all, that's one of the things about kings, isn't it? They have a way of getting assassinated."

"Sire," Priest said, "surely you can't believe that Cutter or Chall, that *any* of us would ever hurt you."

Matt's lip snarled back from his teeth at that. "Can't I? You would do well, Priest, to not assume you have any idea what I might believe. Now, leave me. I am sick of you looking over my shoulder, sick of feeling your judgement, your disapproval."

"Sire—"

"*Leave me!*" Matt screamed, rounding on him, his eyes wild.

"Very well," Priest said, focused on keeping his voice soft, calm, as if he were talking to a frightened animal. Which, just then, he might as well have been. "I will leave, Highness, but I will not be far—I will be outside the door, should you need me."

"Oh, that I do not doubt," Matt sneered, and left with nothing else to do, Priest turned and left.

***

Matt watched the man go, feeling both angry and ashamed all at once. It wasn't fair, perhaps, to take out his anger at his own misfortune on the man, but then neither was it fair that such misfortune had fallen upon him.

He waited, wondering if Emma might speak, might scold him—she often did. But for the moment, at least, she said nothing. Not that her silence was much comfort. For silent or not, she was there, in his head. Always she was there, and though she did not speak, he could feel her, could feel the bit, like those used on horses, in his mouth. Were his words even his, any longer? Or did they belong to the woman? He sighed heavily, telling himself, as he had so often of late, that he would apologize to Priest the next time he spoke to the man but knowing that he would not.

For the truth was that while he loved Priest and Chall, Maeve and Cutter, he hated them also. Hated them for what he had become. Perhaps it was not their fault and perhaps it was—in the end, it made no difference. Even the fact that Cutter had saved him from certain death in Brighton was no comfort, for it would have been better for him to have died along with everyone else he'd ever known than to come here and *become* what he now was. A haunted, shell of a puppet who had no free will of its own except that which its master allowed it to pretend at.

A master who, it seemed, was growing stronger, more in control by the day, who was able to exert more and more influence over him, invading his mind like some great army. With each day that passed he felt more and more of himself slipping away, replaced with...something else. Something that was not him. How long, then, before there was none of him left at all? Nothing but his face, his eyes, and even those his no longer. Stolen from him, like his mind, to be used as Emma saw fit. And just like the puppet who was forced, when not being used by its master, to lie and wait until it might be used once more, there was no escape for him. How, could a puppet run without its master making it? How could a man escape his own mind? What, save death, could end such an imprisonment?

A thought struck him then, and he turned back to the window. A month ago, a year ago, such a thought never would have come to him and, if it had, it would have been like no more than one of those empty, errant thoughts that sometimes finds its way into a person's mind. The same sort of thought, in fact, a man might have when standing at the precipice of a great cliff. Thinking to himself, *Oh gods, what if I fell off? Oh gods...what if I jumped?*

This, though, was different. This was no errant thought to be carried away like a fallen leaf on a breeze of reason. In normal times, such a thought would have seemed dark. It did not seem so now. He was in pain, always in pain, pain that a statue might feel, if it could, while it was slowly torn down, what comprised it chipped away bit by bit. And what was the only good thing to be said about pain? The only comfort one might seek while experiencing it? That eventually, sooner or later, it would end. That was all a person in pain could hope for.

An ending.

Matt took a slow, deep breath, then stepped toward the window once more. Four feet in height, he judged, two in width. Larger than any of the windows he might have ever seen in the village of Brighton, even those which had bedecked the house of Mister Landam, the richest man in the village. Still, it seemed pretty small for his purpose and that was not the only problem. The window was bisected with a cross-frame of thick, hardy wood. It would not be easy to break such a thing, if a man set about trying to. But then, what in life ever was?

Had the frame been built in such a way for safety? So that should a man or woman stumble into it, it would not give way to their weight but would keep them from falling the hundred-foot drop to the ground below? Likely it had been, but that made little difference. Matt thought that, given enough force, enough motivation—and that, at least, he had in abundance—a man *could* break his way through.

No, the window would not stop him, thick frame or not, and there was no one around—Priest, for example—who might do it either. The only thing left, then, was the courage to get the thing done and done quickly, for while Emma's attention might be somewhere else now, likely on whatever manner of chisel she used to work away at his will, his *self,* she would return. Always, she returned.

He put his hand on the rough stone of the windowsill, meaning to climb up, then hesitated for a moment, all his attention focused on the feel of the stone beneath his hands, the slight imperfections in it. He glanced once more back at the door. Priest would be on the other side of it. A dozen feet away, no more than that. Emma was not here. Might he not rush to the door and tell Priest the truth, tell him what was happening? Perhaps the man might even be able to help him, and if not him, then Chall. Chall was a mage after all.

But...no. No he had tried to tell them before and always she had stopped him. Even in those moments when he had been sure she was gone, she would appear, would rip the words out of his mouth before he was ever able to voice them. No, if he went for help, she would know—he did not know *how* she would, but she would. And like the other dozens of times he had tried to tell his friends what was happening to him, he would fail.

There was only real option, only real choice. He turned back to the window, putting his other hand on it. He did not stop this time, did not *allow* himself to stop. Instead, he hoisted himself up so that he was kneeling in the small sill, his head inches from scraping the top of the window. He did pause then, gazing out of the window at the people milling about below, going about their lives.

Did they find comfort in having him as their king? Did they believe that things were going to get better? Fools, if so, for Matt had seen enough of the world to know that things only ever got worse. Men's lives were like a great mountain in the beginning, a mountain that would never grow any taller, any grander than how it had started. Instead, wind and rain and time would do their work, carving away at it bit by bit, until, in the end, nothing would be left as testament to that once great edifice, nothing but dust.

"I'm sorry," he whispered, and in that moment he could not have said to whom he spoke. Perhaps it was to Cutter—his father—who had tried to save him and in doing so had taken upon himself a task that could only end in failure for he, like all men, was doomed. Perhaps it was to Maeve who had treated him so kindly, or Chall who had made him laugh when he needed it. Perhaps it was to Priest who was always a calm, confident presence at his shoulder or to the people in the city below who had already been through so much. What would they think, he wondered, when they woke to hear news that their king was dead, his life taken by his own hand? What could anyone think?

The same, likely, as they would think when, should they find themselves sailing upon a ship, they saw the captain regard an approaching storm only to draw his belt knife and slit his own throat. But he could not think of them, not any of them. He could not help them, could not even help himself. Except to leap, to bring an ending to the pain.

Matt took a deep breath, preparing himself to ram against the window...and then hesitated. He did not hold a knife, certainly not one poised at his throat, and yet...he did. He could feel the kiss of its steel against his neck, knew that but one move would end it all. Would bring oblivion, yes, but peace, too. He knew that...and yet, he did not move.

For despite the knowledge that he might find peace, one simple truth stood firm against it—he did not want to die. Perhaps they all *were* doomed, perhaps life was nothing but the slow erosion of a man, the slow giving way to the inevitable chiseling of time. And yet...he did not want to die.

He gritted his teeth, willing himself to dive against the window, imagining it in his mind, and yet his body failed him, and he could not move. Finally, his forehead covered in a cold sweat, he climbed back down, sat with his back against the wall, buried his face in his hands, and wept.

Is that it?

He knew that voice. How could he not? It was the voice, after all, that had haunted his dreams and his waking moments since Two Rivers. A voice that, as the days went on, was slowly changing, becoming *his* voice. And when that changing was complete, he knew that so, too, would be his doom.

"You...you were here all along."

It was not a question, but she chose to treat it as one. *Of course, Matthias. I am always here. It is my* home, *after all.*

"Then...why? Why did you allow me to...to..."

To what, exactly? You did nothing, Matthias, and you would do nothing. *Even had I not been prepared to stop you—which I would have—still you would have never done it. Face it, Matthias, you are a coward, and cowards are not the doers of great things. By leaping from the window, you knew that you might save yourself, might, in turn, save your kingdom, and yet you balked at it. And do you know why?*

"Just leave me alone," he sobbed, hating the weak, scared sound of his voice but unable to change it. "Please, gods, just leave me alone."

That I cannot do, Matthias, for we are one, inseparable. And the reason you could not take your own life is because of one thing and one thing only—hope. It is a mortal construct, Matthias, hoping when all point of it is gone, and it is ever the tool of the coward, the man who, too weak to face what he must, tells himself that perhaps things will get better. But they will not, Matthias, not for you, at least.

"Why won't you just kill me then?" Matt demanded. "Gods, why won't you just *kill me?*"

In time, Matthias, I will allow you to die, but only when the changing is complete. Until then, know that you are powerless against me. That you can do nothing but what I wish for you to do. Now come, Puppet. There is something in the dungeons which demands our attention.

Matt rose then, wiping the sleeve of his jerkin across his eyes and took a deep slow breath. And then he did the only thing he could do—he obeyed.

***

He woke to a hand on his shoulder, a hand which acted as a tether, pulling him out of the dark depths of dreamless sleep and into the world once more. Cutter blinked, looking up to see Maeve standing over him.

"Prince," she said softly, giving him a small smile.

"Maeve."

"It's time."

He nodded, slowly rising and wincing at a lance of pain that went through him as he did. Still, he consoled himself with the fact that he was able to sit up without aid. She watched him, close enough to help, if he needed it, but not doing so, thinking, likely—and likely being right—that he would be frustrated if she did.

A good friend, always there when he needed her. The best of friends and one far better than he had ever deserved. And what had he ever shown her for that friendship? Nothing but pain and loss. "Maeve..." he began, "I'm sorry. For...well. For everything, I guess."

She frowned. "Prince?"

He winced. He had never been good at this sort of thing, had been far better at causing harm than doing good, and so he did not know how to even go about it. "What I mean...you've always been beside me, all of you, supporting me. You, Chall, Priest, and Matt, you're the best things in my life..." *the only things, really,* "and I am sorry that I have brought so much pain to you. That I made you go down this road."

She gave a soft laugh, shaking her head. "Gods, Prince, but you are not nearly half as clever as you think yourself. Still, I suppose I can't hold it against you—you're a man. It's not your fault."

He blinked at that. He wasn't sure what response he had expected from the woman, but that had not been it. "I'm sorry?"

She sighed. "Men. Gods help you, you're all good enough at swinging your sword at something—or an axe, come to it—but none of you ever stop to question why, do you? Look, Prince, I'm a grown woman, alright? Anything I've done, I've done because *I* wanted to, not because you made me. I mean...do you really think you could make me do anything I didn't want to?"

Cutter grunted. "Well. No."

"Exactly," she said. "I make my own choices. And sure, more often than not, those choices seem to be, in retrospect, just about the worst I could have made, but that's just part of being human. And while many of my choices were a mistake," she went on, leaning in and cupping her hands gently around his face, "staying with you and the others, that wasn't one of them." She sighed heavily at that, sitting back. "You know, Prince, back in Daltenia, I had a husband, a child too. And they were everything to me."

"Maeve," he said, "you don't have to—"

"No, I think I do," she interrupted. "You see, when the Skaalden showed up, those giant demons of frost and death, they took my world from me, Prince. The same way they took yours, the same way they took everyone's that day. I'm old enough now to know that the world doesn't just take from me, but from us all the same. When I got on those ships...I didn't know where we were going and, honestly, I didn't care. The fact is, if I'd have been in my right mind, I probably would have stayed in the city, let those damned creatures finish what they started. But everyone was pushing and shoving, yelling 'this way, hurry' and so I just...followed."

She shrugged, taking a hitching breath. "Didn't think I'd ever have anything worth living for again, not after losing my family." She paused at that, wiping a hand at the tears gathering in her eyes. "But then I met you, you and Chall and Priest, and I found a new family." She gave him a half-hearted grin. "A far cry from the one I left behind, true, but a family nonetheless. And with that, I found a reason to wake up each morning, a reason to keep breathing. I've talked to Priest and Chall, and they feel much the same. You did that for us, Prince. *You*. Oh sure, you were a bloodthirsty bastard, there's no denying that, but you gave me something I can never repay you for. You gave me my life back. Not as good as the one I lost maybe, but pretty damned fine just the same. So no, Prince, you don't owe me anything—it's me that owes you."

Cutter stared at her in shock for several seconds, unsure of what to do, what to say. Finally, he nodded. "Thank you, Maeve."

She shrugged. "Sure."

"Maeve," he said after a time, "about Layna—"

"Oh gods," she said, "you're not going to go apologizing for that again, are you? Look, Prince, it was a long time ago. Sure, you made a bad decision, but you ain't the first man to dip his wick in—"

"No, no," Cutter interrupted, "it isn't that."

"Oh," she said, frowning. "Well. What then?"

"I was just going to ask...you knew her pretty well, didn't you?"

She frowned. "You never asked me about this before."

"No, I...I suppose I didn't. It was...too painful, I think."

She nodded slowly. "And now?"

He gave her a small smile. "I guess I'm getting used to pain."

She watched him for a moment. "Well. To answer your question, yes, I knew Layna pretty well. Or, at least, I tried to. She was a quiet one, as you well know, kept herself to herself as my mother would have said. Still, I'd like to think that we were friends."

Cutter nodded. "And...her parents. Did you ever meet them?"

Maeve cocked her head curiously. "What's going on, Prince? Why are you asking me about Layna's parents?"

"Please, Maeve. Just...did you meet them?"

She frowned, a thoughtful expression on her face. "Well, as I said, Layna kept to herself. Wasn't exactly the type of person that invited you over for dinner. But then, I guess you know that." She glanced at him, and he said nothing. After a moment, she nodded. "Well, yes. To answer your question, I met her mother and father. Once, before your brother asked for her hand, she asked me for my help with..." She winced.

"Help?" Cutter asked.

"Well, you know, of course, that Layna came from common stock, don't you?"

"I...I had heard as much."

She nodded. "Well, it was true. As common as dirt, I believe her father said to me." She shook her head, giving a soft laugh. "A funny man, her father. At least..." She frowned, a dark expression coming over her face. "At least, he was that time."

It was Cutter's turn to frown then. "That time?"

Maeve waved a hand, frustrated. "I'm doing this badly. Anyway, her father *was* a funny man, a good one, too. And I don't care what anyone says, her father, her mother, they were both some of the finest people I've ever met, far better than the nobles that turned their noses up at Layna, that's for sure. Anyway, her father...what was his name..."

"What about her mother?"

Maeve raised an eyebrow. "Her mother?"

Cutter cleared his throat. "That's right."

"Well now," Maeve said slowly, "her name, at least, I remember. Ladia, I think it was."

Cutter nodded slowly. "Ladia."

"That's right. She was a good woman, too, quiet, like her daughter, but kind. The sort of kind that you didn't need to hear her say anything to know it. Just a comfort." She shook her head. "It must have been real hard for Layna to leave her behind, to go and stay at the castle around people who scowled at her every time she passed. Still..." She shrugged. "She loved your brother, there's no doubt about that." She winced. "Sorry, Prince, I didn't mean—"

"No apology necessary, Mae," he said. "If anyone's in the wrong, it's not you. Anyway, what I meant to ask...did you have any reason to think that maybe, well that Layna was adopted?"

Maeve frowned. "Adopted? What would make you ask that?"

"I had a dream, not long ago, about that time, I mean. About Layna. And...in the dream, she said something about her 'real' mother."

"Which got you to thinkin' that maybe Ladia wasn't her real mother? And what would that matter, if it were the case?"

Cutter shrugged. "Probably it wouldn't. I don't know, I just...well, I didn't remember it. Not at least until I had the dream."

She nodded slowly. "Well. I wouldn't get too worked up over it, Prince, though no doubt those damned nobles would have had a time with it back then. Anyway, probably it was just a dream or you are misremembering. I once heard Chall say that dreams aren't much better than illusions, only they're just the ones we cast over ourselves and considerin' the number of times I've dreamed about my husband and daughter only to wake and be alone again, I got to say that on that, at least, I'm inclined to believe him, lying scoundrel though he is."

"So you're saying you don't remember her ever saying anything? About being adopted or anything, I mean?"

Maeve considered that for a few moments then finally shook her head. "No, no I can't say that I do. Sorry. If Layna was adopted, she never told me, that's sure."

Cutter nodded and was going to let it go then another thought struck him. "Maeve?"

"Hmm?"

"What about the second time you saw her father?"

She winced. "You sure you want to get into all that, Prince? The others'll be ready soon—that's why they sent me in here, to get you. Any minute now one of 'em will be walking through, wondering where we've gotten off to. If we're not careful, folks will start to talk, what with you still sittin' in that bed and all."

Cutter grunted a laugh. "You don't have to tell me if you don't want, Maeve. Besides, you're probably right—likely I just misremembered."

She sighed. "It's not that I don't want to...or well, I suppose maybe it is. But if you want to hear it, Prince, I'll tell you it, though I can't promise it won't be painful to hear."

"I told you," Cutter said, "I'm getting accustomed to pain."

She watched him for a few seconds then finally nodded. "Well. The last time I saw Layna's parents was at her funeral."

Cutter winced, a fresh wave of guilt roiling through him. A funeral which he had not attended, for he had already been well on his way with the boy he had sworn to protect, on a journey that would, in time, lead him to the small village of Brighton, a village which would be destroyed because of him some fifteen years later.

She nodded. "Well, as maybe you remember, it wasn't much of an affair. After Feledias heard of Layna and you...well, suffice to say that he wasn't prepared to throw a funeral for his bride. More ready to throw a funeral for a bunch of other folks, namely anyone who he thought was involved, if you catch my meaning."

"I catch it."

"Well," Maeve said slowly, "it was a long time ago, but let me see..." Her eyes took on a faraway cast then as she thought back to more than fifteen years before. "It was raining," she said, her voice sad, "I remember that. Remember thinking that even the gods themselves wept for Layna, and why not? She was a fine woman, Prince. The best I've ever met. As I said, there weren't many people there—it had to be done in secret, understand, what with your brother ready to kill anyone he thought might have had anything to do with Layna...or you."

"I understand."

"Right," she said. "Anyway, there were few enough there. Just Layna's mother, Ladia, and her father...*Erwin!* That was his name. And...well, me, of course."

Cutter blinked. "That was it? Just you three?"

She gave him a sad smile. "Yes. As I said, Layna was a private woman."

"You...spoke to them? Her parents, I mean?"

Maeve winced. "Briefly. You see, I hadn't exactly been invited to the funeral...no one had. And I won't say that her parents were all that happy to see me."

Cutter blinked. "But...why? I mean, it wasn't your fault."

"Wasn't it?" she asked, her voice suddenly sharp. "Oh, Prince, I'm no fool. I was close to Layna, as you said, and so too was I close to you. Close enough to see the way you looked at her. And yet...I did nothing."

Cutter stared at her, surprised. "You...you mean you knew?"

She gave a laugh that sounded very close to a sob. "Of course I knew. As did Chall and Priest. Why, I think even your brother would have known had he not...well..." She winced. "Had he not loved you so much." She paused, running a finger across her eyes where tears had begun to gather. "Anyway, I knew I was guilty, guilty for not saying something...for not *doing* something, and Ladia and Erwin, well, they knew too."

Cutter winced. "Gods, Maeve. I'm sorry that you had to do that alone. It doesn't...it isn't..."

"Relax, Prince," she said. "It was a long time ago. Anyway, Erwin...he didn't say much of anything, really. Just stood over her grave and wept. I've seen tears like that before, Prince, but not since a long time ago. Not since the Skaalden came to Daltenia have I seen such grief. As for Ladia...well, she wept too, but she didn't only do that. She saw me, and...gods, Prince, the look on her face, such hate..." She paused, then gave a ragged sigh. "I've never seen so much hate. She walked over to me, asked me what I was doing there. I told her I came to pay my respects. She laughed then, Prince, but it was not a laugh like any I've ever heard before and one that I would never wish to hear again. A terrible, wailing laugh of grief and hate and pain with no humor in it. *'Respects,'* she said. *'You came to pay your respects.'* But where were you when my Layna needed you? She liked you, Maeve, loved you, said that you were her friend, her only friend. And then...for you to let this...to let this happen...'"

Maeve trailed off, clearly struggling with the memory.

"Maeve," Cutter said, "you don't have to—"

"No, but I do," she said softly. "I've never spoken of that time, Prince, not with anyone. I guess maybe I thought, *hoped,* that if I didn't talk about it, I might forget. But such things...such things can't be forgotten, can they? They're like sores, ones that inattention only serves to make fester. Perhaps...perhaps speaking of it will be better."

"If you say so, Maeve."

She gave him a fragile smile. "If I say so. Very well, then I do. I told her, then, Prince, that I was sorry. Sorry for what I'd done, for what *you* had done. And do you know what she did then, Prince?"

He frowned. "I don't—"

"She laughed. That same, terrible laugh. She said that the gods would deal with you and me both and that your affair and my inattention were far from our greatest crimes. She said that I allowed Layna to be taken from her."

"Taken..." Cutter said. "She was referring to Layna taking her own life?"

Maeve shook her head slowly. "I don't think so. It almost...it was strange, Prince. You see, I thought like you. I told her that I was sorry for what had happened, sorry that I had not protected Layna, had not kept her alive. And her mother only shook her head, spitting at my feet. And then...then she said something I'll never forget."

"What?" Cutter said, finding himself leaning forward, a mixture of anticipation and dread within him.

"She said that all those who walk the earth must die, Prince, and that even one so precious as her daughter was no different. She said she did not hate me, did not hate *you* because of Layna's death. She said that she hated us because we allowed her to be taken, to be changed."

"But...what does that mean?"

"I...don't know," Maeve said. "I tried to ask her, you see, what she meant, but she refused to answer. Instead, she turned and walked back to her husband, but she said one thing more, turning to look back at me. She said, 'Your pain has only begun, *Maeve the Marvelous,* for deeds done in the darkness bear fruit in the day.'"

Cutter stared at her, found that his breath had caught in his throat. Those words. They were the same words Layna had said in his dream. "What happened then?" he croaked.

Maeve shrugged. "Nothing. I paid my respects, as much as I could, and then I left, for I saw that my presence only caused them more pain."

Cutter nodded, his mind racing, trying to put it together. But if it were a puzzle then it was one beyond his ability to solve.

"What is it, Prince?" she said.

"Hmm?"

"You're thinking about something, worrying at it like a dog with a bone. Seems to me you've been worrying at it for some time. So...what is it?"

Cutter considered that. Indeed, he was worrying at something, worrying *about* something, but he wasn't sure exactly what, wasn't sure why the thought that Layna might have been adopted bothered him so much, only that it did. He thought, probably, that he would appear foolish telling Maeve as much, that she would only scold him or tell him it was nothing, and he thought, too, that she would likely be right to do so. Still, he knew that Maeve was clever, cleverer than him by far, and so he opened his mouth, preparing to tell her.

That was when the door opened, revealing Ned, the carriage driver. The man gave them a tight smile and nodded. "Prince. Lady. It's time."

Cutter nodded, at once relieved and disappointed. "Well," he said as he worked his way laboriously to his feet. "Best not keep them waiting."

"Why do you look like a man that just got a pardon minutes before his execution, Prince?"

"It's nothing, Maeve," he said. "We'll talk about it later."

She grunted, frowning at him and studying him as if she could see his thoughts. "Very well, Prince, but we *will* talk about this later."

It wasn't a question, but Cutter nodded. "Of course. Now, would you help me? I'm still a bit...well, exhausted, I guess."

She sighed. "Come on then," she said, moving and draping his arm over her shoulder.

The others were in the common room waiting for them as they came out. Ned was speaking quietly to his wife, Guardsman Nigel to his. Chall sat apart, looking just about as grim as could be. Cutter wondered if the mage, like himself, was wondering what it would be like to have someone who loved you the way the two couples loved each other. Cutter wondered, also, if the man was wondering what he had done, what mistake he had made in his life to find himself alone. For his part, Cutter did not have to wonder at what he had done to end up alone, for he knew well enough, and it had not been one single mistake but seemingly a lifetime full of them.

"Are we ready?" he asked.

Ned and Guardsman Nigel finished talking to their wives then moved to stand with Cutter and the others. "Ready, Prince," the carriage driver said. "Sorry—the old hag was just lecturing me about this and that. I swear, she acts as if I'd forget my head if she wasn't around to remind me to carry it with me."

Cutter had seen enough of Ned and the love he and his wife shared that he smiled at that. "Is she right?"

The man grunted, putting on a sour face. "She's always right. What does that have to do with anything? Anyway..." He made a show of bowing and waving his hand toward the door. "Your carriage awaits, Your Highness."

Cutter glanced at Chall. "Ready?"

"Oh, of course," the mage said glumly, "when is a man not ready to travel in a plague-wagon with the gods alone know how many assassins seeking to poke some fresh holes in him?"

"Well," Ned said, grinning, "not a *real* plague wagon, of course. There's a bit of a difference."

Chall frowned. "Nowhere near as much of one as I'd like."

The driver grinned. "I bet you're a blast at parties. It's funny, what from what I heard of the great mage Challadius, well, I always figured you'd be a bit more..."

"Charming?" Maeve offered with a grin.

"Why, that's it!" Ned exclaimed. "That's it exactly!"

"Forgive me," Chall said sourly, "but facing certain death, I'm afraid, brings out the worst in me."

"Consider it forgiven," Ned said, clapping the mage on the back as if he was completely unaware of the sarcasm. "Now, if you all will follow me, we'll be on our way. Unless," he went on, raising an eyebrow at Chall, "you've got anything else you'd like to say?"

"Lots," Chall muttered, "but no one will listen."

"Right then," Ned said, "on we go."

And with that, they started toward the door, Cutter bringing up the rear. He paused by Emille, noting her worried expression as she stared after her departing husband. "I will do everything within my power to keep him safe. You have my word."

She nodded. "Thank you, Prince."

Cutter watched her for a moment then nodded and followed the others.

It was night again, the lot of them having decided that it would be best to travel under the cover of darkness, a sentiment to which Cutter agreed. The problem, of course, was that while the blanket of night served to better conceal them, so too did it conceal any who might be waiting in the shadows, watching their movements.

The wagon, as Ned had promised, was parked in the street in front of his home, and even in the poor moonlight, the black plague banners with the red markings denoting the wagon bearing them as carrying the corpses of those possessing contagion stood out.

He glanced over at the others, and Chall gave him a sickly look, clearly not loving the idea of riding in the back of a plague wagon, even if it wasn't actually carrying bodies with the plague. "Why don't you ride up front?" Cutter offered.

Chall got a hopeful look at that, but he winced. "Are you sure, Prince? If anything should happen, perhaps it would be better if you were the one—"

"If anything should happen," Cutter interrupted, "your magic would serve us far better than anything I might do, particularly considering the fact that even standing is a chore for me right now. It's the best decision, Chall, for everyone."

The mage clearly wanted to accept the offer, but he was also clearly reluctant, glancing at Maeve's back where the woman was climbing into the carriage. "Are you sure..."

"I'll tell her it was my idea, Chall," Cutter said softly, "which, of course, is nothing but the truth. Besides, it seems to me that it would be nice for you and your new best friend to spend some quality time together."

The mage winced, regarding the driver where he was climbing up in the carriage. "I know he's risking his life just like we are...only...does he have to be so damn chipper about it?"

"You're right," Cutter said, schooling his features to keep the smile off his face, "far better for him to show a respectable amount of dread."

"Exactly," Chall said, then he heaved a heavy sigh and walked toward the front of the wagon.

Cutter watched him go, shaking his head, the grin that had threatened finally on his face now, then he started toward the wagon where the others waited.

***

The trip to the castle was uneventful but no less onerous for all that. The wagon, while a good size, became quickly cramped when everyone had climbed into the back, and Cutter's body was a conglomeration of aches and pains, not to mention exhaustion.

Guardsman Nigel was faring little better. The man sat with his back propped against the carriage's inner wall, his knees in front of him as there was no room to stretch them out. His head was leaned back, his eyes closed, but it was obvious by the grimace of pain on his face that the man had not been lucky enough to find his way into the oblivion of sleep.

That, Cutter understood for while he was still exhausted, weary in mind, body, and soul, the aches of his abused body demanded his attention, refusing to allow him even the brief respite that sleep might provide.

Still, despite the aches and the pains, of which there were many, he counted himself lucky for each minute that passed where Ned or Chall didn't cry out from the front of the wagon to warn of impending attack. Not that he thought it likely he would have done much good if a fight had come, for Maeve had been right—he'd pushed himself too hard. True, he hadn't had a choice, but that would make no difference if they were attacked, and he was unable to protect Emille's husband as he'd promised.

The others also seemed all too aware of the danger, saying nothing, and so they waited in tense silence for the shout of alarm that they hoped would never come, Cutter doing his best to avoid grunting as each bump or jostle of the rolling carriage sent a fresh spike of pain through him.

The trip seemed interminable. The minutes dragged into hours, hours into days and days into years, but Cutter cautioned himself to relax, told himself that it was only the tenseness of their situation which made it feel so.

Yet, despite the logic of it, he was surprised when the wagon finally began to slow. He leaned forward.

"What is it, do you think?" Maeve whispered. "Have we gone far enough to reach the castle?" Her eyes were wide orbs in the darkness of the carriage, and her voice betrayed that she was as tense as he was.

"I don't know," Cutter said, gripping his axe. Always, since Yeladrian, the Fey King, had gifted it to him—a gift that in many ways, had become more of a curse—the weapon had felt like an extension of Cutter. Not a separate item forged of metal and heat, but a part of himself. Now, though, it was heavy, and it took an effort to lift it. Still, he managed, grabbing hold of the obsidian haft and raising the weapon, his arms across his knees as he held it in both hands. "If they come at us, I'll take the front."

Her eyes were afraid in the darkness, but she snorted. "No, you won't. You might be a prince but that doesn't give you a right to be a fool—we both know it'd be all you could do to stand, let alone swing that axe, and the guardsman over there is little better off. No, if they come, Prince, it'll be me who meets them first." And suiting action to words, she stood in a half-crouch, as high as the wagon would allow, drew two blades from where they were secreted about her person and moved to the front of the carriage where the flap of cloth now lay closed, concealing the world beyond from view.

They all waited, tense, listening to the muffled sound of conversation. Footsteps thudded outside the carriage as someone moved to its back. Cutter gripped his axe and wondered if he would even be able to muster the strength to raise it in his own defense.

A moment later, the flap of cloth was thrown open, revealing Chall. The mage noticed Maeve standing with her blades bared and let out a squeak of surprised fear as he staggered back. "Stones and starlight, Mae!" he hissed. "You scared the shit out of me."

"Keep cursing at me, Chall, and I'm liable to get a lot more than that out of you," the woman growled, but Cutter could hear the relief in her tone, a relief he felt as well. "Why are we stopped?" she demanded.

"Why else?" the mage said, still eyeing the blades in her hands warily. "We're here."

Cutter waited as Maeve climbed out of the carriage, watched as she helped the weary guardsman, Nigel, out as well.

"Well?" she asked finally, looking back at him. "You coming, Prince, or do you want me to see if I can round up a few men to carry your royal ass to the castle?"

Cutter grunted, giving her a small smile. "I'm coming." But as he tried to suit action to words, rising from his seat, his legs nearly gave way beneath him, and he was forced to put a hand on the side of the carriage to keep himself upright.

"Prince?" Maeve asked, and he could hear the worry in her voice.

"I'm fine," he lied. "Just tired, that's all."

It was an effort of will to shamble forward and a greater one still to climb out of the wagon without tipping over and collapsing onto the ground, but he did it. The Crimson Prince might not be known for his compassion or mercy, not even decency, but will...that he had in abundance, though it seemed to him that the world was only poorer for it.

After a few exhausting moments he was standing at the back of the wagon, gazing at the gate and the castle beyond. It wasn't until he was standing there, looking at it, noting the guardsmen who waited, silently, for his command, that he realized something. He hadn't expected they would ever make it this far.

Despite what reassurances he'd offered the others, he had felt certain that they would be attacked and killed long before ever reaching the castle.

"Welcome home, Prince."

He glanced over at Chall, at the crooked smile the man wore and grunted, turning back to the castle. "Doesn't feel much like home."

"No?" the mage asked. "Well, likely the fact that it was nearly the site of your assassination has something to do with that."

"Likely."

"Anyway, guess I ought to thank you," the mage offered quietly. "Didn't think we'd make it back, if I'm being honest."

"It's not me you've to thank," Cutter said, eyeing the driver, Ned, as he walked toward them, smiling.

Chall winced. "I have to?"

Cutter shrugged. "They don't call you the Charmer for nothing, do they?"

Chall frowned at that then turned to the approaching driver, the man's grin going nearly from ear to ear. "Thanks," he muttered, "anyway, I'd best check on the guardsman."

He hurried away then, and they watched him go before Cutter turned back to look at the driver. "A plague wagon."

The man grinned, giving him a wink. "Plague wagon."

Cutter nodded. "Look, Ned, I want you to know...that is..." He winced. He wasn't good at this sort of thing. He never had been. Never had been good at being human. Always, Priest, Maeve, Chall, even Feledias had been there to fill in the gaps, to be what he could not. But a quick glance showed that Maeve and Chall stood a few feet away, holding up Guardsman Nigel who was barely conscious.

There would be no help there, then. He cleared his throat, trying again. "What I mean, Ned, is that by helping us, by helping *me*, well...I know what you risked. And I just wanted to say...thank you."

Ned blinked. "Well, I'll be. The Crimson Prince, world's greatest warrior, telling me thanks." He grinned, shaking his head. "Why, that's a thing, isn't it?"

Cutter winced. "Yes, but...it's more than thanks, Ned. Without you, without your wife—"

"Oh that's alright, Prince," he said, raising his hands. "Don't go bowin' on my account. You ask me, bowin', well, that don't come easy for a man like you, does it?"

Cutter said nothing to that, and the driver grinned wider. "Anyhow, we were happy to help. Leastways, I was. That hag back at the house? I can't say as I know what'd make her happy. Exceptin' maybe my funeral."

Cutter grunted, giving the man a small smile. "She loves you."

"Sure and how not?" the man asked with a laugh. "Anyway..." He paused, leaning in, his expression serious. "Can I tell you a secret, Prince?"

"Sure."

"I love her too—why, fact is, she's the best thing that ever happened to me, far better than an old carriage driver like me deserves, truth to tell. But don't go spreadin' that around, eh? My luck, she'd find out and be downright insufferable."

Despite his weariness, despite his worry, Cutter laughed. "I won't, but if you ask me, Ned, I'd say she already knows."

The man winced, then hocked and spat. "Probably you're right. The old witch is a clever one and that's a fact."

Cutter shook his head, looking at the man. "It's a game, isn't it?"

The man's eyes sparkled, and he winked. "Sure, Prince. What else is there?"

Cutter nodded. "Well. Probably it's best if you get back. If you say she's a witch then I don't want any curses cast over me for making you late for dinner."

"And wouldn't that be a blessin'?" the man said, cupping his stomach. "Why you've tasted her cookin'." His grin faded then, and he met Cutter's eyes, a rare, serious expression on his face. "You ever need anything, Prince—anything at all—well, you know where to find me."

"Yes," Cutter said, "I do. Thanks again, Ned."

The driver shrugged as if risking his life and the life of the wife he adored was no great matter. "Sure."

And with that, he turned and started back toward the front of the wagon. Cutter watched him go, and despite all the danger they—and the kingdom—were in, he found a small smile coming to his face. True, the kingdom was in danger, but he thought that with enough men like Ned, enough women like his wife, that they'd be alright in the end.

He continued to watch as the man clucked at the horses, turning the carriage around. The driver gave a wave, tipping an imaginary hat, and then the carriage was rolling down the street back the way they'd come.

"Bit of a bastard, isn't he?"

Cutter glanced over at Chall, raising an eyebrow. "If he is, then the world could do with more bastards."

The mage frowned. "Doesn't have to be so...so damned *likeable* though, does he?"

"Is the word you're searching for 'charming?'"

Chall blushed crimson. "Anyway, what now?"

Cutter's smile faded as he turned to regard the castle, as his thoughts turned to the problems they faced. A war with the Fey, one that was happening all around them. The gods alone knew how many assassins, and a king that, a few months ago, had been no more than a young boy in one of the kingdom's smallest villages.

But that isn't what really bothers you about Matt, is it?

The thought came to him as if of its own accord, but it was his thought, and it was a true one. No. It wasn't the fact that Matt had been a village boy months ago that bothered him. At least, it wasn't only that. Not so much what the boy had been as what he had become.

Since he'd been crowned king, Cutter hadn't had much time to spend with Matt, not with trying to root out the conspiracy in the castle and the city, but something was changing in the boy and not for the better. The innocent, kind-hearted youth he had known—had loved—was being replaced by...something else. It wasn't just in his words, often harsh and sharp, defensive as if he thought everyone was against him. It was also something in his eyes, a sort of sneakiness, like he were hiding something or up to something. What that might be, though, Cutter had no idea. Still, he promised himself that he would talk to the boy, alone if he could, as soon as he was able.

"What now?"

He turned and glanced at Chall. He had been so lost in thought that he had almost forgotten the mage was there at all. The man must have seen something of the thoughts plaguing him in his face, for he frowned.

"Everything okay, Prince?"

"Fine," Cutter lied. "As for what now..." He wanted to talk to Matt, thought maybe that he *needed* to, but first he had to see to getting Guardsman Nigel safe in the castle—if anyone *could* be safe now—and then, there was Belle to think of. The woman had promised to tell him more as soon as she was pardoned, and so he would need to see to getting her released as soon as possible. He sighed. And once all of that was done, perhaps then he would have an opportunity to speak with Matt, to figure out what was bothering the lad so much. "Come on," he said, "let's see about finding the guardsman a bed." He paused, glancing over at where the man's arm was draped over Maeve's shoulder, his gaze wavering as if he was nearly unconscious. "He's earned it."

"Haven't we all," Chall muttered.

CHAPTER NINE

I am fire
And all I touch turns to ash.
—Prince Bernard, known as "The Crimson Prince."

Half an hour later, Cutter stood with Maeve and Chall, watching as the same healer that had seen to him so recently—and who had given him a disapproving frown as he saw him up and about—examined Guardsman Nigel.

For his part, Nigel offered no complaint, mostly because he had fallen into sleep or unconsciousness practically the moment his head hit the bed's pillow. For reasons Cutter could not understand, the man seemed to be doing worse than he had been hours before, and by the time they'd made it into the room, he'd been wheezing for breath, a green tinge to his skin that Cutter did not like.

So he and the others waited tensely as the healer performed his examination. And why not? The guardsman was in a bad way, a man didn't need to be a healer to see that much, and should he die, not only would they be forced to watch the passing of a good man, but they would also lose their best chance—perhaps their only one—of rooting out the conspiracy in the castle and learning what guards, if any, were still loyal and which had been seduced by the Fey.

And so they did not speak as they stood near the door of the room they'd appropriated for the guardsman. They only stood and waited. And hoped, that most of all. Finally, the healer let out a heavy sigh, rising and knuckling his back as he turned.

"Well?" Chall said, sounding practically as if he were about to burst with impatience. "How is he?"

"Well," the old man said, his voice unmistakably surly, "he's been stabbed enough a man might think someone intended to make a kebab out of him, and I'd say he's lost more blood than he's got left. Fire and salt how do you *think* he is?"

"Uh...not good?" Chall asked.

The man rolled his eyes, walking away from the guardsman's unconscious form and moving to Cutter. "From what I've seen, Prince—and from what I hear if the rumors of assassins in the castle are true," the man said, "it seems to me that folks that get around you have a habit of dying."

"Hey, that's not fair," Chall said. The three of them turned to regard him, and he fidgeted. "Well. I mean. The guardsman isn't dead...is he?"

The old healer gave another sigh. "No, not dead. And if the fates will it, he might yet pull through. The poison has had some time to work its way through his system. I have taken measures to stop it, but whether or not I was in time..." He shook his head.

"Poison?" Chall asked. "But how could—"

"The assassins," Cutter said, frowning with anger. "Back at Nigel's house. I thought I saw a strange sheen to their blades, but I didn't stop to think on it."

"*Damn,*" Chall hissed. "That's the last thing we need. But then...how didn't..." He cut off, glancing at the healer before turning to Cutter and Maeve, whispering. "How didn't Emille see it when she examined him?"

The healer cleared his throat. "Because Challadius, such poison as this is detectable only by its symptoms. Whoever this Emille is, she might be the most skilled healer in the world and still it would have gone unnoticed until those symptoms began to present themselves."

"Shit," Cutter said. "What can we do?"

The healer shrugged. "I'd say that *you* should get some rest, but as you seem bound and determined to refuse common sense, Prince, then...for the guardsman...pray. The rest is in the hands of the gods now. If we are lucky he'll pull through but I warn you that, even if he does, he will be weak for some time."

"Great," Chall muttered.

Cutter nodded slowly. "Thank you," he said to the healer.

The man raised a bushy gray eyebrow. "You want to thank me, listen to my advice and get some rest. You dying isn't going to help the guardsman's chances any."

Cutter nodded. "Thanks for the advice."

The old man shook his head slowly. "But you won't listen, will you?"

"Soon," Cutter said. "Only, there's something I need to do first. Will you come back and check on him again?"

The healer glanced back at the man in the bed then frowned at Cutter again. "Why not? Maybe if I'm careful I might even be able to keep him from doing anything foolish—you know, like getting up and walking around and getting into *another* scrap..." He paused, eyeing Cutter's bloody, smoke-stained clothes. "Unless, of course, I completely miss my guess."

"You don't."

The man gave another disapproving shake of his head. "Well. There's some medicines in my shop I'm going to go grab. I'll be back soon. Think you can keep that big axe of yours in its sheath until then?"

"I'll try."

The man heaved a weary sigh then turned and left. Cutter and the others watched him go.

"Have I ever told you, Prince," Chall said once the man was gone, "that you've got a way with people?"

Maeve snorted a laugh. "He isn't wrong, Cutter. Anyway, what now? I imagine we'll all be going to see Belle?"

"Not all of us," Cutter said, meeting her gaze.

She watched him for a minute then sighed. "You mean for me to stay here."

"I do."

"Oh, don't look so upset, Maeve. It only makes sense," Chall said. "The gods know if I was needing babysitting, I couldn't think of a better one for the job than you."

"I don't guess you would," Maeve said, "considerin' I been doing just that for more than fifteen years. Anyway, are you sure?" she asked, turning back to Cutter. "Why not leave Chall? If anyone knows how to *rest*, it's him."

"And what if an assassin comes?" Cutter asked.

Her frown deepened at that. "You think they will?"

Cutter shrugged. "Maybe. What I think is that it would be better not to take any unnecessary chances. Don't you?"

She rolled her eyes. "Fine. I'll stay. But you might regret that choice if an assassin comes for you instead—with the way you're barely able to stand up, your best hope'll be that Chall talks long enough and they decide suicide is preferable to listening to his blather."

Cutter didn't bother answering that. After all, if he ended up regretting the choice, it wasn't as if it would be the first time. Instead he nodded. "Thanks, Maeve. Lock the door behind us."

She nodded. "Just...be safe, alright? Both of you."

"Of course!" Chall exclaimed. "Safe as a kitten in its mother's paws."

As they walked out, the mage leaned in, muttering low so that Maeve wouldn't hear as the door closed, "Assuming, of course, that the mother is a cannibal and the kitten in question has been very, *very* bad."

Cutter offered the man a distracted smile, but he could spare no more than that. Now that Guardsman Nigel was safe—or, at least, as safe as Cutter could make him—he needed to talk to Belle. The woman had promised to tell him more of what she knew regarding the conspiracy in the castle and the assassins who had come for him as soon as he'd pardoned her. He didn't like the idea of setting a known crime boss loose on the streets once more, but the simple fact was that the woman's crimes were small evils when compared to the threat the Fey represented. No matter how much he hated the idea of setting her free, he had questions that needed answers, answers that only she possessed, and so he started down the castle hallway heading toward the dungeon.

The castle's corridors were surprisingly silent, even given the time of night, and what few servants they passed shied away from him and the mage as if they were wild animals that might choose to bite at any moment. Cutter was used to such treatment of course, had earned it in one bloody battle after the other, in one cruelty after the other, but they seemed even more scared than usual, a thought echoed by Chall as they walked.

"Skittish bunch, aren't they?" the mage asked as another servant's eyes went wide at their approach and the servant in question, a young woman barely in adulthood, disappeared through the nearest door, obviously fleeing at their approach.

"Yes," Cutter said, "yes they are."

The door slammed shut an instant later, and Chall glanced at it as they passed. "Think they heard rumors about the assassins? That old crotchety healer knew about them."

"Maybe," Cutter said, frowning at the door as he walked by. Another problem, then, one he would have to deal with and soon. After all, the kingdom was in a bad way if even those who worked in the castle, in the very heart of the Known Lands power, didn't feel safe. He promised himself that he would look into it. But first, there was Belle to see to.

They turned a corner in the hallway, and Cutter nearly stumbled over a woman knelt in the floor, wiping at it with a rag. He let out a grunt of surprise, thrusting an arm out to stop Chall from trampling over her.

A moment later, the woman realized her danger and let out a squeak of fear and surprise, sliding her backside across the floor.

"Excuse us," Cutter said, "we mean no harm."

The fear on the woman's face did not fade, though. Instead, if anything, it grew worse as she gazed upon them. "I—forgive me, Prince. I'm a foolish old woman, please forgive me for—"

"It is we who should be asking to be forgiven," Cutter said. "We were moving in haste and not watching where we were going. Are you alright?"

The woman, who appeared to be in her fifties, her gray hair pulled into a tight bun, met his eyes for only a moment before her gaze drifted back to the ground. A moment later, she was on her hands and knees, bowing so low that her forehead practically scraped the floor. "I...I'm fine, Highness, yes, thank you."

Cutter watched her trembling with fright and glanced at Chall. The mage met his eyes with a frown, and Cutter turned back to her. "Please, rise," he said, offering her his hand. She glanced up slowly, carefully, as if she suspected she might be struck, looking at his hand as if it were a snake preparing to bite.

Cutter only continued to stand with his arm out, doing his best to not look threatening, a job no doubt made significantly more difficult by the blood-stained bandages wrapped around various parts of him.

Yet he remained still, his arm out, making no sudden movements the same way a man might act when dealing with a frightened animal, for that was what the woman seemed then, like a hare preparing to flee. An image only enhanced when, looking at her, Cutter saw that she had a swollen lip, as well as a long scratch along one side of her face, one which appeared recent, not to mention the fact that one of her eyes was black.

Finally, though, the woman timidly reached out, taking his hand, and he pulled her gently to her feet. "Are you sure you're alright?" he asked softly.

"Y-yes, Highness, I-I'm fine," she said, offering him a shy smile.

"Good, and look—" He paused. "I'm sorry, I didn't get your name."

She blinked, as if shocked to be asked. "M-my name?"

"Yes."

She blushed then, and the smile she gave was a little less timid than the one before it. "I-it's Claudette. If it pleases you, Highness."

"Claudette," he repeated. "A good name."

She smiled again, and despite her battered appearance, the expression transformed her face into something fine. "T-thank you, Highness."

He returned the smile. "Claudette," he said, "if you don't mind my asking, what happened? To your face, I mean."

The smile immediately vanished from the woman's face, and she grew pale. "Th-this? I-it's nothing, Highness. I'm just an old fool who fell, that's all."

"You fell?"

"Yes, Highness, that's right. Nobody's fault, just my own at least," she said, offering a soft, breathless laugh.

"Claudette?" he asked, waiting.

"Y-yes?"

"People don't often get black eyes from falling."

"N-no?"

He gave her as gentle of a smile as he could muster. "No."

"Oh. Well...maybe...I ran into a door?"

"You can tell me the truth, Claudette," he said. "Who did this to you? Was it a guard? Another servant? Whoever it was, I can promise you that, if you tell me, you won't have to worry about them any longer. Whoever it is will have to find employment elsewhere."

She gave a weak snort at that. "Kicking a king out of his own castle, that'd be a tri—" She cut off suddenly, her eyes going wide, her face paling even further as she realized what she'd said.

Cutter tensed, feeling as if he'd been struck by lightning. Slowly, he turned and looked at Chall, the mage staring at him in disbelief.

"Wait a minute," the mage said to the woman, "do you…that is, do you mean to say that the *king* did this to you?"

The woman shook her head furiously, a look of horror on her face. "I—that is, please, sir, I didn't, I meant—"

"The truth, Claudette," Cutter said, doing his best to keep his anger from his voice. "Please."

The woman fidgeted, clearly wanting nothing more than to turn and flee. "I-it was my fault, Highness. His Majesty is a busy man, none busier, and I was in the way. My fault entirely and—"

"No, Claudette," he interrupted. "No. Violence is never the victim's fault. That is a truth it took me a long time to learn…or, perhaps, to accept. But it is true for all that. Have you seen a healer?"

She winced. "N-no, my lord, forgive me but the price—"

"Will be covered by the castle treasury, of course," Cutter said. "Now, go and see the castle healers—tell them I sent you. And Claudette? I promise you that this will never happen again."

The woman nodded. "As you say, Majesty," she said, bobbing her head in a low bow, then she turned and hurried away.

"A promise you can keep, do you think?" Chall asked quietly from beside him.

Cutter watched the departing figure of the woman until she turned down an intersection, then he looked at Chall, frowning. "A promise I mean to."

"But…she…she must have been lying. Right?" Chall asked, a desperation in his voice. "I mean, the lad, he would never…"

"No," Cutter said quietly, "no, I do not think she was lying."

"Then what?" the mage asked. "Surely you can't think that Matt would do such a thing?"

"Not the Matt I knew in Brighton, no," Cutter said. "That boy cried every year come slaughtering time." He gave a small smile as the memory came over him. "One year—not so long ago at all, really—he ran to my house demanding that I save the hogs as they were prepared for slaughter." He shook his head, remembering the tears streaming down the boy's face, remembered thinking, at the time, that the boy was too soft. Too soft for a world that seemed to Cutter made only of hard, sharp edges, edges he couldn't help but run into no matter which way he turned. He remembered thinking that the lad would make a poor butcher indeed, that perhaps it had been a mistake to come to Brighton in the first place, the boy not being cut out for the rough life of living on the edges of the kingdom.

And now he had taken that same boy and made him king. Foolish, perhaps? Was the bloodied lip of the serving woman no more than proof that Cutter had thrown the boy in far over his head and that, in his flailing, not dissimilar to those desperate struggles of a drowning man, she had been struck? Were those wounds indeed the lad's fault or were they, like so many others before them, to be laid at Cutter's feet? More blood to add to the river that followed in his wake.

"So...what should we do then?" Chall said after they had stood in silence for over a minute.

He sighed heavily. Perhaps it had been a mistake to make the lad king. It had seemed smart at the time, when Maeve had recommended it, but then, when coming out of the clever woman's mouth, most things did. And if it *had* been a mistake, it had not been hers but his, for he had known the lad his entire life while she had only been with him for months. "We do the best we can," he said finally. "I'll speak to Matt but first we need to see to Belle. Come on."

He did his best to ignore the aches and pains of his abused body as they set off once again, now with a greater sense of urgency. They had set out to make Matt king, and against all odds, they had managed it, but instead of making things better for the kingdom and for Matt, somehow, they seemed to have only made things worse. He had to speak to Belle, to figure out just how bad the corruption in the city was. After all, to defeat his enemy, a man first had to find him.

***

They arrived at the dungeon entrance a short time later. It took them no more than half an hour to navigate their way there, yet by the time they'd arrived Cutter was out of breath, exhausted. Worse than that, his body was covered in a cold sweat, and he felt feverish.

The two guards assigned to the dungeon must have seen some of his suffering on his face, for they shared a glance before looking back at him. "Prince Bernard?" one asked. "Is everything okay?"

"Fine," Cutter managed. "Show us to the cell of the crime boss, Belle."

The two men shared another glance. "Prince, are you sure that—"

"I'm sure," Cutter interrupted, his pain and exhaustion making his words come out harsher than he intended. "Sorry," he said, "but...yes. I'm sure. Forgive me but I'm in a bit of a hurry."

"Of course, sir," the man who'd spoken said, then met his companions eyes before retrieving the keys and starting down into the dungeon.

Cutter looked at Chall who frowned, giving a small shrug of his shoulders, and then they were following behind the man.

It didn't take them long to reach the crime boss's cell which was a good thing as Cutter counted it a victory that he was able to keep his feet under him. But whatever relief he felt at that small victory was quickly destroyed as he gazed into Belle's cell. Or, at least, what *had* been the woman's cell. He doubted it could be counted as much now considering the fact that she was no longer there.

"I-I don't understand," Chall said. "I thought...I thought she was here?"

Frustration and fury suddenly roared through Cutter and, before he knew it, he'd spun and lifted the dungeon guard off his feet by the front of his tunic, slamming him against the wall. *"Where is she?"* he growled. *"What have you done with her?"*

"H-Highness?" the man asked, shocked.

"Are you part of it?" Cutter demanded. "Did you think to be rid of her and steal from us whatever knowledge she might have given?"

"I-I don't understand, Prince," the man said. "Honest, it wasn't me who ordered the woman removed from the cell, I swear it!"

The man was sweating, his face pale with fear. Cutter studied him, aware that his lips had pulled back from his teeth in a silent snarl. He knew this anger, knew it well, but he had thought himself rid of it. The anger demanded that he hurt the man, kill him, but Cutter had promised himself long ago that he would not be ruled by his anger, not anymore. He had been, once, and the consequences of that were ones not suffered by him alone but by the entire kingdom of the Known Lands. So he took a slow, shaky breath, his eyes never leaving the guardsman. "Then tell me who was it that ordered her release? For I swear to you that the man responsible for this will suffer before he dies."

"Why, but Prince, it was...it was the king."

Cutter rocked as if he'd been struck a blow, and he blinked. "What...what did you say?" he managed, his voice a thready whisper.

"I-I thought you knew," the man stammered. "I had thought, perhaps you wanted to look over her cell to see if anything was left behind, perhaps to send to her family or...or..."

Cutter's thoughts were a jumbled mess of confusion, but his mind latched onto the last bit of what the guardsman had said. "To send to her family?" he asked. "Why would we do that?" he finished, suddenly terribly certain that he knew the answer already.

The guardsman cleared his throat. "Forgive me, Majesty, but isn't...isn't that how it's done? After...after executions, I mean?"

And there it was. Some part of him had known that must be it, but the realization that he was right was ill comfort. "Where?" he demanded. "Where was she taken? The town square?"

It was the usual place, where all executions had been held since his father's time. His father had believed that the townspeople should be given a chance to lend their voices to the proceedings, so that, should any feel the execution was in error or unjust, they might be given opportunity to say as much.

"N-no, Prince," the guardsman said, "sh-she was taken to the king's courtyard, here in the castle."

"His private courtyard?" Chall asked, the tone of his voice making it clear that he was as surprised by that as Cutter himself.

"Y-yes, my lord," the guardsman said.

"But why would she be taken—"

"It doesn't matter," Cutter interrupted the mage. "When was she taken?"

"Highness?" the guard asked.

"*When?*" Cutter demanded.

"N-not half an hour ago," the guardsman said. "F-forgive me, Prince, but I thought you knew."

Cutter let go of the guardsman's tunic, allowing the man to drop, then turned to Chall. "Half an hour," he repeated. "If we hurry, maybe we can stop this folly before it's too late."

Had someone asked Cutter, before that moment, if he had it in him to run, he'd have told them there was no chance. And he'd have been wrong.

***

As they hurried through the castle corridors, blood began to seep through the bandages Emille had wrapped around Cutter's wounds, dripping from his fingers and leaving a bloody trail behind him. But Cutter was all too aware of what was at stake, so he gritted his teeth against the pain and, in time, they came to the hallway leading to the king's private courtyard.

Cutter took a deep, ragged breath, and started in the direction of the two guards stationed at the courtyard's entrance and the familiar figure—currently standing with his back turned to Cutter and Chall—who appeared to be speaking with them.

"—I'm your king, damnit!" Feledias was shouting as Cutter and Chall drew closer.

The guards winced, clearly embarrassed. "Forgive me, Prince," one said, "but that is no longer true. I was present for King Matthias's coronation and—"

"*Fine,*" Feledias growled, "but I'm still your *prince,* and I demand you let me through!"

The guards looked apologetic—that Cutter saw on their faces—but he also saw that they didn't look in any danger of moving from where they blocked the door to the courtyard.

"Feledias."

His brother turned to look at him, raising an eyebrow. "Bernard," he said, exasperated, "these, these *men* won't allow me—" He cut off, eyeing Cutter and, more specifically, his wounds, closer. "I hope you don't mind my saying so, brother, but you look like shit."

Cutter gave him a small, weary smile. "Must be improving then. Anyway, what's going on?"

"What's going on," Feledias said, "is that these *guards*—" he gestured angrily at the two men—"think to tell me where I can and cannot go in my own castle!"

"Well," Chall offered, "I mean, it isn't exactly yours anymore, though...is it?"

Feledias turned an angry frown on the mage but before he could say anything Cutter held up a hand, glancing at the guards. "Listen," he said, "a woman has been taken through here to be executed—Belle is her name. We need to speak with her. It's important."

The guard who'd spoken to Feledias winced, shaking his head. "Forgive me, Prince Bernard, but I'm afraid that's out of the question. As I was telling your brother, Prince Feledias, His Majesty was very clear that the proceedings should not be disturbed except by his order and his order alone."

"Fire and salt man, it's a mistake!" Chall said. "That woman whose head you're about to lop off is the key to fixing the problems with New Daltenia! You do *want* to fix those problems, don't you?"

The apologetic expression left the guard's face at that to be replaced by one of anger. "Forgive me, *my lord*," he said in a tone lacking any contrition, "but what I want is irrelevant. His Majesty has given his orders, and I mean to see that they are carried out."

Chall let out an angry huff, opening his mouth again, no doubt to venture some scathing comment, but Cutter put a hand on his shoulder. "He's right, Chall," he said wearily. "These men have their orders. Now come on—let's leave them to it."

"But, Prince," Chall said, shocked, "you can't be serious, it—"

"I am serious," Cutter said. He turned to the guards. "Sorry for the trouble, Guardsman…"

"Alec, Prince," the man said, surprised.

"Guardsman Alec," Cutter said, nodding. "Come," he said to Feledias and Chall, then he turned and walked away.

A moment later, the two followed, obviously surprised and more than a little angry. No one spoke until they got out of ear shot of the guards then Chall let out an angry huff. "Forgive me, Prince, but as I understood it, it was imperative that we talked to this Belle, woman. You can't seriously plan on just letting them kill her!"

"No, Bernard's right," Feledias said wearily. "What choice do we have? If we tried to force our way through, we'd have to hurt those guards, maybe kill them, and even then we wouldn't make it far. I saw more escort the woman through the hall—a dozen at least. Enough even to cause my dear brother here problems were he at his best and…"

"And I'm far from it," Cutter finished.

"So what then?" Chall demanded. "We're just going to let her be killed?"

"No," Cutter said. "That we also cannot do. Still…" He turned, glancing meaningfully at the mage. "Where the direct approach fails, sometimes a more…indirect method might better serve."

Chall blinked. "You mean some sort of…trick?"

Cutter gave the man a small smile as they turned a corner in the hallway then halted. "Or an illusion."

Chall winced, and Feledias gave a grunt. "The Crimson Prince recommending subtlety," he said, shaking his head. "What *would* your fans think?"

"Doubt I have any of those," Cutter said, then turned to Chall. "Can you do it?"

Chall sighed heavily. "You should pay me more."

"Chall? I don't pay you at all. Now, can you do it?"

The mage gave a huff. "Just give me a minute, alright?" he asked. "It isn't as if I can just wave my hands and create an illusion, is it?"

"I'm no expert," Feledias said, "but it seemed to me, on those occasions when I saw you use your magic, that that was exactly what you did."

Chall scowled. "Trust me, Prince, there's more to it than just muttering some words and making something appear—anyone can do that." He noted their two incredulous looks and sighed. "Fine, not *anyone,* but the thing about illusions is they're only as strong as the belief of those they are used against. It wouldn't do, for example, for me to spot a likely wench and suddenly appear a hundred pounds lighter and like the most handsome man in the world, would it? Because it wouldn't be *believable.* The mind wouldn't be able to accept the change, what it was seeing, and the illusion would fall apart."

"Plus," Cutter offered, "it seems that such a thing would be...well, a bit morally suspect."

"Interesting words coming from you," Chall snapped, then winced. "Sorry. Anyway, a man—even a fat one—has needs, doesn't he?"

"Do you mean...do you mean to say you've tried it?" Feledias asked.

"Wouldn't you?" Chall demanded. "Now, quiet, both of you—let me think."

The mage closed his eyes, lost in thought, and Cutter waited impatiently, fighting back the urge to tell him to hurry. After all, the mage knew their situation as well as he did, and while Chall might make a mockery of most things, Cutter knew that, beneath his flippant exterior, the man hid a concern and empathy for his fellow man that was greater than most.

Still, he felt a heady sense of relief when the mage looked up. "Alright," he said, "I think I've got it. You two, stay here. And whatever you do, stay *still,* damnit."

Before Cutter or Feledias could respond, Chall walked back to the corner of the hallway, glancing around it at the two guards still stationed some distance away. Then the mage took a slow, deep breath and closed his eyes.

"Follow orders, do you?" Cutter heard him mutter. *"Let's just see."*

The mage continued to stand there, nothing happening so far as Cutter could see, and Feledias let out a quiet, angry hiss. "We don't have *time* for this," he whispered. "We need to—" But he cut off at the sudden sound of shouting from somewhere down the hallway.

A moment later, a figure in a guardsman's uniform rushed past the opening to the hallway in which they stood, yelling as he did.

"*To arms!*" the figure roared in a voice that thundered in the hallway, "*The king is attacked and calls for aid! Assassins in the castle! Come on, damn you!*"

The figure turned then, hurrying back the way it had come, deeper into the castle. For several seconds, nothing happened, and Feledias let out another angry hiss, starting forward, "This is ridiculous, we need—"

"Quiet," Cutter said, catching the man by the arm, "don't move."

A few seconds later they heard the sound of footsteps, and the two guards they'd spoken with were hurrying past. One of them, the one named Alec, glanced in their direction but seemed to look through them, proof of the mage's magic, then he hurried on with his companion, the two men drawing their swords.

Cutter stood listening to the sounds of their departing footsteps until Chall let out a weary sigh, turning back to them. The man's face looked pale and, when he spoke, he did so in a dry croak. "That ought to...do it."

"You alright?" Cutter said, moving forward.

"Me?" the mage asked. "I'm fine, never been—" He cut off as the strength seemed to leave his legs, and he would have fallen had Cutter not reached out and steadied him with an effort that nearly made him fall instead. Feledias was there a second later, steadying them both.

"A yelling soldier conjured out of thin air. I must admit," Cutter's brother said, "that was damned impressive."

"Sure," Chall muttered, "and without so much as a single farmer's daughter here to see it."

Feledias grunted. "All in all," he said, glancing at Cutter, "I find I much prefer being on this side of his illusions."

Cutter nodded in agreement. "Come on—we have to hurry."

And so they did, rushing down the hallway as quick as Cutter's wounds and Chall's exhaustion would allow. Less than a minute later, they were at the door to the castle courtyard. Cutter didn't hesitate, slamming the door open and walking inside.

The smell of grass and flowers struck him immediately as he stepped through the door. The king's courtyard was so different from the stone castle hallways that it almost seemed as if he walked into another world. Green grass swayed in a slight breeze, flowers, planted and maintained by the castle servants, rose in a profusion of color all around, and a small fountain bubbled beside a bench.

The courtyard was meant to be a place of relaxation and calm, where the city's ruler might find a quiet moment in the demanding schedule of a king to meditate and find some solace from the many decisions and problems which plagued him. Cutter could count on one hand the times he'd visited the place, for during the time before his exile from the city, the man he had been had cared nothing for calm or relaxation. What solace, what peace he had found had only been that which came from defeating his enemies, from hewing them down with his axe.

The half a dozen guardsmen who now stood in a circle in the center of the courtyard also seemed immune to the tranquility the place offered. They paid no attention to the carefully maintained grass and flowers, nor did they seem to take any notice of the fountain's gentle burbling. Instead, all their attention was focused on a figure who knelt at their center, her head placed on a headsman's block. A figure Cutter recognized immediately as Belle, despite the fact that judging by the woman's bloodied, bruised face, she had been ill-used since last they'd spoken.

A mixture of emotions ran through him then. There was relief, yes, relief at finding the woman alive, at discovering that they had not been too late. But mostly, as he stared at her bruised and battered face, there was anger. An old, familiar anger, one that had ruled him for most of his adult life. Yet as dangerous as he knew that anger was, he could not let it go. The woman had been set to be executed but, apparently, that had not been enough. Someone had given her a bad beating, so bad that the one administering it could only have enjoyed it. True, Cutter had a reputation for violence—one he'd earned a thousand times over the years—but even he had never sunk so low as to beat a woman in chains.

And while that anger was the greatest of what he felt, there was something else too...shame. He had promised the woman his protection in exchange for her help, and even a blind man could see that, whatever she had been through in the last hours, it had *not* been protected. As he hurried forward, he found himself thinking of the time he'd first met her.

So what are you then, Prince? she had asked him. *Are you fire or are you ice?*

He had not answered her then, had been unwilling to play her game, but he had considered her words, later, and now he knew the answer. *I am fire,* he thought. *I am fire and all I touch turns to ash.*

"—and so, Belle Eskral, criminal known in the city as 'The Scorpion,'" said one of the men, marked as a captain by the badge on his uniform, "for your crimes against the city of New Daltenia and its people, for your trespasses against the kingdom of the Known Lands and King Matthias, its rightful ruler, you are hereby sentenced to—"

"*Wait!*" Cutter yelled as he half-ran, half-shuffled forward.

The guardsmen turned, several of them drawing their swords as they did. "What is the meaning of thi—" the captain began, then his eyes went wide. "Prince Bernard?" he asked, confused.

"It's me," Cutter rasped as he came to stand in front of the man.

"B-but Highness," the captain asked, "what are you doing here?"

"There's...been a mistake," Cutter panted.

"Mistake, Prince?"

"This woman," he said, gesturing at Belle who was staring at him with an unreadable expression on her bloody face. "I offered her a pardon for her help. She is to be released into my custody at once."

The captain glanced at his guardsmen then finally turned back to Cutter. "Forgive me, Prince, but I can't do that."

"Can't?" Chall demanded from beside Cutter. "Listen, Captain, I don't know if you're aware how all of this works, but your *prince* just gave you a direct order. Now, release her and—"

"I will not," the captain said, staring at Chall with disgust before turning back to Cutter. "I am sorry, Prince," he said in a voice that indicated he wasn't sorry in the least, "but I have orders from His Majesty King Matthias himself to execute this prisoner."

"No, listen," Cutter said, "there's been a mistake, alright? This woman—"

"This *prisoner*," the captain interrupted, "has been the bane of New Daltenia for many years, a disgusting individual who has well-earned the king's wise sentence. Now, if you will excuse me—"

The man cut off at the sound of high-pitched, rasping laughter, and they all turned to regard Belle where she sat with her neck still placed in the headsman's block. "I am a bane, is that it, Captain Revan?" she rasped. "I wonder, did you say as much these last five years? Surely I was not too disgusting for you to refuse the coin my men bribed you with each month."

"Shut up, wench!" the man growled, and the woman let out a cry of pain and surprise as he slapped her hard across the mouth.

Belle hocked and spat out a mouthful of blood. "Oh, a big man aren't you, Captain? Hitting a woman while her hands are chained and—"

"*Enough!*" he roared, rearing his arm back to strike her again but, before he could, Cutter grabbed his wrist, stopping him.

"Don't do that," he growled. The anger was close now, so very close, and he felt his chest rising and falling in labored, rapid breaths.

"My, my," Belle said as the captain stared at Cutter, a mixture of emotions—anger chief among them—chasing their way across his features. "I wonder, is this what the princess feels like as she watches the valiant knight charge toward the castle on his horse, intent on slaying the dragon therein and rescuing her from her imprisonment?"

Cutter ignored her, watching the captain instead and, after a moment, the man jerked his arm away with a look of disgust. "You overstep yourself, Prince," he said. "This execution *will* take place, on order of the king himself. Or..." he went on, his eyes narrowing and a small, humorless smile coming to his face, "would you defy the king's own order?"

The threat was clear enough in the man's tone, but he chose to emphasize it anyway, glancing at the other guardsmen meaningfully before looking back at Cutter.

"What do you want to do, brother?" Feledias asked quietly from beside him, and Cutter glanced at him to see that his brother's hand was on his sword.

Bloodshed was close, then, so very close. Cutter had seen enough of it, after all, to recognize its coming. And the truth was that part of him, the angriest part and, likely, the largest part, welcomed it. Violence. Blood. Victory. A struggle in which there were no doubts or worries to plague him, where who was in the right was determined only by the one left standing when the thing was done.

Still, he fought against the temptation, taking a slow breath. "Of course I would not defy the king," he said quietly, meeting the captain's eyes, "but, as I told you, there has been a mistake. The crime boss Belle is working with the crown and so has been pardoned. If you would but wait, I will speak to the king of it—he will send an order for you and your men to stand down."

The captain stared at him for several seconds, thinking it through and, by the expression on his face coming to a conclusion that would not be to Cutter's liking. But it was Belle who spoke. "Oh, Prince," she said, and he turned to see her give him a humorless smile, "do you not see? Life is no storybook, and I am no princess. As for the dragon...well, it is real enough, but it is the world itself. And even you, for all your talents, cannot slay the world."

"Shut up, you filth," the captain growled.

"Or what?" Belle asked. "You'll kill me?" She gave a soft laugh then winced as if in pain. "I am reminded, Prince," she said, turning to Cutter, "of the time we first met. Do you remember?"

Cutter frowned. "I remember."

"In my own castle, was it not?"

"So you called it," Cutter said, wondering what she was getting at.

She inclined her head. "You thought me a dragon then, didn't you? And perhaps you were right. A dragon in her den, nesting on her hoard. Coins, yes, but not just that, for in this world of doubt and fear, coins are not the finest of treasures, are they?"

Cutter glanced at Chall, and the mage gave a small shrug of his shoulders as if to say that he had no idea what she was talking about either. "What is, then?" he asked.

"Oh, but you know, don't you?" she asked. "It is what all men seek—you as well. It is what brought you to my cell and what, in turn, has brought you here, to my grave. Do you understand?"

And then, Cutter did. What could be more valuable to a crime boss than coin? Well, that was an easy enough question to answer—information. Information regarding which guards could be bribed and which could not, the dirty secrets of men and women, used to blackmail them to her own gain, information used as a shield to keep her safe. "Yes," he said finally.

"Good," she said. "Perhaps not so big a fool as I thought. And I know what treasure it is that you seek, Prince, know it better, perhaps, than even you know yourself."

"And what treasure is that?"

She favored him with a bloody smile. "Why, the most important of all, of course—the truth. They call me criminal, Prince, and no doubt they are right to do so, but I have spent my life dealing with truth. It is, after all, far more...*marketable* than lies. And I know some truths that you might find...most interesting."

"What truths?"

She glanced at the guardsmen surrounding them then gave a shake of her head. "Come, Prince. Do you know nothing of dragons? They do not carry their hoard with them—they keep it some place safe."

"In their den," Cutter said.

"Just so. Now, if you—"

"*Enough!*" the captain growled. A metallic ringing filled the air as he drew his sword and Cutter braced, mustering what little strength he had left as he prepared to defend himself. But the man did not rush after him, as he'd first thought; instead he took several quick steps forward, raising his blade.

Cutter realized then, what the man meant to do. He lunged forward, but his wounds slowed him, and even had they not, he doubted he would have been fast enough, for the blade seemed to move with its own deadly imperative, little more than a metallic blur cutting through the air. Then, before anyone else could react, it cleaved into the woman's neck in a crimson spray.

Cutter stared in disbelief as the headless body slumped to the ground. Behind him, he heard a gasp, heard someone else—likely Chall—growing sick, but he barely noticed. All his attention was on the woman. The woman who had held the answers to the many questions plaguing him. The woman he had promised mercy.

"There," a voice said, "now that nasty job's finished, by the king's order."

The voice pulled him out of his stupor, and his eyes drifted up to the captain who was running a rag down the crimson-stained blade of his sword, a look of faint disgust on his face.

"*You*," Cutter growled, the word, even to him, sounding barely understandable, as if it came from the throat of some wild beast.

The man paused in his labors, turning to Cutter. At first, he looked annoyed, but he must have seen something in Cutter's face, for he paled. "I did what I did by the king's order," the captain said hurriedly. "I cannot be faulted for that, for I am only showing my loyalty to—"

Wounded or not, exhausted or not, Cutter found himself moving forward, lumbering toward the man.

"N-now you just wait a minute—" the man said, backing up then letting out a startled cry as he fetched up against one of the ornamental statues placed in the gardens. "I—"

The man managed nothing else before Cutter's hands were on him, jerking him up in the air. "*I promised her mercy*," he growled.

"Mercy is for the innocent," the captain said and a moment later, hot, sharp pain blossomed in Cutter's side, and he stared down to see that the man had plunged a dagger into him. It hurt, but even that pain was a distant thing next to his anger. Cutter remembered, later, looking at the statue, made of hard stone, meant to last for generations. He remembered, also, grabbing hold of the back of the man's head. But that was all. Then a red haze descended upon him, and he knew nothing else.

CHAPTER TEN

What's the worst part of being a soldier, you ask?
Well. The rations are pretty shit.
Fine, fine, you really want to know?
I guess I'd say it's the waiting
Waiting for the battle to come, for it all to begin.
Oh, and I hear dying's bad too...
Not that I've tried it yet.
—Unnamed soldier interviewed during Fey War

It was late and Maeve was tired. Since Cutter had left, she had sat in the single chair placed in the corner of the room they had found for Guardsman Nigel, watching the man quietly writhe, moaning from time to time. She had watched him, willing him to wake, praying for the gods to heal him for hours now. So far, her prayers had gone unanswered.

When Cutter and the others had left, she had been so full of nervous energy that despite not having slept well in days—months, truth be told—rest had been the last thing on her mind. After all, if Cutter was right—and while the prince was many things a fool could not be counted among them—then the crime boss, Belle, held the answers to all their problems. She and the guardsman, assuming, of course, that the man lived. Maeve was no healer, but she'd spent enough time listening to the poisoned guardsman's moans, watching him twist and shift and sweat in his sleep, that she thought Belle was their best chance at getting the information they needed.

So she sat, and she worried, waiting to hear news from Cutter or the others, hoping that the guardsman would wake before then, hoping that *something* would happen and soon. She hadn't been sleepy when Cutter and the others left, but that had been hours ago now, and the days and weeks of little sleep were beginning to tell. It was all she could do to keep her eyes open, and so she decided that she would just have to risk disturbing the guardsman's fitful sleep. Better that than she fall asleep as well.

She rose, stretching as she did. That helped, at least a little, and so she decided to give pacing a try. The room was not large and so she quickly reached the other end, only to turn around and go back again. Waiting. It was the most damning thing. She had never been known for her patience. Likely it was the reason why she'd been such a terrible gardener.

She just wished that *something* would happen. In the quiet room, the only sounds the moaning of the injured guardsman, *injured but not dying, please gods,* she almost felt as if she were going mad. Besides, being alone, in the relative quiet, gave her time to think, and since losing her husband and child so long ago, she had tried to avoid that, when she could. In fact, she sometimes thought that her entire life since that day had been led only to serve as a means of distracting her from what she had lost.

She sighed, turning around again to start back toward the other side of the room then froze when she heard the sound of the door's latch being tried.

Maeve grinned as relief swept through her and turned to the door. But instead of opening, the handle moved slowly back and forth, so quietly, in fact, that she would not have heard it had the room not been nearly completely silent.

Maeve stared at the handle as it moved, frowning. The door was locked of course, just as Cutter had told her to lock it when he left. Obviously he knew that, so why, then, would he try the door? Why didn't he just knock instead and ask her to let him in?

Maeve could think of only one reason why and that was that the man outside in the hallway wasn't Cutter at all. And a person didn't have to be particularly clever to imagine why someone would try the door so stealthily. Even as Maeve stood there, she began to hear metallic scrapings, what could only be someone trying to prise the latch open.

Maeve had been in plenty of fights before, faced countless threats, but that didn't stop her heart from speeding up in her chest as she silently drew two of her blades from where she kept them secreted.

Perhaps she was being paranoid. Perhaps the visitor was only a servant come to clean the room, perhaps the healer returning to check on his charge, but she didn't think so. She'd led a life that would make anyone paranoid and, so far at least, she was still living it largely *due* to that paranoia. Anyway, she could think of no reason why the healer or a castle servant wouldn't knock or announce themselves.

Quietly, she moved to stand at the side of the door so that, when it opened, it would block her from view, and then she waited for what would happen. She didn't have to wait long. Whoever was on the other side of the door might not have gotten the knack for knocking, but they seemed pretty talented at picking a lock as, less than a minute later, it swung open slowly, indicating that someone was easing it open, no doubt in order to keep it silent lest the sound of its creaking give them away.

Maeve watched as first one shadowed form, then another, glided into the room. It was dark in the room, the only illumination coming from the spatters of moonlight that made it through the small window along one wall, and so she could not discern any defining features of the visitors. But then, she didn't need to, for she could make out what they held in their hands clearly enough. Just shadowed silhouettes, but in her experience there weren't many things that had the silhouette of daggers save daggers.

Maeve remained still behind the door, holding her breath, while both figures stepped into the room.

The two figures started toward the bed, as she'd known they would, and Maeve skulked forward. Then, when she was close enough, she buried one of her blades in the back of the figure nearest her. The man let out a grunt of surprise as the dagger quested forward, piercing his heart. Only a grunt, no more than that, but in the silent room it sounded like a crack of thunder.

Maeve stepped away from the first, leaving her blade in his back as he collapsed to the ground and by the time the second had fully turned, her blade was waiting at his throat.

"Hi," she said softly. "Sorry to disturb you—I couldn't sleep."

The man shifted the blade he held in his hand, baring his teeth, and she shook her head. "I wouldn't," she said. "I'm old, slower than I used to be, it's true, but I think even I'd be able to move my knife a couple of inches before you can bring yours around."

The man hesitated, seeming to think about it but finally he let the hand holding his blade drop. "What do you want, bitch?" he growled.

Maeve gave a slight shrug of her shoulder, a shrug that just so happened to nick the man's throat, causing him to hiss. "I told you—I've been around for a while, and I've been called a lot worse. Words don't hurt, you see? But knives...well, knives can hurt a great deal. As for what I want...how about we start with why you're here? You know what? Never mind. That seems obvious enough, doesn't it?" She paused for a moment, as if considering. "How about this? Why don't you tell me your name?"

"Fuck off," the man growled.

Maeve sighed. "Must be tough introducing yourself at parties. Anyway, I'd think you could be a bit more polite. Here I am, being just as cordial as you please, and you insist on being rude." She shook her head. "It makes a woman wonder what the world's coming to. Fine, we'll try a different question. Who sent you here?"

The man said nothing this time, choosing instead to scowl. Might have even been a good one, but it was hard to say for sure as she could see little of his features in the shadows save for his eyes, studying her.

"You may not like my questions, and I understand," Maeve said, "truly I do, but there are others who will be here soon, some friends of mine. They'll ask their questions too, and I'm afraid they—one in particular—have a tendency to ask a lot harder than I do. Trust me, it would be easier for us both if you answered me."

"You speak of the Crimson Prince," the man growled. "The Destroyer. The traitor to his people, the breaker of the peace."

The man's voice shook with anger, but Maeve nodded. "That'd be the one. So. Fancy letting the *Destroyer* ask you questions, or would you rather be a good chap and answer mine?"

"You think I fear you or your Crimson Prince?" the man growled. "You, all of you, are nothing. Soon, very soon, you will all be dead."

Maeve grunted. "Maybe. The gods know I've got more of my life behind me than I do ahead—it's one of those hard facts a body has to come to terms with as she gets older. Still, I don't know if I'd be so comforted by that as you seem to be. After all, everybody dies. Some folks, though, well some folks die a lot sooner than others." She let her gaze travel to the man's dead companion on the floor to accentuate her point, then looked back to him. "Now, I'll ask you again—who sent you?"

She couldn't see much of the man's face, but she could see enough to see his eyes narrowing, his body tensing as if in preparation for something. "I really wouldn't," she said, "I told you, I'm old, but I'm not that—"

But the man chose not to listen, diving to the side and, with a shout, bringing his knife around to stab her in the side. Or, at least, he meant to. Instead, as soon as he began the motion Maeve slid the dagger across his throat, pivoting out of the way of the man's own questing blade.

The assassin grunted, staggering and bringing a hand to his throat, the blood sluicing out of it nearly black in the gloom. He stared at her with wide eyes, as if he couldn't believe she'd done what she'd promised she would, then he collapsed to the ground at her feet.

Maeve sighed, staring down at the two bodies. Not the first men she'd killed—far from it—but being familiar with the pang of sadness, regret, and shame that always accompanied such an act did nothing to stop its coming. "Why wouldn't you just listen?" she asked of the dead man.

The dead man, unsurprisingly, did not respond.

A moment later, though, there was a gasp, and Maeve looked up to see Guardsman Nigel staring at her from the bed. Or, more accurately, staring at the bloody blade she still held clenched in one fist. "Ah," she said, "you're awake. Well...fancy an early breakfast?"

CHAPTER ELEVEN

They say that the worst scars are the ones a man carries on the inside.
Maybe that's true and maybe it isn't, but say this for those hidden scars—
They damned sure don't bleed as much.
—Healer interviewed after battle during the Fey War

Cutter came awake to be greeted by a host of aches and pains, some minor, most not. He opened his eyes slowly. It was dark, and he could make out footsteps padding closer to him. Someone leaned down over him, no more than a silhouette in the darkness, and he reached out, clamping his hand around the figure's throat.

"*Prince...it's...me...*" a strangled voice gasped.

Cutter grunted, letting go. "Chall?" he croaked.

"S-sure," the man said, coughing, "or what's left of me. Stones and starlight, but for a man who nearly died you've got a damned strong grip on you."

"Sorry about that," Cutter said. Then with a grunt of effort, he rose to a sitting position. As his eyes slowly adjusted to the gloom, he was able to make out more of his surroundings, and he glanced down at himself and the fresh bandages wrapped around...well, just about everywhere.

"Like your new outfit?" Chall asked, rubbing at his throat. "The healer came by and saw to you. I don't mind tellin' you, you missed a lot of headshaking and muttered curses. Not that I know what the man's complaining about. Long as you're around, there's plenty of job security for the crotchety old bastard."

Cutter winced then noted another figure sitting on the floor in the corner of the room, his arms draped across his knees. "Fel?'

"It's me, brother," the man said. He gave a rueful smile, only just visible in the darkness and held his hands out to his side. "Accommodations fit for princes, are they not? Still, all things taken into account, I think I prefer them to the throne just the same."

Cutter grunted. "Where are we?" he asked, thinking he knew the answer already.

"The dungeons," Chall said.

"The dungeons," Cutter repeated, then turned back to the mage. "What happened?"

The man winced, avoiding his gaze. "Well. Now I can't be for sure as you didn't tell me—weren't really in much of a talking mood, at least before you passed out. But it seems you took a bit of offense to that bastard of a captain killing Belle out of hand."

Feledias snorted from his spot in the corner. "A bit of offense? Gods, mage, but you're underselling that a bit, aren't you? I'd heard you were an accomplished liar—no surprise, considering you're an illusionist—but that's a damned bold one."

Cutter cleared his throat, rubbing at it.

"You alright, Prince?"

"Sure," he said. "Just...well, my throat hurts."

Feledias gave a second snort. "And so it would after all that screaming."

"Just leave him alone, will you?" Chall asked angrily. "It's not like he doesn't have enough on his plate just now."

"Screaming?" Cutter said. Then a sinking feeling overcame him. "Where's the captain...Revan, wasn't it?"

Feledias barked a harsh laugh. "Which part? Last I saw—before you fell unconscious and we were spirited away with such fervor by the remaining guardsmen—you'd scattered pieces of him damned near over the whole courtyard." He shook his head. "If you hated the décor so much, brother, you could have said as much; why, we might have even hired someone to do the work—no need to have set about the task of doing it all yourself."

"You mean...I killed him?" Cutter asked.

Feledias finally winced, as if ashamed. "Yes, brother," he said quietly. "You killed him most...convincingly. I must confess that, since meeting you again after these long years, I had begun to wonder if the beast you carried inside you had expired. Now...now I do not."

I am fire, Cutter thought. "What happened next?" he asked, turning to Chall.

"Prince," he said hesitantly, "are you sure you want to..."

"It's fine, Chall," he said. A lie. "*I'm* fine." A bigger one. "Now, tell me what happened."

The mage nodded slowly. "Well, the guardsmen took a bit of offense at you goin' after their captain and all. They were all set to kill you—you passed out about the time you...finished up—but I talked them out of that much at least, said the king would make any man suffer who dared to lay a hand on his father."

Cutter wasn't at all sure that was true, not considering the way Matt had been acting lately. In fact, he wasn't at all sure that it *should* be true. He thought perhaps it would have been better if the men had been left to do their work, but he nodded. "And then?"

Chall shrugged. "Some still wanted to kill you, but they had a bit of a talk and decided on the dungeon as a sort of...compromise."

"I see," Cutter said. "But...then why are you both here? You didn't hurt anyone."

Chall winced. "I wouldn't say that was *exactly* true. Some of the guards, before the talking was done, got a bit...excited about the whole killing you thing. Me and your brother here...well, we sort of...I guess you'd say we talked them out of it."

Cutter blinked. He wasn't surprised that he had screwed up again, wasn't surprised that the anger he always carried around with him had gotten the better of him once more, but the idea that Feledias had helped him *was* surprising. "You mean...the two of you...Feledias..."

"I did nothing," his brother barked. "Don't take it to heart, brother—I wouldn't have been all that upset to have seen those men bring their blades to bear on you. Only...well, I thought the best way of figuring out this whole conspiracy was to keep you breathing for a bit longer."

It was Chall's turn to snort. "Did nothing, is it? Well, there's two guardsmen, one with a broken nose and another with a broken arm that'd likely disagree with that."

"I see..." Cutter said. "And...I'm sorry. To both of you. You didn't deserve to be put here and...well. Thanks."

Feledias grunted. "Save your thanks and your apology both, brother. One is useless and the other silly. After all, only a fool would expect an apology when he sticks his head in the lion's mouth and finds its teeth clamped around him. All manner of creatures, beasts and mortals, even the Fey, I think, act according to their nature. And your nature, brother, is blood. It always has been."

"He's wrong, Prince," Chall said, but the weak sound of his voice made Cutter think that that was a lie hard to swallow even for one of the world's greatest illusionists.

Cutter knew, in fact, that his brother wasn't wrong, just as he knew that Chall knew it, but he decided to let it go for now. After all, there were other things to think about. "What of Maeve and Guardsman Nigel? Any word?"

Chall winced again. "I'm...not sure."

"What the fat man *means,* brother mine," Feledias said, "is that, as it turns out, jailers are rarely free with information to their prisoners."

"Right," Cutter said.

"Do you...do you think she's okay?" Chall asked, doing his best to sound casual but botching the job completely.

"I'm sure she's fine," Cutter said, also doing his best to sound casual and, he suspected, botching the job completely.

"But...if it's as bad in the castle as we think," Chall said, "then it wouldn't be out of the realm of possibility for someone to send assassins after Guardsman Nigel, and we left her alone with—"

"Easy, Chall," Cutter said, rising slowly and putting a hand on the man's shoulder. "Maeve can take care of herself—better than most. Likely better than any of us. If an assassin *was* sent, then I pity the poor bastard."

The mage nodded, giving him a small, fragile smile but saying nothing. "Why don't you have a seat," Cutter said, "relax." He motioned to the cot that he'd been lying on when he'd woken. "You look exhausted. I'd get some sleep, if you can. There's no telling how long we'll be here."

The mage grunted. "Don't think I'll manage any sleep, not with Maeve out there somewhere, but probably my feet could use the rest."

He sat down, leaning back against the stone wall of the cell, and despite his words he was asleep within minutes. Cutter watched him, making sure he was sleeping, then, started toward the corner where Feledias sat, keeping one hand along the wall to maintain his balance.

"You've looked better, brother," Feledias said as he drew close.

"We both have," Cutter agreed. "Anyway...about the captain. That is...you're sure he was dead?"

Feledias stared at him for several seconds as if seeing him for the first time then, finally, he nodded. "Yes, brother. I'm sorry but he was dead, there is no mistaking it."

Cutter nodded, sliding down to sit with his back against the wall beside his brother. "I see. Well...thanks, Fel. I know you said you don't want it but...thanks anyway."

His brother gave a grunt. "Anyway, what's the plan now? Beyond being executed, I mean."

Cutter shook his head. "I don't think we need worry about being executed. Matt wouldn't let that happen."

"No?" Feledias asked, meeting his gaze. "Look, Bernard, I don't know the boy, not like you do, but from what I've seen of him, he's changed quite a bit since he got here. Why, I hardly recognize him as the youth we put that crown on."

Cutter winced, not offering any argument. Mostly because he couldn't think of one. "I'll admit," he ventured finally, "that Matt has been...acting strangely." He paused, remembering the castle servant with her bruised face and busted lip. "Been acting...badly," he went on. "He's been going through something, though I'm not sure what. But going through something or not, there's no way he'd have us killed."

Fel gave a slight shrug of his shoulders. "If you say so, brother. And if he does, well, I suppose there could be worse things. After all, if the Fey have infiltrated the entire kingdom as much as they have seemed to then it might be best we die. Wouldn't do to be two princes without a kingdom, would it?"

"That's not going to happen," Cutter growled.

"My brother the optimist," Feledias said then gave a snort. "It's an odd look on you, Bernard. Anyway, what do you mean to do?"

"What I can," Cutter said. "And it's not as bad as you seem to think, Fel. We've got Guardsman Nigel back to the castle, and Maeve's watching out for him. When he wakes—"

"You mean *if* he wakes," Feledias corrected. "Your mage told me some of this guardsman. I don't know much about poisons, but it seems to me that the whole point of using them is so that people will never wake again, isn't it? And if the poison doesn't kill him, well, whoever is behind all this has already proven that they don't mind taking the more...*direct* approach to silencing those who stand against them."

"He's got Maeve watching over him," Cutter persisted. "She'll—"

"Fight bravely and with great *honor*, I'm sure," Feledias said, his tone thick with sarcasm, "but what difference will that make, in the end, brother? We have no idea how many men this unseen conspirator commands—for all we know, the entire castle guard and staff might serve him. Is the woman supposed to somehow stand against so many, should they come for the guard? Assuming they even do, of course. Were I the conspirator, I think I would stop hacking away at the snake's body, as it were, and aim for the head."

Cutter frowned. "The head? What do you mean?"

His brother gave another small shrug. "Why, the king, of course."

The king. Matt. The thought sent a chill of terror through Cutter. He couldn't allow anything to happen to Matt. Not just because he had promised Layna that he would protect him but also because he was his son. His son and, his strange, recent behavior excluded, the realm's best chance of having a leader worthy of it. "No," he growled, tightening his fists. "No. I won't let that happen."

"And how would you stop it, brother?" Feledias asked, not mocking now but earnest, almost sad. "You are strong, yes, but even you are not so strong that you might bend iron bars and walk out of here. No, Bernard, I am afraid that we, and the kingdom, are doomed."

Cutter considered that. Things looked grim, that was true. A king acting erratically, conspirators in the castle, guardsmen seeming to be trying their best to cover it all up. "No," he said again. "You're wrong, Fel. Things are bad, but they've been bad before, for both of us. How many battles did we fight, battles that looked to be lost only to turn around in the end?"

"Too many," his brother answered. "But while winning battles is all well and good, brother, you only have to lose the once."

"Yes," Cutter agreed, rising to his feet and doing his best to ignore the pains that shot through his body as he did, "but we won't lose—not this time."

"And what of Maeve? Do you really believe that she'll be okay? That she and the guardsman will survive the night?"

"Yes," Cutter said.

"But...why?"

Because I have to, Cutter thought. "If you knew Maeve as well as I do, you wouldn't have to ask me that question. I'd get some rest, if you can, Fel. Tomorrow's shaping up to be a long day."

"Aren't they all?" his brother countered, but he leaned his head back, closing his eyes and, in moments, was asleep.

***

The half-conscious guardsman's weight was growing heavier and heavier by the moment, his arm draped over her shoulders feeling as if it were made of stone, and Nigel himself muttered intelligible words that Maeve did not understand, likely ones that he himself didn't understand.

She paused at a corner, glancing around it and down either direction of the hallway. Empty, at least for the time being, but she couldn't count on it remaining so for long. It was too much to hope that the two assassins were the only ones in all the castle that intended her and the guardsman ill. Far too much. So she clenched her jaw, shifting and pulling at the man's arm in a vain effort to disperse some of the weight pressing down on her as she hurried around the corner.

Panting breaths hissing between gritted teeth, she shuffled down the hallway until she came to the door she'd been looking for. Maeve heaved a sigh of relief and gave it a knock. No one answered and, after a moment, some of her relief began to fade. Had the man chosen now, of all times, to go for a midnight stroll?

Readjusting the guardsman's arm on her shoulders—which ached as if she'd spent the better part of the day dragging an ox cart behind her—Maeve tried again. Still no answer came, and she began to feel the first rumblings of panic. She glanced back down the hall. Still empty, for the moment at least.

"Come on, damn you," she growled, knocking a third time, hard enough that her knuckles ached where they'd rapped on the door.

This time, she heard muttered words from inside the room followed by the soft sound of footsteps. A moment later, the door slid open a crack.

"I'll have you know that you are interrupting the chronicling of the kingdom's history, a most important task and—" The voice cut off, and the face of Petran Quinn, the once-exiled but recently reinstated Historian to the Crown leaned forward, blinking at her.

"Fire and salt, Lady Maeve, is that you?"

"It's me, Petran."

"But...what are you doing at so late an hour and who is your...companion?" he asked, frowning as he stared at the delirious, slumped guardsman.

"Oh, you know," she said through gritted teeth, "I just thought I'd take a stroll and this fine gentleman offered to accompany me."

"A...a stroll?"

"That's right."

"And you are aware, I'm sure, that it is several hours past midnight?"

As she stood there, exhausted and afraid, sure that any moment an assassin—or likely several of them—would appear in the hallway to finish what their companions had started, Maeve couldn't help but marvel at the fact that the historian had survived as long as he had. "The thought had occurred," she managed. "Now, are you going to let us in or not?"

The man blinked, his eyes wide. "O-of course, please...come in."

He moved aside, swinging the door wider, and Maeve brushed past him, struggling under the weight of her burden. She heard the sound of the door shutting behind her as she guided the guardsman to the bed. "You'll want to lock that."

"Lock it?" Petran asked, as if she'd spoken a different language. "Why um…why is that?"

She heaved a heavy sigh as she lay the guardsman down, stretching in an effort to work some of the stiffness out of her shoulder and back. Then she shrugged, turning to look at the historian who still stood by the door. "Well, we wouldn't want to make the assassins' jobs too easy for them, would we? This way, they at least get that warm feeling of accomplishment after dedicating the few seconds it'll take them to break it down."

"Break it…down?"

"Sure," she said. "A lot harder to stab us to death from the other side of the door, don't you think?"

"Stab…" The man cleared his throat, his face paling in the light of a lantern sitting on the room's desk. "Forgive me, lady, but…would you like a drink?"

"What I'd like is a good night's rest, but since that doesn't appear on offer…yes, a drink would be fine."

Petran moved to the desk, sliding open a drawer and retrieving a decanter then set about the task of pouring their drinks, obviously making an effort to remain calm. "Forgive me for pressing, Lady Maeve, but who did you say your friend is?"

"You mean the not-quite-but-very-nearly dead man currently unconscious on your bed?"

"I…yes," the historian managed in a croak. "That'd be the one."

"A loyal guardsman, that's what."

"I…see."

"I know, I was surprised too. I thought they stopped making them. Anyway. You heard of the assassination attempt on Cu—that is, Prince Bernard?"

The glass slipped from the historian's fingers, smashing on the floor, and he let out a yelp of surprise, though whether at her words or at the broken glass it was hard to say. "An…assassination attempt, you say?"

"I do," Maeve said, frowning. "Wait a minute, do you mean to tell me this is the first you've heard of it?"

The historian's back was to her, but she saw him tense. "Well. I mean, I've been a bit busy, you understand."

"A bit busy," Maeve repeated. "Too busy, it seems, to notice assassins running amuck in the castle?"

The man gave an embarrassed laugh. "Well, I'm sure you must be exaggerating a bit, surely not amu—"

"Amuck," Maeve repeated. "I know what I said."

He cleared his throat, his hand shaking as he poured the first drink. "And...what...that is, is everyone okay?" he managed in a dry croak as he reached for a second glass.

"Maybe you finish pouring our drinks before I tell you the rest," Maeve suggested. "Otherwise, like as not, we'll both be drinking straight from the decanter."

The historian winced but gave a nod. "Likely a wise suggestion." He continued pouring the drinks and, if Maeve was any judge, doing just about as slow a job of it as he was capable. Finally, though, he was finished, and walked back to the table, placing the drinks on its surface with exaggerated care. "Please, have a seat," he said, gesturing to the table's single chair. "And tell me all about what's happened."

"I appreciate the offer," Maeve said, "but if you really don't know what's been happening lately then maybe it's best if you're the one who sits. No offense, Petran, but you don't seem all that steady on your feet."

"Are normal people steady when hearing of assassins in the castle?" he asked.

Maeve shrugged. "Probably not, but then I don't know a lot of normal people, more's the pity."

The historian inclined his head as if to acknowledge a point then sat. "So," he asked in a timid voice, looking at her as if she was about to pronounce his death sentence, "about what's happened..."

"Are you sure you want to know, Petran?" Maeve asked. "You're just a historian after all. Chances are you could remain safe enough in this room—I don't imagine anyone would bother you overly much. No need to trouble yourself."

"Ignoring the 'just' for a moment," the man said, offering her a small smile, "I would have to disagree with you, Lady Maeve.

You see, it is exactly *because* I'm a historian that I must know. I admit that I am no warrior, but just because the truth scares us does not mean it is not worth pursuing. It is always better to seek it, always better to *know*."

Maeve frowned, considering his words. "You really believe that?"

"I hope so," he said, giving her another timid smile. "After all, it is an idea that I have based my entire life's work around."

Maeve nodded. "Very well, Petran, but understand that knowing the things that I will tell you…it might put you in the bad graces of some very powerful people."

The historian favored her with a crooked smile, a bit more confident this time. "Forgive me, Lady Maeve, but I have spent the better part of the last fifteen years in a cell, being beaten regularly for no other reason than the guard's amusement, eating moldy bread when I ate anything at all. I know something of the disfavor of powerful people."

Maeve winced. "Right. And I know…that is, I know what you went through, Petran, it must have been terrible, but understand that the people behind what's been happening…if they decide you're a threat, I don't think it's likely you'll see the inside of a cell again."

"Well, that's good at lea—"

"They'll just kill you instead."

The historian's face paled at that, and he cleared his throat. "Ah. Right."

"Still want to know?" she asked.

The man took a slow, deep breath. He looked scared—and that, at least, Maeve couldn't hold against him for given what was happening with the kingdom, any sane person ought to be. Finally, though, and to his credit, he gave a single nod. "Yes, Lady Maeve. I would hear what you have to say—if you would tell me."

"Very well," Maeve said, and then she began recounting the events that had transpired in the castle in the last days, telling the man of the assassination attempt on Bernard, then moving on to the rescuing of Guardsman Nigel at his home—at least, what she *hoped* was his rescue, there was still no way to know whether the man would succumb to the poison or not. Then she moved on to discussing their meeting with Ned, though she left out the man's name, seeing no need to put the driver or his wife in any more danger than was necessary.

When she finished, she leaned back, tired and exhausted and more than a little scared herself.

The historian said nothing for some time, his face pale as he struggled to process everything she had told him. He was still, statue still, and the first movement he made was to reach for the glass and finish the drink in one long pull. He set it down, spilling droplets on the table. "Forgive me," he said in a whisper, "I...I am usually tidier than that."

"Sure," Maeve said, "but just this once—don't go making a habit of it." She said it lightheartedly, or at least as much as she could, hoping to inject some much-needed levity into the conversation.

Apparently, it worked, as the historian let out a heavy sigh. "Thank you, Lady Maeve," he croaked. "For...telling me."

Maeve sighed. "Don't thank me yet. Anyway, that's where we're at."

"And you have no news of Prince Bernard or Challadius?"

She frowned. "No, I don't, and I thought they'd be back by now. I'm...worried."

"And...what of the assassins? Did they have anything that might tell you who they worked for or..."

"Not so lucky as that," she said, offering him a small smile. "Speaking as a one-time assassin, I'm afraid they generally make it a rule not to carry around something that would betray who they work for. At least not in the open—such things are usually kept in a secret, hidden place in case their employer decides to do anything...rash."

"Right," the man said, swallowing, "I apologize...sometimes it is easy to forget that you were once the most celebrated assassin in the realm."

Maeve shrugged. "Times change. Besides, it isn't a part of my life I'm particularly proud of, if you want to know the truth."

"Well, I would not worry overly much about Prince Bernard and Challadius surely. As for the prince, well, he can take care of himself, can't he? And Challadius..."

"Challadius can barely take care of getting out of the bed every morning," Maeve said, doing her best to hide her worry for the mage and failing miserably, even to herself. "As for Bernard, he's strong, sure—none stronger. But even he needs other people, needs friends...even if he won't admit it."

The historian nodded at that, his brows drawn down in thought. "Still, I find it strange..." he said, speaking quietly, almost as if to himself.

"What's that?" Maeve asked.

"Well..." He paused, clearing his throat, "I, of course, do not know anywhere near as much of the assassins' art as you, but it seems to me that if these men were able to so easily infiltrate the castle—not once, but twice, you understand—and if their goal really is to destabilize the kingdom so that the Fey might more easily overtake us...well. It seems to me that they would be better served going directly for King Matthias."

Maeve frowned at that. She'd been so busy reacting over the last several days that she'd given the situation little thought other than how to get her and her friends out of it alive. Now that the historian had pointed it out though, it seemed like the most obvious thing in the world. "You're right," she said. "That would be the easiest way to hurt the kingdom. Killing the lad would force the kingdom to look to Bernard or Feledias to rule and neither of them are exactly loved by the people of the Known Lands. Why, there'd likely be riots in the streets. But...if that's the easiest way then why wouldn't they use it?"

"Perhaps..." The historian paused, thinking. "Perhaps it is because they know that the king will be better guarded, and they don't think it would be possible to make it to him?" he ventured.

Maeve considered that for a moment then shook her head. "No. No, these men, whatever else they are, aren't afraid, that much is sure. They wouldn't let a couple of guardsmen stop them."

"So...why?" Petran offered. "What reason would they have to avoid going for the king?"

"I can't think of any," Maeve said after a moment, but that wasn't exactly true. She could think of at least one, but the very idea made her sick to her stomach. The only reason she could think that the men wouldn't go for the king was if the king were in on it somehow. But...no. That couldn't be possible. True, Matt had been acting strange lately, but he had only arrived in New Daltenia with her and the rest of them. Even if the lad *had* wanted to take part in a conspiracy to overthrow the realm—ridiculous by itself—he was from a small village on the outskirts of the realm. He didn't *know* anyone in New Daltenia. How would he have even begun such a thing? And even more to the point, how would he have had the time?

No, it couldn't have been Matt. There was simply no way it was possible for the lad to have orchestrated the assassination attempts on Cutter or Guardsman Nigel. Not to mention the fact that, beyond *any* of that, Priest had been with the boy the entire time, his shadow. If Matt was up to anything, Priest would have known and told her and the rest at once. "Damn," she said. "What a damned mess."

Petran nodded. "Yes," he agreed. "And I think, perhaps, that we could both use another drink."

He rose then, headed toward the desk to retrieve the decanter. Maeve watched him for several seconds and then came to a decision. "I'll have to skip that drink, Petran." She said, rising.

"Oh?" the historian asked, turning back to look at her.

"Yes," she said. "And I need to ask a favor—I wonder if you couldn't watch over our friend here for a while?"

The historian blinked, turning to regard the unconscious guardsman lying in the bed. "O-of course, Lady Maeve, but...are you sure you wish to venture into the castle once more after so soon facing the assassins?"

"I have to," Maeve said. "For one, I need to find Cutter and Chall—they should have reported back by now and the fact that they haven't..." She paused, giving her head a shake and doing her best to push her fears aside. After all, they would serve no purpose now. "Besides, the longer I'm here, the greater chances the assassins—if there still are any—start searching and find us. And somehow I don't think these are the type of men who let a little something like a locked door keep them from doing their jobs."

The historian nodded reluctantly. "Still...perhaps I could go with you?"

"No," Maeve said. "I need you here, watching over Guardsman Nigel. Besides, if it comes to a fight—and I don't mean any offense, Petran—you'd just get in my way."

The man sighed. "I suppose you're right. But...at least let me summon some of the castle guards. There's greater strength in numbers after all and—"

"Castle guards like the ones who tried to assassinate Prince Bernard so recently?" Maeve asked. "No thank you, Petran, I think I'm better off on my own."

The man seemed mollified by that, and he gave a nod. "As you say, Lady Maeve, but I still confess that I feel most terrible, allowing you to go out into the castle amidst such dangers by yourself."

She gave him a small smile. "If it's any consolation, Petran, you couldn't stop me if you wanted to. Besides, like I told you," she said, patting her tunic to make sure the knives she had secreted there were secure and easily accessible should she find the need to draw them, "I work better alone."

And with that, she opened the door, turning back to look at the historian who resembled nothing so much as a frightened child. "Keep this door locked and don't open it for anyone except Prince Bernard or myself. Understand?"

"Y-yes."

Maeve gave the man a nod and, with that, turned and walked out the door, closing it behind her. Standing in the hallway, out of Petran's sight, she stared at her hands, saw the tremor there. She had not wanted to admit it to the man as it would have done no good and only served to worsen his own fear, but Maeve was afraid. Bernard and Challadius were late, and assassins were seemingly coming and going in the castle as they pleased.

Still, she told herself that she had faced worse in her time and survived, even if she had been a lot younger and a lot dumber then. But even that did little to console her. After all, most of the time, during the war, she had not been alone but had been able to count on Bernard and Chall and Priest to have her back. And despite the words she'd said to Petran, no one worked better alone.

But Chall and Bernard were missing, and the only lead she had on their whereabouts was the dungeons. And considering the fact that the two had headed there and, since, had been conspicuously absent, she didn't much like those odds. After all, anything that was enough to deal with the world's greatest warrior and one of its greatest mages—even if he was a perpetual pain in the ass—was more than enough to handle an old woman well past her prime.

As for Priest, he had not left the king's side since Bernard had given his orders and, likely, was there even now. An idea began to form then. True, she didn't like her chances of going to the dungeons in search of Bernard and Chall alone, thought it far more likely she would run into assassins before seeing either of her friends. But if she made it to Priest and Matt, then they could decide what to do together. After all, Priest was a clever man, not to mention one of the best in a fight she could hope for. And as for Matt, well, it was true that he'd been acting strange lately, but was that any real surprise, given how much his life had changed recently? It couldn't be easy realizing that the people you thought were your parents weren't and going from being just another village boy to king of the Known Lands. And whatever might be bothering him, he loved Cutter, that much she knew.

Yes, that was it. She would find Matt, find Priest, and together they would discover what had happened to Cutter and Chall. The decision made, she felt better, safer, but not so safe that, as she began making her way down the castle hallways, she neglected to keep her hands near her knives, in case she needed to draw them.

CHAPTER TWELVE

Deeds done in the darkness bear fruit in the day.
—Queen Layna of the Known Lands

Cutter stood at the bars of their cell, gazing out the dimly lit hallway. He had been standing so for some time while Feledias and Chall slept. He knew that he, too, should try to get some rest, for he was exhausted, mind and body both, and his wounds were paining him. He had heard, often, that sleep was the best medicine, and he knew that it would do him good. But he knew also that even should he try, there would be no chance of getting any rest, not while Belle, the woman he had promised a pardon, remained dead, nor while Maeve was left to protect the guardsman alone.

So he stood in the darkness, thinking dark thoughts, and he waited.

Eventually, he heard a metallic creak and craned his neck to peer down the dungeon corridor toward the entrance. A moment later the door was thrown open and orange light, painfully bright after so long in the near-darkness, blossomed at the end of the corridor. Cutter shielded his eyes but did not turn away, for one of the lessons his life had taught him was that, just because something was painful to look upon didn't mean that a man shouldn't. Another was that in an attempt to avoid pain, men often found worse waiting for them.

He saw several figures, what appeared to be five in all, walking down the corridor. One walked at the front, a lantern held aloft, and as they drew closer Cutter saw that it was the guardsman he had spoken to about where the crime boss, Belle, had been taken what felt like a lifetime ago. The uniforms of the other four marked them as castle guardsmen.

The group made their way to in front of their cell, the dungeon guard wincing. "Sorry, Prince, for...for you being in here, I mean," the guard offered apologetically. "Wasn't up to me and—"

"*Enough talk*," one of the four guardsmen barked. "Unlock the cell, jailer, and speak no more to the prisoner."

"Prisoner?" the guard asked in disbelief. "Fire and salt, man, he's your prince!"

"Is he?" the guard answered. "Even if so, it matters not, for we are come on order from King Matthias himself, *our* king. He is your king too, is he not?" the man asked, a dangerous tone to his voice.

"O-of course," the guardsman said, "but—"

"Leave it," Cutter said quietly. "Please, open the door."

The dungeon guard glanced at him, nodding, an apologetic look on his face. "As you say, Prince."

Cutter stood, regarding the four men as the jailer retrieved the key and unlocked the gate and they, in turn, regarded him with looks of undisguised hostility.

"Where are we off to then?" Cutter asked as the gate swung open with a metallic creak. "The King's Courtyard for another execution?"

The spokesman of the group sneered, making it clear that, were it up to him, that was *exactly* where they'd be headed. "His Majesty, King Matthias, requires your presence in the audience chamber."

"I see," Cutter said. "Well then, best we not keep him waiting."

"You're not giving the orders here, *Prince*," the guard said. "Now, step out of the cell and keep your hands at your sides."

Cutter did as he was told, moving slowly so as to give the guards no excuse to draw the blades their fingers seemed itching to pull out.

The guard who'd spoken watched him, a small, humorless smile on his face, then he nodded to the jailer. "Shackle him."

"Oh, come on," the dungeon guard said, "is that really—"

"Do it," the man barked, "or do you want to try out one of those cells you've guarded for so long?"

The jailer stared, incredulous, then turned to Cutter who gave the faintest of nods. With a shake of his head, the jailer retrieved a pair of shackles from where they'd been hanging on the wall and went about the task of binding Cutter's hands and feet together with the heavy iron manacles.

When he was done, he turned to the guards' spokesman. "Anything else?" he said, his anger clear in his tone. "Maybe want me to make him stand on one leg and hop?"

The guard ignored the man's words, nodding his head at the sleeping figures of Challadius and Feledias. "We'll be wanting them as well."

Cutter felt a thrill of panic course through him at that. "Look, whatever your business is, it's with me. There's no need to—" He cut off with a grunt as the guard backhanded him hard across the face with a gauntleted fist. Cutter staggered, the coppery taste of blood filling his mouth, and he would have fallen had the jailer not reached out to steady him.

"Just who do you think you are?" the dungeon guard demanded.

"*I* am Sergeant Selladross, of His Majesty's personal guard, on orders from His Highness, and should you think to stand in my way again, *jailer*, then you will find that no man is safe from the king's justice."

The sergeant leaned forward, so that his face was beside Cutter's. "Captain Revan was a friend," he whispered. "The king told me to bring you and your companions to him, and so I shall, but I doubt very much if you will enjoy the experience, Prince. And should you get any ideas, know that your brother and your fat friend will suffer for it."

Cutter said nothing, was too busy wrestling with the anger inside him, anger that was threatening to get out of control. Instead, he only gave a nod, running an arm across his bloody mouth.

The sergeant leaned back, smiling, then motioned to his men. "Wake them and bring them out."

"Shall we manacle them as well, Sergeant?"

"I don't think that will be necessary," the man said, turning and giving Cutter a humorless smile. "Do you, Highness?"

Cutter said nothing, standing as the guards woke Feledias and Chall and ushered them out into the hallway.

"What...what is it?" Chall asked sleepily. "What's happened?"

"We are being brought to see the king," Cutter said.

"Oh," the mage said. "Well, that's good..." He paused, frowning at the manacles on Cutter's wrists and ankles. "Isn't it?"

"I guess we'll find out soon enough," Cutter said.

"Enough talk," the sergeant snapped. "Another word, and you will discover that the only title you own that means anything just now is 'prisoner.' Now, let's move—the king waits."

With that, the other three guards took up positions around Cutter and his companions, one on either side, the third behind them. The sergeant himself moved to walk at their front.

"Seems you made some new friends while I was sleeping," Feledias whispered from behind Cutter.

"You know me," Cutter answered quietly, "a real social butterfly."

"I must admit, brother," Feledias said as they started down the dungeon corridor, "that I am glad to see that you have finally discovered your sense of humor. It is only a shame that it is of the gallows' kind."

"Is there any other?" Cutter asked.

As they made their way through the castle, Cutter and his two companions received several pokes and prods—and more than a few strikes—from the sergeant and his men. At first, these blows came either because they walked too slowly or too quickly but, eventually, the guards gave up even those pretenses of excuses, striking them from time to time for no other reason than that they clearly enjoyed it.

Cutter weathered these unexpected, random blows as he had weathered so much other hardship in his life, silently, some part of himself, the angry part—what he thought of as the *red* part—vowing that he would get his vengeance, sooner or later.

By the time they finally reached the door to the audience chamber, he and his two companions were sporting several bruises and scrapes—Chall even having a black eye swollen nearly shut—that they had not when exiting their cell less than an hour before.

"Fire and salt," one of the two guards stationed at the door said as they regarded Cutter and his companions. "What happened to them?"

"Tripped," the sergeant said.

The guard stationed there grunted. "That so? Seems they must have tripped a lot."

The sergeant shrugged. "This group of prisoners is, I'm afraid, particularly clumsy."

The guard studied him for a moment, and Cutter had the brief hope that the man might call him down for his actions. Instead, after a moment, he gave a nod. "Well. Best you be gettin' 'em inside. The king's not a patient man at the best of times, and he seems to be in a particularly foul mood today."

He proceeded to knock on the door in a series of rapping blows and, a moment later, the great doors of the audience room swung open.

Cutter wasn't sure what he'd expected when he had been summoned by the king, but he was surprised to find that the audience chamber no longer looked like an audience chamber at all. Instead, it looked like a dining hall. Tables had been set up on either side of the room, tables at which half a dozen men and women sat on either side of the room, laughing and drinking.

On the throne itself, Matt sat, and flanking him on either side, were four guards. Priest, who Cutter had asked to watch over the boy, stood below the raised dais the way a servant standing in readiness to fill the king's wine goblet might. Close enough to see to the king's needs but far enough away that he might be forgotten.

Cutter didn't like the look of that, didn't like what it said for Matt's current state of mind that he had chosen strangers to guard his person over Priest. Nor did he like the flagrant drinking and laughing from those present at the tables, as if now, of all times, when the kingdom sat at the edge of collapse, was a time for celebration.

He frowned over them, not recognizing a single one, he was surprised to find, until finally his gaze settled on Maeve, sitting apart at one end of the table, farthest from the throne. Was it happenstance, he wondered, that had found her sitting there, or was it by design? And if by design, then whose?

Matt sat on the throne with one leg draped over one of its arms, grinning like a fool, his face flushed from drink, a large wine stain on the front of his tunic. As he noted Cutter and his companions' arrival, he lifted a golden goblet casually, spilling some of the liquid on the floor as he did, then tapped on it with a fork, sending a chime in the air.

A chime that was largely ignored by the, for lack of a better word, *celebrants* in the room. Matt's smile faded in an instant then. "*Shut up!*" he shouted, and the buzz of conversation abruptly cut off.

Matt stared around at those people gathered at the tables, all of them avoiding his eyes, studying their plates and drinks like chastened children, then slowly he smiled. "Forgive me, worthies, but it seems that my errant father has arrived, along with his...*friends.*"

There was something about the way he said "friends" that Cutter didn't like, just as he didn't like the look in Matt's eyes, a look of malice and scheming. "Ah, Father, please come forward that I might see you better."

Cutter glanced at the sergeant who angrily motioned him forward, then started toward the throne. In the suddenly silent room, the metallic sounds of his manacles shifting as he moved seemed as loud as peals of thunder.

"Stones and starlight what did you do to him?" Maeve demanded, half-rising out of her chair as Cutter drew close enough for the light of the lanterns to reveal evidence of the guards' attention.

"Sit, please, Lady Maeve," Matt said, "I will see to this. I am sure there was just some misunderstanding or—"

"*Misunderstanding?*" Maeve demanded. "It looks as if they beat him and the others nearly half to dea—"

"*Enough!*" Matt roared. "You will sit, Lady Maeve, or you will be escorted from these chambers—do you understand?"

Maeve, her face plastered with incredulity, turned to Cutter who gave a faint shake of his head. Then she gave an angry huff and sat.

"Now then," Matt said, running a hand through his hair as he turned back to Cutter. "It is good to see you, Father. I hope that your stay in the dungeons was not too...difficult."

"It was fine," Cutter said, glancing around the room. "I see a lot of new faces."

"Your Majesty," Matt said.

"You've got to be—" Maeve began, but Matt thrust up a finger, and the woman subsided into silence.

Cutter bowed his head. "Of course. Forgive me—Your Majesty."

"Better," Matt said, smiling. "I don't mean to be a stickler, of course, Father, but rules are rules, aren't they? And rules, well, they're everything, the very thread which keeps this wonderful kingdom of ours together. Why, without them..." He paused. "Well. I suppose everyone in this room knows well what happens when one of their rulers chooses to ignore the rules and say...has an affair with his brother's wife."

Cutter tensed at that, fury and shame running through him like a lightning strike, but he forced himself to remain calm, nodding. "You are right, of course, Majesty."

There was a snicker from beside Matt, and Cutter looked to see that it had come from one of the guards. The man was young, appearing to be in his early twenties and apparently Matt's sudden interest in rules didn't apply to him, for his uniform was wrinkled, his shirt untucked, and he had his sword belt hitched at what Cutter could only imagine he thought a rakish angle. Still, none of that was what struck him the most. Instead, it was the man's face. There was something familiar about it. At first, Cutter couldn't place it but then, in another moment, he did, and he let out a grunt of surprise.

Matt glanced at the man beside him then grinned, turning back to Cutter. "Ah, yes, I see you have recognized Rolph."

"Rolph," Cutter repeated. "The same man, unless I'm mistaken, that attacked you in Two Rivers? The same man who was helping the Feylings take over the town, the one who meant to watch you and the rest of us be executed?"

Matt winced. "Yes, that's the one. And true, Rolph has made some regretful decisions in the past but then..." He met Cutter's eyes. "But then who among us hasn't?" He let the words hang in the air for a moment before sitting back, waving his hand casually. "Anyway, Rolph was bewitched by the Feyling who went by the name of Emma, as you well know. He and the rest of the town. It would be unfair to blame him for what transpired there anymore than it would be fair to blame a puppet for heeding the string pullings of its master."

Cutter nodded. "As you say, Majesty. Still, I'm surprised he was able to make it here so quickly."

"So quickly?" Matt asked, raising an eyebrow. "I sent for Rolph the day following my coronation. You see, given the current circumstances in New Daltenia, I thought it best to search for guardsmen from...*outside* the city. Do you not agree?"

Cutter said nothing to that, for there was nothing he could say. After all, he had been the target of an assassination attempt by several of the guardsmen only days ago.

"Anyway," Matt said, "let us leave that for now."

"And these others?" Cutter asked, waving a hand to indicate those seated at the tables on either side of the room. "Are they also members of your personal guard?"

One of the people seated at the table—a man, Cutter judged, though it was not so easy to tell as he wore his hair long and had on more face paint than most women Cutter had ever seen—snickered.

"These?" Matt asked. "Oh, no, no, these are my *advisors*. They might not be too useful on a battlefield, I'm afraid, but they are quite useful in matters pertaining to the running of New Daltenia and its future."

"The...running of New Daltenia, Majesty?"

"That's right," Matt said, holding up his hands as if he were helpless. "After all, I needed help from *someone* didn't I? And what with you and my uncle seemingly too busy to ever be around since my coronation, I thought I had best find it elsewhere."

Cutter winced. "Forgive me my absence, Majesty, but I have been investigating the assassination attempts and—"

"Oh, I am *well* aware of your investigations, Father," Matt interrupted. "Just as I am well aware of the fact that you have, without any authorization, killed a member of my household guard—a Captain Revan, I believe."

Cutter tensed at that. "He killed Belle, the woman who was our best chance at finding out exactly what's going on in the city and—"

"*Executed,*" Matt snarled, leaning forward in his throne and gripping the arm rests as if he meant to rip them off. For a moment, his face was twisted with an insane rage, and Cutter thought that he would rush him and attack. He mastered himself a second later, though, sitting back in his throne and taking a deep breath. "Forgive me—it has been a trying few days. Captain Revan, Father, was acting under *my* orders and as such you had no right to attack him out of hand."

"Out of hand?" Chall said from near the door. "You can't be ser—" He cut off with a cry of pain as one of the guards struck him, knocking him to his knees.

The guard who'd done the striking stared at Cutter, a small smile on his face. For his part, Cutter controlled his expression, refusing to give into the anger roiling in him, but also he marked the man's face so that he might remember it, so that later, should the opportunity arise, he might find him again. "The woman he killed," he said, turning back to Matt, "had information that would have gone a long way to rooting out the members of the conspiracy in the castle."

"Is that so?" Matt asked, glancing around at his "advisors" sitting at the tables with a smile and they grinned and snickered obligingly.

"Yes," Cutter said simply.

"And if that is the case," Matt said, "if this woman really was as important to our cause as you say, why, then, did you not come to me and tell me of her importance the moment you learned of it?"

Cutter frowned. "I meant to," he said. "But I got busy. She told me of a guard, Guardsman Nigel, who could help, told me, too, that the man was in danger."

"You got busy," Matt said. "Too busy, it seems, to include your *king* in your plans."

"There was no time," Cutter repeated. "Even rushing as I did, I only just made it to the guardsman's house in time to help him deal with several assassins that had attacked him."

There was a disbelieving snort from one of the king's "advisors" but the man cut off his laughter as Cutter turned to look at him.

"Assassins, you say," Matt repeated.

"Yes, Majesty."

"I see. And do you have any proof of this?" Matt asked. "Their bodies, perhaps?"

Cutter winced, remembering the flames engulfing the guardsman's home, remembering, too, that had it not been for Chall and Maeve's intervention, he never would have made it out alive. "They burned," Cutter said. "In the fire."

"I see," Matt said again. "Rather...convenient, isn't it?"

"Not if you're the assassins."

"Perhaps not," Matt said, "but if you are, let's say, an exiled prince recently returned to his city's capital, one intent on covering the tracks of his doings...well, few things erase evidence better than fire."

"I didn't start the fire. The assassins did."

"Ah, yes. And no doubt you have proof of that?"

Cutter said nothing, for they both knew he did not.

"Well?" one of the advisors sneered. "Do you mean to ignore His Majesty, *prisoner?*"

The man's grin faltered as Cutter turned to stare at him and, after a moment, Cutter looked back to Matt once more. "I did what I believed best at the time, what I thought necessary to protect the kingdom." *To protect you.*

For a moment, the devious cruelty that seemed to lurk in Matt's gaze faded, and Cutter thought that perhaps his words had reached him. A moment later, though, it returned. "Is that so?" Matt asked. "Well, of course, why shouldn't we believe that you acted in the best interests of the kingdom? After all," he went on, raising an eyebrow, "you entertain such a powerful reputation for your...altruism."

"Forgive me, *Majesty,*" Maeve said, her words simmering with anger, "but wouldn't a better use of our time be to try to discover how so many assassins have made it into the castle instead of interrogating Prince Bernard here?"

One of the guards watching Chall started toward the woman, drawing his sword, but froze as Matt raised his hand. The king did not so much as glance in the woman's direction. "Speaking of guardsmen," he said, still watching Cutter, "I hear tale that you brought this guardsman you spoke of, the one who was supposedly attacked by assassins, back to the castle, is that right?"

Cutter glanced at Maeve who gave a single, covert shake of her head, then back to Matt. "Yes, Majesty. I thought, all things considered, it would be the wisest course."

"Another decision made without any consideration to the will of your king," Matt pointed out. "And where, I wonder, is this guardsman now?"

Cutter glanced at Maeve again and the woman watched him. Though she said nothing, he thought he saw a world of meaning in her gaze. "Last I saw, Majesty," he said, "the guardsman was in the room we found for him, resting after the healer's attention. It seems that some of the assassins coated their blades with poison, and the man was having a hard time of it. The healer seemed uncertain as to whether or not he would recover at all. I can only assume he's still there...recuperating as well as he is able."

"You might assume as much," Matt said, "just as I might assume that my father would respect the crown he himself placed upon my head but you, like me, would be wrong."

"Wrong, Majesty?" Cutter asked.

Matt's eyes traveled slowly between Maeve then back to Cutter. "Lady Maeve told me something of this guardsman who you deem so important, and so I sent men to retrieve him from the room. What they found were two dead men, neither of whom was the guardsman. Curious, don't you think?"

Cutter avoided glancing at Maeve, but he thought that he could feel her gaze on him. "That is curious, Highness."

"Even more so Lady Maeve's word," Matt went on, now looking at Maeve again, a distrustful expression on his face, "her *assurance* that she knows nothing of how those two dead men came to be there just as, apparently, she has no knowledge of the guardsman's current whereabouts. Strange, wouldn't you say? Stranger still considering that, by her own admission, she was set the task of watching the guardsman by you, a man her loyalty to whom I have seen with my own eyes."

Maeve shrugged, her gaze locked on Cutter's. "Sorry, Prince," she said. "I'm loyal, of course, but the older I get the more I find that my bladder is not quite as cooperative as it once was."

Several of those in the room blushed or gave faintly disgusted looks at that, as if Maeve mentioning a biological imperative was somehow more disturbing than a room full of revelers when the kingdom appeared to be on the brink of destruction.

"Not so strange after all, Your Majesty," Cutter said. "Anyway, I'm sure that a search of the castle grounds will—"

"A search that has already begun, at my command," Matt interrupted. "It seems, Father, that the rest of us are not quite as big of fools as you take us for."

Cutter frowned at that. "Forgive me, Majesty, but I have never thought you were a fool." Truth be told, he couldn't say as much for the rest of the people scattered about the tables, save Maeve, for "fool" was likely the word he would have chosen to describe them.

"Is that so?" Matt asked. "So then all those lessons you sought to teach me on our journey from Brighton, all those times when you treated me like a child, I was meant to take them some other way?"

"Begging your pardon, Majesty," he said, meeting Matt's eyes. "But you *were* a child." *You still are,* he thought. *You're my child.* "As for what I did, I did it to protect you."

"And so you did," Matt snapped angrily. "For now I am here, am I not?" He gestured around the great audience chamber with both hands. "Here in this...*place.*"

He sounded angry, furious, in fact, but Cutter had no idea what might have made him so, so he said nothing, only stood and waited.

Matt took a slow, deep breath as if to gather himself, then ran a hand through his hair again. "As I said, the search for the guardsman has begun. I have my men combing the castle in search of him, checking every closet and every cellar. They *will* find him, sooner or later," he said, then paused to look at Maeve. "And when they do, we will discover the truth of our missing guardsman. I would very much not like to be the person who stood between his—or *her*—king in the matter. Not at all."

"Are you sure that's wise, Majesty?"

Matt shifted his frown from Maeve to Cutter, as Cutter had intended. "Once more, it seems, that you question your king."

"What I question, Majesty," Cutter said, "is if the guardsman is to be protected, whether it is wise to send guards in search of him. After all, it was castle guards who tried to kill me. I believe it would be safe to assume that not all those who claim to be your men, your friends—" at this it was his turn to pause, sweeping his gaze around the room—"actually have your or the kingdom's best interest at heart."

Matt sat back, nodding slowly, a small smile on his face that made Cutter feel as if he had unwittingly stumbled into a trap. "You speak of loyalty."

"I do."

"You, the Crimson Prince, the man who had an affair with his brother's wife, my *mother*. Isn't that right, Uncle?" he asked, turning to stare at the door where Feledias and Chall still stood flanked by guardsmen. "Or did I get that wrong?"

"No, Your Majesty," Feledias said, his jaw tight, "you did not get it wrong."

Matt nodded. "I didn't think so." He turned back to regard Cutter once more. "You speak of loyalty, Father, and you speak of Fey conspiracies to overthrow the kingdom, but it seems to me that you did a fine enough job of that on your own, fifteen years or so ago, the date of my...*conception*."

Matt watched him then, his head cocked, examining him as if he were a child poking at an animal with a stick and waiting to see if, and more importantly, how *much* he had hurt the creature. And the answer to that was simple enough—plenty. Still, Cutter had lived with the shame of what he'd done for fifteen years, and he could not allow it to cloud his judgement, not now. "You are right, of course, Majesty," he said, aware that his words came out in a strangled croak. "I have done a lot in my life that I'm not proud of..." In truth, he had done little else. "Things I would take back, if I could," he went on, turning and glancing at Feledias who met his gaze, his expression unreadable. "Yet, my past crimes, terrible as they are, change nothing. We are at war, Highness—" He turned a disapproving frown on the people at the table, some of which were even now picking at their food. "We are at war regardless of whether we act it or not. And if we don't start fighting it soon, we will lose. Already we are well on our way."

"War," Matt said. "And tell me, Father, at whose feet might that be laid? After all, it was *you*, wasn't it, you and none other who slayed the Fey King, Yeladrian?"

Cutter winced. "Yes."

"You, also," Matt continued, "who, due to your indiscretions with your brother's wife, set the two rulers of this kingdom against each other, its *people* against each other and, in so doing, served to greatly weaken the kingdom when it was in dire need of strength."

Cutter said nothing to that, made no argument, for there was no argument to be made as Matt spoke nothing but the truth.

Feledias, though, spoke up. "It isn't fair to put it all on Bernard," he said, seemingly surprising everyone in the room, not least of all Cutter himself. Everyone, Matt included, turned their gazes upon him, and Feledias shrugged. "True, my brother has done many bad things..." He paused, looking at Cutter. "Some things that I, for a long time, thought unforgiveable. But the slaying of the Fey King...he did that not because he wanted to take life but because he wanted to save it. And since my life is the one in question...I cannot fault him for it."

"I see," Matt said, "well, perhaps you cannot, Uncle, but *I* can. Yes, Father," he went on, frowning at Cutter, "we *are* at war. Despite your obvious dislike for everyone present, including myself, we are well aware of that fact. Just as we are aware that it is a war *you* caused. And what, I wonder, should be the punishment for the man who is solely responsible for bringing our kingdom to the brink of destruction, for driving us into another war without even giving the us time enough to lick our wounds from the Skaalden invasion that drove us from our homeland?"

Cutter blinked, surprised to hear the youth reference that considering he hadn't been alive at the time. Matt must have seen some of his surprise on his face, for he gave a sharp nod. "Oh yes, Father, I have taken some small bit of time since accepting the crown to try to educate myself on our kingdom and its history. I was surprised to find just how much you neglected to mention...or *chose* to keep from me. Another fault, perhaps, that might be laid at your feet but certainly not the greatest." He turned to look at the people at the table, his gaze traveling back and forth. "What would you advise then, advisors? What would be the appropriate way to deal with such a man, one who brought war to our very door?"

Cutter saw Maeve staring in disbelief as if she had taken Matt for a young man and had discovered instead that he was some ravening beast. Perhaps she was right to do so, perhaps not.

Cutter found it difficult to think on it. The youth's words had brought up a well of emotions in him, a well that was always waiting, ready to erupt, and chief among those emotions was shame. He found it difficult to think of anything, just then, except for the many ways in which he had failed. Failed himself, failed Chall and Maeve and Priest, even Matt, and, of course, failed the kingdom.

"Execution!" someone shouted.

"Lashes!" someone else screamed.

Matt frowned, shaking his head. "Execution. If that is a joke, it is not a very funny one, Pondus. After all, what sort of man, what sort of *king* would take the throne and, within weeks, murder his own father? No," he said, shaking his head, "that is impossible. As for lashes...no doubt they would be painful, but the pain would be over quickly enough and the problems the kingdom faces would remain. That, I fear, may not be strict enough of a punishment to seem fair to those in the city, those *many* of its people who seek some redress for my father's crimes. I doubt very much if such an action would appease them but would likely only incense them against the crown further in a time when what we need, more than anything, is some stability, some...trust."

"There is another way, Highness."

Matt's gaze, and that of the rest in the room, traveled to a man seated two spots to Maeve's left.

"Is that so, General Falder?" the king asked.

"General Falder?" Feledias asked. "Who is that?"

Matt raised an eyebrow. "Forgiving, for a moment, Uncle, your interruption and distinct lack of my title, General Falder is, of course, the new commander of the capital's troops—recently instated as the position became vacant."

"Vacant?" Feledias asked. "What of General Malex?"

Matt sighed, shaking his head in obviously feigned regret. "Yes, well, following the events in the city and castle, particularly the fact that your very own regent, Uncle, was one of the Fey in disguise, I thought it prudent to have my men pursue inquiries into all those who held positions of power in the city. Malex, I'm afraid, was found to be a traitor."

"Traitor?" Feledias demanded. "But that's impossible!"

Despite the fact that Malex had been among those aiding in Feledias's pursuit of Cutter and his companions, Cutter found himself agreeing. "He's right, Majesty," he said, drawing Matt's frown. "Malex has always been a good man—loyal."

"You of all people would say that to me?" Matt asked. "After he and his men tried to kill us less than a few months ago in that little village...what was its name—"

"Ferrimore, Highness," Cutter interrupted, surprised that Matt might have so easily forgotten it and the people whose lives were lost there. "And Malex is not loyal to me, nor should he be. He is loyal, though, to the crown, to the kingdom. He served under our father years ago...he would never betray his memory."

"And yet...he did," Matt said simply. "For my men discovered documents in Malex's possession, documents which revealed all too clearly that the general was colluding with the Fey in an attempt to bring down the kingdom. Why, it is my understanding that he was instrumental in the creatures' undermining of the kingdom here in New Daltenia over the last years."

Feledias grunted. "How could he be? Malex was with me searching for my brother for the last year or more. He wasn't even *here*."

"Nor did he need to be," Matt said. "After all, Uncle, there is nothing about traitors that make them incapable of putting their traitorous orders in letters and sending them to their agents in the city, is there?"

Feledias stared, dumbfounded, his mouth opening and closing, clearly shocked that Matt was claiming Malex was a traitor.

"What will happen to him?" Cutter asked.

"Malex?" Matt said, then gave a shrug. "Execution, likely, though first the questioners will have their time, will seek to discover just exactly what the general was up to so that they might undo his work."

"Execution," Cutter repeated.

"Well...yes," Matt said. "It is, after all, what is done to those who have committed treason against the crown, is it not, Father?" He gave a small, humorless smile then. "At least...most of the time it is." He gave his hand a wave then as if the fate of a man who had spent his entire life pledged in service to the kingdom made no difference.

"You would kill him on the strength of some documents found in a desk drawer?" Feledias demanded. "Documents which could have been placed there by anyone in the world?"

Matt's eyebrows drew down in a frown. "I would watch your tone, Uncle. You are family, it is true, but family or not, you will accord the crown, will accord *me* the respect I deserve. As my father has so recently said, we are at war, and in war there are casualties. It is unlikely, nearly impossible that Malex is innocent for the evidence found against him was quite damning, but even should he be, I cannot concern myself with it any longer. We are at *war* and one man's life, no matter whose, cannot be weighed against the lives of every man and woman of the Known Lands, men and women who look to *me* to protect them."

"Men and women like the serving woman with the black eye and bruised face?" Cutter asked.

For the first time, since Cutter had entered the audience chamber, Matt seemed caught off-guard, as if up until now, everything that had been said had been part of a play he'd read many times over but here one of the actors had foregone the script to improvise instead. He recoiled in his seat as if struck, and for a brief instant, his face was twisted with a wretched, terrible grief that was difficult to look upon.

A moment later, though, and the instant passed. The look of surprise, of shame, vanished from the youth's face as if it had never been to be replaced by one of clearly feigned confusion. "I'm sure I don't know what you mean, Father," he said. "If there has been some sort of abuse in the castle, please bring it to my attention, and I will see to it."

"Maybe later," Cutter said, watching him.

"Now then," Matt said, clearly struggling to overcome his shock as he turned back to the general, "General Falder...you were saying?"

The general in question—whose nervous, almost shy demeanor was a very unusual look on a man who was meant to oversee the troops of the entire kingdom—cleared his throat, bobbing his head in an anxious nod. "Yes, of course, Majesty. I was saying that there might be a third solution to the problem of your father's...punishment."

"Oh?" Matt asked, and something about the way he asked the question, something about the surprised look on his face, made it all seem practiced to Cutter, as if he had rehearsed this conversation, rehearsed his expression, a dozen times before now. "And what might that be?"

The man shrugged. "Well, Majesty, it seems to me that the best solution now might also be what was deemed—by your father, I mean—to be the best solution fifteen years ago after his...indiscretions. I speak, of course, of exile."

"Exile," Matt said thoughtfully, as if tasting the word. "Hmm...and where might you exile him to, General Falder? Surely not Brighton, for that place exists no longer. My father and uncle saw to that most...thoroughly."

"There is only one place I can think of, Majesty," the man said. "The Black Wood."

There were hushed whispers from those at the tables at that and those, too, sounded rehearsed to Cutter, just as the nods and murmurs of agreement put him in mind of actors—and not terribly good ones—playing at their roles.

"My advisors like this...idea?" Matt asked.

Another, the one who'd advocated for Cutter's execution moments ago, rose, giving a sloppy bow. "The general has a marvelous idea, Majesty. After all, as you rightfully said, it is your father's doing that we are at war with the Fey in the first place. Perhaps...perhaps his going might even be used as a sort of...olive branch. A means by which we might finally find peace with the Fey creatures."

Feledias snorted. "Peace. Sure, and why not have all the healers in the kingdom start using battle axes instead of their needles, eh?"

Matt raised an eyebrow. "You have a point, I'm assuming, Uncle?"

Feledias looked around at the faces in the room, an expression of clear disdain on his own. "My point, *Majesty*, is that if it's peace you're after, you don't send the realm's most famous warrior, not anymore than you'd hire a blind man to build a house."

"I see..." Matt said. "But then, according to my father, according to all of you, he has changed, has he not?"

Feledias frowned, clearly caught off-guard by the question. "Well, yes, but what does that have to do with anything?"

"Why, it has everything to do with it, Uncle," Matt said. "After all, if my father really *has* changed, then he is no longer the bloodthirsty brute that slayed the honorable Fey King Yeladrian without provocation. Nor, then, is he the man who slept with your wife, *my* mother. He is a new man, and while that warrior of years gone by might have sought only blood, perhaps the man he has become could be used for something else. Perhaps he could be used for peace."

"If you're going to send him then at least have the balls to call it what it is!" Maeve snapped. "Not exile at all but execution! They'll kill him the moment he sets foot in the Black Wood and you know it!"

"Guards," Matt said, clearly annoyed. "Remove Lady Maeve from my audience chamber." Several started forward, and Matt held up a hand. "But do not harm her," he went on, turning and glancing at Cutter. "Despite my father's insinuations, I would not like to see an old woman harmed."

Maeve hissed, rising from her chair. "Forget it—I'll remove myself. I think I've long since grown bored watching a child play-act at being king and fools pretend at wisdom."

The guards nearest her growled in anger at that, several starting toward her as she walked toward the door, but Matt raised a hand and they hesitated. "Let her go," he said, a small smile on his face. "Lady Maeve is a kind soul, she is distraught that is all, and how not? Given these current times, it is no surprise that one of her age might find herself...distressed."

There was laughter from those at the tables at that, and Cutter saw Maeve's back tense as she moved past him. She met his gaze for a moment then walked to the door and, in another moment, was gone.

"Now then," Matt said once the door was closed behind her, "where were we? Ah yes, my father's punishment. Exile..." he said again, tapping his chin in thought. "Well, there is a certain...symmetry to it, is there not? After all, who better to send on a mission to the Black Wood, a mission to stop a war, than the man who started it?" He watched Cutter with a cunning look in his eyes he did not like. "What better way to atone for risking the lives of the entire kingdom in starting a war than by risking your own life in the pursuit of peace? Of course," he went on, "the man my father used to be...why, such a man as that would balk at the idea of being *sent* anywhere, I imagine. Would likely meet such an idea with hostility, perhaps even outright violence." He paused, raising an eyebrow at Cutter. "Tell me, Father, what is your thought on all of this?"

He waited, and there was something in the way he asked it that made Cutter think he almost *wanted* him to grow violent, was *hoping* he would. "I am not that man any longer," Cutter said finally. "But if I go on this...peace mission...what will become of Chall and Feledias? They had no part in the murder of your captain—responsibility for that lies with me and me alone."

"One might argue that they did indeed have a part in it," Matt said thoughtfully. "After all, they were with you, and none of the guards testified that they tried to stop you from your bloody course. Still..." He paused, shrugging, "I suppose it might be said that they could not have stopped you, even had they wanted to. After all, Father, your determination when you choose the path of blood is famous, isn't it? Or...perhaps *infamous* would be more correct." He rubbed at his chin as if considering but here, too, Cutter got the impression that the decision had already been made, had likely been made before Cutter had even asked. "Very well," Matt said in a tone of voice a parent might use when indulging a willful child, "if you agree to accept your mission willingly, without any violent reprisals against anyone, myself included, then your companions will be pardoned."

Cutter blinked. "I would never hurt you, lad," he said. "Surely you know that."

The cunning look left Matt's face again and, for a moment, he was the same, naïve, innocent youth Cutter had known in Brighton as he met Cutter's gaze, his eyes brimming with tears. "I know," he rasped in a voice thick with emotion, "Father, I—" he began, but abruptly he cut off, staring down at the floor so that his hair covered his face, his hands gripping the edges of the throne so hard they shook.

Then he jerked his head up, a furious snarl on his face. "A good attempt," he spat. "But not enough."

"Attempt?" Cutter asked uncertainly. He glanced back at Chall who gave a small shake of his head to indicate that he had no idea what Matt meant either.

"Forget it," Matt said, taking a deep breath and clearly gathering himself. "It...it's nothing." He gave his head a shake as if to clear it. "Now, then, Father, if there is nothing else, the sooner you begin your journey the better. The Black Woods are far away, after all, and if things are really as bad as you think then the sooner you can speak to the Fey about reaching some sort of accord the better."

"There is one more thing," Cutter said.

"Oh?" Matt asked with obvious impatience. "And what's that?"

"Before I go, Majesty," he said, "I would speak with you alone."

There was some snickering from several of those gathered at the table at that. "Surely you can't be serious," one said, a man who appeared to be in his twenties with slicked back hair and ruffled sleeves. "Do you mean to say that the same man who has counseled caution, who *claims* to have discovered a conspiracy within the castle—"

"Claims?" Chall said. "The bodies of the assassins sent to kill him are still warm!"

The man sneered at the mage before turning back to Cutter. "Assassins you may well have hired for all we know. Perhaps this was your plan all along, is that it, *Prince* Bernard? To cause confusion in the castle so that you might get the king alone and kill him yourself?"

Cutter had endured much in his life, had endured plenty of mocking and scolding in the last half hour as he stood in this room, but the insinuation that he would ever intentionally hurt Matt hit him in a way that none of the other things could. He'd taken a step forward before he knew it, his hands balling into fists at his side.

"*Halt!*" one of the guards shouted, but Cutter barely heard it, just as he barely noted the sounds of footsteps as several hurried forward.

"Don't be ridiculous," Matt said hurriedly, and his voice, at least, cut past the storm of Cutter's sudden anger, "my father, whatever his faults, would never harm me, of that much I am sure. Very well, Father, I will see you in my chambers."

Cutter did pause then, his great chest heaving with his rapid breaths as he fought his anger back down. It did not go willingly but finally, it did go.

Matt rose from his throne. "Come, Father," he said, "we will speak."

And with that, he turned and moved toward a door at the back of the audience chamber. Cutter watched him, then turned back to the "advisor" who had claimed that he meant to hurt Matt. "What is your name?"

The man gave a scoffing laugh, looking around as if for help, but those others gathered at the tables pointedly avoided his gaze and, after a moment, he glanced back at Cutter. "It…" He paused, lifting his chin, a sneer on his face. "My name is Ladrian Eliart."

Cutter gave a single nod, meeting the man's eyes. "I will remember it." The man's face paled, but Cutter paid it little attention as several of the guards walked up.

"This way," one said, and then he was being escorted toward the door at the back of the audience chamber, then through it. The guards led him down the castle corridor until they came to a door with two of the king's own guards, including the man, Rolph, stationed at it. The young man from Two Rivers sneered at Cutter but said nothing as the second guard opened the door.

"Allow my father in—alone," came a voice from inside.

"Majesty," one of the guards said, "surely you can't—"

"Do as I say!" the youth screeched, and the guard paled, swallowing.

"Try anything," Rolph said to Cutter, "and I'll finish what we started in Two Rivers. Understand?"

Cutter said nothing, for he had heard far stronger threats from far more threatening people. Instead, he only stepped through the doorway.

The room was usually used for meetings of the king's inner council. There was a large table at the center, a dozen chairs scattered around it, but Matt was not sitting. Instead, the king stood in front of a window at the back of the room, staring out of it, his hands clasped behind his back.

"Shut the door," Matt said without turning, and the guard, Rolph, shot Cutter one more angry sneer before doing as ordered.

Once the door was closed, the king let out a heavy sigh as he stared out of the window. "New Daltenia," Matt said, almost as if he were talking to himself, "the capital of the Known Lands, the pride of its people and heart of their strength. It is something isn't it, Father?"

"Yes."

Matt turned to look at him, a look of disgust on his face. "Well enough designed on the outside, with streets kept clean, people smiling and laughing. But underneath that thin veneer, the city and its people are filthy with guilt, covered in it. They cheat and lie, murder and steal as all mortals do."

Cutter frowned at that. "All mortals." he asked. "Including kings?"

Matt gritted his teeth then opened his mouth as if to reply. Instead, he paused, taking a slow breath before he spoke. "You wished to speak with me?"

He had, he still did, but now that he was here, alone with an opportunity to speak with the boy without an audience, Cutter found it difficult to find the words he meant to say. On a battlefield, his enemies standing before him, he had always been at ease, but speaking from the heart had never been his strong suit. Likely many would have said that was because he didn't have one. Still, battles were simple. People, though...there was nothing more complex.

"I did," he said. "Majesty...son, I wanted to ask...is everything okay?"

"With the kingdom?" Matt asked. He shrugged. "Well, that depends on who you ask, doesn't it? Certainly you don't seem to think so, but then—"

"I don't mean with the kingdom," Matt said. "I mean with you. Is everything okay with you?"

Matt's eyes widened in surprise at that, then his features twisted, contorting as if he were straining against something. After a moment, he mastered himself and gave Cutter a small smile, one that never touched his eyes. "I'm fine, Father. Thank you for asking. Now, is that all?"

"Not quite," Cutter said. "I wanted to tell you…Matt, I know I'm not a good man, know, too, that I haven't been a good father. I will go to the Black Wood as you asked, but…well, in case I don't make it back, I wanted you to know that…I love you. I always have, ever since your mother first put you in my arms. I know it was wrong, what I did, to Feledias, to…to your mother. But know this—you are the thing in my life of which I am the proudest. You are the best thing I have ever done. Perhaps the only truly *good* thing."

Matt blinked at that, and Cutter thought he saw tears gathering in the youth's eyes. "Father…about what I said in there…I mean, about you being guilty of…"

Cutter shook his head. "It's okay, Matt. You were right. I *am* guilty. Anyway, I didn't come to talk to you about me or my sins. I just wanted to check on you, to make sure that everything's okay."

"What…what do you mean?" Matt asked, sounding defensive and scared all at once.

Cutter shrugged. "You've been acting strange lately, lad. Not yourself. Threatening guardsmen, hitting the servants…I know it's a lot of pressure, being the ruler of an entire kingdom. And I know…well, I know it wasn't fair for us to put you in this situation. I'm sorry, lad. Truly, I am."

A look of such anguish came over the youth's face then, and Cutter moved forward, putting a hand on his shoulder. Slowly, Matt raised his eyes to meet his. "It isn't…it isn't your fault," he said. "And it isn't the pressure either. It…it's my fault," he managed. "Back…" He paused then, wincing as if straining or in pain, "Father, back in, in Two Rivers, I…" He let out a gasp of pain then, bringing both his hands to his temples as he whimpered. The strength let out of his legs, and he would have fallen had Cutter not caught him.

"It's okay, lad," he said as the youth sobbed in his arms. "Everything's okay. And what's not…well, we'll figure it out, alright? I'm here for you."

The youth tensed then, and his whole body seemed to tremble with some great emotion. Suddenly, he jerked away from Cutter's embrace, wiping angrily at the tears streaming down his cheeks. A change seemed to come over him then, and when he took his hands away that sly, cunning look was in his gaze again. "Here for me, are you?" he asked. "The same way you were there for your brother? The same way you were there for your kingdom? Or what of your father? The one you let be murdered by those creatures, the Skaalden." He gave a sneer. "Prince Bernard, the world's greatest warrior, its most notorious *murderer*, fleeing on a ship while his father the king dies, too scared even to avenge him."

Bernard stared in shock at the transformation in the youth. And it *was* a transformation, for it almost seemed that he was speaking to a completely different person than he had moments ago. "Matt," he said softly, reaching out, "I—"

"*Enough*," the youth growled. "We have talked, Father, as you asked. Now I think it is well past time you began making preparations. That is if you still intend to leave for the Black Wood in the morning."

Cutter stared at him for a moment, thinking, wondering at what he had said to set the youth off, but the truth was there was no telling. Matt was right—he was a murderer. Not a man for soft speeches, not a man to offer comfort to those who needed it. He was a blade unsheathed, one liable to cut any who touched it.

I am fire, he thought, *and all I touch turns to ash.*

Finally, he nodded. "I will go but...only one thing more, Matt. I know that I'm not a great man...I know that I'm not even a good one. But I promise you—if you ever need me, I'll be there. All you have to do is ask. Okay?"

Matt met his eyes again and for the briefest of moments, he seemed to be *him* again. But then it was gone, and he nodded, waving a hand dismissively. "Sure, sure. Are you finished?"

He was going to the Black Wood then. A place inimical to mortals, a place full of the Fey who hated all mortals but hated him most of all. "Yes," he said. "I'm finished. Good night...son."

And with that, he turned and walked out of the door to the guards who waited there, prepared to escort him to his rooms.

CHAPTER THIRTEEN

The most important words in the world
Are often those that go unsaid.
    —*Scholar Kelden Marrimore*

Matt watched his father walk out into the hallway, watched the door shut behind him, trembling with need. The need to tell him that he hadn't meant it, not any of it, that it wasn't *him* who had insisted on him journeying to the Black Wood just as it wasn't him who had struck the serving woman. It had been his body, yes, but it hadn't been *him.* He was a puppet—that and that only.

A puppet who now knelt within a cage inside his own mind, grasping the bars in two tight, sweating hands, the metal rough beneath his grip. He knew that, in truth, that metal was not rough, was not metal at all. He knew that, in truth, it, like the cell in which he was imprisoned, was not a thing of the real world but of his mind. And yet...this knowledge served no purpose except to tease him, to mock him with his helplessness. For real or not, the bars would not bend, and the cell remained around him, unmoving.

For a moment, though, when he'd been speaking with his father, the bars had slipped, had bent and shifted out of his way, and he had darted through them, meaning to tell his father everything, to tell him the truth. He had been just about to do as much when *she* had shown up. Emma. His puppet master. He had tried to fight her, to get the words out despite her, but it had been no use. She was the puppet master, he the puppet. She needed only to give a yank on his strings, and he was silenced. Moments after that, the cage had returned, forming around him as if by magic. And if it was magic, then it was a very dark magic indeed.

You will suffer for that, Matthias.

He stared after the door for a moment, the door through which his father had left moments ago, then turned away. There was no point in looking any longer, after all. He'd had a chance, and he had failed. His father was gone now. Gone to the Black Wood. Gone forever.

There were tears in his eyes, blurring his vision, as he turned and saw her standing a short distance away, regarding him. "W-why?" he asked. "Why did you make me do it?"

You know why, she said.

And he did. Cutter, his father, was a problem for the Fey. And while they hated all mortals, while *Emma* hated all mortals, she hated him the most. Matt knew that, not because she had told him but because he simply...knew. Whatever link Emma had created within them that allowed her to control him, to know his deepest thoughts, his most hidden secrets, that link seemed, to a degree at least, to work both ways.

Often, since she had taken up residence within his mind, Matt got flashes of her feelings, of her thoughts. Thoughts and feelings he felt sure she meant to hide, ones she did not know he could possibly be privy to. Over the last several days, he had thought that, perhaps, there might be some answer there, some means of fighting her, but now he knew that even the idea had been ridiculous.

She was in control—it was as simple as that. What difference whether the puppet knew the puppet master's mind? As long as the master held the strings, the puppet could do nothing but dance.

"You're...you're evil," he said.

Evil, she said, as if tasting the word. *Good. I told you, Matthias, these are only words. Words you mortals use to condemn those whose ideals do not agree with your own or to reassure yourselves that you are in the right. But they mean nothing. When your people have been laid waste, when your great cities and towns are naught but scattered rubble, your people rotting in the ground, their names forgotten, then who will be left to decide whether what transpired was good or evil? The victors, that is all, and victors, Matthias, are always right. Are always good.*

"That's...that's not true," Matt said.

"Ah, so you speak then of *absolute* good? Of *absolute* evil?"

"I...I don't know. Yes. Yes, I do."

"A morality which exists beyond the bounds of human understanding or, for that matter, Fey understanding? One that was here before us, which will remain long after we are all turned to so much dust?"

"Yes."

She gave one of her soft, musical laughs at that. "Fiction, Matthias. As much fiction as the bogeymen so many of your young believe lurk in their closets, underneath their beds. Fiction, and one which is dispelled by the cold light of reason."

"You're wrong," Matt said, meeting her eyes. "The bogeyman exists—I've seen him. Only, it's not a him at all. It's a her."

She gave him a small, humorless smile at that. "Very well, you have had your say. You hate me, Matthias. I can feel that hate coming off you in waves. But in the end, it will make no difference. Perhaps the spider hates the boot that crushes it, but its hate, no matter how strong, will do nothing to stop the boot's descending. You are like that spider, Matthias, you and your kind. Or, perhaps, you are more like roaches. But hate or not, in the end, you will all be squished. It is, after all, the roach's destiny. At least—" she paused, giving a small laugh—"in so much as the roach might be said to *have* a destiny."

"And...Cutter? My father? What will you do to him?"

She smiled. "Isn't it obvious? Why, we will squish him, of course. But I would not worry overly much about your father, if I were you. After all, you have problems enough of your own. I do not know how you managed to break loose of my control there, for a moment, but it does not matter. I told you that you would suffer for it, and so you will. You will, you *must* be punished. And that punishment...begins now."

Pain, terrible, shocking pain rushed through Matt's body at that, and he collapsed to his knees, screaming. Or, at least, he meant to scream. But on the outside, in the real world, he only gritted his teeth, unable, through her control of him, even to attain the small victory of voicing his agony onto the world, for the cage was tighter now, its bars stronger now than they had ever been. And so Matt struggled uselessly, hissing and writhing in pain on the ground while the guards, still waiting outside the close door, knew none of their king's despair.

The Matt of the real world struggled, twisted and shifted as pain coursed through his body, an unending tidal wave of it.

Meanwhile, the Matt who was a prisoner in his own mind screamed. He screamed, but the only one who heard him was Emma, and her only response, as the pain grew worse and worse, was a small, satisfied smile.

CHAPTER FOURTEEN

*Men don't always get what they deserve...
In fact, it seems to me that they rarely do.
But that doesn't mean they shouldn't.*
—Unknown author

Cutter's walk back to his quarters felt as if it took forever. His wounds were part of it, wounds that had not been given a chance to heal. Another part was his worry over Guardsman Nigel. He understood that Maeve had not wanted to tell Matt, likely suspecting that to do so would be to put the guardsman's life in unnecessary jeopardy. After all, it was all too possible that one of those "advisors" in the audience chamber was part of the conspiracy.

And even had they been alone, with only Matt in the room, still Cutter thought it would have been best for Maeve to keep her knowledge of the guardsman's whereabouts to herself. A week ago, he wouldn't have thought twice about sharing such news with the boy, trusting him completely. Now, though…now he wasn't so sure. He knew that Matt, the *real* Matt, would never harm anyone, but something was happening to the boy, something that made him erratic, mercurial, so that his moods, his thoughts, couldn't seem to be predicted from one moment to the next. One second he would be the youth Cutter had known since he was a baby and, the next, he would be someone…else.

Yes, partly what troubled him was the guardsman, partly it was his wounds but mostly it was Matt. He had thought, for a moment, that he had reached the boy, that his words had reached him and, for that brief moment, he had hoped. But then the *change* had come again.

Finally, he and his escort of half a dozen guards reached his quarters.

"Get a good night's sleep, *Prince*," the sergeant sneered. "From all I hear of the Black Wood, you're going to need it." The sergeant motioned to one of his guards and the man stepped forward, straining with obvious effort as he held out a familiar form to Cutter.

Cutter stared at the axe, the black obsidian of its blade seeming to shine with deadly promise in the ruddy glow of the lanterns hung in the hallway. He hesitated for a moment, but only that. He did not want it, not in truth, but if he were going to the Black Wood, what he wanted had little to do with it. Need, that was what he had to focus on now. Slowly, he reached out and took it, and the guard who'd held it sighed with obvious relief as he was freed of its weight.

"A fine weapon," the sergeant said. "One that looks as if it could slaughter dozens and, from all the stories, it has. But then..." He paused, grinning. "I suppose it would need to slaughter hundreds, thousands—if you're to have any chance of surviving the Black Wood, that is. I wonder, Prince, can it kill so many?" He grinned wider. "Can you?"

Cutter looked at the man, saying nothing, then took the key to his room from his trouser pocket with his free hand and unlocked the door. He started to step inside when the sergeant spoke again.

"I would not leave my rooms tonight, if I were you, Prince," the sergeant said. "Not for anything...not for your life. Why, if you did," he went on, smiling, "then me—or one of my men—might take it that you meant to flee, going against the king's order. And that would not be good, Prince. Not good at all. Do you understand?"

Cutter met the man's eyes, still saying nothing, then turned and stepped through the door. He closed it, locking it behind him. Not that he expected it would do much good. The assassins he'd so far seen in the castle had not seem all that perturbed by anything so simple as a locked door. Still, a man could only do what he could and hope that it was enough.

Now, back in his room, alone and way from prying eyes, Cutter allowed his shoulders to hunch in exhaustion. He glanced at the bed for a moment then forced his gaze away—it did not go easily. He was tired, more tired than he remembered ever being, but he knew that while the bed looked inviting enough, should he lie in it, should he give in to the sleep that his throbbing headache seemed to demand, then that bed, with its soft coverlet and softer pillows, might well turn out not to be a bed at all but a coffin. After all, assassins had broken into the castle not once but twice—that they knew of—and somehow he didn't think that the guards stationed outside would be all too bothered about defending him. In fact, it was more than a little possible that they themselves would *be* the assassins.

Instead of moving toward the bed, he walked to the room's small table, sighing as he sat in one of the chairs. Then he propped his axe against the table. Hopefully, he would not need it, but one of the bits of wisdom his father had taught him long ago—and that had held up time and again over the course of Cutter's life—was that a wise man hoped for the best and prepared for the worst.

So he sat, and he thought, and he prepared.

Now that he was alone with an opportunity to think, Cutter found himself remembering Belle's odd words in the courtyard, before the captain had taken her execution into his own hands. He scolded himself for not considering them before now, but with all that had happened since, he had allowed himself to fall into a state of reaction instead of *action.*

He knew that to do such a thing was dangerous, for if there was anything the many battles he'd been in had taught him, it was that a man—or a kingdom—who spent his time only reacting to his enemy with no thought to his own actions was a man, a kingdom, doomed to fall.

He had not spent so much as a moment since waking in the dungeons to consider Belle's words, but he considered them now, considered them very carefully. He was still thinking on them when he heard a shout from somewhere outside in the hallway then listened to the sound of the guards' footsteps as they faded away in the distance.

A few moments later, there was the sound of a soft knock at the door. Cutter rose, leaving the axe where it was, and moved toward the door to unlock it. He swung it open with a nod. "Chall. Maeve." He raised an eyebrow in surprise as he noted the third figure. "Priest. Please, come in."

"How did you know it was us?" Chall said, surprised. "And not an assassin?"

Cutter gave the man a small smile. "Assassins don't often knock."

"Ah," the mage said, wincing. "Right."

Cutter stepped out of the way, and the three walked inside. Then he closed the door.

"We'd best hurry," Chall said. "The illusion I placed will last for a little while, but we don't have time for tea, if you understand my meaning."

"I think I do," Cutter said. Then he glanced at Priest. "Won't the king miss your presence?"

Priest shook his head. "Forgive me, Prince, but I doubt Matthias will even notice. He has his own guards now and has made it clear that he cares nothing for my services."

Cutter winced at that. "Right. So, what brings you all here?"

Chall snorted, but it was Maeve who spoke. "I think you know well enough. So what's the plan?"

"The plan?" Cutter asked.

She rolled her eyes. "You heard Chall, Cutter—we don't have time for you to play the fool. Now, what's the plan?"

"The plan is that, tomorrow morning, I travel to the Black Wood."

Chall snorted again. "While I enjoy a good joke as much as anyone, Prince, I find that, with such things, timing is everything."

Cutter only stared at him, and the mage's eyes went wide as he glanced to Maeve. "I mean...it is a *joke,* isn't it?"

"No," Maeve said, watching Cutter. "No, Chall, he isn't joking."

"No, I'm not."

"Wait," Chall said, "then...that is, you mean to actually *go* to the Black Wood?"

"I do."

"Of course you're not going!" Maeve snapped. "I don't know if you're only pretending to be a fool or actually *are* one, but you can't go. They'll kill you!"

"Probably."

"Prince," Priest said, "she's right. Matt—that is, the king—he isn't in his right mind. I have been watching him over the last several days, as you asked, and...I think, perhaps, he's sick. He gets headaches, sometimes—bad ones—and he's been acting very oddly. Normally, he would never ask you to go."

"Yet he did," Cutter said. "I have been given an order by my king, and I intend to follow it."

"A king who is little more than a boy!" Maeve snapped.

"Yet king nonetheless," Cutter countered.

"B-but it's a stupid order!" Maeve said. "The Fey don't *want* peace—everyone in that damned room knew that! If you go, they'll kill you—likely before you get a dozen words out."

"Maybe," Cutter agreed.

"No," she said, shaking her head angrily. "Of course you won't go. You can come with us. The guards are fools, after all, not to mention all new. We know this castle better than any of them. We can take one of the back ways and—"

"No, Maeve."

"*No?*" she asked.

"I won't run."

"Even if it means you'll die?" she demanded.

"Especially then," he said. She opened her mouth to speak, but he held up a hand. "I don't intend to give my life up cheaply, Maeve, or at all, if I can help it. All I mean is, if a man doesn't believe in anything enough to give his life for it, then he's no man at all."

"And the man who gets killed for no reason isn't a man either," she snapped. "He's just a corpse and corpses can help no one, Prince. Except the worms, maybe, and I doubt they're hurting for food."

"So what would you council me to do then, Maeve?" he asked. "Leave? Flee the castle?"

"Yes!" she said. "If it means that or dying then of course!"

"And what do you think the people of the city, of the kingdom, would think," he said slowly, "when they learn that their prince disobeyed a direct order from their king?"

She frowned. "What does that have to do with anything?"

"Everything, Maeve," he said softly. "The Known Lands are in a bad place now, and mostly they are there because of me. They have learned not to trust their leaders, and why not? We have spent at least the last fifteen years training them to do just that. Now, they have hope—hope that things will be different. Hope that *Matt* will be different. What do you think will happen to that fragile hope, then, if they learn that I disregarded the direct order of their king?"

"But...I mean, well it isn't as if you haven't done it before," Chall said slowly.

"Yes," Cutter agreed, "and how did that work out, Chall?"

The mage winced at that, and Cutter turned back to Maeve. "I have to do this, Maeve."

"Because of the kingdom," she said, frowning.

"Not just that," he said. "It...I have failed Matt, failed the kingdom, too many times already. I have failed all of you, too. If he wants me to go to the Black Wood...then I mean to go."

"And what are we supposed to do then?" Maeve demanded. "Just sit around and wait until Matt comes up with some elaborate way of killing us as well? I don't know if you noticed or not, Prince, but we don't seem to be the most popular people right now."

"I've been thinking on that," Cutter said. "Belle, before she died...I think she told me something."

Chall snorted. "You think? Gods, the woman kept going on and on about dragons and hoards and, fire and salt, who knows what else."

"Dragons and hoards?" Priest asked.

The mage shrugged. "Who knows. She wasn't making any sense—out of her mind with fear, probably, and who can blame her?"

"You're right, Chall," Cutter said, "she wasn't making much sense. But then...I don't think she intended to. At least not on the surface."

Chall frowned, clearly confused, but it was Maeve who spoke. "What does that mean?"

"All that talk of dragons and treasures, of dens, I think she was trying to tell us something," Cutter said.

"Something like what?" Maeve asked. "What treasures?"

Cutter considered that, thinking back over the conversation, trying to remember exactly what the woman had said.

"The truth," Chall said. "She said the greatest treasure was truth."

"That's right," Cutter said, "well done, Chall."

The mage smiled at that, clearly pleased.

Maeve snorted. "The truth, huh? Funny that, coming from a crime boss and all."

"I thought so too," Cutter agreed. "But she stressed it, made it sound really important, whatever truth she meant."

"What truth then?" Priest asked.

Chall shook his head, clearly frustrated. "She didn't say."

"And do we know where to find this truth?" Maeve asked.

The mage winced. "She uh...she didn't say that either."

"Of course she didn't," Maeve said. "Because she was just talking! Stones and starlight the woman couldn't be trusted at the best of times and just then she was getting ready to be executed. It's no surprise she was talking nonsense!"

"I don't think it was nonsense," Cutter said, remembering. Then he grunted as an idea struck him. "And I think I know where to find the truth she was talking about."

"Oh?" Maeve asked doubtfully. "And where is that?"

"Well," he said, glancing at Priest, "the same place where all dragons keep their treasures of course—their dens."

"You mean..." Priest began.

Cutter nodded. "That's right. The tavern you took me to—she was telling us to go there."

"But why?" Chall asked. "If she knew something, why wouldn't she just tell us?"

"Because she didn't want the guards to know," Cutter said slowly, thinking it over.

They all were silent for a moment at that, and he nodded. "Listen," he said, his gaze traveling between the three of them, "I know I don't deserve to ask it of you, but...when I'm gone—"

"I'll look into it," Priest said immediately.

"*We'll* look into it," Maeve corrected. "If, that is, I still can't convince you not to go. It's a long way to travel just to die when you could do that easily enough here in New Daltenia."

Cutter gave her a small smile. "Sure, but then I wouldn't get to see all the sights." A thought occurred to him then. "And, what of Feledias? Did...did any of you see him? Did he mention anything about coming by?"

Chall winced. "Well, I'm sure he wants to, Prince to...you know, see you off. But he said there was something he needed to see to. He uh...he sent his regards."

Cutter shouldn't be surprised by that. After all, he had wronged Feledias as bad as anyone could wrong anyone. It shouldn't shock him that his brother hadn't come to see him before he left. But the fact that it wasn't a surprise did nothing to keep it from hurting. "Right," he said, trying to give a smile.

"One more thing," he said.

"Name it," Chall said, then cleared his throat as Maeve and Priest turned to look at him in surprise.

"I was wondering...once I'm gone, if you all couldn't look after Matt for me."

Chall snorted. "Seems to me he's got plenty enough guards to do that already."

"Yes," Cutter agreed, "but I don't trust any of them—I trust you."

The mage colored at that, and Maeve grunted. "See, now you've gone and embarrassed him, Prince. A lot more comfortable being chased by half-naked women then being treated to any real human interaction, is our Challadius."

"Hey, that's not true," Chall said.

"Isn't it?" Maeve asked, raising an eyebrow.

"Well," he said, grinning, "usually they're all the way naked."

She rolled her eyes at that, and Cutter laughed. He wouldn't have thought, with everything going on, that he would have been capable of a laugh just then, but he would have been wrong. It felt good, that laugh, a brief moment of respite amid the worries and fears that had been plaguing him for days. It was a gift, though just how fine of one he doubted they could have known. "Thank you," he said, "all of you. For everything. The time we've spent together...it has been the best—"

"Not another word," Maeve said, holding up a hand, and he saw that there were tears gathering in her eyes. "Shaping up to sound way too much like a goodbye for my tastes. Anyway, whatever you've got to say, you can tell it to us when you make it back."

Cutter watched her for a moment, then finally nodded. "When I get back," he repeated.

She studied him for a few more seconds, her face contorting as she obviously struggled to control her emotions, then gave a tight nod, wiping a finger across her eyes. "Well then," she said, trying to make the words sound light as she turned away to look out of the room's small window, "what now?"

"Now," Cutter said, "you three should leave. The guards will be back soon enough, and in case they decide to check in on me, I think it would be best if they didn't find you here with me. The gods know I've already caused you enough problems—I'd rather not make it worse."

"No."

Cutter and the others turned to stare at Priest. He had known the man for a long time, sometimes, it felt like for *all* time, and he had never known the man to sound so abrupt. So...demanding.

But the man did not look away, only met his eyes and gave his head a firm shake. "No. You say, Prince, that you must go to the Black Wood, and if you believe it to be so, then I will not argue with you. But you need rest—anyone with eyes can see that you are about to fall over where you stand."

Cutter grunted. He thought he'd been doing a pretty fair job of covering his exhaustion, but then he had known Priest long enough to know that the man didn't miss much. Or anything, really. "I'm fine."

"No," Priest said again. "You're not. We cannot change your mind about going to the Black Wood, cannot go with you, as you have said, but the least we can do is watch over you to make sure you get a good night's sleep."

"Look, Priest," Cutter began, "that really isn't necessa—"

"Yes, it is," Maeve said. "Priest's right. Now, no more arguing. It's late and getting later. Go and lie down—we'll take shifts watching you."

"And if the guards come back?" Cutter asked quietly.

"Then we'll deal with it. Quietly," Maeve said, giving him a small smile, one that held within it a challenge. "Wouldn't want to wake you."

Cutter sighed, then nodded. "Thanks," he said again, then moved to the bed. He sat, pulling off his boots, and then lay back, thinking, as he did, that there was no hope of him getting any sleep, not with all that lay before him, not with the many worries and troubles plaguing his mi...

He was asleep before the thought was finished, sinking down into the peace of the waiting darkness.

CHAPTER FIFTEEN

The best comfort for any man is his friends.
And the more the better.
That way, there's plenty of people to throw in front of you once the dying starts.
—Challadius the Charmer

While Prince Bernard slept, Maeve, Priest, and Chall sat at the small table in his room.

"Well," Chall said, glancing at the prince's snoring form, "that didn't take long, did it?"

"Good," Maeve said, "he needs his rest."

"Don't we all," Chall muttered.

There really was no disagreeing with that, so she didn't try. Instead, she glanced at Priest, the man sitting quietly, staring at the table top as if some great secret lay hidden within the wooden grains. "What do you think? About the prince's thoughts on the woman, Belle? About her keeping some secret hidden?"

Priest considered for a moment then shrugged. "I knew Belle for a long time, and it sounds like something she would do. She was cruel, it's true, only after her own self-interests, but she was also clever—it was the second which made her the most dangerous. She told me once, long ago, that while swords and knives had their places, it was a person's secrets that were the most dangerous."

"What sort of secrets?" Chall asked.

The man shrugged again. "Different things for different people. Different...levers. It was what she called them. For some men it was a hidden affair, for others it was money skimmed from their employer, that sort of thing."

Chall grunted. "None of those seem important enough for the woman to be talking about moments before she was executed."

"No," Priest agreed, "no they do not."

"Do you intend to go?" Maeve asked.

"Of course. The Prince has asked it of me," Priest said, as if it were as simple as that. And Maeve knew that, for him at least, it was. Yet, she saw within his gaze, his reluctance to do that, his reluctance to once more venture into the world of his past, and Maeve thought she understood. After all, she'd done plenty of things in her own life that she wasn't proud of, that she'd just as soon forget.

"I don't like it," Chall said. "Priest going—alone—to deal with men and women whose qualifications for their jobs revolve around the fact that they are more than willing to kill, cheat, and steal. And..." He paused, glancing back at Prince Bernard's sleeping form before turning back. "Now, the lad is sending the prince away. What do you think those involved in the conspiracy in the city will do when they learn that the king has sent away the kingdom's greatest warrior? Somehow I have a hard time imagining that it will make them *less* bold."

Maeve winced. She hadn't thought of that—more proof, if any were necessary, that while Chall was an incredible pain in the ass just about all the time, the man was no fool. "Nothing good," she said reluctantly.

The mage snorted softly at the understatement.

"Still, it isn't as if we have any choice," Maeve said. "Bernard won't be talked out of going—you saw that. Anyway, whatever is wrong with him, Matt is no fool—I'm sure he's smart enough to know that the fact that Bernard is being sent on a...*mission* should be handled quietly."

"I hope you're right, Maeve," he said. "I really do because the gods know we've got more than enough to deal with already."

Well, there was no arguing with that, and so she didn't try to. She rose, glancing at Cutter once more. "Can you two keep the watch for a while?"

Chall frowned. "And where are you going? Out for a stroll with assassins roaming the castle, is that it?"

"Careful, Chall," she said, giving him a small smile, "it almost sounded as if you care just then."

"Of course I care," the mage said. "Why, if something happens to you, that's one less person I have to throw in front of me when the dying starts."

Maeve sighed. "Petran has been alone with Guardsman Nigel for several hours—I fear to leave him so any longer. It's unlikely that the king's guards would think to check the historian's rooms but...well, I'd rather look in on him anyway. To be sure."

Chall nodded. "Fine," he said, rising, "if it's that important, I'll go with you."

"No, Chall," Maeve said, shaking her head before the man was finished. "You stay here. Better if I go alone." She turned to Priest then. "When will you go?"

The man had a grim expression on his face. "Tomorrow, after the prince departs."

She nodded, turning back to the mage who still stood, a worried expression on his face. "Relax, Chall," she said. "I'm just going to go check on Petran and Nigel—I don't mean to get killed." With that, she turned and started for the door.

"No one does, Maeve," he said softly.

She paused then, her hand on the door's latch. She knew that she had to hurry. After all, the guards would be returning soon from chasing Chall's illusion, and they would no doubt have some very pointed questions if they saw her walking out of a room that was meant to contain Prince Bernard and him only. Still, she considered telling Chall the truth then, about how she felt about him, about how she'd felt for a long time, a truth she had kept so hidden that she had barely even recognized it herself.

People always told themselves that they had more time, that they could afford to put off, for today, that thing that they were scared of doing. But then that was the thing about time, wasn't it? Sooner or later, it ran out. Time did not stop its march for anyone, not for a commoner in the street, not for the richest king or prince, and especially not for an old washed-up assassin with more years behind her than ahead. Likely, if things kept going the way they were, a lot more.

But the guards would return soon, and there were things that needed to be done so now, like so many times before in the years since she had known the mage, Maeve told herself that she would tell him her feelings later. If, that was, there *was* a later. She took a deep breath and stepped out of the door, gratified to see that, for now at least, the hallway remained empty, then she closed it behind her, starting toward Petran's room.

CHAPTER SIXTEEN

Fear the man—or woman—willing to take coin to kill someone. But more than that, fear the one who is willing to do it for free.
—Maeve the Marvelous

He stood at the small window of his room, looking out on the city of New Daltenia and its people. *His* people. He had stood so for half an hour or more after waking to find Maeve and the others gone. Stood staring out at the city, at the people, that he had failed.

He had hoped that perhaps Feledias might visit him before he left, for he doubted very much that he would ever return, and there were things he wished to say, things he needed to say. But there was no sign of his brother and when the door swung open without so much as a knock, he turned to see that it was not Feledias but Sergeant Selladross.

"Ah, you're awake," the man said with clear disappointment in his tone, as if he'd been looking forward to forcing him awake.

"Yes," Cutter said, watching as several guardsmen filtered into the room one of whom, he saw, carried two sets of manacles.

He turned back to the sergeant, raising an eyebrow. "Am I to travel to the Black Woods in chains, then?"

"Oh, of course not," the man replied, smiling. "Only, His Majesty thought it best if you remained so until we reach the edge of the city. Less chance, then, of any..." He paused, glancing pointedly at the axe sheathed on Cutter's back. "Misunderstandings."

"I see," Cutter said, noting that the man remained in the doorway as he motioned the two guardsmen carrying the manacles forward.

Cutter glanced at them as they approached, saw them watching him warily, even starting as he turned, offering his wrists.

One hesitated then moved forward, licking his lips nervously as he clasped the manacles around Cutter's arms. When that was done, the second knelt and clasped his own around Cutter's ankles, the two manacles linked with a chain that was no more than a foot long.

"What else?" Cutter asked, looking at the sergeant. "Am I to ride in a cage?"

"Oh, of course not," the man said, grinning, "that's no way to treat royalty, is it?"

Cutter said nothing to that, following as the guards ushered him out the door and into the castle hallway. Castle servants hurried out of their way as he was marched down the corridor, and he noted, among them, the woman who Matt had struck. She stared at him with a look of pity on her face as they passed, and Cutter considered telling her that she should save that pity for one worthy of it.

In the end, though, he said nothing, knowing that acknowledging her would do her no favors with the guardsmen. In time, they reached the front doors of the castle, and Cutter followed his escort out into the morning light.

He was led down the path to the front gate then stood in shock, gazing beyond it into the street. He had thought himself incapable of being surprised any longer, but he was wrong. Both sides of the street, for as far as he could see in either direction, were packed with people. Hundreds, thousands of them, what seemed to be the entire population of New Daltenia, all gathered as if to witness a parade or some grand spectacle.

Which, he realized as the sergeant turned and glanced back at him with a smile, giving him a wink, they were. The spectacle of their prince—or, at least, the man who had once been their prince—being marched through the city street in chains. "Does the king know of this?" he asked.

The sergeant's grin widened. "Know of it? Why, it was His Majesty's idea. After all, what point in punishing a member of the royalty to demonstrate his fairness if no one witnesses the demonstration? Now, come, Prince," he said, gesturing widely as the castle gate swung open, "your people await."

***

"What in the name of the gods are they *thinking?*" Chall demanded.

Maeve glanced over at the mage, then at Priest. The older man didn't speak, but then he didn't need to—his troubled expression told her all that needed to be said. She looked back at the crowds gathered in the street and shook her head. "I don't know, but I don't like it."

The mage hissed angrily. "So much for getting the prince out of the city quietly." He grunted as someone in the crowd bumped into him—not an uncommon occurrence when the streets were as packed as they were. "You ask me, every man, woman and child in the damned city is out here."

"Or near enough as to make no difference," Maeve agreed. She had been relieved, last night, to find Petran and the guardsman still undiscovered, still safe, just as she had been happy to know that Cutter had made it through the night without any attempt on his life. Now, though, staring at the teeming crowds, crowds that might have been mistaken for those that gathered to witness a parade if it hadn't been for the angry scowls and mutterings all around her, whatever relief Maeve had felt vanished.

So many people, and none of them looked all that happy to her. What they looked like, in truth, was trouble waiting to happen. "Shit," she said, her assassin's instincts—dulled by the passage of years but recently resharpened—kicking in. Of course there hadn't been an attempt on the prince's life. After all, why bother sneaking into the castle, risking getting caught, when you could simply gather in the crowded streets where one might fire a crossbow and disappear into the throngs of people without a trace?

Ideas for what to do rushed through her mind one after the other, discarded one after the other. Then, finally, she hissed. "We need to split up."

Chall frowned. "Split up?"

"That's right," Maeve said, then she leaned in close, speaking in a hushed whisper to the two men. "The prince is in danger. There's no telling who in the crowd might be part of the conspiracy."

The mage's eyes widened at that. "You mean…"

"I mean that if there's a better place to effect a man's assassination then I don't know it!" Maeve snapped. "Now, unless I miss my guess, the guards will march him down main street, out the northern gate of the city. Chall, you watch from the castle to the end of Merchant's Row. I'll take from Merchant's to Crafter's, Priest—"

"From Crafter's to the gate," Priest said grimly, "I've got it."

"Got it?" Chall demanded. "Got *what?* What are we supposed to look for?"

Maeve hissed. "How about anyone waving a sword and screaming bloodthirsty murder?" she said. "Start there."

"Now, we need to get going before it begins and—" She cut off at the distant sounds of shouting. *Too late,* she thought. "*Go, now!*" she snapped.

Priest nodded, disappearing without a word into the crowd.

"But…Maeve, what are we supposed to *do?*" Chall demanded.

"The best you can!" she said, and then she was off and running.

***

Maeve came to a panting halt at the end of Merchant's Row, scanning the street around her for anything or anyone that seemed out of place. The problem, of course, was that despite her snappy remarks to Chall, assassins rarely advertised their presence. In fact, staying unnoticed sort of went with the job description. Still, she could think of nothing else to be done, so she continued to study the people around her as the distant shouts of the crowd grew closer, informing her that the prince and his escort were drawing near and that he had at least not been assassinated yet.

Not that she had expected him to be. Any assassin worth their salt would know better than to attack the moment the prince set foot outside the castle walls. Certainly she wouldn't have done so. No, she would have waited, given it time. After all there was no hurry, for the man had to traverse this entire half of the city, a trip that would have taken well over an hour even had the streets not been packed near to bursting as they were.

No, a smart assassin would wait until the guards, and Cutter himself, began to let down his guard. Of course, the prince never *did* let down his guard, but then the assassin wouldn't know that. He—or she—would wait until they were well on their way, too far from the castle to retreat to it or to call for guards. For that same reason, he would not want to wait too long, lest his quarry escape out of the city.

All of which meant that, likelier than not, if there *was* an assassin, he, or she, stood somewhere among the crowds all around her, might be any one of those men and women who were staring down the street, waiting for the prince and his escort of guardsmen to march past. "The fools," she hissed again, angrily. It was almost as if they *wanted* the prince killed.

She blinked at that, cursing herself for a fool. Of course they wanted it. Why else would they parade him down the street? True, a trip to the Black Wood meant almost certain death, but why leave anything to chance when a crossbow bolt shot out of the crowd could guarantee it? It simply wasn't credible to think that the guardsmen leading him hadn't thought of that which meant only one thing—they *had* thought of it and had decided to lead him through the city anyway, and it didn't take a genius to figure out why they would do such a thing.

At least she remembered enough of the assassin's art to anticipate the attack, but anticipating it did no good at all if she couldn't stop it. And despite how she'd responded to Chall's concerns, the simple fact was that the mage was right. There was too much ground to cover and too few of them to cover it. She did a quick scan of the street, looking for anything out of the ordinary—like someone holding a sign that said, "assassin on the job," maybe.

She saw nothing untoward—no great comfort—so she began making her way farther down the street. Or, at least, she tried to. After ten minutes of forcing her way against the crowd, of hot, sweaty struggle as she fought her way through the packed streets, Maeve could glance back and see, quite clearly, the place where she'd started.

The noises of the crowd—boo's, mostly—were growing louder by the minute and a quick look down the street showed the prince's escort drawing closer. In another five minutes, maybe less, they would pass the spot where Maeve now stood. And if there were an assassin, the man would have an easy enough job of remaining hidden until he made his attempt. If, that was, he could navigate his way through the crowd, for the one small consolation available to Maeve was that the man would have to struggle with the busy streets as much as she did.

Unless he isn't on the street at all.

The thought seemed to come out of nowhere, but as soon as she'd had it Maeve decided that it made sense. After all, the streets were so teeming with people that it was nearly impossible to move through them, a fact she could attest to personally considering she'd spent the last half hour trying, and largely failing, to do just that.

And as distracted as those people were by the approach of their sovereign prince, a prince for which, it was clear, they held little love, still she thought it likely that they would notice someone in their midst drawing a sword or crossbow. If, that was, the assassin in question even had enough room to pull the weapon in the first place.

So how, then, could the man count on getting the job done?

"Shit," Maeve hissed, pulling her eyes away from the streets and up to the rooftops of the buildings flanking the avenue on either side. Growing more panicked by the moment, she turned in a circle, eyeing the rooftops, searching for any sign. She was just beginning to think that she'd been wrong after all when her eyes caught on a figure standing on the roof of a nearby tailor's.

At first, she thought that she might have imagined it, for the rooftop on which she believed to have seen it was situated so that, anyone looking at it, was also forced to stare into the brightness of the early morning sun. Which, of course, is exactly the sort of place she would have stood, had she meant to commit murder and not be seen doing it. The figure, if indeed there *was* a figure and what she saw was anything more than a dark smudge in her sight caused by the brightness of the sun, seemed to be wearing a dark robe, the hood pulled down.

Her hand held up in a vain effort to keep the sun from her eyes, Maeve watched the smudge for several seconds, trying to decide if it were an actual person or not, knowing, as she did, that if she raced all the way to the rooftop only to find out that she was wrong, then there would be no more time to do anything else.

Just when she was about to decide that the smudge was no more than a smudge after all, it turned. An almost imperceptible movement—but not quite, and she noted that the figure was regarding the approaching group of guards, and one royal prince, coming down the lane.

The smudge disappeared for a moment, and when it came back it was holding a second, smaller smudge, one that, when she looked closely, bore a remarkable resemblance to a bow. "*Shit*," Maeve hissed.

And then she was running. Or, at least, trying to. The state of the streets was such that her intended run turned into a sweaty, cursing shuffle as she shoved her way through the crowds of people, ignoring their shouts of outrage.

The tailor's shop was situated on the other side of the street. On a normal day, it would have taken only moments for her to reach it, but for all the men and women in her way it might as well have stood a mile distant.

I won't reach it in time, part of her mind despaired as she continued the process of shoving her way through the crowd.

I have to, she told that part as she slung an elbow into a fat man who, judging by his clothes, was some sort of merchant. She moved past him as he gasped, but her foot caught on something and then she was stumbling out of the crowd and into the street. A quick glance showed the front of the prince's procession in the distance. Maeve shot a look up at the tailor's rooftop, but the figure was out of her sight now, and she started across the street at a run.

It was hard work, pushing her way through the crowd to the tailor's door, but she finally reached it, sweaty and out of breath. She tried the latch and was unsurprised to find it locked. Perhaps she might have knocked, but it was likely that the owner wasn't inside but somewhere in the street, assuming he was still alive at all, and very *un*likely that he would have heard her knock over the tumult even if he was inside. So instead, she chose the expedient of drawing one of her knives and ramming the blade into the crack of the door. She worked it around for a moment, cursing her old, stiff hands and fingers which had once been so nimble as she felt the seconds slipping away.

Finally, after what felt like an eternity, there was a metallic *click* and the door swung open. Maeve rushed inside only to come up short at the sight of two men standing a short distance away, swords in their hands.

"Hi there," one said.

"Shop's closed," the second said. "In case you couldn't tell, you know, on account of the locked door."

Maeve froze then, studying the two of them. There had been a time when two men, particularly two shabbily dressed men as these, who held their swords as if they'd never seen one before, wouldn't have given her any pause. Not Maeve the Marvelous, legendary assassin and companion to the Crimson Prince. But she was not that woman anymore—far closer to Maeve the Ancient, even though it didn't have quite the same ring. So she did pause.

She could leave, she knew. The men would let her go, she believed that. She could leave, could live, but if she did that then she would have to keep walking, out of the tailor's shop, out of the city altogether, and she wouldn't be able to walk far enough to get away from her shame. A person's shame followed them, always—Cutter had taught her that. Besides, Cutter was her friend, and the gods knew she didn't have enough that she could spare any to a couple of two-bit assassins like those now watching her.

"Well," she said with a sigh as she drew a second blade, companion to the one she still held, "Best we be getting on with it—I've got places to be."

"Yeah, like the cemetery," one said, grinning as if he thought himself the height of wit as he motioned to his companion and the two slowly started encircling her.

Maeve sighed again. It seemed that her looks weren't the only thing that had diminished with the passing of time—even the class of criminals she now faced had declined. As she watched the men move, awkwardly and with clearly no understanding of footwork, she grew confident that she could take them. The problem, of course, wasn't that she just needed to take them—she needed to do so quickly. For every second that passed gave the assassin on the roof more time to finish his task, and it was too much to hope that he was as useless with the crossbow he carried as these two looked to be with their swords.

Maeve had been in countless fights over the years, but her talents did not lay, as Cutter's did, in barreling headlong into her enemies, counting on superior strength to overcome her foes. Nor did she rely on her speed, like Priest, or her magical gifts like Chall. Hers had always been a danger of cunning, of outwitting her foes. Better, she had always thought, if her enemies didn't know they were in a fight at all until they were dead.

Still, despite her best efforts, she had found herself in plenty of standup fights over the years, so she counted on that experience to keep her alive as, instead of waiting as she would have done, given the chance, she charged at the man on the right. He let out a startled yelp, swinging his sword in what might have been an attack, if one squeezed one's eyes closed tightly enough.

Maeve didn't close her eyes, though. Instead, she sidestepped the blow, letting the man's awkward swing pass within inches of her. Her attacker grunted in surprise at this, supposing, she guessed, that she would stand there and let him cut her in half, something even he could have managed given enough time. He stumbled, off-balance, and so it was an easy enough thing for her to slip her dagger into his throat. Too easy, in truth.

The man let out a gurgling wheeze, bubbles of blood forming on his lips before she pulled the knife away and he collapsed to the ground.

Maeve turned, knowing that the second man would be coming at her, but while her blades might have been as sharp as they ever had been, she was slower, and by the time she'd spun he was already on her, barreling into her, shoulder first. The man was big, muscular, and the blow sent her flying backward until her back struck painfully against some wooden shelves, scattering folded linens across the floor. Not that Maeve noticed, for she was too busy dodging blows from the man. Not blows from a sword, for the man, like many amateur swordsmen—if even that title could be given him—had foregone his blade, counting, instead, on his large, muscular frame, his strength to finish her quickly.

But while the man might have been strong, he was slow, and even off balance as she was, Maeve managed to evade the heavy-handed blows he landed around her, blows meant to crack bones but which only managed to crack the wooden shelving instead.

Still off balance, she saw an opening after one such swing and lunged for it, meaning to put some distance between her and her attacker. She was nearly there when her foot caught on one of the linen piles now strewn about the floor, and she tripped. Not badly enough to fall, but it might have been better if she had, for instead she only stumbled, slowing down enough for the man to reach out and grab her, wrapping his thick arms around her as if he meant to squeeze the life out of her. Which, judging by his angry growl as he bared his teeth and, more importantly, by the pressure on her sides as his thick arms constricted, was exactly what he intended.

It hurt, badly, and Maeve felt as if her bones were being ground to dust. But then, she had been hurt before, more times than she cared to count, so she endured the pressure long enough to lunge forward and clamp her teeth around the man's throat, sinking them in as deeply as she could. Blood filled her mouth, sour and coppery, and the man screamed. He didn't release his hold on her, at least not completely, but loosed it enough for her to slip her hand into her tunic and retrieve another knife to replace the two she'd dropped when the man struck her.

The man was still bellowing in pain as Maeve drove the blade into his stomach. He did let her go then, and she slammed the knife in deeper, pulling it up, toward his heart.

Her attacker let out a tortured wail then lashed out blindly with his hand, this wild, panicked blow connecting where the others had not, striking Maeve hard in the face. The next thing she knew, she was lying on her back, blinking up at the ceiling of the tailor's shop, the side of her face aching terribly.

The taste of blood filled her mouth, though whether it was the man's or her own she had no way of knowing. She worked her tongue around in her mouth as she climbed to her feet, feeling for any loose teeth and, thankfully, finding none.

Still, the room seemed to swim, and she drunkenly turned to check on her attacker only to find that the man had fallen on his back nearby, her knife still protruding from his stomach. Maeve hurried toward the corpse. Keeping one arm on the ruined shelves for balance, she knelt and retrieved the knife.

A Warrior's Curse

She froze at the sound of shouting, spinning and expecting to find another of the men barreling down on her but the room was empty. At least, that was, save for her and the dead. A moment later she realized that the shouting wasn't coming from inside the tailor's at all but, instead, from somewhere out in the street. Which could only mean one thing—she was out of time.

Hissing a curse, she scanned the shop as quickly as she could, her eyes alighting on an open door behind the counter. She hurried toward it, using the wall for support, nearly slipping on the blood puddled on the floor as she did.

Stepping through the door, she came into a small room. There was a safe in one corner, and a table where the tailor likely took his lunch or went over the business's numbers. She was just beginning to panic, to believe that she had chosen wrongly after all, when she caught sight of a ladder in the corner. She moved toward it and glanced up.

There was a hatch which no doubt led to the roof, but it was currently closed. She suspected so that the assassin could be warned if anyone should mean to interfere and could take measures to rectify it—likely in the form of an arrow to the face for the poor fool who meant to climb up it. A poor fool which, just then, was her.

There was no time to waste, no time to search for some other way onto the roof. Maeve gripped a knife in her teeth, thinking it best to have it ready in the unlikely event that the bowman allowed her to get close enough to use it, then started up the ladder as quietly as she could, a task made more difficult by the dizziness she felt and the ache in her jaw.

She reached the hatch and then lifted it as quickly and quietly as she could which just meant that the creaky wood sounded like the wail of a dozen banshees instead of twice that number. Suddenly, she heard screams and panicked shouting from the street below.

Too late, Maeve thought in a panic. Realizing that stealth was out of the question and that her only ally now was speed, she threw the hatch open the rest of the way and scurried up the ladder as fast as she could.

As she reached the top, she rolled to the side on the off chance that the archer was an amateur who had no idea of how to lead is target. The roll took her to her feet and she started forward at a sprint in the direction she'd seen the figure only to come up short, freezing and staring in awe.

The figure that she had seen from the street sat propped against the rooftop along with a second figure who wore similar clothing. The two might have been asleep, had the front of their brown robes not been coated with blood, their heads lolling at unnatural angles. Or, at least, unnatural for anyone living.

Still, she only paid them a brief moment of attention. What caught her eye—and held it—was a third figure. A woman who stood facing Maeve, a bloody knife gripped in each hand. "Oh, hello," the woman said.

Maeve blinked in shock, her mind unable to believe what her eyes were telling it. "E...Emille?" she stammered.

Ned's wife nodded. "Hello, Maeve," she said, then winced, flushing as if embarrassed as she glanced back at the two corpses and the blood-stained rooftop. "Sorry...that is, about the mess. I would have cleaned up but—"

"*Emille?*" Maeve said again.

The woman cleared her throat. "Forgive me, Lady Maeve, but I would appreciate it if you weren't quite so loud. Ned is in the street somewhere, waiting on me, and if he knew I was up here he'd...well, he'd have some questions, let's say that."

"But...but...what are you doing here?" Maeve asked in a croak.

The woman shrugged, kneeling beside one of the bodies and wiping her blades clean on the dead man's brown robes before lifting the blue dress she wore—and which somehow didn't appear to have a drop of blood on it—and sliding them into sheathes at her calves. That done, she rose, looking back to Maeve. "I admit that I don't often play the hostess, but it seemed...well, rude to allow the prince to be killed so soon after he visited my home."

"But...but..." Maeve began, unsure of how to finish. "You...that is, you killed those men."

The woman raised an eyebrow as if to say that Maeve were one to talk—a fair point, of course—then shrugged. "Well. If it helps, they didn't seem like particularly *nice* men."

"But how did...how did you do it?"

The woman gave her a small shrug again. "The usual way, I suppose." She motioned her head to the knife Maeve had taken out of her teeth and now held in her hand. "Similar, I suspect, to what you had in mind."

"What I mean," Maeve said, some of her wild thoughts finally settling, "is who are you?"

The woman blinked. "I'm Emille, lady. We've met before. Now, if you mean who am I to kill these men...well, in my experience killing doesn't require any particular credentials." She turned, regarding the corpses. "More's the pity."

"But...you're a healer...aren't you?"

"Of a sort," the woman said. "Anyway, who do you suppose would know better how to take a life than those tasked with saving it? It's the same job, really, you understand. Just...well, in reverse."

"Forgive me," Maeve managed, "but...you don't seem all that shaken up. Like maybe you've done this sort of thing before."

"Well," Emille said slowly, "I wasn't always a carriage driver's wife. Anyway..." She gave another shrug. "A woman has to have her hobbies, doesn't she?"

Maeve shook her head in wonder. "And Ned? Does he—"

"No," the woman said quickly, turning on her with an angry flash in her eyes, "Ned knows nothing of it, and he will not. Do you understand?"

Maeve stared, shocked by the sudden change. "Emille, I have no intention of telling your husband anything. In fact, I just want to say thank you—for saving the prince, I mean. He's...well...that is...he's..."

"A good man?" the woman asked, raising an eyebrow again.

Maeve considered that then shook her head slowly. "Maybe. I don't know. But he's trying."

The woman gave a single nod. "The most that can be asked of any of us."

"Well, thank you, Emille. Again."

"Listen, Lady Maeve," Emille said, moving closer. "These assassins, their job couldn't have been made easier. Not with the town criers sent out to tell everyone about Prince Bernard's punishment—being sent to the Black Wood." She shrugged. "It seems to me almost as if someone *wanted* him killed."

"Yes," Maeve said, frowning, "I was thinking the same thing." She moved to the edge of the building and looked down, trying to figure out the source of all the pandemonium since Emille seemed to have handled the two assassins. She saw Bernard walking past with his escort of guards and clenched her jaw in anger as she noted his manacled wrists and ankles, as if the man were some common criminal of the city, a city that wouldn't even *exist* had he not defended it in the Fey Wars.

But while many of those in the crowd shouted after him, several throwing rotten fruit, there was a circle of people across the street from where she stood that seemed intent on something else, and it took her a moment to realize that a man who looked very much like the fat merchant she'd bumped into on her hurried way to the tailor's shop was lying on the ground, an arrow sticking out of his thigh.

"I wasn't fast enough," Came Emille's voice, and Maeve turned to see the woman standing beside her.

"Fast enough to foul the shot," the woman went on, "but not fast enough to keep it from striking someone else. I need to go see to him."

"You mean to help him?" Maeve asked.

The woman nodded. "If I can. It's my fault he was shot, after all."

"No," Maeve said, glancing at the dead men on the roof top. "Not your fault."

Emille shrugged. "I should have been faster. Will you come with me?"

Maeve nodded, following silently after the woman as she started back toward the ladder, thinking that one of the hardest lessons she'd had to learn in her life was that, when it came to stopping tragedy, no one was fast enough.

***

As they stepped out of the tailor's shop, Maeve caught sight of Cutter and his escort disappearing around a corner farther down the street. She frowned after it, but Emille wasted no time, moving through the crowd with such ease that Maeve felt herself feeling impressed and more than a little jealous as she fumbled after her, forced to push and shove her way through in an effort to keep pace with the woman.

They reached the scene of the injured merchant in short order.

"*Oh, gods, get a healer! I'm dying, here, can't you see that? I'm dying!*" the fat merchant was shouting as Maeve forced her way out of the crowd, panting and looking at Emille who stood, taking in the gathered people and the fat man on the ground with a business-like efficiency.

A crowd encircled the man, but none of them seemed inclined to help and that much Maeve understood. She knew much of hurting, had learned plenty during her years, but she knew very little of healing. Emille, though, didn't seem daunted in the least, approaching the man and kneeling beside him.

"A-are you a healer?" the man gasped. "I need a healer!"

"Of a sort," Emille said distractedly as she first laid a hand on the man's head, then grabbed his wrist, cocking her head as if listening to something only she could hear.

"O-of a sort?" the man asked in a voice that was somehow scared and demanding all at once. "What does that mean?"

"I help animals," the woman said, continuing her ministrations.

"*Animals?*" the man demanded. "Do you know who I am? I am Merchant Elfedius, one of the highest-ranking members of the guild! I am no, no *pig* to be experimented on!"

"*Coulda fooled me,*" someone from the crowd whispered, and several others snickered.

This did draw Emille's attention and she turned, scowling at the man who'd spoken. She said nothing, but then she didn't seem to need to as the man in question blushed and pointedly avoided her gaze.

Emille watched him for another moment then turned back to the merchant. "If you wish, you may wait for another healer," she said, her voice not cruel or particularly kind, only as if she were speaking of the weather. "Though, there is no knowing how long one might take, and you have lost a fair amount of blood already. Still, if you are lucky and the wound does not become infected, perhaps you may live until they get here."

The man groaned. "Y-you mean, what? That I might *die?*"

Emille shrugged, glancing at Maeve and meeting her eyes for a moment before turning back to the man. "I know little of such things but, as I understand it, that is largely the point of arrows."

"B-but who would want to kill me?" the man said. "I am one of the highest ranking—"

"*Better question is who wouldn't,*" someone from the crowd asked, and Emille had not even managed to turn halfway to stare at him before he spoke again, "S-sorry," he stammered.

"So?" Emille asked, turning back to the merchant.

"S-s-so what?" the man stammered.

"Would you like to wait for a 'real' healer, or would you prefer I tend to the wound? It's your choice, though I would recommend you make it quickly before you lose too much blood. Hesitate too long, and the choice will likely make itself."

"H-help me then," the man said, "p-please, oh gods I don't want to die."

She gave a business-like nod at that, reaching into her shirt and retrieving one of the knives Maeve had seen her holding when she'd climbed to the rooftop. In fact, Maeve saw that there was still a small bit of blood on it, but if anyone else noticed they gave no sign. Except the merchant, of course, who while he may not have noticed the blood, most certainly noticed the knife.

"H-hold on a minute," he stammered, "wha-what do you mean to do with that?"

"I mean to cut out the arrow," Emille said, "I mean to save your life. Now, would you prefer to continue talking or to leave me to my...what was it you called it? Oh yes, experiments?"

The man said nothing, only groaned, turning his head as if not seeing the knife would somehow make it hurt less. Maeve watched the woman work, stunned that someone who was so obviously skilled at killing could somehow be as skilled at healing, too. And she *was* skilled. Even Maeve who knew little of healing could see that much in the efficient, confident way she cut out the arrow from the writhing merchant before retrieving a small bottle from somewhere inside her shirt and beginning to apply it to the wound.

Maeve stood watching her like those others gathered, and as she did, she wondered if she could have been something else in her life besides a killer. Or, failing that, if she could have, like Emille, been both.

"What happened?" a voice asked from beside her, and Maeve jumped, startled. It was rare that someone managed to sneak up on her without her knowing, but she'd been so engrossed in the woman's work that she turned and was surprised to find Ned, the carriage driver, standing beside her, a grim expression on his face.

"He was struck by an arrow," she said.

"That'd explain the arrow in his leg, sure," Ned said. "What I meant was, *how* did it happen?"

He asked the question off-handedly, as if it was of no great consequence, but there was something in the way he asked it that made Maeve think that it had been asked anyway but off-handedly. She considered telling the man the truth but quickly dismissed the idea. For one, there were too many people around, people who might overhear her but, more than that, she knew that answering the question with the truth would only lead to more questions. Questions that would, in time, revolve around how Emille had come to be with Maeve, and as a woman who had spent the last fifteen years of her life in hiding, married to a husband who hated her and whom she hated in turn, Maeve understood the importance of secrets. In the end, she just shook her head. "Came out of nowhere."

"That so?" the man asked, turning away from his wife at her labors for a moment and meeting Maeve's eyes. The carriage driver might act like a good-hearted fool, but in that gaze Maeve could see that he, like his wife, was more than he let on.

"Yes," she said. "Just flew out of the sky."

"Huh," he said. "Might be we ought to get underneath somethin' then," he said, still watching her. "You know, in case it decides to rain anymore arrows."

"I...I don't think it will," Maeve said.

The man gave a single nod. "Well. S'pose that's good then." Then he turned away, back to his wife, and Maeve was glad to be relieved of the weight of his knowing stare. "She's something, isn't she?" he asked softly.

"Yes," Maeve agreed as she turned back to regard his wife at her work, "she's something."

"So gentle," he said, the words so low she didn't know if he was talking to her or to himself, doubted even he knew. "So soft."

Just then, the merchant let out a scream of pain, reaching as if he meant to interfere with Emille's work. The woman didn't even so much as pause, swatting his hands roughly away.

Ned grunted. "But hard, too. Soft and hard all at once."

You have no idea, Maeve thought. But then, for all she knew, perhaps the carriage driver did. After all, the man, despite his attempts at appearing a fool, was clever. He was similar to Challadius in that regard. The thought of the mage sent a trill of panic through Maeve. Cutter might have survived this assassination attempt—no thanks to Maeve but all to Emille—but that didn't mean there wouldn't be another. Assassins, in her experience, were a damned stubborn lot.

"Listen, Ned," she said, "I have to go."

The carriage driver turned to her again, raising an eyebrow. "Marvelous things to be about, eh?"

Maeve winced. "Something like that." She leaned in close. "The guards will be by sooner or later, to ask questions about the arrow and all. I think it might be best if you and Emille weren't here when they arrived."

Ned nodded. "Might be you're right. I'll wait 'til Emille finishes up here then we'll leave."

She gave a nod of her own then turned to go, stopping when the carriage driver grabbed her arm. "I wonder, Lady Maeve, if you wouldn't mind tellin' the prince, when you talk to 'em, that I said hi?"

"Of course," Maeve said, meeting the man's eyes, and there was that clever look again, as if the man, while appearing casual on the surface, was thinking far more than he let on.

Ned smiled. "And tell him, too, that I meant what I said. If he needs me, or my wife, he has only to ask."

Maeve's first, uncharitable thought, was that with all that was going on with the kingdom, they needed warriors far more than they needed carriage drivers, but after a moment's reflection, she decided that was wrong. The world, after all, could do with more carriage drivers, assuming they were anything like the one standing before her and also assuming that their wives were even half the women that his was. "Thank you, Ned," she said softly, "truly."

The man shrugged, as if it were of no consequence. "Well. I best go see if Emille needs any help, though like as not she'll curse me for gettin' in the way. Still," he went on, grinning, "what are husbands for if not for bein' there when their wives need to get some good cursin' done, eh?"

And with that, he turned and walked away, kneeling beside his wife.

Maeve watched the two of them for a moment then with a smile turned and stepped into the crowd.

CHAPTER SEVENTEEN

*Surviving...well that's the easy part.
It's getting on with the business of living that's hard.
—Veteran of the Fey War*

Cutter had been through battles that lasted for days, had taken part in the Fey War until the creatures were driven back into the Black Wood. He knew something of exhaustion, of the pervasive weariness that crept not just into a man's limbs, but his heart, his soul. Or at least, he thought he did.

The trip through the city had taken only a matter of hours, but they had been some of the longest hours of his life, and the exhaustion that suffused him was as bad, if not worse, than any he had ever experienced before. He had *known,* of course, that the people of New Daltenia must hate him. After all, how could they not? He, their prince, who had betrayed his brother but, more than that, had betrayed *them.* The man who had, by his actions, very nearly ripped the kingdom apart. Yes, he had known they hated him, had thought of it often in his years spent exiled to the small northern village of Brighton. But knowing a thing was far different than *experiencing* it. It was one thing to think of how they must hate him. It was quite another to see that hate in their twisted expressions of rage, to hear it in their screams and shouts.

He had questioned, at first, Matt's decision to send him to the Black Wood, had wondered at it, thinking perhaps that it was another part of the conspiracy, that someone—perhaps one of the youth's new advisors—had convinced him to send Cutter away so that he could not help defend the city against what was coming.

But he believed that no longer, had stopped believing somewhere along the road leading out of New Daltenia, somewhere amid the screams of those he had so wronged. The truth was that, however much he might want to help them, he could not. The truth was that his staying in the city would only make it worse. Either he would do something evil—on purpose or not—or he would draw that evil to him like a lodestone. Certainly, looking back on his life it seemed to him that he had done as much, that and little else.

The city of New Daltenia, the kingdom of the Known Lands, was sick, that was true, but he was not the man to heal it—he never had been. What good was a warrior, after all, a man who knew war and that only, in a healer's tent? He did not know how to heal, only how to hurt. It was the warrior's curse that even in attempting to protect, to save, he could cause only pain, only death.

I am fire and all I touch turns to ash.

By the time he caught sight of the northern gate of New Daltenia, the words had become a mantra, repeated over and over in his head, not to stave off despair, but to revel in it. For, he thought, he deserved nothing else. So he endured the scornful, hateful shouts from the crowd, accepting them as his due just as he had accepted the spatterings of rotten fruit which had struck him on their walk through the city or the occasional, almost distracted blows from the guards.

He shambled toward the city gate, stinking of rotten fruits and vegetables, blood oozing from a cut on his head, either from one of the guards' blows or from a rock thrown by one of those who had marked his progress. He did not know and he did not care. Wherever it had come from, he deserved it, that and far more. He had accumulated a great debt over the years, reaping it with his axe, and it was one that he could not, could *never* repay.

"So, Prince," the sergeant said, turning and grinning, "what do you think, I wonder, of the attention of your people?"

Cutter said nothing, not because the man was obviously taunting him but simply because there was no point.

The sergeant watched him, his grin slowly changing into a frown. "Come on then," he said, hocking and spitting on the street.

"I'd just as soon be done with this filth—the gods know I need a bath."

They marched him toward the city gate, and though he did his best to keep up with the increased pace, the manacles on his ankles made the task difficult, if not impossible. Each time he stumbled, he was rewarded with a fresh cuff to the head from one of his escort, sometimes even when he did not stumble, as if the men knew that the time for their cruelty was nearing its end and they intended to milk it for all it was worth.

Cutter made no move to defend himself, accepting each blow as his due just as he accepted the pain, for while each blow hurt, the pain it caused was as nothing compared to that which gripped him. He had done what he could, and most of it hurt, not helped. Now, the kingdom would fall or it would not and, if it did, there would be no one to blame save him.

They reached the gate proper and one of the guards stationed there walked up to them, a look of shock coming over him. "Is that Prince Bernard?"

The sergeant leading Cutter's escort nodded, seeming to regain some of his good humor as he glanced at Cutter's stained, bloody figure. "So it is."

"Fire and salt what *happened* to him?" the man said in shock.

The sergeant shrugged. "Justice, though not as much as a bastard like this deserves. Now, open the gate."

The man hesitated, glancing uncertainly between Cutter and the sergeant but, in the end, he hurried away to comply and, in another few moments, the gate began to swing open.

"Well, you've escaped the *love* of your people, Prince," the sergeant said, "but I wouldn't rejoice too much. As much as the people of the Known Lands hate you—and they *do* hate you—I suspect that your reception in the Black Wood will be far more...interesting." His grin widened. "And likely considerably shorter."

He watched Cutter for a moment, but when Cutter did not respond, he hocked and spat again, this time on the front of Cutter's tunic. Then he waved at one of the guards. "Get this filth out of the city."

A Warrior's Curse

One of the men moved forward, grabbed Cutter's manacled wrists, and began leading him toward the gate.

"And remember this, Prince," the sergeant shouted after him, "should you think to flee, to run and hide, we have men everywhere. We will find you, and you will be made to suffer—as will those you care about the most!"

Cutter paused then, glancing back at the man, and this time, he did speak. "Don't worry, sergeant," he said. "I'm done running."

They led him to the city gate and then outside of it. Cutter stood as one of the guard's went about the task of unclasping the manacles from his wrists and ankles.

"Oh," another said, walking up with a bundle in his hands. "Your things, *Highness.*" The last was clearly a taunt, and he tossed a bundle at Cutter's feet.

The bundle landed with a thud, the ragged cloth that had been wrapped around it revealing the obsidian handle of his axe as well as the sheath.

"Might be short a few coins," the guard said, grinning, "I'm afraid I dropped 'em somewhere along the way."

Cutter stared at the man who fidgeted, then sneered, and finally hurried away. When he was gone, and those guards removing his bonds had finished, Cutter was left standing alone, regarding the axe where it lay.

How long, he wondered, had he hoped to be rid of it? Of what it meant? Now, he realized that it made no difference. The axe was not the weapon—he was. And those deaths he had claimed with it were not its fault but his own. He knelt and retrieved the axe and its sheath, securing them at his back.

He turned back to the city gate, still open, taking it in one last time. His city, the city he had failed, yes, but the city he loved for all that, the *people* he loved. He told himself they would be better with Matt as their leader—certainly the youth could do no worse than Cutter had, and the people deserved better.

The guards began to swing the gate closed, but paused at a shout.

"*Wait!*"

The guards turned and Cutter did as well to regard the group of people running down the street. Cutter saw Priest, and Maeve, Chall, and was surprised to see Feledias among them.

245

The guards moved to block the way, but Feledias didn't pause as he marched forward. *"Out of my way, I come by order of the king!"*

The guards did move at that, hurrying to either side of the gate and opening an avenue through which Feledias and Cutter's companions walked.

Cutter waited until they all came to stand in front of him, Chall bending over with his hands on his knees, gasping for breath.

"Thank the gods we reached you," Maeve said.

"Right?" Chall panted. "I thought I was about to die."

Maeve scowled at the mage. "You'll have to forgive Chall," she said, "we had to hurry to catch up with you—you all moved pretty fast."

Not fast enough, Cutter thought. "What can I do for you, Maeve?"

She frowned at that. "Listen, Prince, you can't go."

Cutter sighed. "Maeve, we've been through this—I have to go."

"No, you don't understand," the woman said. "There was another attempt on your life when you went through the city. Whoever's behind this, Prince, they're motivated, and they want you dead badly. Likely, because they know if you're dead then their conspiracy will be—"

"How do you know, Maeve?" Cutter interrupted in a soft voice.

The woman glanced, confused, at Priest. "Know what?"

"How do you know that the people who tried to kill me are part of the conspiracy?" he asked. Another shared look of confusion between the two, this time including Feledias and even Chall who seemed to have gotten some of his breath back.

"Prince," the mage began slowly, speaking as if Cutter had just claimed he could fly, "it seems fairly obvious that whoever is behind the assassination attempts—"

"Does it?" Cutter interrupted. "Does it, Chall?" The mage cut off, looking at Maeve helplessly, but Cutter pressed on. "You're my friends, all of you, better friends than a man like me deserves, but let's be honest, alright? There doesn't need to be some grand conspiracy for someone to want me dead—I've earned it. That and more. There's no telling the numbers of wives I've made widows, of sons and daughters that have grown up without their fathers because of me."

"What are you saying, Prince?" Maeve asked.

Cutter shrugged. "I'm saying that I've come to terms with who I am, Maeve, with *what* I am. All that thinking I'd changed, *hoping* I had, it was just that...hope. And a useless one at that."

The woman glanced back at the gate where the guards watched, several of them frowning, their hands on their swords, and shook her head angrily, turning back to Cutter. "Listen, Prince, we don't have time for this, alright? We can sneak you back into the city and talk about it la—"

"No."

"Are you saying," Priest said, "that...you still mean to go?"

"I do."

Maeve scoffed. "You've got to be kidding me! No offense, Prince, but that's just about the most damned fool thing I've ever heard. They'll send assassins after you as soon as you're out of the city! Stones and starlight for all we know they could be waiting outside the city already!"

"Maybe they are," Cutter said. "But I'm going."

"But...*why?*" she demanded, and he saw that there were tears in her eyes.

Cutter felt a wave of guilt at that. He was a monster, yes, but even monsters might offer some small comfort. He stepped forward, gently wiping her tears away with a finger. "Listen, Maeve, the Known Lands is in trouble, the worst trouble the kingdom's been in since the Skaalden and—"

"But that's exactly why we *need* you," she said. "Prince, we—"

"No, Maeve," he said softly but firmly. "I'm a killer—it's all I am. And by that measure I think I'm probably just about the last thing the Known Lands needs right now. What the people need is a chance to heal, to rebuild. With Matt as their king, they have a real opportunity to do that now, and the quickest way to screw that up would be for me to make the selfish choice and stay when I should go. As long as I remain in the city, I can only cause harm." He glanced over at Feledias who stood with an unreadable expression on his face. "What about you, brother? Have you also come to talk me out of leaving?"

Feledias looked at the other three before turning back to Cutter. "No, brother. I have known you long enough to know that once you've set your mind to something you're as stubborn as a bull." He paused, offering him a small smile. "As ugly, too, but I suppose that can't be helped. But no, Bernard, I have not come to talk you out of going. I've come to go with you."

"What?" Chall asked.

"You've got to be joking!" Maeve said.

"I'm not," Feledias said.

"Fel?" Cutter asked, surprised and relieved all at once. "But...why?"

His brother shrugged. "Because I think you're right, Bernard. The kingdom needs an opportunity to heal, and it can't do that, not while the two men who wounded it so badly are still sitting in the capital. I don't know about this son of yours, my nephew..." He paused, shaking his head in wonder at that. "It seems to me he's having some issues...acclimating to the throne, maybe. But what I do know is that, however bad he is, he can't be any worse than us."

Cutter nodded slowly. "But Fel, a journey to the Black Woods...it..."

"Is almost certain death?" his brother said casually, then shrugged. "Sure, but then I've faced certain death before. Anyway, you need a minder to come along." He offered another small smile. "The gods know what sort of mischief you'll get up to on your own. Like as not you'd wind up running around the woods naked, eating raw rabbit and crouching in some cave or another. Besides, for fifteen years I promised myself that I would see you dead. It'd be a shame to miss it."

Cutter watched his brother then gave a small smile of his own, offering his hand. A surprised look came over his brother's face and a moment later he took it. "Thanks, Fel," he said.

"Don't thank me yet," his brother murmured as he came to stand beside him, facing the others, "I've heard the Fey like to play with their food before they eat."

Cutter nodded, moving forward and offering Chall his hand. "Thanks, Chall," he said. "For everything."

The man's face twisted as if he might break into tears at any moment, but he took a slow, ragged breath, gathering himself before taking Cutter's hand. "Y-you're sure?" he asked.

"I'm sure."

The mage winced. "I could come along, too. Maybe I could—"

"No, Chall," Cutter said. "Your place is here. I need you and the others to watch after Matt, to keep him safe and to look after that..." He paused, glancing at the guards. "After that thing we spoke about."

The mage gave another ragged sigh and nodded. "I'll do my best, Prince."

Cutter smiled, clapping him on the shoulder. "Your best is a damned sight better than most."

He moved to Maeve then, the woman frowning at him as if she would have liked nothing more, just then, than to use him as target practice for the knives she always kept secreted on her.

"Maeve," he said.

She let out a sound that was between a growl and a whimper. "I still think it's a mistake," she said.

"Maybe," he said softly, "but it's mine to make."

"And so you're just going to leave the kingdom defenseless then? Because of...what? Some sort of guilt?"

Not some sort of guilt, he thought. *I am fire, and everything I touch turns to ash.* "Not defenseless, Maeve," he said, giving her a small smile. "They've got you."

She snorted. "Maeve the Marvelous. A washed-up old woman who looks more like a troll than the supposed world's greatest beauty, more likely to attract a mob than a man."

Cutter glanced at Chall then back to her. "I think we both know that's not true." She flushed at that, looking at her feet and Cutter put a finger on her chin, lifting her face. "Things will get better once I'm gone, Maeve, trust me."

She sighed. "I've always trusted you, Prince. That's never been the problem."

He nodded. "I'll miss you, Maeve."

"And I you."

Perhaps it still wasn't right between them, but it was as good as he could make it, so Cutter gave her another nod then moved to Priest. "Valden."

The man gave him a sad smile. "Prince."

"You'll look after them? And Matt?"

"Of course," the man said. "As best as I am able. But...are you certain, Prince? That this is the best way?"

Cutter considered that. "No, I'm not. But I think maybe it's the only one."

The man watched him for a second then nodded. "Is there...anything you need? Anything I can do?"

"You're doing it," Cutter said.

"I...I do not know what we will do without you," Priest said.

"Survive," Cutter said, "how about starting there? Anyway, don't look so sad, Priest. I have come through the Black Wood before, more than once. We will see each other again."

The man nodded, but it was clear from the look on his face that he didn't believe the lie anymore than Cutter himself. And why not? True, he had traveled into the Black Woods and come out again before, but those had been relatively quick trips when his goal was to push back an already beaten foe or, in the second case, attempting to go unnoticed. Now, the foe was strong, perhaps stronger than it had ever been, and this time, to follow the king's orders, he would not only have to forego stealth, he would have to march into the very heart of the Fey kingdom and attempt to negotiate a peace treaty. It might not be suicide exactly, but then Cutter didn't think it was all that far off.

Based on the grim expression on his companion's face, the man was having similar thoughts, so Cutter forced a smile he didn't feel. "It'll be okay, Priest. Either way, it'll be okay. After all, the world needs its priests a lot more than it needs its killers."

Before the man could say anything more, Cutter gave him another nod then turned and walked back to where Feledias stood. "Ready?" he asked quietly.

Feledias raised an eyebrow. "To venture into the homeland of creatures out of nightmare and attempt to negotiate a peace when we have nothing with which to bargain?"

Cutter considered that then, after a moment, nodded. "That sounds about right."

His brother shrugged, grinning, and in that grin Cutter could see some of the child he had once been, back before Cutter's betrayal, before the Skaalden had come to Daltenia, slaying thousands of its people, including their father, back when they still believed that the world was mostly good. "Well," Feledias said, "I suppose I've got nothing else going on."

Cutter turned back to the others, all standing and watching them, Chall snuffling as tears streamed freely down his face. "Goodbye, friends," he said. "Knowing you has been my honor."

Then with that, he turned and walked away, leaving his friends, his world, behind him.

***

Priest watched the two brothers walking away and, as he did, said a silent prayer to Raveza, the Goddess of Temperance, to keep them safe. As he watched them leave, Priest thought of the prince's final words to him. *The world needs its priests a lot more than it does its killers.*

He shook his head sadly. The statement was, no doubt, a true one, taken objectively, but the prince had presupposed something in the saying of it which made it in error. For one, Prince Bernard was not only a killer—he was much more than that. And Valden was not only a priest...he was much less.

"Do...do you think they'll be okay?"

Priest turned to regard Challadius, the mage snuffling and running an arm across his face. He considered trying to comfort the man with one of the common platitudes of his order, ones in which he himself had often sought comfort. *All things by the goddess's will,* perhaps, or *the path to peace is taken one step at a time.* But in that moment, such words felt empty, bereft of any meaning, if even they'd had it in the first place. So instead, he met the man's eyes and slowly shook his head. "I don't know."

"But...what can we do?" Maeve asked, and there was such uncertainty in the normally sure woman's tone that Priest's heart went out to her, wishing that he could comfort her, could say something that might give her some peace. But the last few months had shaken him, shaken him more than he would care to tell the others. "Priest," Bernard had called him, but Valden was not sure that such the title was accurate anymore. It was like a shirt a man had outgrown, one that didn't seem to fit quite right, for if he had not lost his faith, he felt sure that he was beginning to.

Still, he took a slow breath, gathering the remnants of that faith, that *hope* the way a man might, upon finding his house burned to the ground, fall to his knees and scoop the ashes of his old life into his arms. "For the prince?" he asked softly. "Nothing. Except, that is, what he asked."

Maeve met his eyes then, her own shimmering with tears. "You still mean to travel to Belle's hideout?"

"I do," Priest said, "and I mean to do it alone."

Maeve heaved a heavy sigh, shaking her head. "It seems that it is my lot to be surrounded by suicidal fools."

"But...what is it exactly that you hope to find?" Chall asked, sniffling.

"We don't even know if there's anything *to* find," Maeve said exasperated. "Priest, the woman was about to be executed. She was likely out of her mind with fear. Probably she didn't even know what she was saying."

"Maybe," he agreed.

"And yet you mean to go anyway," Maeve said.

It wasn't really a question, but Priest nodded. "Yes."

"But *why?*" Maeve demanded. "They're *criminals,* Priest. Thieves and murderers and worse. You and Bernard were lucky to survive your first trip there and somehow I doubt relations have improved considering that we just *executed* their *boss.*"

"Wait a minute," Chall said, "we weren't responsible for that—stones and starlight, Maeve, we tried to stop it!"

"Uh-huh," Maeve said, "and do you think that they know that?"

Chall fidgeted. "Well, I mean, I'm sure if we were to explain..."

"Sure," Maeve said, rolling her eyes, "because criminals are known for their understanding. He'll *die,* Chall."

Chall winced, seeming to consider that then, finally, he nodded, glancing at Priest. "You might die."

"There is much I am uncertain about," Priest said slowly. "I have begun to...question things, lately, things that I once took as absolute truth. But there is one thing that I know, friends, one truth that holds when all else falls away. If we are alive, there is always a chance that we will die."

Maeve snorted. "A damned better chance if you go sticking your head into lions' mouths."

Priest inclined his head. "Yes, such beasts will bite—it is all that they know, that they *are,* and I pity them for that. Yet, such beasts, while dangerous, are also predictable and in that predictability lies their weakness."

Maeve shook her head. "I doubt that's much consolation to the fools who are bit, not that they're likely to be consoled by anything, being dead and all."

"What did you mean, Priest?" Chall said abruptly.

He turned to regard the mage. "I'm sorry?"

The other man fidgeted, clearly uncomfortable. "I mean...about beginning to question things? What did...what did you mean by that?"

Priest stared at the man, surprised to find that he looked almost frightened. He had spent years mocking Priest's calling, his beliefs, but now the thought of Priest foregoing those beliefs seemed to fill him with an almost childish, superstitious fear. Valden hesitated for a moment. The truth was that he understood the mage's feelings, for discarding such beliefs, beliefs he had dedicated the latter half of his life to, was frightening, particularly because if he did not believe in them, that meant that the world, and all that happened within it, was random, that there was no power greater than their own looking after them. It meant that, in the end, they were alone.

Priest could not find the words of his belief as he once had, words that might give the mage comfort, but he decided there was some little bit of comfort he could still offer the man. "Forgive me, Challadius," he said, "I misspoke. I only meant that I have been afraid, but I will pray to the goddess for guidance, and I am sure that all is well and all will *be* well."

The mage let out an almost imperceptible sigh at that, nodding his head and apparently accepting the lie. "Ah, right."

Priest watched him for a moment. The man still seemed afraid, uncertain, but he had done what he could. He turned back to Maeve. "You ask me, Maeve, why I will go, knowing the dangers, and so I will tell you. I will go because Prince Bernard asked us to."

And while I may have lost my faith in many things, I have not lost it in him.

She sighed. "I still think it's a mistake, but if you think it's worth it…"

"I do."

She nodded and, before he knew it, it seemed to him that before even *she* knew it, she had pulled him into a tight embrace. "Be careful, okay?" she asked.

"As careful as one can be while sticking his head in a lion's mouth," he said smiling.

She pulled away after a moment and then Chall walked up, fidgeting and looking at his feet like a child preparing for a good scolding. Priest found himself smiling. "This is not goodbye, Challadius," he said softly.

"You don't know that," the mage said.

Well, that was true enough—there were many things Priest did not know, now in particular—so he only nodded, offering his hand. The mage blinked, staring at it for a moment and then, before he could react, Priest was pulled into a hug so tight it took his breath away. He grinned, hugging the man back.

Then Chall pulled back, ending the embrace as quickly as it had begun. "You're a good man, Priest," he said, refusing to meet his eyes. "A good…friend."

"As are you," he said, "but for the task ahead, Chall, I am not Priest. I am Valden—that and that only." *Perhaps forever.* He turned to Maeve. "I will meet the two of you at the castle as soon as I may. However this turns out…there are things we need to discuss."

And with that, he turned and left.

CHAPTER EIGHTEEN

Sometimes, the hardest thing to do is nothing.
—General Ichavian, famed military strategist

"What do we do now?" Chall asked as they watched the man's departing form walk down the street.

Maeve sighed. "We'd best be getting back to the castle to check on Petran and Nigel. The historian is a good man, but he's no warrior, and I fear what might happen should he be found harboring the guardsman."

Chall nodded, frowning, and Maeve raised an eyebrow. "What is it?"

The mage shook his head. "I just...I just wish there was some way we could help him, that's all."

"Who?" Maeve asked. "Cutter? Or Priest?"

"Either," he said glumly. "Both."

Maeve had known the mage for a long time, and while he complained often enough, and loudly enough, that anyone who had only just met him would surely think he was a grim man, she knew that nothing could be further from the truth. The man's cynical, often abrasive exterior hid an optimistic side of him, and so it hurt her to see the look of abject grief on his face. She moved forward, taking his hand in hers. "We can help them, Chall. By looking after the guardsman. After all, depending on what Priest finds out, the man is our best chance of rooting out the conspiracy in the castle. Now, will you come with me?"

He gave a weary sigh then, finally, treated her to a small smile. "Of course I will." He grunted. "For whatever good it'll do."

She smiled back. "More good than you could ever know, Chall." There was a moment, then, when their eyes locked, and Maeve felt something stirring within her. The man was grossly overweight, it was true, and rude—almost as if he were participating in some sort of competition and, whatever that competition was, he was winning. But then, even when he *had* been Challadius the Charmer, it had never been his looks that had attracted her to him. They had meant no more than the rudeness, just dressing covering the man underneath, and it was that man for whom she cared so much.

"Listen, Chall," she said softly, "I..." She hesitated then, surprised to find that she was afraid. As afraid as she could ever remember being, more afraid, even, than she had been when dealing with the assassins. She wasn't sure what that said about her, that intimacy should scare her more than the threat of death ever could, but thought that probably it was nothing good.

"Yes, Mae?" he asked. *Mae.* She had always told him she hated that name and, certainly, it was true that she *had* hated it, at least when anyone else said it. But coming from him, there was something sweet about it, something...*intimate.*

So just tell him, part of her thought.

And then what? What interest would he have in someone like you, an old woman whose beauty is nothing more than a memory? And even if he was *interested, what good would that do? Likely, you'll both be dead within the week.* Finally, she shook her head. "Later. For now, we'd best hurry."

"You're...you're sure?" he asked, and in his gaze she thought she saw some understanding.

She hesitated for a moment again then cleared her throat. "I'm sure. Come on."

***

The trip back to the castle was blessedly uneventful as the majority of those who had gathered to watch the prince's procession had retired, either to their homes or, more likely, to one bar or another. What few people remained in the street laughed and joked as if they were at some sort of party, at least until some of them saw Maeve and Chall and frowned. It was no great surprise, she supposed, that the people who had hated the prince might also hate his companions. Still, Maeve paid their scowls no more attention than she did their laughs and smiles as she hurried to the castle.

In time, they reached the castle gate and the four guards stationed at it eyed them as they approached. "What do you want?" one demanded.

Maeve frowned. "I'm Lady Maeve, and this is Challadius. We have been lent rooms at the castle."

If anything, the man's openly hostile look grew worse instead of better. "Friends with that criminal, aren't you? The one they exiled from the city not two hours gone?"

Maeve gritted her teeth. "That *criminal* is your rightful prince."

"Not *my* prince," the man said. "Now, how about the two of you turn around and march your asses back into the city bef—" He cut off as one of the other guards stepped forward and whispered something in his ear, his words too low for Maeve to make out.

Maeve glanced at Chall and saw a look of unpleasant surprise on his face to match her own. She had known things had gotten bad, but this didn't seem like a good turn of events. If she couldn't get into the castle, she wouldn't be able to check on Petran. If that happened, it was only a matter of time before he and the recovering guardsman were found.

Finally, the guard finished listening to whatever his companion had been saying and turned back to her. "I apologize, Lady Maeve," he said in a tone that would have been convincing had it not been for the anger shimmering in his eyes. "I spoke out of turn. I fear today has been a very difficult day for all of us."

"Some more than others," she said, "but there's no harm done."

The guard smiled at that but, once again, the expression came nowhere close to touching his eyes. "You and Challadius the mage may, of course, be granted entry to the castle, for I am told that you are also dear friends of King Matthias the Virtuous."

Or at least we were, Maeve thought, but she nodded, returning the smile as the gates swung open. "Thank you," she said.

The guards moved to either side, flanking them, and Maeve glanced at Chall before starting toward the gap between them. It was ridiculous, she knew, but Maeve found herself thinking that, the moment they were between the two groups, the guards would draw their swords and cut them down. Impossible, of course, for while there might be a conspiracy in the castle, there was a big difference between assassins sneaking into people's rooms at night to kill them and four guardsmen committing murder in broad daylight where anyone in the city might witness it.

But ridiculous or not, the feeling did not abate, and she moved slowly between the men, tracking them as best she could out of her peripheral vision as she did, ready to draw her knives if her fears came to pass. Only a dozen paces, no more than that for her to be outside of arm's reach of the guards, yet they were some of the longest steps of her life, and Maeve found that she was surprised when she was outside the range of their swords and she and Chall had not been attacked.

She glanced at Chall and by the look on the mage's face, he was equally disturbed. "Come on" she said, "let's get out of here."

The mage didn't seem inclined to argue, so she hurried into the castle. Once the door was closed behind them, Chall let out a breath. "You almost get the impression we're not welcome?"

"I'd say so."

The mage shook his head. "Thought sure they were going to poke us full of holes, see what came out."

Maeve nodded, not trusting herself to do too much more just then. Her mouth was dry, and her forehead had broken out into sweat. "Let's go find Petran," she said quietly, "and best not say anything you wouldn't want overheard until I tell you otherwise."

Chall frowned at that. "What is it, Maeve? Think the castle has ears?"

"I *know* it has ears," she countered. "I'm more concerned about what those ears might be listening to. Now come on."

They started down the hallway at a fast walk, Maeve resisting the urge to run, wanting as she did to put as much distance between them and the guardsmen at the gate as she could. But then, that was the thing about castles—there were always more guards. They passed several on their way through the corridors, and while none moved to accost them, many of them studied her and the mage with hostile expressions.

It seemed that, in the space of hours, she and her companions had become the targets of hatred for nearly every person in the castle, including the serving men and women who watched them with expressions at least as hostile as the guards. At least, most of them. There were some guards and serving people who did not scowl at them as they passed as if they could think of nothing they'd rather do then attack them out of hand, tear them limb from limb. But those few gave her little comfort. In fact, they concerned her more, for while there might not have been open hostility in their eyes, there was *something* there, a sort of cunning thoughtfulness that she did not like as they marked her and the mage's progress, as if they were plotting behind their bland expressions.

She didn't need to ask Chall if he felt as tense as she, for she could practically feel the anxiety coming off the man in waves. It felt as if they walked through the heart of enemy territory instead of the castle of the kingdom they had spent their entire lives fighting to defend. Part of her thought that she was being silly, like a child waking from a nightmare only to see phantoms where there were none. The problem, though, was that she knew she wasn't.

Things were bad in the castle, worse, somehow, than they'd been only hours ago, as if the departure of the two princes had left the guards to abandon even the pretense of accommodating kindness they had shown thus far.

While Maeve was thinking on this, part of her mind—the part that had been honed over years practicing her craft—became aware of something or, more particularly, someone. A serving person who seemed to be wherever they went. A middle-aged woman with no features or clothing to distinguish her from any of the other serving people they passed and one who seemed to try to hide her face every time Maeve looked. It seemed impossible that the woman should so easily be able to match their route without being obvious, but after a moment realized that she must be making use of the servant's corridors that ran like veins through the castle.

The woman was good, blending into the surroundings and always managing to be turned the opposite direction when Maeve glanced, seemingly innocently, in her direction. But while she might have been good, Maeve had once been counted as the best assassin in the kingdom, and she didn't get that title by missing things. While the woman's appearance, her dull brown hair that seemed to be the province of every serving woman in the castle, and her clothes, might not have been contrived to avoid standing out, there were ways to be sure.

She made use of one such way now, reaching casually inside her tunic, surreptitiously to scratch an itch but, in actuality, she drew one of her blades from its sheath. Not much, just enough to expose the bared steel which she proceeded to use to prick her finger. A small cut, nothing dangerous certainly but enough to draw blood.

She continued walking, drawing the hand back out and curling the finger up so that the bloody nub would not be exposed. Then, when who she thought was the same woman showed up in their path once more, this time knelt on her hands and knees, scrubbing at the floor, Maeve pretended to slip. Not much of a slip but one that required her to reach out and catch herself on the woman's back with one hand.

"Oh, fire and salt, excuse me," Maeve said, "I tripped."

"My fault of course, mistress," the woman said, scurrying out of the way and never exposing her face as she did.

Maeve slowed no more than that, continuing on until they reached an intersection in the hallway then she turned right.

"Maeve," Chall said curiously, "are you sure we're going the right way? I thought you said—"

"Quiet," she hissed in a whisper, smiling at a guard patrolling the hallway who watched her with obvious dislike. "I think we're being followed."

"Followed?" he asked in a return whisper. "Are you sure?"

He started to turn and Maeve caught him by the arm, gripping him hard and leaning in to hiss in his ear. "I swear by the gods, Chall, that if you turn and look, I will stab you this very instant." The mage paled at that but nodded. "Now laugh," she hissed.

"What?"

"Laugh as if I said something funny," she whispered as they moved past two more guards standing at the entrance to a hallway, "do it now."

Chall finally seemed to get the idea and he leaned back, laughing as he walked. Maeve winced at the obvious fakeness of it. For an illusionist, the man was a damned terrible actor. Still, she thought it might be good enough to fool the guardsmen at least, and the serving woman too, if she was somewhere nearby.

"What do we do?" he asked once they were past the guards.

"Well, first you stop looking around like you expect an army to be hiding behind every door to rush out and hack us down when we pass."

"But...but they might, mightn't they?" he asked breathlessly.

"Maybe," she said, "but if they're waiting on us and have dedicated that much time to it then I don't see that seeing it coming will do us much good."

"Fine, I'll stop looking. Or I'll try anyway. I've got to be honest, Maeve, I've never been cut out for this sort of thing. I know I hide it well, but I'm pretty much terrified just now."

"You're not hiding it all that well, Chall."

He frowned. "You could have lied."

"Yes," she said as she led them down another castle hallway at random, "I could have."

She continued on until she saw who she thought was the woman again—it didn't take long. This time she wasn't in the hallway itself but standing in an open doorway, a duster in her hand as she set about—or at least *appeared* to set about—the task of dusting out the cobwebs in the door-jamb.

Her back was to them, as Maeve had known it would be, and so it was easy to spot the small drop of blood, tiny enough that it might go unnoticed by most, but not if you were looking for it, and Maeve was.

Maeve waited until they were past the woman then took a corner, glancing around to make sure they were out of sight of anyone before stopping. She counted slowly to three, giving it a moment, then nodded. All too aware that the timing had to be perfect, she hooked her arm in Chall's, and began moving back in the direction they'd come. "Follow my lead," she whispered.

"Sure," the mage mumbled, "why not? Seems I've been doing it all my li—"

"Quiet," Maeve hissed.

She slowed down then, as if they were out for no more than a leisurely stroll, and she glanced at the guards a short distance ahead out of the corner of her eye. Now was the time. "Challadius," she said, loudly enough that the guards could hear as she turned to look at the mage, "there was something I wanted to speak to you about. Something I've wanted to speak to you about for a long time actually."

The mage winced at how loud she was speaking. "Whatever it is, Mae, can't it wait?" he asked in a hushed whisper. "This doesn't seem like the best time."

They drew in front of the guards then, and she stopped, turning and putting her hands on either of the mage's arms. "It has waited, Chall," she said, softly but not so softly that the guards could not hear. "For fifteen years and more it has waited, *I* have waited, and I will wait no longer."

The mage seemed to pale at that, though whether it was the fact that they had drawn the attention of both guards as well as a castle servant, a man who was currently cleaning one of the paintings hung on the wall, or from her words, there was no knowing.

"A-are you sure?" he said. "I mean, maybe there's a better time to—"

"No, Chall," she said. "There *is* no better time. We always think we have all the time in the world, always think that we might do the thing we want to do, the thing we *need* to do, tomorrow, but that's the thing about tomorrow's, isn't it? They're never promised. *This* is the time, Chall. The only time."

She focused on her words, on making eye contact with him, on loving him. It was not hard. Not hard at all. "I love you, Chall," she said softly but, again, loud enough that the guards, only feet away now, might overhear. "I think that, perhaps, I have always loved you."

The mage froze, his face paling, his mouth opening and closing. "Maeve," he said finally, his voice a dry croak, "I don't know, I mean, what to say—"

"You don't have to *say* anything," she interrupted, pulling him closer, running her hand through his hair. "I love you, Chall. And I *want* you. Oh yes," she said at his shocked expression, "I am not so old that I do not still want, do not still *feel*. And what I feel, what I *want*, Chall, is you."

He stared at her, dumbfounded, and Maeve hoped, prayed, that he would catch on, that he would say the right thing. And as she waited for the flustered mage to manage some words, she realized that the anxiety that she felt, anxiety she didn't remember feeling since her husband, many years ago, had first began courting her, wasn't only due to the plan she had in mind.

"Maeve," he said, licking his lips nervously, his face as pale as if he faced some great army. "I...I love you too. I...I *want* you too."

"Do you?" she asked breathless, telling herself that it was only the acting which made her heart begin to hammer in her chest. Telling herself that but not really believing it. "Then take me." She held her arms out to either side, and the mage blinked.

"Um...take you?" he asked, glancing around the hallway. "That is...here?"

She laughed then, and even she could not tell whether that breathless laughter was part of the act or a thing all its own. "We're in a *castle*, Chall. I think we might find somewhere more...more *appropriate*, don't you?"

He cleared his throat. "You mean...like...like an empty store room, maybe, or—"

"Or a *bedroom*," she said. "Come—I have waited long enough. I will wait no longer." Then she hooked his arm in hers again and began leading him down the hall, backtracking down the path they had taken. They walked past the guards, her practically dragging the dumbfounded mage behind her. Maeve noted the guards watching them just as she noted that the castle servant had left off his task and was now staring, wide-eyed at them. She felt her face flush with heat, but she pressed on, turning a corner.

She could not hope to know the servant's corridors as well as the woman following them. After all, there was no telling how many months, how many years the woman had worked at the castle, using them every day, but she thought maybe that was okay. After all, she might not know all the secret corridors used by the servants, but those corridors were not the only secrets the castle held.

She continued on, pulling the mage beside her, trying to remember the location of the room she searched for. The problem, of course, was that she had not seen it for over fifteen years and even then only the once. Twice she thought she'd found it only to open the door and be disappointed.

"Maeve," Chall said after she hissed in frustration closing the door to the second bedroom. "Maybe if you told me what we were looking for, I'd be able to—"

"A room, of course," Maeve said, doing her best to hide her frustration as she backtracked. She knew that the room was somewhere on this side of the castle, knew that, given time enough, she would be able to find it. The problem, though, was that they didn't *have* time. Any minute now, the woman following them would realize her mistake and would no doubt return to the guards to ask where she had gone.

Then it was only a matter of time before the woman found her way into their path again which was good—perfect, in fact, since Maeve *wanted* to be found, but needed to be found at the right *time.*

"I don't mean to quibble, Mae," Chall panted as he followed in her hurried footsteps, "but those last two looked a lot like bedrooms to me, and—"

"Not just *any* room," she snapped, "a particular one."

"Like…like a special room?"

"Exactly," she said.

She was just beginning to despair that she would ever find it when suddenly she caught sight of another door and hurried to it. "This is it," she said, staring at the door, a grin spreading on her face.

"It is?" Chall asked, curiously. "Very well, I'll—" She slapped his hand that had been reaching for the door handle.

"Not yet," she said.

"Ow," he said. "Not…not yet? What do you—"

"Just wait," Maeve said, turning to him. "Put your arms around me."

He blinked. "Um…yes, ma'am," he said, then did as she requested.

They stood there for several seconds, Maeve looking at him, but not *really* looking at him. Instead, she was waiting, listening.

"So..." he began uncertainly, "do um...should I kiss you or—"

"Not yet."

"Ah. Right."

As they waited, standing in each other's arms, Maeve thought of how many chances she was taking. She thought this was the room, but then it *had* been fifteen years. What if she were wrong? Worse, what if the serving girl didn't manage to find them soon? Each moment they spent here was one where Petran was left alone with the guardsman, and if the conspirators were checking each castle room—something she was confident they would do, for they would know the importance of silencing the guardsman—then it was only a matter of time before they found them.

"Maeve, this is a bit strange, isn't it?" he asked. "Just standing here, I mean—"

"Do you trust me, Chall?" she asked.

"Of course," he responded, and she was surprised by how gratified she was at his fast response.

"Good," she said, and she did not have to fake the smile that came to her face. "Then wait."

No sooner had she gotten the words out than she heard the soft, almost imperceptible sounds of footsteps from somewhere down the hall, coming from the direction they had traveled moments ago.

She waited until she judged that the woman—if indeed it *was* the woman—would be coming down the hall, then she met Chall's eyes. "Kiss me."

He blinked. "Here? Weren't we going to go in the room or—"

"Kiss me, damn you," she hissed, and he did.

It was a good kiss, better than she had expected, likely due to all the practice the man'd had, and for a brief moment Maeve forgot what she was doing. Forgot everything except the kiss, except the feel of him against her. Chall. A pain in her ass, yes, but a man who she knew was honest and, though he tried to hide it, kind. A man who worried more than he let on and one who would do anything for anyone—even if he did bitch the entire time.

She felt a wild storm of emotions rise in her, a mixture of nervousness and excitement, and, for a moment, she was no longer an old woman with her best years behind her. Neither was she Maeve the Marvelous, the feared assassin, beautiful and terrible all at once. Instead, the kiss transported her to another time, another *her*, one who was only just a woman grown, and the excitement she felt, in that moment, was the excitement that young woman had felt when she had first kissed the man who would become her husband.

Snap out of it, damn you, the old part of her scolded the young woman. *You can kiss later—assuming you're alive. Damned harder to do as a corpse.*

She forced her eyes open then and caught sight of the serving woman at the end of the hall. The woman's back was to them as she wiped at an imperceptible spot on the wall, but Maeve knew that she was marking each movement, each word. "Come on," she said, pushing the door open. "Show me what I've been missing all these years."

Then, still embracing, the two of them stumbled inside. She closed the door shut with her foot then paused a moment to lock it. Once that was done, she pulled away, moving to the other side of the room. "We'll have to be quick," she said over her shoulder as she scanned the room, wracking her memory. "Get ready."

"Alright," the mage agreed from behind her.

The room, like many of the castle rooms made for visiting guests, was well-appointed, with a silk coverlet on the bed, a divan in one corner, a desk in the other and a fireplace. Her eyes caught on the fireplace and Maeve grinned as she turned back to Chall. "It's here, it—" She paused, her eyes going wide as her face heated. "What are you doing?"

The mage finished pulling off the second leg of his trousers, stumbling as he did and hissing a curse, just managing to catch himself on the door to avoid falling. "Y-you said get ready," he said, left holding his shirt in one hand and his trousers in the other.

"Not *that* kind of ready," she snapped. "Now hurry up and get your clothes back on."

"This is all very strange," he said, frowning, but he began to dress again.

Maeve watched him, unable to keep herself from it. He was overweight, sure, the gods knew the man could do with some exercise, but she wasn't exactly a prize herself, and there was something thrilling about seeing him naked.

He frowned. "Ought to charge you for that," he said once he was finished dressing. She grinned. "Not much, surely?" Then she told herself to focus, turning back to the fireplace and feeling around the bricks with her hands.

"Maeve, I have to ask, what in the name of the gods are you doing?"

"Looking for the switch."

"The...switch?"

She let out an exasperated sigh, turning back to the man. "Bernard brought me here to this room, years ago. You see, Bernard was not always as...*reserved* of a man as he is now—" she paused as Chall snorted—"and this room has a, well, a sort of secret passage to what were once his own chambers."

Chall frowned. "Why would he have a secret passage from this room to his chambers? Unless—" He grinned. "Ah, I see."

"Right," Maeve said. "We just have to find the right brick, and the fireplace slides away, revealing the passage." She frowned. "Assuming I've got the right room."

"Wait a minute," Chall said, "you mean to tell me you don't even know if we're in the right *room?*"

"It was more than fifteen years ago, alright?" she snapped. "I wasn't exactly taking notes, so just help me look, damn you!"

"Alright, alright," Chall said, moving to the other side of the fireplace and feeling around at the bricks.

Maeve went about her task then, after a moment, the mage paused, glancing at her. "Wait a minute, Maeve. You said that Cutter used this room for his liaisons, correct?"

"That's right," she said distractedly, running her hands along the bricks, searching for some imperfection.

"And...and you said he took *you* here...right?"

Maeve frowned at that, turning to look at the man. "Is this really the time for this conversation, Chall? In case you've forgotten, the kingdom's nearly overrun with Fey and those working with them. We're being followed in the castle, and poor Petran is watching over Nigel by himself, the man who is our best—perhaps our *only*—chance at figuring out what's happening and stopping it before it's too late."

"Right, no, I get all that," the mage said, fidgeting. "I just meant...I mean, why did the prince show you this room? That is, unless—"

"Is that what you think of me then, Chall?" she demanded. "Just some...some *whore* out to bed a prince?"

Chall winced. "I mean, no, but...well, he was sort of known for that kind of thing back then and—"

"You're one to talk!" she snapped. "How many farmer's daughters, Chall? How many farmer's *wives?* Or are you even able to count that high?"

"Hey, I can count," he said defensively.

Maeve let out an angry hiss. "Just look for the damned switch." A moment later, she felt it, a slight give to one of the bricks. She grinned, pressing it, and Chall let out a satisfying squawk of surprise, stumbling backward as the entire fireplace began to shift almost soundlessly to the side.

"It's...really quiet," the mage said.

"Yeah, well," Maeve said, "I think that was sort of the point. Now, come on—if we hurry maybe we can reach Petran before they do."

The mage didn't bother asking who "they" were, as there was really no need. "Oh, one more thing," Maeve said. She moved to the bed, pushing on the headboard a few times to make it strike the wall then let out a moan. She gave a nod. "That ought to do it." She turned back to see Chall watching her. "What?"

"N-nothing," he said. "Just...um...are we ready?"

She rolled her eyes. "Men. It's like you only think about the one thing. It's a wonder anything gets done and you all don't just spend your days lying around in bed with one woman or the other."

Chall cleared his throat. "Well, I mean, if given a choice—"

"Come on," Maeve interrupted, and then stepped into the tunnel. There were no torches on the walls here, for even the servants were not privy to this tunnel—it would have largely defeated the purpose if they had been—and so the tunnel itself was nearly pitch black. When Maeve hit the switch on the wall which made the fireplace slide back into place, there was no light at all.

"Stones and starlight but it's dark," Chall said.

Maeve thought that was probably just as well, for she was thinking about Chall again, about the kiss, about him naked, and the bed which had looked so damned inviting, and she knew that she was blushing. "This way," she said, starting forward, her hands out before her like a blind woman which, just then, she might as well have been.

"*Which* way?" Chall said, his voice sounding slightly breathless and afraid in the dark. "I don't know if you know this or not, Maeve, but it's as black as a tomb in here."

"Sure, but with less corpses, one hopes," she countered. "Here, just give me your hand."

She heard some fumbling and, in a moment, the mage's hand interlocked with hers. It felt natural there, right, but Maeve forced herself to keep her mind on the task at hand, inching forward through the darkness, one hand out in front while the mage latched onto the other with a death grip.

She heard water dripping somewhere, and the only other sound was the ragged breaths of the mage. "What's the matter, Chall?" she asked, "you scared of the dark?" But the truth was that she was not so comfortable with it herself. There was darkness, like that of the night where the only light came from a pale moon, and then there was that through which they now walked, a darkness as different from the other as day was from it, for here there was not even the faintest trace of light to silhouette the walls and tunnel around her. It was a pervasive, all-encompassing darkness, and after only a few minutes traveling she regretted her quip about the corpses. It had seemed funny at the time, but it did not now—she doubted anything would have.

Men thought themselves civilized, thought themselves *progressed,* but as she and the mage made their slow, shuffling way through that darkness, she thought that it was no more than a sham. Only take away the lights, the torches and lanterns, and they were but beasts, hissing and snarling at any sound they couldn't immediately identify.

"Gods, how long is this damned tunnel?" Chall moaned from behind her, and this time Maeve did not make a joke.

"Too long," she said, and that, at least, was the truth. She was glad, though, that Chall was with her, for she thought that walking these corridors alone would have driven her mad.

Gritting her teeth, she forced her way onward, then paused as she felt a slight stirring of air in the suffocating tunnels. She frowned, feeling around her only to realize that the walls were gone. "Shit," she said.

"What?" Chall asked in a panicked voice. "What is it? Rats? Fire and salt, Maeve, if I feel a rat I think I'll go ma—"

"It's not a rat," she said quickly. "We're at an intersection."

"Well. Which way do we go?"

"How in the shit should I know?" she snapped.

"You're the one that came down here!" Chall said. "You and the prince. Or did you not get past the damned bed to—"

"I never went into the tunnels," she snapped back. "Now shut up for a minute, let me think."

"Too busy being in the bed," he muttered, but Maeve ignored him. Let the mage think what he would—if they made it out of here, she would correct him. Likely with her fists. For now, though, there were more important things to worry about. She forced herself to even her breathing, bringing up a mental map of the castle. She hadn't been here in a long time, save the last week, but there had been a time when she'd walked the corridors nearly every day.

Finally, she nodded. "This way," she said, turning down the right-branching path.

"Are you sure?"

"Sure, I'm sure," she said. *Or at least as sure as I'm going to be.* If she was right, the path would bring them closer to the room where the historian and the guardsman sheltered. If she was wrong...well. Better not to think of it, not with the darkness so close, seeming to press in all around her.

She didn't know how long they spent in those tunnels, in that darkness, for there was no way to mark time save the slowly rising fear—not panic, not yet, but getting closer to it—that grew in her as they walked. *Ridiculous,* she scolded herself, *the Known Land's most famous assassin scared of a little darkness.* But then, that was the problem, wasn't it? It wasn't a *little* darkness. It was *all* darkness, everything, everywhere, nothing but darkness.

Her outstretched fingers brushed against something cold and slimy and she let out a hiss of surprised fear.

"What?" Chall moaned, his grip on her hand tightening further until it felt as if the bones were being ground into dust. "It's rats, isn't it? I knew it—gods be good, Maeve, I can't—"

"It's not rats!" she said, her fear making the words angrier than she'd intended. "Just...just hold on a minute," she said, softer this time.

She reached out again, tentatively, sure that she had touched a snake or wet rat or...*or maybe a corpse.* Holding her breath, she extended her arm further and then there it was again. Not a rat or a snake at all, and, thank the gods, not a corpse. No, it was only a wall, and that cold wetness she had felt was no more than moss which had grown on its untended surface.

"What is it?" the mage whimpered.

"A...a door, I think," she said. "Feel around for a latch. There's got to be one somewhere."

"O-okay," Chall said, and Maeve thought he sounded a little better than he had, no doubt thrilled at the prospect—as she was—of getting out of the damned tunnel.

"Hey, I found something," Chall said a moment later.

"Well, hit it for the gods' sake!" she snapped, struggling to keep her rising fear under control.

The mage did and suddenly there was a rumbling, grinding sound as the wall in front of them slid away. Light, blessed, wonderful light pushed the darkness away. Still holding hands, the two of them stumbled forward, into that warm glow, something that would have been considerably more gratifying had Chall not tripped—and the next thing Maeve knew, he was falling and, more distressing, taking her with him.

They struck the ground, rolling, and by the time they finished Maeve was lying on top of the mage who was blinking up at her, his face pale and waxy looking in the light of a lantern.

"Hi," he said.

She grinned. "Hi yourself." She climbed up, glancing around, and saw that they were in a store room and that what the mage had tripped over had been a bag of flour. A bag which had ripped and went a long way to explaining why they were both covered in white dust. Sighing, she offered him her hand.

He took it, and after a few seconds of hissing, grunted curses, they managed to get him to his feet. "Well," Chall said, making a show of ineffectually dusting himself off. "Where are we?"

"Who cares?" Maeve said. "Just so long as we're out of those tunnels. Still, if I'm remembering right, we ought to be somewhere close to Petran's room."

"And if you're remembering wrong?"

She shrugged. "Then at least we're out of the tunnels." She stepped over the spilled bag of flour, moving toward the door at the other end of the room.

"Maeve?"

She turned back to him. "Yes?"

"What if...I mean, *if* you're wrong, and they find us..."

She shrugged again. "Then I think Petran and the guardsman will have to worry about themselves. Still, we can't hang around here all day, and I don't much fancy going back in those tunnels. Do you?"

The mage shot a quick look back at the tunnel entrance as if he expected some great hand to reach out to pull them back in. "Gods no," he said quickly, shuffling toward her, "better the headsman's axe than that."

"Careful what you wish for," Maeve muttered, then she swung the door open. She eased out of it, glancing in both directions, the hand not gripping the door's handle ready to go for one of her knives at the least provocation, but she was grateful to see that the hallway was empty. Grateful even further when she realized that she recognized it.

She turned back to the mage and grinned. "Petran's close—this way."

They hurried down the castle halls, seeing no one, and minutes later they were standing outside of Petran's door. Maeve knocked softly.

"Wh-who is it?" came a voice from the other side, managing to sound both weary and terrified at once.

"It's me, Petran." Maeve hissed. "As a general rule, assassins don't tend to knock. Now, let us in, will you?"

"Oh, thank the gods," she heard the historian say from inside the room and moments later the door was swinging open. The man stared at their flour-covered figures, his eyes wide. "What happened to the two of you?"

Maeve shared a look with Chall then shook her head. "Later, if there's time." She pushed her way inside, closing and locking the door.

Inside the room, she looked at the guardsman on the bed, still unconscious. Maeve frowned. "How is he?"

"Oh, he's better," Petran said, giving her a smile that looked more than a little forced before raising a trembling hand which held a glass of wine and taking a long drink. "H-he woke an hour or two ago. I told him where he was, all that had happened, and...well, he promptly fell back to sleep."

Maeve frowned, looking at the man. "He needs a healer."

The historian winced, nodding. "I considered that but...after our last conversation, I was afraid to tell anyone where we were. Lady Maeve did...did I do wrong?"

"No, Petran," she said, "you were right to be cautious. Things are bad—worse than I would have thought."

The historian let out a heavy sigh at that, nodding. "Well...that, that's good. About me being right, not the things being bad, I mean...I must be honest with you, Lady Maeve, Challadius, I am not cut out for this heroing business, not at all."

Maeve snorted. "None of us are. Still, we do what we have to, and you did good."

The man smiled gratefully then walked to the table and began to refill his glass out of the decanter he'd used before, the contents of which, Maeve saw, were significantly diminished since the last time she'd been here.

"S-so, what do we do now?" Petran asked as he shakily poured the drink.

"We have to get out of here, as quick as we can," Maeve said.

"This room?" the historian asked, wincing as he glanced at the desk, heavily-laden with papers. "I suppose, if you think it best, though the transporting of my papers might be—"

"Not this room," Maeve interrupted, "the castle itself."

"Ah," the man said. "Is...do you think it's really necessary?"

"No," Chall said before Maeve could respond, "not necessary. Not so long, at least, as you don't mind writing your next entry on executions." He shrugged. "You'll have some firsthand experience, after all, though I can't say I know whether or not they have parchment and ink in the afterlife."

The historian blinked, his face going pale, and Maeve shot the mage an angry look. The man was already frightened, and there was no reason to make it worse. "Is...is it really so bad as that?" the historian asked in a shaky voice.

"I'm afraid so," Maeve said, still scowling at Chall who pointedly avoided her gaze. "The guards—and assassins too, no doubt—are scouring the castle searching for our unconscious friend. Maybe they just want to have a talk with him but somehow I doubt it, and I think it best if we're not around to find out. Now, pack your things, quick as you can, we need to—"

"Hello?"

Maeve started at the unexpected, rasping voice, and they all turned to see that Guardsman Nigel had sat up in his bed and was staring around the room confused. And if anyone had a right to be confused, Maeve supposed it was him. After all, it wasn't everyday that a person was poisoned and then woke up in a room they never remembered entering.

"You're awake," she said.

The man nodded. "I suppose so, Lady Maeve."

"How do you feel?" she asked, hurrying to his bedside.

He gave her a small grin. "Well, I won't lie to you, lady—I've felt better."

Chall snorted. "Just be thankful you're alive to bitch about it. Not every day a man gets poisoned and survives."

The guardsman blinked. "Poisoned?"

"We'll tell you about it later," Maeve said. "Can you stand?"

She watched as the guardsman strained, working his way to his feet. She stood ready to catch him should she need it but, in the end, he managed it on his own, though he had to use the wall and bed for support more than she would have liked. "It...it seems so," he panted.

"Good," Maeve said. "If you can stand, you can walk. We've already wasted too much time—we need to get out of here. Now."

"Oh, it's too late for that, I'm afraid," a new voice said. "Much too late."

Maeve spun, drawing two knives from inside her tunic as she did, and saw that the newcomer was none other than the serving woman who had been following them. Not that she looked much like a meek serving woman now. She wore the same servants' whites as she had, but her entire demeanor had changed. Gone was the nervous, scraping servant they had seen in the hallways.

The woman stood in the open doorway, leaning on the frame with one shoulder, her ankles crossed as if she didn't have a care in the world. Maeve noted, too, that she had drawn no weapons.

"You," Maeve said, unable to keep the shock from her voice.

The woman inclined her head. "Me."

"What do you want?"

The woman gave a small shrug of her shoulders, smiling. "Well, to kill you all of course. So how about you make my job easier and put those knives down. I promise to make it quick."

Maeve frowned, her anger eclipsing her surprise. "How did you find us?"

The woman sighed, rolling her eyes. "Come now, *Maeve the Marvelous,* I'm no fool—I know well enough when I've been marked. Anyway, I did enjoy your show in the hallway—quite nice. "But that's the thing about men—when they think they're going to get laid, they rarely pay attention to anything else. Certainly, they don't look around them like they're on their way to their execution...which of course, you were, but then you didn't *know* that, did you?"

Maeve winced.

"Gods, Mae, I'm sorry," Chall said.

"It's not your fault, Chall," she said, not daring to take her eyes off the woman.

"That's true," the woman said. "I would have found you anyway. Still, I did quite enjoy watching you fumbling around."

"Who are you?" Maeve asked.

The woman shrugged. "Does it matter? Very well, as you're about to die, I will tell you—my name is Felara Alderich, and I am the best assassin of the age."

"Huh," Chall said, doing his best to sound confident, but Maeve could hear the undercurrent of fear in his voice, "never heard of you."

"Perhaps not, fat man," the woman said, her eyes traveling to him for a moment before coming back to Maeve. "But that changes nothing. It's no easy thing for an assassin to make her name. Still, I think single-handedly dispatching the famous Lady Maeve as well as the renowned Challadius the Charmer might go some way to rectifying that."

"Single-handedly," Maeve repeated. "You mean you came alone?"

"Of course," the woman said.

"A mistake," Maeve said. "There are four of us and only one of you."

The woman grinned. "You are correct that someone is mistaken, dear Maeve, but it isn't me."

Maeve should have felt confident. After all, the woman was alone. But there was something about the way she stood so casually in the doorway, smiling as if she didn't have a worry in the world, that gave her pause. "Others have tried and failed," she said, forcing a confidence into her tone that she did not feel.

The assassin sneered. "You mean those fumbling idiots? I am as far above them as...well...as I am above you. Now, enough talk." She stood then, drawing two knives of her own and stepped further into the room, away from the doorway.

Maeve glanced at the door, no longer barred by the woman, and Felara gave a soft laugh. "Oh yes, Lady Maeve. Escape, safety, lies just there. You need only deal with me, and you and your companions can flee the castle, none the wiser."

"Maeve," Chall said softly, and she saw that the mage had edged his way closer to her, "I've got a bad feeling about this. Maybe if we—"

"Relax, Chall," she said quietly and with far more confidence than she felt. "She's alone. As soon as it starts, you get Petran and Nigel out of here, understand?"

The mage blinked. "But...what about you?"

"I'll be along directly," Maeve said, still eyeing the woman who was waiting patiently as if she already knew the outcome of the approaching fight and was in no particular rush.

"But it's not necessary, Mae," he said, "I could use an illusion to—"

"No," Maeve said. "There's still a lot of ground to cover getting out of the castle. You need to save your strength to get Nigel and Petran to safety."

"But, Mae, I don't like this," he said.

Neither do I, she thought, but she turned to him. "Be ready."

Then she stepped away from the mage, walking the short distance across the room to stand a few feet in front of the assassin.

The woman smiled. "Done saying your goodbyes?"

Maeve glanced behind her at the others, still watching her, then motioned angrily toward the door before turning back to the woman. She said nothing. The time for talking was past. Instead, she only waited, flexing the stiff fingers gripping the handles of her knives and inwardly cursing old age which did not feel it sufficient to steal a woman's beauty but thought to steal her grace and dexterity as well. Despite her assurances to Chall, she did not like her odds. The woman was confident, yes, that was part of it, but not all.

Maeve had seen a lot of killers in her time, and there was something in the way the woman stood, in her eyes, that told her that the woman before her was an experienced one. She could only hope that she might buy the others enough time to at least escape. Of course, the problem was that, when it came to duels between assassins, they were a far cry from duels between warriors. No heavy armor to blunt the blows and slow the action, not here. Here, a single, quick thrust or slash would finish it.

You don't have to win, she told herself, *you only have to not die too quickly.*

Not exactly a comforting thought, and she tried again. *You are Maeve the Marvelous, the greatest assassin in the Known Lands, feared by all. Parents once used your name to scare their children into behaving. You are not nothing.*

"Ready?" the woman asked, her eyes flashing in anticipation.

Maeve chose not to respond, at least not with words, for a lifetime of painful, bloody experience had taught her that it was often the person who struck first who struck last. She lunged forward, calling on every ounce of strength and speed she possessed, aiming one of her daggers directly for the woman's heart in a blow so swift that it was impossible to dodge.

Only, the woman did. She sidestepped the strike and swiped out with one of her knives in an almost casual gesture. Maeve hissed as she felt a line of pain trace down one side of her face, and her lunge became a stumble. She nearly struck the wall before regaining her balance and turning to eye the woman.

Felara was smiling again, though the truth was Maeve wasn't sure the expression had ever left her face. "Oh my," the woman said, "it seems that I have spoiled the looks of Maeve the Marvelous." She shrugged. "At least what old age and infirmity have left of them, at least."

Maeve brought the back of her hand to her face, checking it. A shallow cut, one that didn't bear thinking upon save for the sharp pain it brought. A distraction, no more than that. She circled to the side, away from the door, hoping to at least open up an avenue through which the others might make their escape.

The woman's smile widened as if she knew exactly what Maeve intended. "Are you ready for another go?" she asked.

Maeve wasn't, would have chosen a nap instead or a nice hot bath, if she'd been given an option, but as so often was the case in a person's life, being ready really had nothing to do with it. Growling, she moved forward again, not lunging this time, but coming at the woman in a flurry of steel, her two knives dancing in her hands as they came at her from every angle.

Yet despite her efforts, the woman moved like the wind, swaying and ducking around her blows with seeming ease, not countering but only enduring the assault without receiving so much as a bloody nick for Maeve's efforts.

Maeve's breath was rasping in her lungs but finally the woman *did* counter, her hand flashing out almost too fast to follow, like a serpent's strike. Before Maeve had even fully realized that the blow had landed, she felt a line of white-hot pain up her arm, and she cried out, stumbling away.

The assassin didn't pursue, choosing instead to stand and watch as Maeve hissed in pain, panted in weariness. This cut was also shallow, though not so shallow as the first, and blood leaked down Maeve's arm, staining her tunic sleeve crimson. But that was not the worst of it. The worst was that her left arm, where the woman had struck, felt numb, so numb that she had to glance down to see that she had dropped one of her knives.

"Uh oh," the assassin said. "Are you quite alright, Lady Maeve?"

"*Fine,*" Maeve growled.

The woman shook her head, a disapproving look on her face. "Honestly, I must say that I'm disappointed. I expected quite a bit more from the world's most feared assassin." She sighed again. "Oh well. You'll forgive me if I wrap things up—other things to do, other people to kill, I'm sure you understand."

The woman flowed forward like water, her blades flashing, and Maeve knew that she was outmatched. The woman would have likely been able to take her even at her best, and she was far from her best. She couldn't remember the last time she'd gotten any real sleep, and her muscles felt sluggish, awkward. Still, left with no other option, she held her lone blade in front of her and watched the woman come.

"*Maeve!*" a shout came, and before she managed to turn to look, a figure charged at the woman's side.

The figure resolved itself into Challadius, but before the man's tackle struck her, the assassin stepped away, spinning and lashing out with one foot that struck the mage in the face.

He cried out in pain and careened into the desk on which the historian's neatly-stacked papers sat, sending them and the desk itself flying.

Felara hissed in disgust and anger and moved toward the fallen mage who lay on his back, groaning and blinking at the sky.

Maeve thought she had been scared before but watching the woman moving toward Chall, her bloody blades bared, sent a terror greater than she had ever experienced racing through her. "*Leave him alone!*" she screamed, starting forward, but the woman was already standing above the mage, and she knew that she would be too late.

"I'm...sorry, Mae," the mage said, then the woman grinned and time seemed to slow as she brought her blade down into the mage's stomach.

Chall screamed, and Maeve screamed with him, charging into the woman who managed to draw her blade again, fending off Maeve's slash.

Maeve growled in fury. She had only one knife now to the assassin's two blades, but she didn't let that deter her as she came on, switching grips in her hand from one moment to the next, coming at her from all angles. The smile did leave the woman's face then, as she frantically dodged and parried the blows, forced back toward the room's window.

Maeve began to think that she might take her after all, when suddenly the woman growled and ducked, spinning. The next thing Maeve knew, she was lying on her back much as Chall had, staring up at the ceiling with little to no idea of how she'd got there.

"Better," the woman said from above her, and Maeve was gratified to see that now, at least, she did seem to be breathing heavier. "But not good enough." She raised her blade, but before she could bring it down there was a shout and Maeve and the woman both looked to see the guardsman, Nigel, charging the assassin, brandishing a chair.

The man attacked ferociously, shouting as he did, but it was obvious that his ordeal had stolen much of his strength. The woman dodged the ungainly blows easily until she finally planted a boot in his stomach, sending the guardsman, and his makeshift weapon flying backward to strike the bed.

In the brief moments that Nigel and the woman fought, Maeve had taken advantage of the assassin's distraction, starting to her feet, but she had only managed to make it to her knees before the woman turned, placing her blade at her throat.

Her chest rose and fell with her labored breaths, but the assassin still managed a smile. "And so ends the life of Maeve the Marve—" But before she could finish a figure appeared behind her, bringing something down on the woman's head with a loud *crack*, and the assassin let out a grunt, collapsing to the ground in front of Maeve.

Maeve looked up to see Petran standing above her, his face as pale as parchment, his eyes wide with terror. The man held the decanter—or at least the remnants of it—which went a long way toward explaining the powerful smell of alcohol and the shattered glass strewn on Maeve and the floor.

"Petran?" she said, surprised.

The historian winced as if he were a child caught acting out. "Sorry," he said. "I was taught never to strike a woman but...well, she isn't a very *nice* woman, is she?"

Maeve grunted, looking at the unconscious form. "No, no, she's not. Now, help me to my feet." The man did and a moment later, Maeve was standing on wobbly legs, her face and arm where the woman's blades had scored her aching, but the worst pain was in the back of her head that had struck the floorboards when she fell. She meant to finish it then, to make sure that the woman would no longer be a threat, but Chall moaned in pain. "Shit," she rasped.

She started to turn to Chall but hesitated, kicking the assassin's blades away first. Then she hurried to the mage who lay on the floor gasping and groaning in obvious pain. Maeve fell to her knees beside him, trying not to pay too close attention to the blood staining his shirt where the woman's blade had stabbed him. "Oh gods, Chall. How bad is it?"

"Not...good," the mage hissed through clenched teeth. "That's for sure."

There was a breathy, bubbly rasp to his voice that Maeve did not like, and she lifted his shirt, examining the wound.

"Always dreamt...about...you undressing me," Chall rasped. "Though...it was never...quite like...this."

"Don't talk, Chall," Maeve said, struggling to keep her rising panic down as she tore a piece of her tunic and used the fabric to wipe the blood away. At least most of it—it was still coming. She turned toward the bed. "Nigel!"

The guardsman had only just managed to right himself, and he turned to her. "The sheets," she said, "tear them into a long strip—we need to bandage the wound. Now."

The guardsman nodded grimly, going about the task, and while Maeve knew he was moving as quickly as she could, knelt with her hands pressed to the wound, applying what pressure she could, she felt a rising panic.

"Maeve..." Chall said, "listen...if I'm to die, then...there's something...you should know."

"No, Chall," she said, his face blurring as tears gathered in her eyes, and she gave her head an angry shake. "No, you're not going to die. You're too much of an asshole for that. Now, stop milking it and—"

"Maeve," he said softly, so softly she could barely hear, and while a louder voice might not have made her stop, that one, so weak and frail, did. He gave her a small smile. "In case...well. I just want to tell you...I love you. Really."

The tears came then. "I love you too, Chall."

He grinned, opening his mouth to speak but the words, whatever they had been, turned into a cough, and when he was finished Maeve saw blood on his mouth. "Not...acting...this time?" he rasped, a small, bloody smile on his face.

Maeve forced herself to smile back. "Not acting," she said.

"Well," he said, closing his eyes. "Well, that's fine then."

"Stay with me, Chall," she said desperately. "*Where are the damned bandages?*" she shouted, only to turn and see that Nigel had just walked up and was offering them to her.

Maeve took them, grunting and hissing and crying as she levered the mage up so that she could wrap the long fabric around him. Chall said nothing as she worked at least, that was, until she gave the makeshift bandage a hard yank, and he groaned.

"Lady Maeve—"

"Not now, Petran," she said, working to tie the bandage.

"But, lady, I think—"

"*What?*" she snapped. "What is it?"

"I hear footsteps," he said from the doorway. "And shouts. I think...I think the guards are coming."

"*Shit,*" Maeve hissed, her mind racing as she finished tying off the bandage. The assassin might not have managed to kill them all—a close thing—but if they were still there when the guards arrived, at best, they could be expected to be put in the dungeons. At worst, they'd all find their necks perched on a headsman's block before the day was through. Assuming the men could even be bothered and didn't just cut them down here.

She wanted to stay with Chall who seemed to have fallen unconscious, to offer what comfort she could, but she knew that if they didn't get out of here, now, they were all dead. So she rose. "You two, get him to his feet," she growled.

"And you, Lady Maeve?"

"I mean to make sure this bitch doesn't bother us anymo—" She cut off as she turned to where the woman had fallen only to see that she was now standing, her hands, at least, empty of any knife. The woman wobbled uncertainly as blood leaked down her face.

"We're not finished yet," she hissed.

"You're damned right we're not," Maeve said, drawing a blade and starting toward her, but instead of responding in kind, the woman moved to the window, swinging it open and climbing into the ledge before turning back to Maeve with a smile. "Another time, Lady Maeve."

Maeve gave a shout, charging toward her, but before she could reach her the woman did something almost incomprehensible to Maeve's mind—she stepped out into the thin air and dropped.

Maeve charged toward the window, leaning out, and looking down to see that the woman had caught herself on another window outcropping a short distance below. The assassin grinned as she levered herself up. Maeve cursed, wanting, *needing* to follow her, but she knew that to try to track down the assassin would only mean her death—likely *all* of their deaths.

"She...she jumped," Petran said. "Is she...?"

"Escaped," Maeve hissed, and she turned to see that the two men had managed to lever the unconscious mage to his feet, each of them standing with one of his arms draped over their shoulders, huddled beneath the weight.

"Come on," she said, leading them into the hall. She glanced down either side, expecting to see an army of guardsmen approaching, but so far none presented itself. Which wasn't as much of a comfort as it might have been for Petran was right—she could hear them approaching. Any moment, they would round the corner and see her and the others, and with the burden of the unconscious mage, not to mention their collective exhaustion, there was no way they would be able to escape them.

"What do you want to do, lady?" the guardsman asked, grunting with the effort of holding up the mage.

Maeve shook her head angrily. "We'll just have to hurry, hope we don't run into any of them in the hallways. Now, come o—"

"Or we could take the servant's corridors," Petran offered.

"What?" Maeve asked, spinning on him so quickly that the man recoiled, nearly dropping the unconscious mage.

"Th-the servant's tunnels," the historian stammered. "I thought…if we wanted to avoid the guards, perhaps—"

"You know the tunnels?"

The historian's chest puffed out slightly at that, and he raised his nose in the air. "Why, of course, as Historian to the Crown it is my duty to know such—"

"*Show me,*" Maeve snapped, and the man did, glancing around the halls then leading them to one statuette which, with a pull of the arm, made a panel in the wall slide aside and then they were stepping through. No sooner had the hidden door closed behind them then Maeve heard the sound of marching, booted feet, pass through the hallway where they'd been standing moments before.

They all stood still—except for Chall who hung unconscious—barely daring even to so much as breathe lest the guards hear them. Maeve stood with her finger held to her lips in the dimly lit tunnels, staring at the others, until the guards' footsteps faded into the distance. She waited a little longer, to be sure, then gave a nod. "Okay, stay quiet. Petran, lead the way."

"Of course, Lady Maeve," the historian said, "only…lead it where?"

It was a good question, and Maeve took a moment to consider. They weren't safe in the castle—that much was painfully obvious. More important, they needed a healer and quickly. She thought—*hoped*—that Chall's wound wasn't immediately fatal, but if he wasn't seen to, and soon, there would be no doubt. True, they might try to hide in the city, but Cutter's treatment as he was escorted from the city was still fresh in her mind, just as she remembered the scowls the people had given her as she and Chall had passed. No, counting on the benevolence of New Daltenia's citizens was out of the questions. Besides which, even if they did venture into the city, where would they go? To some inn, only then to call on a healer and hope no one chose to tell the town guard about a man who looked as if he'd been thoroughly stabbed?

She found herself thinking of Emille and her husband Ned. The two had done much, had *risked* much for them already. Were she and the others to return to them once more, she knew that they would again be putting the couple's lives at risk. A couple who had gone out of their way to help them. Yet, it was the only safe place in the city that she could think of. The two would be more than willing to help, had offered as much, but that would be little comfort if Maeve's decision led to their deaths. Still, Chall was losing more blood by the minute and, in the end, there really was no choice.

Finally, she gave a heavy sigh. "I know a place."

CHAPTER NINETEEN

*I do not ask men to believe, for all men believe in something.
The problem is that, more often than not, it is the wrong thing.
—Priest of Raveza*

Priest walked the streets of the poor district. People who lived in the finer parts of the city often talked about the dangers of New Daltenia's crime-ridden streets, many of them too afraid to even consider setting foot here. And Priest knew enough to know that they were right to be afraid, for the shadows lingered everywhere here, even in the daytime, shadows that might, at any moment, reach out and snatch the unwary, pulling them further and further into darkness. It had happened before, and it would happen again. Priest knew this well, for he had once been one of those shadows, had once been that darkness.

Only when he had been recruited by Prince Bernard, only when he had met him and Chall and Maeve, had that begun to change. The prince spent his life weighed down with guilt for the things he had done, and indeed he *had* done things for which a man might be ashamed, yet Priest had him to thank for the man he had become. Bernard had been brutal, yes, perhaps even cruel, but there was goodness in him too. Goodness that had given Priest, for the first time in his life, something to believe in besides the blades he had always carried. Bernard had given him belief, had given him *purpose,* and for that Priest owed him a debt that he knew he could never repay.

And so now he ventured into a place he had promised himself that he would never come again, but that was not the worst of it. For he had also promised himself that he would never again become the man, the *creature,* who had worked for Belle, the one whose only joy was in spilling the blood of others. Yet, he needed that man, that creature now. Not for himself, but for the others, Bernard most of all. Because the prince had asked it of him. He could not save Bernard from whatever fate awaited him in the Black Wood, but he would do whatever he could to save the others, to save Matt. That, at least, he could do for him.

So as he walked down the street, noting the shadows that lurked in the alleyways, aware of the eyes following him from the doorways and windows of the buildings he passed, he called on the man he had been, the one the people of the poor district, of the city, had known as Valden the Vicious, Belle's favorite pet. Belle was dead now, but the creature was not, and when he went looking for him in his mind, he did not have to go far, not far at all. The creature lay before him, ready, waiting, as if it had always been there, some great abyss which he had spent the last years striding along the edge of, so close that one single misstep might have sent him hurtling into it.

He called, and the creature answered. He pulled the creature about himself like a mantle one might wear, but this mantle was one, he knew, which would be far easier to put on than to take off. And then, in that moment, he was Priest no longer. He was Valden the Vicious. The man he had once been. Perhaps, some dark part of him thought, the man he had *always* been.

The creature, unlike many of New Daltenia's citizens, did not fear the dangers of the poor quarter—it welcomed them. That creature did not worry over the shadows but bared its teeth at them, *hoping* they would choose to rouse themselves, to reach out and try to claim him. But perhaps *because* of that hope, none did, and Valden the Vicious strode down the street toward the place that had once been the closest thing to a home he had ever known. He did not draw a weapon to dissuade any who might accost him, for the man, the *creature* he was did not *want* to dissuade them. He walked the streets the way a lion might tread through the prairie grass, confident that it was in its home, its place, and that in that place, it ruled.

In time, he stood in the street, staring at the rundown building that served as Belle's headquarters, the building where he had once come again and again, first to retrieve a name, and second to mark it off the list. He was aware of shadows gathered in the street behind him on either side, but he did not fear the shadows. If they were wise, it was they who feared him.

He walked up to the door. He did not knock, for knocking was a thing only done by those who came to this place without invitation or welcome and so was as good as a death sentence. Instead, he only stood, waiting. The door remained stubbornly closed to him, and in time, he became aware of two shadows drifting closer.

Valden turned, baring his teeth in a humorless grin, not going for his knives, not yet, but ready to. He silently regarded the two figures as they drew closer.

"Valden?" one asked. "That you?"

"Why don't you come and find out?" Valden said, still grinning.

The figure grunted, removing its hood. "Yeah, I'd say that's you alright. I'd say I've missed you but, then, I wouldn't lie to you."

"Ah," Valden said. "Cautious Catham. Why am I not surprised?"

"There was a time, years gone now, when that name used to bother me, when it used to sound like a taunt to my ears." The man gestured to a jagged scar at his throat, then shrugged. "Not so much anymore. I learned, the hard way, that a man can never be too cautious."

That didn't seem to require a response and so Valden gave none, only watching the man, a ghost from the past. He had not had friends then, for the man he had been was incapable of such things, but Catham had come the closest.

"This is him?" the second shadow asked, removing its hood to reveal a young man that appeared to be in his mid-twenties, a sneer on his face.

"Yes, lad," Catham said, "this is Valden the Vicious."

The young man sneered deeper, turning on the older man. "Told you not to call me that, you old bastard. The name's Dashen. Dashen the Deadly."

Catham glanced at Valden, giving his eyes a small roll where the younger man couldn't see then nodded. "As you say," he said, his voice full of contrition. "Dashen the Deadly. My mistake, sir."

Valden grunted. "It seems the years have not changed you, Catham."

"My experience, Valden," the man said, "they rarely do."

"I could take him," the young man said, his eyes going up and down Valden like a man examining livestock he was considering purchasing, a look on his face that said he wasn't impressed with what he found.

"That so, Deadly?" Catham asked softly.

"You're damn right it's so," the younger man snapped. "You doubt me?"

Catham shook his head. "Wouldn't dream of it. Though, there's only one way to find out, isn't there? And what, with you not havin' a contract, standin' to earn nothing from it, only blood, well, seems to me that's a pointless pursuit."

"A name," the young man growled in what Valden supposed he considered his most menacing voice.

"What's that now?" Catham asked.

"Might not get a coin, but I'd get a name alright," the young man said, still eyeing Valden. "The man who killed Valden the Vicious—everyone'd hear, everyone'd know it."

"Well, suppose that's true," Catham said carefully. But then, the man always was careful. It was the reason why, in a world of brutal killers, he had outlived nearly all his contemporaries. "Still, can't say I'd recommend it. Give it some time, you'll get your name right enough. More of it than you'll want, I'd wager."

The younger man snorted. "And just what do you know of it, you old bastard? Catham the *Careful*. What kind of name is that for a killer?"

The older man shrugged, clearly not put off in the least by the younger man's ire. "It's my name, is what it is, and I'm still breathin' to have it."

Dashen the Deadly hissed. "Catham the Coward, more like. What about it, old man?" he asked, turning back to Valden. "You think you can take me?"

Valden glanced at Catham and gave a small shrug. "Only one way to know for sure," he said, echoing the other man's words.

The young man seemed to take that as an invitation and, with a shout, he drew the sword sheathed at a jaunty angle at his hip and charged. Valden watched him come. It was only the space of seconds, but in those seconds, he sized him up, learned far more than most could have about the youth and his fighting ability if they'd been given a day for the task.

The man was fast, charging at him, and Valden took a moment to step off the door's stoop. It wouldn't do to sully the doorway or the building. Even beasts, after all, knew never to shit where they ate. The youth gave a cry and lunged at him, his blade flashing in the air. He was fast, but Valden was faster.

He stepped to the side, just enough that the blade missed impaling him by no more than an inch, then he drew one of his knives and, in one quick motion, slammed it into the man's chest.

Dashen the Deadly turned to the side, staring at Valden, his eyes wide with shock. "*Gurr...*" he said, but no more than that before he collapsed, dead, at Valden's feet.

Valden stared at the body for a minute then turned back to Catham.

The other man nodded sadly. "Like I said—people rarely change." He motioned in the air and the shadows gathered in the street began to fade into the nearby alleyways like phantoms. "See ya around, Vicious." And with that, the older man turned and followed the others.

In moments, he was gone, and Valden turned at the sound of a wooden creak to see the door swinging open as if of its own accord. Valden gave no thought to the corpse lying at his feet, no more than a lion, killing for sport, might wonder at its prey. He stepped through the door.

The inside of the building was the same as it had been when he and the prince had come here weeks ago, the same as it had been for fifteen years and more.

"Vicious," a voice said, and he turned to regard the old woman sitting behind the desk, a small, loaded crossbow held almost casually in one hand.

"Nadia."

"You've got a lot of balls, showin' your face around here after what you and yours did to Belle."

Valden could have told the woman that it wasn't his fault, that they had, in fact, tried to save the crime boss, but there was no point. The woman no doubt already knew everything there was to know about what had transpired. "I've come to talk to the boss."

A Warrior's Curse

The old woman gave a snort. "Well, now, that'd be some trick, wouldn't it? 'Fraid you might be out of luck there, Vicious, exceptin' you got a means of talkin' to the dead, that is. Unless my information is very, very bad Belle's a bit worse for wear—a sword to the neck'll usually do that."

"I mean the new boss."

"Ah, right," the woman said. "What is it, the headsman's got a vacancy, has he?"

"I don't mean any harm," Valden said. "Belle sent us here."

"No harm, that so?" she asked, smiling. "I wonder if Dashen the Deadly'd say as much. Or, I suppose, Dashen the Dead is closer to the truth now, isn't it?"

"He came at me," Valden said. "You know what they say about a man goes looking for blood."

She sighed. "He finds it. Anyway, you done us a favor there. Dashen's a pain in the ass...or well, *was*. Grew up hearin' too many stories, I guess."

"He should have listened closer then. The thing about those stories is that someone always dies."

She inclined her head like a fencer acknowledging a point. "True enough. Anyway, enough about Dashen—what is this you say about Belle sendin' you here?"

"She said she had information about the conspiracy in the castle."

"Conspiracy?" the woman asked, her eyes going wide in mock surprise. "Surely not. Not in our fine city."

"I'm afraid so."

She sighed. "And this information, you figure you want to talk to the boss, and he'll just...what, give it to you, that it?"

"Something like that."

She shook her head, staring at him. "Never took you for an optimist, Vicious."

He said nothing to that, and finally she gave another sigh, sitting back in her chair. She reached under the desk with one hand but he didn't miss the way she continued to hold the crossbow in the other.

Valden waited until, a few moments later, the door beside Nadia's desk opened, revealing one of the biggest men he'd ever seen, one who, in size, at least, rivaled even Prince Bernard himself.

"And just who the fuck are you?" the man growled by way of greeting.

"Valden."

The man frowned. "Wantin' to talk to the leader, are you? Well? What is it then?"

Valden raised an eyebrow then glanced at Nadia. The man was a far cry from Belle, that much was sure, had more in common with the corpse lying outside than the crime boss. Oh, Belle had been dangerous, one of the most dangerous people Valden had ever met and that in no small amount of competition, a poisonous snake but one that had kept her fangs hidden until she saw need to use them. This man, though, with his barrel chest and arms like tree trunks, the scowl on his face and the way those arms were currently folded across his chest, the hands knotted into fists, seemed to be going to great lengths to exude menace. After a moment, Valden realized why.

"You can go now," he said to the man, his eyes going back to the old woman sitting behind the desk.

The man let out a sound somewhere between a growl and a grunt. "What's that?" he demanded.

"I said you can leave," Valden said. "Your services won't be required."

The man frowned at him for several moments as if he wanted nothing more than to cave his head in and was giving serious consideration to giving it a go. Valden only turned to watch him, waiting for what would happen. Finally, perhaps realizing that his scowling was doing no good, the man glanced at Nadia.

The old woman sighed. "Well, you heard him, Ox. Go on then and whip us up a couple of drinks, will you? Vicious here has something he wants to talk about."

The man frowned, scowling at Valden again. "You sure, boss?"

The woman glanced at him. No more than that, but the big man's face paled, and he sketched an awkward bow before retreating through the door as if his life depended on it. Which, likely, it did.

A Warrior's Curse

Valden waited for the door to close then turned back to the woman behind the desk. "Boss, is it?"

She rolled her eyes. "Well, someone has to be, don't they? Anyway, you've no idea the amount of shit involved in it. I've a mind to order you cut down here and now just for the bother of it all. S'pose I've got enough to get the job done well enough, though, frankly, I can't afford losin' the numbers, not with a good third of our men takin' Belle's death as an opportunity to look for more gainful employment elsewhere."

"I imagine some of them found a sight more than they bargained for."

She shrugged as if it made no difference. "Some examples had to be made. It's a dangerous time, Vicious. What with Belle's death, everybody and their cousin is tryin' to desert or make a play for power. Shit, if it weren't for me promisin' Belle years ago, I'd let the bastards have it. And that's all before you take into account that the city itself is goin' to shit, not least of all the castle."

"And here I thought you didn't know anything about that."

She gave him a smile. "Maybe I was puttin' you on a bit before, though you can't blame a woman for bein' careful, things the way they are."

"No, you can't."

"Anyhow, I suppose you'll be wantin' to know who it was put the mark on your friend the prince and the guardsman—Nigel, isn't it?"

"Yes, it is. And yes, I would."

She nodded slowly. "And what's in it for me then? I like you, Vicious, always have, but in case you didn't know, career criminals, as a rule, don't tend to do much for free. What do you intend, to give us all pardons, is that it?"

Valden shook his head. "No. What you all have done, what *I've* done, it's long past pardons. Anyway, what would you do with it, if you had it but keep doing what you always do? No, it isn't in my power to offer pardons and, even if it was, I wouldn't."

"Not in your power?" the woman blinked. "Well, that's a bit of a surprise, isn't it? I mean, you bein' best friends with the prince and all."

"Prince Bernard departed for the Black Wood this morning, as I'm sure you well know."

She grinned. "Caught again, though you might be sellin' that a bit short. Not so much departed as exiled, wouldn't you say?"

Valden said nothing to that and she studied him. "You really do care for him, don't you?" she asked, sounding genuinely surprised for the first time.

"I owe him everything," he said simply.

She watched him for a minute then finally nodded. "I believe you, but that doesn't address the question of recompense."

"If we don't figure out what's going on in the castle, Nadia—and soon—then it isn't a question of *if* the city will fall, only when. What do you think, that the Fey will stop their invasion at the borders of the poor district?" He shook his head. "They do not feel fear the way we do, Nadia, and they cannot be bought or threatened. If the Fey come, *when* they come, then you and your family—such as it is—will be killed along with the rest of us."

"You would appeal to my self-interest," she said, "thinking, likely, that I, like most criminals, will be unremittingly selfish."

"Yes."

She sighed. "The most damning thing is, you're right. I'm old, Valden, was old even back when you went by Vicious and *were* vicious. Yet I am as scared now of death as I ever was. Perhaps more so." She gestured casually to the door. "It is one of the reasons why Ox there has been fielding much of the visits from people."

"Who is he, anyway?" Valden asked. "I don't remember him from the old days."

Nadia snorted at that. "Nor would you. After all, nearly everyone from the old days is dead, aren't they? You, me, and Catham just about account for it. No, Ox is new. Used to be a farmer, if you can believe it. At least until he lost his farm. Came to the city looking for work and found us." She shrugged. "You know how it goes."

"Yes, I do. Listen, Nadia, I'm in a bit of a hurry and—"

She nodded. "I understand. But I've got to be honest with you here, Vicious, even if I tell you what you want to know...I'm not all that sure it's going to help."

"Maybe not, but it's better to know."

She shrugged. "If you say so, though, in my experience, the knife cuts just as deep whether you see it coming or not...but that's your affair. Very well—you want to know who was behind the assassination attempts in the castle? Well, I can help you there. It was the king himself."

Valden blinked. "You...you mean Feledias? Fire and salt if you're right, I have to go. He went with the prince to the Black Wood. Thanks, Nadia," he said, turning and moving toward the door. "I've got to hurry or—"

"Not Feledias."

He froze, his hand on the door handle. Then, slowly, he turned. "Sorry?"

"It wasn't the old king who ordered the assassination of Prince Bernard," Nadia said, watching him. "But the new one."

Ice cold fear ran through Priest at that, and he felt the breath catch in his throat. "You mean..."

She nodded. "The assassins were hired by King Matthias the Virtuous himself."

Valden felt as if he'd been punched in the stomach, and it was several seconds before he was able to speak. "And...and the assassins who attacked Guardsman Nigel?" he croaked.

"Also hired by the king."

"Are...that is...are you sure?" he breathed.

"I'm sure," she said. "The man I spoke to about it...well, he wasn't really in a position to lie. Anyway, I doubt it helps, Vicious, but I want you to know that those men didn't work for us. Belle meant to do right by your prince, truly. She was cruel sometimes, yes, but she was no fool, and she understood what was at stake. What *is* at stake."

"But why...?" Valden whispered. It didn't make any sense. Matt would have died in Brighton if not for Cutter, and the prince was the only reason why he had been made king in the first place. What possible reason would the lad have for wanting him dead? That got Valden thinking about how strangely the youth had been acting lately, ever since...*ever since Two Rivers*. A terrible, horrifying idea began to form in his mind then, one that made the skin of his arms break out in gooseflesh. "Thanks, Nadia," he said. "I've...I've really got to go. The others...they need me." After all, Maeve and Chall had meant to go to the castle to check on Petran. Which meant...*they're walking right into a trap.*

"Very well," the woman said, then, as he swung the door open, "And Vicious?"

He turned back to her then, and she gave him what appeared at least to be a genuine smile. "Good luck."

"Thanks, Nadia," he said. *I'm going to need it.* When he took to the streets again, he did not walk calmly—instead, he ran.

He didn't know how long it took to make his way through the city, only that it was too long, for each minute wasted brought Chall and Maeve closer to death. *If they aren't dead already.*

He forced the thought away, as he had the other dozen times he'd had it while running through the city but now, like then, it did not go far. By the time he turned a corner and caught sight of the castle in the distance, Valden was exhausted, the breath rasping in his lungs, but he barely noticed. He was too intent on reaching the others, his friends, in time.

He was sprinting at the gate, drawing more than a few stares, when suddenly a carriage pulled out in front of him, and he came to a stumbling halt, catching himself on one of the horses. He glanced past them and saw that the castle gate was only a hundred feet away, no more than that, and that the guards at the gate were watching him strangely. Not surprising, perhaps, considering that he had been sprinting down the street directly at them.

He moved to go around the horses and someone caught his arm. "Excuse me," he said, pulling away, but the hand held on.

"Easy, friend, easy, no rush—you haven't missed your ride. I'm here, and you're here, right?"

Priest frowned, trying to pull away again, "Listen, I really have to go."

"And find your friends, right?" the voice asked, quieter this time.

This time, Priest did turn back, frowning as he started inching his hand toward one of his knives.

The man winced. "Wouldn't do that, if I were you. I'll regret it, that's sure, but I imagine you will too." He offered his hand. "The name's Ned. We met once before, though I can't say I'm surprised you don't remember—from what I hear, you all have had a busy time of it."

Priest blinked as realization dawned. "You're the driver, aren't you? The one that..." He trailed off, wary of saying too much in case he was wrong.

Ned grinned. "The one that saved you lot from torture and death? Sure, that's me. Anyway, your friends sent me here lookin' for you. Or...well, suppose it's more accurate to say that they wanted to come themselves but are...indisposed."

"I see..." Priest said. "Then...you know where they are?"

"I do," Ned said, glancing back at the gate where one of the guards had started toward them down the street, "but if I was you, I'd hop in," he went on, gesturing to the carriage. "I'm thinking you wouldn't like what happened, you waited around for that guardsman to come ask a few questions."

Priest still hesitated. The man seemed trustworthy, likeable even, but he had met enough assassins and killers to know that they often *were* likeable, at least right up until they stuck a knife in you. "My friends...are they okay?"

The driver winced, glancing back at the approaching guard, "Look, friend, I really think we ought to have this conversation later. You see, we're in a bit of a hurry here, and—"

"Are they okay?" Priest repeated.

The driver ran a hand through his hair. "The woman, Lady Maeve, she's fine," he said hurriedly. "The mage...well, he's been stabbed."

"*Stabbed?*" Priest repeated. "How is he? How...how serious is it?"

"I don't know," the man said. "He...there was a lot of blood, but my wife's seeing to him. If anyone can help him, it's her. Now, will you come?"

Priest frowned. If the man was a liar, he was a damned impressive one. But then, Priest had met impressive liars before too, as dangerous, in their way, as assassins. Still, the guard was getting closer, raising his hand to hail them, and Priest didn't think he had much choice. He hopped in the carriage.

"*Hey! Driver, hold that carriage!*"

"Best hold on tight in there," Ned said as he climbed into the driver's seat, "seems we're going to have a bit of a chase." No sooner were the words out of his mouth then he clucked to the horses and they pulled away with shocking force, enough to knock

Priest backward in his seat. Then they were careening down the street, the buildings and people flashing past in a blur, and he thought that surely they must wreck any second. Yet, whatever else he was, the man was obviously a skilled driver, weaving in and out of the traffic, dodging carriages and people as if he'd trained all his life for just such an event.

Left with nothing else to do, Priest held on for dear life, doing his best to fight back his rising gorge as the carriage driver worked his own special kind of magic.

CHAPTER TWENTY

Losing people isn't the type of thing a person gets used to.
At least, if someone has, I don't want to meet the bastard.
—Captain during Fey War mourning the loss of his troops after battle

Maeve stood at the corner of the room, wringing her hands and doing her best to keep from pacing while Emille examined Challadius. They had arrived several hours earlier, and the woman had immediately begun seeing to him, cleaning and rebandaging the wound. She'd also administered several tonics, ones she'd had to pour down his throat as the mage hadn't regained consciousness since the castle.

Meanwhile, Guardsman Nigel and his wife sat in the other room, talking quietly, and Maeve could see the excitement at being reunited in their eyes. Part of her hated them for that, hated them for finding any sort of pleasure while Challadius lay fighting for his life. It seemed a terrible cruelty to her that the guardsman's wife might be reunited with the man she loved while Maeve was forced to consider the very strong possibility that she would lose hers.

And she *did* love him. Despite many years of pretending the contrary—particularly to herself—she was forced, now, to confront the fact that she loved him, that she had *always* loved him. And despite her unjust anger at the guardsman and his wife, she knew that there was no one to blame but herself for the fact that that love had gone unrealized for so long.

Just as there was no one to blame for the fact that the assassin had managed to wound Chall in the first place. The mage had many talents, but hand-to-hand fighting was decidedly not one of them. That was Maeve's territory. He had counted on her, and she had failed him. And because of that, he now lay within inches of death, all because she hadn't been fast enough, hadn't been *good* enough. *Maeve the Marvelous, they called you,* she thought with an angry sneer. *What a pathetic joke.* What good were all her talents if she could not even use them to defend the man she loved? What point in them, in any of it? She had lost one such man, long ago, when the Skaalden had come to their homeland, bringing with them that unnatural frost and fog, had lost him somewhere in the mist, him and her child.

That loss had nearly broken her. *Had* broken her, in fact, and she had only begun to come back together after meeting the prince and Priest...*and Chall.* She knew that, this time, that loss would kill her, and she thought that was okay. If Chall died, then she wanted to die as well. Let the Known Lands, let all of it, be someone else's problem. For years, she and her companions, Chall among them, had risked their lives for the kingdom and what thanks had they received for their efforts? The prince exiled, Chall lying inches away from death, and though he had not said as much, Maeve got the impression that Priest was faring little better. Something had changed in the man in the last days, as if some light that had always filled him, one she had not even noticed until it was gone, had faded.

And then there was her. An old useless assassin who, it seemed, was fated by the gods to watch her friends fall in front of her one by one until she alone was left. And there was nothing she could do about it, not now. She'd had her chance with the assassin that went by Felara, and she had failed. So now she stood in the corner of the room, wringing her hands, her body bathed in a cold sweat, and hoped. *Hoped* in a hopeless world that Emille could do what she could not—that she could save Chall.

After what felt like an eternity of waiting, of starting at each moan the mage made in his sleep as the healer tended to him, Emille rose and walked to her. Maeve watched her, trying to determine by her stride, by her expression, the mage's welfare, but the woman's face was a blank mask.

"How...how is he?" she asked, barely able to get the words out past her fear.

"He's strong," Emille said, "a lot stronger than I would have given him credit for. A fighter. If you would have showed up even an hour later, I would have said he had no chance. As it is..." She slowly shook her head. "He's lost a lot of blood, lady. Thankfully, the blade didn't strike any vital organs but...there's just no way to know for sure. If he makes it through the night, he should be out of the worst of it."

If he makes it through the night.

Those words rang in Maeve's mind like a clarion bell, like some grim pronouncement of certain doom, and a shiver of fear ran up her spine. Her vision went black for a moment then, a black darker even than the tunnel through which she and Chall had traveled.

The next thing she knew, she was in Emille's arms. The healer-assassin said something, but her voice sounded muzzy, as if she spoke through fabric, and Maeve could not make out the words.

If he makes it through the night.

"What?" she said, her voice sounding slurred as if she'd spent a night drinking. "What?"

"Lady Maeve."

The room was spinning wildly, and Maeve's stomach was in knots.

If he makes it through the night.

"Please," she moaned, "oh, please," but if someone had asked her, in that moment, who she spoke to—herself, Emille, the gods—even she could not have said. She closed her eyes, squeezing them shut as if by doing so she might not just block out the spinning room but the reality of what lay within it.

She was trembling, and the strength was gone from her legs, the only thing keeping her upright the healer's arms wrapped around her. The woman spoke to her then. She could not tell, in that maelstrom of emotions which gripped her, what the woman said, but while she could not make out the words, the tone was clear enough. It was a soothing, comforting tone, the sort of tone a mother might use to comfort her child or a stablemaster his horses and, slowly, the worst of the storm began to subside.

Finally, she slowly opened her eyes.

"Lady Maeve," Emille said, watching her carefully, her face full of so much compassion that Maeve felt tears began to gather in her eyes. "Are you alright?"

No, Maeve thought, *no, I don't think I am. In fact, I think I am very, very far from alright.* "I'm...fine," she rasped, her throat feeling unaccountably dry. "Just...just lost my balance for a moment." But then, she did not think it was her balance she had lost, not really. More likely, she thought it might be her mind. Lost or losing and in the end it made little difference which it was.

If he makes it through the night.

"What...what can I do for him?" she asked.

A look equal parts sadness and desperation came over the woman's face then. "Nothing, lady," she said softly. "It...it's up to the gods now."

Nothing. She could do nothing for him now just as she could do nothing for him when the assassin attacked. One woman, one against four and she had beaten them as if it were nothing, would have killed them all had Petran not managed a lucky blow with a whiskey decanter. She was left, then, to hope to benevolence from gods who had never showed her—or, so far as she could tell, any person of the Known Lands—the least bit of it.

"You...you care for him deeply, don't you?"

"Yes," Maeve croaked. "More than he knows." She met the woman's eyes. "More than even I knew, I think."

The healer nodded. "Well, if it helps any, lady, I believe that he will make it through."

"You believe," Maeve repeated, watching the woman.

Emille gave her the smallest of smiles. "I hope."

Hope. Maeve's life had taught her many lessons but hope was not one of them. "I'm afraid I have no hope left in me, Emille," she whispered, studying Chall's unconscious form and the bandages wrapped around him.

"That's okay, lady," the woman said softly as she turned her own eyes to the mage. "I have enough hope for the both of us."

Maeve turned to look at the woman then. Here she was worrying over Chall when the woman's husband was out risking his life to find Priest before the man made it to the castle not to mention the fact that Maeve and the others had endangered her and her husband's lives not once but twice in coming here. Yet, the woman was comforting her, offering not a single word of complaint. "I'm...sorry," Maeve said. "For coming here, for putting you and your husband in danger again."

The woman gave a small smile, but Maeve could see that it cost her. "It's nothing, lady."

"No," Maeve said, "it's not nothing. I have nothing, nothing to offer you in return, but I want you to know, Emille...I won't forget what you and your husband have done for us."

"But you're wrong, lady," the healer said. "You and your companions *do* offer us something. You offer us the chance at a better world, a better kingdom."

Maeve winced. "A slim chance, that is."

The woman gave another smile, this one seemingly easier than the last. "Maybe, but any chance is better than none. And as for my husband, I wouldn't worry too much. That man is too damned stubborn and annoying to do anything so convenient as die."

Maeve found a small, fragile smile coming to her own face then. "Still...thank you."

The woman inclined her head. "You're very welcome, lady."

Maeve was just about to say something more when there was a knock on the door, and she froze. "Oh fire and salt they must have followed us," she said, "they must have—"

"Relax, lady," Emille said, putting a hand on her shoulder. "I know that knock—I'm fairly sure I've had a nightmare about it recently. Come—you will see that things are not so bad as that."

The woman started toward the door but Maeve glanced at Chall. "He will be alright, lady," Emille said.

Maeve gave an expression somewhere between a smile and a grimace. "Hope?" she asked, looking at the woman.

Emille gave her a wink. "Exactly."

Maeve took a deep slow breath then followed her into the house's main room. They arrived in time to see the carriage driver, Ned, stepping inside. And, behind him, a figure that some large part of Maeve had thought she would never see again. "*Priest!*" she shouted, the word out of her mouth before she could help it, and then she was running across the small room, pulling the man into a tight embrace.

The man held her, strong and gentle at once as was his way, saying nothing, unmoving as Maeve shed hot, wet tears into his shoulder. Finally, she pulled away, meeting his eyes.

"How is he?" Priest asked softly.

"Emille says...that...if he makes it through the night, he'll...be out of the worst of it."

The man nodded grimly, putting a hand on her shoulder. "He will make it, Maeve."

"I wonder..." Maeve said, trying to lighten the mood, "if you couldn't put in a good word with your goddess."

The man winced at that, recoiling as if she'd struck him then obviously trying to feign that he had not. "I...will try, lady, though I do not know if the goddess listens to me any longer. In fact..." He trailed off, shaking his head and not finishing. But then, he didn't need to. Maeve could read the remaining part of the sentence as if it were written on the man's forehead. *In fact, I'm not sure that she ever did.*

An exiled prince, a washed-up assassin, a priest who had lost his faith, and a mage who might not survive the night. What chances did such as them have, Maeve thought, of righting all that had gone wrong in the Known Lands? Slim, she had told Emille, but now, looking at Priest, at the anguish that he kept hidden from his features but could not entirely conceal from his eyes, she thought that "none" was far closer to the truth.

"What news do you bring?" she asked, desperate to change the subject, to talk, to *think* about anything but the man who lay in the next room dying.

Priest's expression grew grim at that. "Best we gather everyone—we will all want...*need* to hear this."

A few minutes later they were all gathered around the table. Guardsman Nigel's wife, Paula, with her arms wrapped around her husband, a look of defiant challenge on her face as if she dared him to try to leave her once more. Ned and Emille stood, their hands clasped together and somehow, in that small gesture, demonstrated a love as great as that shown by the guardsman's wife. Maeve sat with Petran on one side of her, the historian looking lost and confused and afraid, much like Maeve felt. Priest sat at the head of the table.

"Before you share whatever news you have," Emille said, "perhaps it would be best if you all explain what happened at the castle."

Maeve was at once anxious and terrified of what Priest might say, but she nodded, quickly recounting the events inside the castle. The others listened without interruption save for gasps of surprise and fear, and by the time she was finished Emille's face had gone a deathly pale.

"Felara, you said?" Emille asked. "Are you sure?"

"I'm sure," Maeve snarled, the thought of the woman who had so badly hurt Chall making anger roil within her. "She made sure we knew—was proud of it."

"As well she might be," Emille said, licking her lips. "Felara...she is an assassin and not just any assassin but one known for being the best in the city."

"And how would you know that?" Ned asked curiously, frowning at his wife.

Emille gave a dismissive wave, leaning toward Maeve. "And you are sure she lived?"

Maeve frowned. "I'm sure."

Emille heaved a sigh, shaking her head. "This is bad. Felara is the best killer in the guild. She has never missed a mark, prides herself on that fact. She will not give up, not until she is dead or..."

"Until we are," Maeve finished for her.

"That so?" Ned asked, raising an eyebrow at his wife. "Make a habit of hanging out with assassins do you, wife? Fire and salt what sort of things do you get up to while I'm out slaving away to make us coin?"

Emille winced, flushing. "It...they're just rumors, that's all. Ones heard at market." She turned to Maeve then. "But ones repeated enough that they must surely be true."

Ned was still looking at his wife strangely, and Maeve decided it best to change the subject. "Anyway, another assassin is nothing new, even if she is the best. Tell us," she said, turning to Valden, "what happened?"

The man nodded grimly. "I went to Belle's hideout," he said without preamble, "and spoke to the new leader of her...organization."

"And did you find out anything?" Maeve asked. "Anything that might help us?" she finished, doubting very much if such was the case.

"I...found out something," Priest said, "but I do not know how it might help us." The man hesitated then, a look of almost physical anguish mixed with fear coming over his face.

"Well?" Maeve asked, her own voice shaky, for she had known Priest for a long time, and the man was not the sort that frightened easy. "What is it?"

"Nadia, the new leader, divulged to me the identity of the person behind the assassination attempts on Prince Bernard and Guardsman Nigel."

"*And?*" Maeve demanded. "Who was it? Some Feyling? Or one of the king's new *advisors?*"

Priest winced. "No, Lady Maeve. It was not a fey creature nor one of the king's advisors. According to Nadia, it was..." He took a slow, deep breath as if to steady himself. "The assassination was ordered by none other than King Matthias himself."

Silence descended on the room then, as loud as a thunderclap, and Maeve found herself staring at Priest, wondering if it wasn't some sort of terrible joke. But the man did not laugh or smile, only returned her gaze with a miserable one of his own.

"But that can't be right!" Ned exclaimed, startling Maeve. "I met the king, if only for a moment, and he seemed like a good enough sort. Young, sure, but that's a crime we're all guilty of at one time or another."

"He tried to kill his own father?" Petran said. "That doesn't make any sense."

"No, it doesn't," Maeve agreed with a desperation in her voice even she could hear. "Matt loves the pri—Cutter. Why, he'd be *dead* if it weren't for him."

"I said as much," Priest said, "but Nadia assures me that it is true. She had it from the mouth of one of the assassins hired for the task."

"Well...it...she has to be lying, that's all," Maeve said. "Matt would never..." She trailed off then, thinking of how the youth had acted in the last weeks. True, the young boy who had once lived in Brighton, the young boy who she had come to know and even love like a favored nephew over the past months, would never have contemplated killing anyone, least of all Cutter, for he had idolized him. But then, that boy had changed. Matt had become something, some*one* different since they'd arrived in New Daltenia, and had, over the last days, seemed to endeavor to put increasingly more distance between himself and Cutter, as well as Maeve and the rest.

"But...but *why?*" she demanded. "Why would Matt do such a thing?"

Priest shook his head grimly. "I have thought long and hard on that myself, Maeve, since first learning of it, and I have come to only one conclusion—he wouldn't."

Maeve frowned. "But you're saying he did. What are you talking abou—"

"*Matthias* wouldn't," Priest interrupted. "But I do not think that the man we know as king is Matthias, not any longer."

"Well, that'd be a neat trick," Ned said. "What are you saying, that he's got a twin and that twin decided to show up, take his place?"

"No," Priest said, his eyes still locked on Maeve, "not a twin."

"So...what then?" Emille asked. "You think he's being blackmailed or...or threatened maybe?"

"No," Priest said again, still watching Maeve. "I fear that what has befallen Matthias is far worse than that."

Maeve shook her head in frustration. "Then what?" she demanded. "Besides, it couldn't be blackmail, could it? It seemed that Matt started acting strangely the moment we arrived in New Daltenia, and he was with us all along."

"I believe you are wrong, Maeve."

She snorted angrily. "I think I would have known if the lad had snuck off somewhere, Priest, or if someone had kidnapped him. I might be old and addled, but I'm not *that* addled. Not yet at least."

"What I mean," Priest said, "is that you are wrong that Matthias has been acting strangely since we arrived in the city. Think back, Maeve. When did we first notice him acting...unusual?"

Maeve frowned, opening her mouth to utter some angry, dismissive remark, but then she paused. Priest was right. Matt hadn't started acting strangely when they arrived in New Daltenia but before then. "You mean...Two Rivers?" she asked.

"Yes," Priest said. "And what happened in Two Rivers, Maeve?"

She sighed, frustrated. "We fought two Fey creatures who were trying to take over, as you well know. One of them a Glutton and the other—"

"The other?" Priest asked softly.

Maeve frowned. "I don't know what she was—I've never seen one before."

"Nor have I," Priest said, "but do you remember what she *did?*"

Maeve nodded slowly, casting her thoughts back to Two Rivers, to the mayor's home where they nearly died. "She...seemed to make the people obey her, cast some sort of spell over them or something."

"Exactly," Priest said.

"And...what?" Nigel asked, chiming in for the first time. "What does it mean, sir? Do you believe that this Fey creature cast a spell over the king?"

"But that's impossible," Maeve said. "We killed it—it couldn't do—"

"Not *we*, Maeve," Priest said, watching her.

"Oh," Maeve said. "You're right. Matt killed it. But...what difference does that make? Dead is dead never mind the hand holding the sword. The creature couldn't do anything, not with her head separated from her shoulders...could she?"

Priest shook his head slowly. "I don't know, Maeve. I have never seen the like of that creature before—there is no knowing what it might do, just as there is no denying that it was following the killing of her that young Matthias began to act...erratic."

Maeve blinked, feeling as if so many pieces of a puzzle were beginning to fall into place. "You're right," she said. "I thought...at the time, I mean, I thought that it was just, you know, the killing that had done it." She hissed in anger. "Damn, I'm a fool."

"If you are a fool then we all are," Priest said, "for we all thought the same."

"But...could it really *do* that?" Maeve asked. "Take...take him over, I mean?"

Priest shook his head, his frustration showing on his expression, and Maeve glanced around the room to see that same frustration and uncertainty mirrored on the faces of the others.

"Damn," Ned breathed finally. "If what you're saying is true, if they can really *do* that, I mean, then who's to say what else they've done, what other terrible things they've been behind?"

"Deeds done in the darkness bear fruit in the day," Maeve muttered.

"What's that, lady?" Nigel asked.

Maeve shook her head, unsure herself of why the words had come to her. "It's...a saying. Or, at least, I think it is. Cutter, he told me that Queen Layna, before...well, *before,* said it." But then, she realized, remembering the odd conversation with the prince, that hadn't been *all* he had said. He had said that Layna had claimed they were words her *real* mother had told her. "*Shit,*" she hissed.

"What is it, Maeve?" Priest asked.

"*Shit,*" she said again as the pieces began to fall into place, as she remembered Ladia, Layna's mother, telling her that they had taken her daughter from her, telling her that they had done it even before she died. At the time, Maeve had thought it no more than a mother's anger, likely justified. But...was it more than that?

She was standing from the table before she realized it, the others watching her. "I have to go," she said.

"Go where?" Petran asked. "Lady Maeve, it isn't safe in the city, you know that."

"He's right, lady," Ned said. "Not the best time to be thinkin' on taking a late-night stroll, if you ask me."

"Maybe not," Maeve said, "but I have to. If I'm right—" *gods please let me be wrong*—"then we never really won the war at all."

Priest frowned. "What do you mean, Maeve? We drove the Fey back to the Black Wood."

"Yes," she said, "and they might have driven our kingdom apart. Now, I have to talk to someone...if she's still alive."

"An old friend?" Ned asked.

Maeve winced. "No. No, I think she'd call me plenty of things, but I doubt 'friend' would be among them. Still, there's no choice, and I need to go now—as I recall, she lived on the far end of the city."

"Well, if that's the case, why not take the carriage?" Ned offered. "I can drive you and—"

"No," Maeve interrupted quickly, glancing at Emille. "No, I have to go alone."

The carriage driver shrugged. "If you say so, lady."

"I do." She moved to the door then paused with her hand on the latch. She'd been so caught up in her thoughts that she had nearly forgotten about Chall. "Wait," she said, "I can't leave, I—"

"I will look after him, lady," Emille said softly. "You have my word."

Maeve met her eyes, trying to convey some of the gratefulness she felt in her gaze, then she gave a nod and, before anyone could say anything to dissuade her—before she herself could think better of it—she opened the door and stepped out into the darkness.

CHAPTER TWENTY-ONE

*Revisiting people from the past is never fun.
After all, there's a reason why you left them there in the first place.
—Challadius the Charmer*

Maeve was glad for the night, the night which might help conceal her from anyone searching for her and the others. That they *were* searching was not in doubt. If Matt really was taken over by a Feyling—and the more and more she thought of it, the more she believed Priest was right—then the creature would not rest until it had killed all of them, eliminating any danger to its designs.

She knew that the others had been correct—it was dangerous to be out, to risk herself, particularly when she should be standing beside Chall, for if anything should happen while she was gone, she knew that she would never forgive herself. But she told herself that she'd *had* to go, that she had no choice. It wasn't as if she could have sent someone else—particularly when she had no idea how dangerous it could be.

But that was only part of it. The truth was that it was something *she* could do. She could not help Chall, could do nothing to countermand Cutter's exile, but this, at least, she could do.

And so she walked, hurrying through the city, keeping her cloak tight about her, the hood drawn to help hide her features from anyone who might be watching. It took the better part of an hour to reach the home, and so different did it look from the last time she'd seen it that she thought she'd remembered wrong. After all, many years had passed since she'd been here.

The home was situated in a modest part of the city, not the poor district, but not far from it either. Yet, the last time she had been here, Maeve remembered being surprised at how pleasant it was, at how much the small dwelling *felt* like a home. There had been a cobbled path leading to the door, and a small garden on either side, well-kept and maintained, certainly far better than her own efforts with a garden had proven. And the house itself, while small, had also been well cared for.

Now, though, she could hardly believe she was looking at the same place. The wonderful gardens had given way to weeds as high as her waist, and vines crept up the side of the house around flaked pieces of mortar. And the decay did not end there. Even the door sat crooked in its frame, hanging askew.

Frowning, Maeve walked down the path, forced to push long shoots of weeds out of the way as she did. Then, standing at the door, she took a deep breath and knocked. The door creaked open a fraction, revealing nothing but darkness from within, and no answer came.

Maeve knocked again, louder this time, and still there was nothing. Hissing with frustration, she knocked a third time, and this time an answer did come, only not from within the house but from her right, on the other side of the garden.

"What's all that racket at this ungodly hour?"

Maeve turned and saw a gray-haired woman who appeared to be in her sixties eyeing her. One of the woman's hands clutched a walking stick, and the other waggled a finger at her as she stood at the door of her own home. "What do you think you're about, woman, waking honest folk up in the dead of night?"

"Sorry," Maeve said, looking at the hunch-backed woman, "I'm looking for someone."

"An old friend, that it?" the lady asked.

"Something like that," Maeve said. "A woman and her husband, Erwin and Ladia, used to live here and—"

"Still do."

"What's that?"

"You said 'used to'" the old woman said. "They still do. Leastways, Ladia does. Erwin, why, he's been dead goin' on a year now, maybe more." She shook her head. "Always thought they were fine people, those two. That was until that harlot daughter of theirs bedded both princes and damned near tore the kingdom apart." She shrugged. "Always liked the girl, too. Just goes to show what a fool I am and that folks can hide a damned sight more than they show."

Maeve found herself frowning at that. "I knew Layna—she was a good woman. Erwin and Ladia were good people too."

"That so?" the woman countered sharply. "Know a lot of good people that are responsible for almost destroyin' a whole kingdom, do ya?"

Maeve frowned, considering saying something to the woman but decided against it, giving her head an angry shake and turning back to knock on the door.

"Oh, you won't find her there," the old woman cackled. "No, ain't much for sittin' in the house, is our Ladia. Not much for keepin' it either, you want to know the truth," she finished, sniffing and giving a disapproving glance at the overgrown garden.

"Well, where is she then?" Maeve said, doing her best to keep her anger from her tone but, judging by the frown on the old woman's face, not doing so fine a job of it.

"And just who's asking?" the woman countered, and Maeve cursed herself inwardly. "Who are you to demand anything of me, showin' up in the middle of the night and talkin' to me like you're some prince on holiday?"

"Not a prince," Maeve snapped, "but I know one. My name, you old hag, is Lady Maeve the Marvelous, the kingdom's foremost assassin."

The old woman paled at that, the hand holding her walking stick trembling so badly that, for a moment, Maeve thought she might fall and good luck finding someone to help her up. In the end, though, the woman managed to keep her feet. "Y-you're Maeve the Merciless?"

Maeve frowned. She had forgotten that one. "Yes, and if you do not tell me what I want to know, and quickly, I assure you that you will see just how merciless I can be."

"Th-the cemetery," the old woman blurted, "just around the corner there." She waggled her cane in the direction she meant then hurriedly retreated into her house. Maeve listened as the door was slammed shut, the latch thrown in place.

She winced, the feeling of satisfaction she'd felt at scaring the old woman vanishing in a moment. Here she was trying to be subtle, and instead she dropped her name to the first person to antagonize her. Normally she didn't think she would have let the woman's cruelty make her act so foolishly, but then with Chall wounded and all that was happening, she wasn't thinking clearly. Not that that would be much consolation if she got herself or the others killed. And it was far too much to hope the woman would keep quiet. There, she didn't doubt, was a bit of news that would be passed on just as soon as there was someone to pass it *to*.

Still, there was no help for it now so she turned and hurried down the walkway in the direction the woman had indicated.

It didn't take her long to find the cemetery, a small parcel of land which held a few hundred tombstones, no doubt relatives of those who lived nearby—or who at least had once. She stepped into the cemetery and after a few minutes of walking among the graves saw a figure kneeling in the dirt in front of two graves. The figure's back was to her, but Maeve knew, instantly, who the stooped old woman, dressed in little better than rags and, in that way, resembling her house, must be.

Maeve watched her for a moment, hating to intrude upon her grief—and her grief, at least, was not in question, for she could see it in the way the woman slumped, her head bowed, tears leaking down her face in the moonlight. Finally, Maeve took a slow, deep breath and started forward.

"Ladia?" she asked softly.

The woman started, turning, her eyes wide and frightened in the moonlight. "Who are you? I don't have any money, if that's what you're after. You bastards already took it all and—"

"I'm not here for that," Maeve said. "It...it's me. Maeve."

"Maeve," the woman repeated as if the word had no meaning. Then, something, some mad glimmer, came into her eyes.

"*Maeve*," she said again, hissing the name this time. "*You.* What in the name of the gods are you doing here? Will you and your *prince* take everything from me and then, seeing it not enough, rob me even of my chance to mourn?"

Maeve winced. Visiting an old friend, Ned had asked her, and no. No, that was certainly not the case. "Ladia, I do not mean to cause you any pain, I came because—"

The old woman let out a shrieking, terrible sound, somewhere between laughter and anguish. "Pain?" she asked. "*Pain?* What do *you* know of pain? Pain is my life, *Lady Maeve*, it is all I know, all I have. There is nothing else. First you and your *friends* take my Layna from me, my girl, then the flux takes my sweet Erwin. And now I am here, alone."

Maeve moved forward. "I...I am sorry," she said. "For Erwin. For...for Layna. I promise you, Ladia, me and the others, we did not mean for it to happen." She put her hand on the woman's shoulder then, and Ladia turned to regard it so abruptly that Maeve suddenly felt sure that she would attack.

In the end, she did not, only heaving a heavy sigh. "No, you have not come to take my time to mourn but to steal my anger, is that it, Lady Maeve? To steal the only thing I have left that makes me feel alive?"

"I...I did not come for that either," Maeve said. "Ladia, I am sorry, truly, for all that you have suffered but...I only came to...to ask you a question."

"Oh?" the woman said, not sounding angry now, her voice devoid of any emotion at all, sounding dead. "And what question is that, Maeve?"

Maeve winced. "You told me, back then, that we took your daughter from you. What...what did you mean by that?"

The woman watched her. "As if you don't know," she said tiredly. "After she met that Prince Feledias, my sweet girl, she...she changed. At first, everything was fine, *she* was fine, but then...Erwin and I didn't hear from her for a while, so we came to visit her at the castle. She..." The old woman shook her head. "She didn't know me. *Me,* her own mother, who raised her from a baby."

Maeve frowned. "Didn't know you?"

"That's what I said," the old woman snapped. "She...changed somehow. I tried to talk to her, but she had us taken out of the castle, Erwin and me both, and she never would see us again. The next time I saw her was at her funeral. You remember," she said, seeming to muster enough energy to sneer, "you were *there,* after all."

"But...how could she not know you?" Maeve asked, thinking that she had been right after all, that she knew the truth already.

"How in the name of the gods should I know?" the woman said. She shook her head then, wretched in her grief. "It was as if...I don't know, as if she were under some kind of spell, or something. Or if...maybe as if she wasn't her at all. Oh, she still *looked* like her, sure, but that wasn't my Layna. My sweet, sweet Layna." She gave a sudden convulsion and burst into tears then, burying her face in her hands.

"Ladia," Maeve said, "gods, I'm so sorry. I—"

"Just leave me alone," the woman sobbed, "leave me to my anger and my grief, Maeve. Do not take them from me—they are all I have left."

"Please," Maeve said, choked with emotion, "I would...I would do something, would help you, if I could."

"*Help?*" the woman shrieked. "*Help?* Can you bring my Erwin back from the dead? Can you bring *Layna* back?"

Maeve recoiled at the madness in the woman's eyes, the anger in her tone. "I...I cannot, but—"

"Then the only help you can offer is to leave me!" the woman said. "Please, gods, just leave me."

Maeve stared at her, helpless. Then, finally, hating herself, she turned and walked away, leaving the woman to her grief.

By the time she retraced her steps and arrived back at Ned and Emille's home, the sun was beginning to creep over the horizon. She walked down the street in the direction of the house, then past it, looking around her as she did. When she saw no one paying her any undue attention, she turned back and made her way up the path to the house, giving a knock.

The door swung open a moment later to reveal Priest. The man was grinning widely. "Maeve, welcome back."

"Well, good morning to you too," she said, surprised to find the man smiling for, when she had left, they had been a grim lot.

"He's awake," the man said, still grinning.

"Awake?" Maeve asked, pushing her way past him. She started toward the room where the mage had been laid then paused as she saw the others gathered at the table. Including, she saw with a powerful shock of relief, the mage.

"Chall?" she said.

The mage turned, wincing as he did. "Hi, Maeve," he said. "I'll tell you, if you've ever considered getting stabbed in the stomach, I really wouldn't recomme—" He never got a chance to finish for Maeve rushed forward, pulling him into a tight hug.

"Not that I don't...appreciate the sentiment," the mage groaned, "but maybe you should let up just a touch."

Maeve did, just a touch, pulling her head back. "Stones and starlight, Chall, I thought you were going to die."

"Well," he groaned, "Not yet, but if I hurt like this for much longer, might be I'll take on the job myself. Or...well, you *are* an assassin after all, I wonder if I couldn't get you to do me a bit of a—"

"Oh, shut up, Chall," she said and then, before he could respond, she kissed him. There was no artifice or design to it, not this time. It was only a kiss, a real kiss, one long overdue, and for a time Maeve forgot everything else, forgot about Cutter's exile, and what she'd learned about Matt and Layna, forgot even the kingdom itself. It was only him and her.

At least, that was, until someone cleared their throat, and Maeve pulled away for a moment, glancing around to see the others all staring at her with wide eyes. She turned back to the mage and saw him doing much the same. "I'm glad you're okay," she said.

"Shit, me too," Chall said, then grinned.

"You saved my life, you know."

He grinned wider. "I'm aware of it. So what was that then, your thanks?"

She laughed. "Part of it. You'll get the rest later. But first...we all need to talk."

"Mean the shows over?" Ned asked.

"Afraid so," Maeve said, and slowly all of them began to gather around the table.

"Priest filled me in," Chall said, "though I can't say I'm sure about it all."

Maeve nodded. "Well, maybe this will help you." She went on to explain to them all that Ladia had told her about her daughter.

When she was finished, Chall frowned. "I'm still not sure, Maeve. I mean, her daughter changed, so what? Money changes people—there's nothing new about that."

"She didn't just *change*, Chall," she said. "Ladia said she didn't even recognize her or Erwin. Money might change people, but they're still the same *people*."

The mage grunted, still not completely convinced. "Well," he said. "I don't guess there's any way to know for sure."

"That's...not exactly true," Priest said.

They all turned to him, and the man shrugged. "Well, it seems to me that there might be one way, at least. To know for sure."

"Oh?" Chall asked. "What's that? You got a crystal ball handy, that it?"

"No," the man said, giving a small smile, "but I *do* have a mage. Battered and bruised, sure, but still a mage."

Chall frowned at that. "I don't like the way you're talking, Priest. Which is nothing new, I suppose, but I *particularly* don't like the way you're talking right now."

Nigel frowned. "I don't get it. What are you thinking of doing?"

Priest continued to watch Chall. "I remember years ago, when we were in the Black Wood, you said that you could *feel* the magic of the place. Is that true? Can you really do that?"

The mage winced. "Yes. Maybe. It depends, alright? It isn't as if I just reach out and touch it. But if the magic is strong enough, or I look close enough..." He nodded. "Probably."

"Then that's it," Priest said.

"What's it?" Maeve asked, not following.

The man glanced at Chall, and the mage shook his head. "Uh-uh. You tell her."

Priest nodded, looking back to Maeve. "We have to kidnap the king."

There were several seconds of silence, broken only when Ned barked a laugh. "Sure, why not? And while we're at it, I've never really cared for where the castle is. Reckon on the way out we could pick it up, maybe move it to the other side of the city?"

"Ned's right," Maeve said. "You weren't there, Priest. The castle isn't safe—Chall nearly died the last time we went. And if we go again, who's to say that woman, that *Felara,* won't be there waiting for us? I won't risk it again and—"

"We have to do it, Maeve."

She turned to look at the mage. "You can't be serious, Chall." She looked at the others, all of them watching her, apologetic expressions on their faces. "No," she said, shaking her head, "no, I won't allow it. You can't go back, Chall. I won't..." *I won't risk losing you, not now.* "There's got to be another way," she finished, turning to look at Priest.

"There isn't, Maeve," Chall said softly. "I don't know if Priest is right or not, but if he is, there's a chance I might be able to detect the creature, and a chance—albeit a small one—that we might somehow be able to get it out of him. And...if there's even a chance, Maeve, we have to take it."

She stared at him, at once feeling betrayed and more in love with him than she ever had. "No," she breathed. "No, Chall, and that's final. Now, I...I need some time alone."

She hurried away, fleeing toward the back room. She stumbled inside, closing the door shut behind her. She looked at the table, still stained with Chall's blood, the table where, only hours ago, he had lain, fighting for his life. The tears came then. Hot and heavy tears that traced lines of grief down her face.

It wasn't fair. She had already given so much to the world, but the world, like some insatiable beggar, had decided, it seemed, that it was not enough. It had stolen one life from her already and now it meant to steal another, to steal even the small chance at happiness that she had managed to gather from the ashes of what it left her the first time.

She didn't know how long she stood there, staring at that table but not really seeing it, the tears flowing freely. Eventually, though, she heard the sound of the door opening. She did not need to look up to know that it was him, for she knew his sounds, the sounds of his footsteps, his breathing. In another moment, he was beside her.

"Look at me, Maeve."

She did not, only stood, staring at the table. "Maeve," he said softly, "look at me."

Finally, she did, turning to him. "You can't go, Chall. I'll go, if that's what needs doing. Me and Priest, some of the others, if we think it'll help. But not you."

The mage gave her a small smile. "That so? And if I don't go, Mae, then who's going to try to sniff out the magic we think might be on the lad? Or did you become a mage yourself, during your exile? Because when I found you, you were practicing pulling turnips, not casting spells."

"Potatoes," she said, sniffling.

"What's that?"

"I was pulling potatoes."

"Right. Potatoes then."

An idea struck her, and she grasped his hands. "I know what we could do, Chall. We could get the king and bring him here. We'll be safe here,"—*you'll be safe*—"and then you can take all the time you need to...well, do whatever it is you're going to do."

He grunted. "So let me understand this, Mae. You want to not only kidnap the king—quite an impossible task—but now you also want to somehow lug him across the entire city while, if what Priest is saying is true, the creature inside him is going to do its level best to get us all killed and get free? Not that it would have to do much—a simple shout would be enough to draw the guards' attention."

She winced. "We could bind him, gag him, maybe, and—"

"No, Mae," he said, gripping her hands gently. "This is how it has to be—you know that, I think."

And the most damning part of it was, she did. She knew that there was no way they'd make it across the city, not without being caught by the guards. "But you're *wounded,* Chall," she said, "you nearly *died."*

"*We* nearly died," the mage countered. "Sure, maybe I came a bit closer than the rest of you lot, but if we mean to do this, I reckon you'll all get a chance to even things up a bit soon enough."

She looked at him, and he was smiling, doing his best to hide his pain, but she could see the way he hunkered over, the way he moved tenderly, carefully, so as not to make it worse. "She was better than me, Chall," she said. "If only I'd been better, faster, then you never would have been wounded in the first place."

"True," the mage said, nodding thoughtfully. "A fair point. Come to think of it, you really did drop the ball, didn't you?" He sighed theatrically. "All these years of being threatened by those knives of yours, turns out that they aren't so dangerous after all."

She stared at him for a second, and he shook his head, smiling. "Look, Maeve, so maybe the woman got the better of you this once, so what? It isn't exactly as if you're at the top of your game, is it? None of us are. I mean, when was the last time you slept?"

Maeve blinked. With everything that had been going on, she'd lost track of the last time she'd managed to get any meaningful rest. "I'm...not sure."

"See?" the mage said. "Anyway, if you want to start passing around blame, why not blame me? After all, if *I* hadn't been so exhausted—and scared, I'll admit it—I could have, perhaps, cast some sort of illusion, got us all out of there. Or maybe we should blame Priest—the man's always talking about that goddess of his, but I didn't see her show up to keep that knife from seein' what my guts looked like. Or how about Cutter for sticking his wick where it didn't belong in the first place?"

Maeve frowned. "There's...I assume, a point to all this?"

"My *point*, Maeve, is that there's plenty of blame to go around, if that's what you mean to do, but it isn't going to help us, is it?"

"I guess not," she said slowly. "But I still don't like it, Chall."

He laughed. "What's to like? This might surprise you, Mae, but I don't much care for the idea of getting stabbed again either."

"But you still want to go."

"Want? Stones and starlight, no, I'm not suicidal, am I? But then 'want' doesn't really have anything to do with it. We'll go anyway."

She raised an eyebrow. "Because it's the right thing to do?"

"A pox on the 'right' thing," the mage said sourly. "No, I couldn't give two shits about that. We'll go because maybe, if we're really lucky, we can help the lad."

Maeve found herself smiling. "You like him, don't you?"

Chall fidgeted, uncomfortable, as always, with the thought of saying or doing anything that might counter his hard-won reputation for being a selfish cynic. "And so what if I do? And to be honest, I'd want to go even if it weren't for that."

"Why?" Maeve asked, genuinely curious.

The mage laughed. "Not going to let me get out of this one, are you? Fine. I'll go because the prince wouldn't hesitate to go if it were one of us and Matt is his son. And if, by some chance, Bernard *does* make it back from the Black Wood, I'd rather not be the guy who let his son go on being possessed by some Fey monstrosity. Being stabbed isn't any fun, but I imagine there's worse things."

Maeve was smiling wider now. "Challadius the Charitable. Has a certain ring to it, doesn't it?"

"More like a death knell," the mage muttered, then he met her eyes. "Anyway, are you okay?"

She nodded slowly. "I think so. Or as close as I'm likely to get. So...are we leaving now?"

"Me and the others talked about that after you left. We're thinking maybe we'd best wait for night but then, you're the one with all the experience—you tell me."

"Night's the way to go," she said.

He smiled slowly, a mischievous look in his eyes. "Well, in that case. Ned and Emille said they've got a spare room, if we want to...you know. Get some rest."

Maeve arched an eyebrow. "Are you sure you're up for it?" She grinned. "Resting, I mean. What with your wound and all."

"This?" he asked, gesturing at his bandaged stomach. "Pshh. Just a scratch."

"A scratch," she repeated, unable to keep the smile from her face.

"Sure," he said, "a scratch. Anyway, I think maybe I could do with some rest."

"Me too," she said. "But I'll warn you, Challadius," she went on, grabbing his hand, "if you think you've risked your life so far, you have no idea what you're in for."

And with that, she led him to the bedroom, uncaring of the knowing looks the others shot them as they passed through the main room of the house. In moments, they were in the room, an urgency within her, and, judging by the way he fell while removing his trousers, Chall as well. An urgency that they might have been forgiven as the both of them had waited on this moment for fifteen years and more.

But they were together then, the waiting done.

In time, they both lay in the bed, staring at the ceiling. "Marvelous is right," Chall gasped.

"Oh, Challadius," Maeve said, turning to him, "you haven't seen anything yet."

CHAPTER TWENTY-TWO

Often, the man left still standing, after the dying's done, is overcome with one feeling
And that feeling, contrary to popular belief, is not victory.
It's loneliness.
—Unnamed soldier during Fey War

"What is it then, brother? Is it that you *pursue* misery?"

Cutter sighed as he pushed another knot of brambles and vines aside and stepped past. He might have held them for his brother, who walked behind, but he had been listening to the man complain since they'd set out through the forest, so instead he let them go and was rewarded with a squawk of indignation from Feledias.

"Shit on this damned forsaken forest," Feledias hissed. "What's so wrong with the road anyway? Seems to me, brother, that after all the trouble you and I went through, all the meeting with engineers and draining of the kingdom's coffers, that it's a damned shame to go gallivanting through the forest when there's a perfectly good road we might walk on."

"You know," Cutter said as he swiped at a thick tangle of undergrowth with his axe, the always-sharp edge making quick work of it, "you and Challadius really ought to hang out more. Seems to me the two of you would get along great."

Feledias snorted. "I've no interest in that fat mage friend of yours, not unless he knows a spell that might burn this whole cursed forest down."

Cutter glanced back at Feledias. "This 'cursed forest' is our land, brother, fought and bled for by our people."

"A damned shame," his brother repeated. "Tell me, what was wrong with the road again?"

"Nothing, at least not with the road itself, though I think the assassins that are no doubt traveling it in search of us might make the journey a bit more arduous."

Feledias hissed, batting at an errant, thorny vine that had nicked him. "Better to die by an assassin's blade then by a thousand scratches from vines that seem dead-set on making what remains of our lives a misery."

Cutter sighed. There didn't really seem much point in arguing with his brother. He had been acting so for the day and a half since they'd departed the capital, and he didn't appear ready to let up anytime soon. Anyway, Cutter knew that the forest was the least of Feledias's worries, and that his brother had only chosen to use the forest as a focal point for his frustrations.

The truth was that, while he might not admit it, Feledias was worried for the kingdom, just as Cutter was. He didn't know what had transpired to make Matt act so or how bad the conspiracy actually was within the capital—hopefully, by now, the others had some inkling—but he felt guilty for leaving when his people so badly needed help. It did not matter that his leaving hadn't been by choice, did not even matter that he knew, deep down, that the people of the Known Lands were far better without him or his brother around.

The two princes of the realm, one who'd had an affair with his brother's wife, who had started a war with the Fey, and the other who had committed untold atrocities to hunt the first down, included the burning of Brighton and the slaughter of its people.

Cutter glanced back at Feledias as the man worked his way through a particularly thick tangle of brush. The man didn't look like a monster, just as he knew he himself did not, and the man, the brother, Cutter had known would never have done to the people of Brighton what he had. Yet, he *had* done it.

No, they did not look like monsters, but they *were* monsters just the same, and the kingdom, the *world*, could only be better off once they were dead. Besides, that was the thing about monsters—all men, Cutter thought, carried them inside them. Sometimes, those monsters did a fine job of hiding themselves, of remaining concealed behind friendly faces, behind the artifices of civilization, but they were there just the same, waiting for their chance to rise up and...well, do what monsters did.

And perhaps Matt was right. Perhaps Cutter really *could* make peace with the Fey. He didn't think so, not really, but it was a fine thought, a fine idea that he might do something good before he died.

"*Vagabonds,*" Feledias spat, "that's what we are. *Vagrants.* Tell me, brother, what is a prince without a kingdom?"

"A man," Cutter answered idly as he continued hacking his way through the brush.

"A *man,*" his brother repeated. "Oh, but we have fallen far, brother mine, plummeted down a precipice to come to this place of unending torment."

"Bein' a bit melodramatic, aren't you?" Cutter asked. "They're just vines."

"*Just* vines?" Feledias demanded. "Fire and salt, Bernard, they're *evil.*"

"Maybe we have fallen down a precipice," Cutter said, "but if we did, it's one we chose to step into ourselves." He paused then, turning back to his brother, meeting his eye. "The kingdom deserves better than us."

Feledias sighed. "You're right, of course. And if it's our lot to die, then die we will. I'll do it and without complaint—"

"I doubt that."

His brother frowned. "Anyway, I know that you and I have earned our deaths a dozen times over, more, but do there have to be so many damned *thorns?*"

"I was wonderin' the same," Cutter said, raising an eyebrow. "Seems to me you're a bit thorny yourself."

"Did...did you just try to make a joke?"

Cutter grunted. "Maybe."

"You have many talents, brother," Feledias said, then paused. "Or, perhaps...just the one." He glanced meaningfully at the axe. "Either way, humor cannot be counted among your gifts. Perhaps it would be best if you left it to others."

"I'll try to remember that."

They traveled on in blessed silence, for another hour until finally they emerged from the woods into a farmer's fields. Or, at least, what once had been. Here, like in so much of the kingdom of the Known Lands, it seemed that things had fallen into disrepair. Weeds had overgrown the lot of it, choking out any plants that might once have grown there.

Cutter could see the road, off to their left, and on the other side, a house and barn. Beyond that, in the distance, the forest began again.

"Thank the gods," Feledias breathed. "Let's go see if we can rent a room for the night. It's getting dark, and the gods know I've had enough of thorns and brambles for the day. For a lifetime, really, but I'll take what I can get."

Cutter frowned at the distant farmhouse. "Better if we stay in the woods. Any assassins searching for us will no doubt check the place out."

"Better if *you* stay in the woods, maybe," Feledias said, "since you seem to love them so much. But I, for one, Bernard, mean to sleep in a real bed tonight, one without any biting mosquitoes or snakes or *thorns.*"

"Fel," Cutter said, "it's not sa—" But he cut off as his brother marched toward the barn with grim purpose.

Cutter glanced around. No killers came rushing out of the woods, waving swords and shouting battle cries, but that was little comfort. After all, from what he knew of them, one of the requirements for assassins was not being seen until it was too late. Still, his brother was already halfway to the road, and it was clear that he had no intention of changing his mind, so Cutter heaved a heavy sigh and followed.

Feledias waited at the farmhouse door for him, a small, knowing smile on his face, and Cutter grunted as he came to stand beside him. "Did you knock?"

"Thought I'd wait on you," his brother said, still grinning.

Cutter frowned and gave the door a firm knock. At first, no answer came, and he was just about to knock again when the door creaked open, revealing a man who appeared to be in his forties, though it was hard to say for sure for the man's skin was waxy, his face lined from clear malnutrition which also showed in the too-thin hand that trembled as it grasped the door.

"Y-yes?" the stranger asked, a look on his face that made it clear he regretted opening the door.

Cutter couldn't blame him. After all, him and his brother likely would have appeared intimidating in the best of times. After nearly two days spent trekking through the woods, their clothes and hair covered in dirt and bits of bracken, they likely looked like two bandits on the run which, unfortunately, wasn't so far from the truth as he would have liked it.

"Forgive us for intruding, sir," Cutter said, "but we have been traveling for some time and spotted your barn from the road. With night coming on and all, we were wondering, if you might have a place we could sleep. We'll pay, of course."

The other man looked at the two of them for a moment, then he smiled. The expression went a long way toward transforming his weary face. "I understand that, strangers. Not wantin' to be out at night, I mean. Times have been tough all around, it's a fact, what with the Fey creatures roamin' the darkness and the taxes bein' raised so high from the capital a man spends all day at work and finishes it poorer than when he started."

Cutter shared a look with Feledias at that, and his brother winced. "Yes," he said, turning back to the man. "Still, as I said, we'd be happy to pay and—"

"Pay?" the man asked, shaking his head. "No, of course not. You're welcome to stay in that old barn for as long as you need—the gods know it ain't much use for anything else anymore."

Cutter nodded his head gratefully. "I appreciate it, really, but still I'd like to pay you."

The man shook his head again. "Wouldn't dream of takin' it. The world the way it is, I figure the only way we can get on is by helpin' one another. Now, please," he said, raising his hand when Cutter started to speak again, "I'll hear no more of it. You take the barn for as long as you need, and that'll be the end of it, alright?"

Cutter nodded. "Alright."

The man gave a single, solid nod of his own, clearly satisfied. "That's fine then. Now, I was just sittin' down to eat. Why don't you fellas come on in, have a bite?"

Cutter glanced around, taking in the barn and the house, the man himself, all three of which looked as if they'd seen far better days. "We wouldn't want to intrude," he said, thinking that the man needed all the food he could get and then some. "Anyway, thank you for the—"

"There's no intrusion at all," the man said, offering his hand. "The name's Alder."

Cutter took the hand, giving it a shake, and while the man himself looked frail, weak from hunger, his grip, at least, was firm. "Thank you, Alder," he said, "truly. You're helping us out, and I appreciate it, but we couldn't ask for your food. It—"

"Well, good thing you didn't ask then, ain't it?" the man said, grinning. "I offered is all, and I still am, though I'll warn you it ain't nothin' fine. Once, my family ate well here, but those times are gone along with my family, too, and the food ain't much. That said, you'd be doin' me a favor. It'd be good to eat and talk proper." He got a wistful look in his eyes then, staring off as if at some distant memory. "Seems I've been alone for about as long as I can remember. So." He turned back to Cutter, a desperation showing in his eyes, if not on his face. "Will the two of you have dinner with me?"

Cutter winced inwardly, glancing at Feledias. His brother's expression showed much of the guilt and shame he himself was feeling, but Feledias gave a covert nod. Cutter turned back to the man. "We'd be honored, Alder."

Alder grinned again. "Might wait on that 'til you've tasted what we're havin', if was I you."

Bernard found himself smiling in return. There was a part of him, the part that had spent the better part of his life killing and trying not to be killed, that didn't want to trust the man's hospitality, his kindness, but there was something about the man, his open, trusting face, that made that nearly impossible. "Lead the way, Alder."

The man nodded. "Well, come on then—I'll warn you, the house ain't much. My wife, the gods look after her, used to keep a tidy house, and I reckon she'd string me up if she was around to see what it's fallen to."

Cutter considered asking the man what had happened to the family he'd mentioned, but he had noticed an almost haunted look in the man's eyes when he spoke of his wife, his family. On the other hand, he had learned over his years in exile that no misery was ever so terrible as that which a man faced alone. But by the

A Warrior's Curse

time he'd prepared to ask about them, the man had already turned, disappearing into the house.

Cutter started through, then realizing Feledias hadn't moved, glanced back. "Well?"

His brother was frowning. "What if he means to kill us? I don't like it, Bernard."

Cutter shrugged. "It was your idea, Fel."

"And you choose *now* of all times to start giving a shit about my ideas?" his brother counted.

Cutter grinned. "Well, better late than never, eh?" Before his brother could say anything else Cutter turned and stepped into the house. He heard Feledias heave a heavy sigh as he stepped into what served as the main room of the home. Despite Alder's words of caution, the place, while simple, was clearly well-kept, the surface of the wooden table and the floors clean of dust or trash.

Alder was at the far end of the room, knelt over a fire above which hung a pot, a wooden spoon in his hand as he stirred the contents, his back to Cutter. Cutter heard the sound of footsteps and turned to see his brother walking up beside him.

"Change your mind?" he asked quietly.

Feledias favored him with a frown. "Thought I'd better eat a real meal while I still can. Traveling with you, likelier than not I'll be eating berries and bugs until we make it to the Black Wood."

"Go on then, have a seat," the man said, turning and gesturing to the table. Cutter turned and looked at it, noting that there were only two chairs.

Alder noted his gaze and waved a hand dismissively. "Go on, take a seat. The gods know I've had enough of sitting and then some, myself. Hadn't been much else to do lately, not since the farm went to shit. Anyway, I prefer standin'."

Cutter didn't like it, making a man stand in his own house, but Alder was insistent, so he nodded, moving to the table and having a seat, though he scooted his chair in such a way that he could keep an eye on the man. Alder was the type of man it was nearly impossible not to trust, but then Cutter had met such men before, and more than once they'd tried to poke a few holes in him when he wasn't paying attention.

So he watched, carefully, as the man stirred the pot. Seemed unlikely that he was hiding a crossbow in there, but then it was often the things a man thought unlikely that ended up killing him in the end.

Cutter removed his axe, setting it propped against the table leg within easy reach.

Alder suddenly turned at the sound of the axe head hitting the wood, and Cutter tensed at the abrupt gesture, sure that the man was about to attack. He didn't, though, only stared wide-eyed at the weapon, what Shadelaresh had called the Breaker of Pacts.

"My but that's a mighty thing, ain't it?" the farmer asked.

Bernard winced. "I...that is—"

"Good for chopping firewood, anyway," Feledias said, glancing at Bernard.

Alder grunted a laugh. "I imagine it is at that. Well," he said, turning back to the pot, "I reckon it's as edible as it's likely to be." He rose and began rooting through a cupboard. A moment later, he retrieved several dusty earthenware bowls and spoons. He winced as if embarrassed, wiping the dust off with his simple linen tunic. "Sorry about that. As I said, it's been a while since I had company."

He bent then, ladling stew into two bowls then bringing them back to the table. "Hope you like cabbage," he said apologetically as he placed the bowls, along with the spoons, in front of Cutter and his brother.

Cutter glanced at the stew—mostly water with only a few scraps of wilted cabbage in it—and hesitated.

While his physical health might have been in question, Alder's mind worked well enough, for he noted the hesitation, grinning. "You're thinkin' maybe I poisoned it?"

Cutter winced, for that was pretty much exactly what he'd been thinking. "I don't mean to offend, it's just—"

"Oh, no offense given," Alder said, waving a hand dismissively. "The world bein' what it is lately, I can't blame a man for not taking any chances. Hold a moment." He went to the pot over the small fire and returned a moment later with his own bowl, then ate a spoonful, making a sour face as he did. "Not poison, though I don't reckon it's all that far from it neither. My wife, Hilda, she used to cook a fine meal—never had much of a talent for it myself, though I like to think that's got at least a bit to do with a shortage of ingredients."

The cynical part of Cutter, the animal part, thought that it would have been possible for the man to have poisoned their two bowls while keeping his own safe, but then logically he knew that would have been nearly impossible. After all, he'd been watching the man the entire time, and he would have noticed had the farmer tried to pour anything into their food. Still, Cutter had never been much good with trust. But the man was watching him, as was Feledias, apparently having chosen to take his cue from him.

Cutter still hesitated, but in the end he told himself that it didn't matter. They traveled to the Black Wood, a journey that could only end in their deaths, and if the food was poisoned—which he doubted—it could be no worse than what awaited him and his brother. He took a spoonful, ate it. It was one of the hardest things he'd ever done, but while the stew tasted sour, he did not think it was poisoned, and the grin that came to Alder's face made it worth it.

"I told you," the farmer said, "not poison, but then not so far off either." He met Cutter's eyes. "Not an easy thing, trusting people, is it?"

"No," Cutter agreed. "It isn't."

The man sighed. "A damn shame, that, but what can you do? Gotta trust someone sometimes—otherwise, what's the point of anything? Or so Hilda used to tell me."

"She sounds like a wise woman, your wife," Feledias offered.

Alder grinned. "Oh she was that, that and more, a damn sight better than a man like me deserves and that's a fact. Question is, do you reckon she's wise enough to have a bite of that stew you're eyein' like it's a snake ready to bite you?"

Feledias winced, glancing at Cutter, then, finally, his brother shrugged. "Why not?" He took a bite of the stew, tensing as he did. When nothing happened, he sighed, visibly relaxing, and Alder laughed.

Cutter hadn't realized how hungry he was until he tasted the stew. Not the finest he'd had—bland and more water than cabbage—but after two days eating what they could scavenge in the woods it tasted good, and before he knew it, his bowl was empty.

Alder grinned. "Go on then, there's more," he said, gesturing to the pot. "Help yourself."

"Thank you," Cutter said. He rose, walking to the pot and glancing in. The man was right—there was more, but not much. Two bowls left, he judged. "Come to think of it," he said, "I'm just about full."

"Oh, go on and get some," the man said, laughing. "Don't suffer on my account. Fact is..." He gestured at his wilted frame. "I don't eat as much as I used to. Anyway, two bowls, and I'd spend the night camped in the privy—that I know from hard-won experience."

Cutter winced. Not good with trusting but then not good with kindness either. "Thanks," he managed, then he poured another bowl, keeping the portion small.

He made his way back to the table and, for a time, the three of them ate in companionable silence. As they did, Cutter realized that he was comfortable. He couldn't remember the last time he felt truly comfortable, felt *safe*. Ridiculous, of course, for while the man Alder might not be an assassin, there were certainly others who would like nothing more than to see him and his brother dead. Yet, sitting there, in the small, well-kept house, the warmness of the stew filling his belly, he felt a greater peace than he could remember feeling in a very, very long time, perhaps even since before the Skaalden came and drove his people from their homeland.

After a time he finished the last bit of his stew and as Feledias began on his own round of seconds, Cutter sat back in his chair. "If you don't mind my asking, Alder," he said, "what happened? To your farm, I mean? That is, I saw that it's in a bit of disrepair."

The man grinned. "Noticed that, did you? Aye, well it'd be hard not to. As for what happened?" He shrugged. "Life, I guess. One day, a man's got everything he could ever want or need, the next—" he snapped his fingers—"it's gone. The most damning thing is that, most of the time, people don't really know how good they got it until it's taken away." His eyes got that distant look then, and he sighed. "I did, though. I knew. Didn't stop life from happenin' but then, nothin' does, does it?"

Cutter gave a sigh of his own. "No, no, I suppose it doesn't."

Alder shrugged. "Anyway, there's no point for a man to spend his life thinkin' on what he's lost. Better, you ask me, to think about what you have, what you've had. Everything fades, life, stars, all of it, but some of those shine damn bright while they're around."

"Your wife?" Cutter asked. "She shone?"

Alder smiled again. "Like the sun itself. Anyway, I got a question of my own, if you don't mind. I been lookin' at that axe of yours." He nodded his head to it. "Seems to me I might've seen it before. Or heard of it maybe, though I can't think of where."

Cutter did his best to mask his wince. He didn't want to lie to the man, but neither did he want to tell him his true identity. If anyone came around asking questions about them, it would be better if the farmer didn't know. Better for everyone. "Picked it up a few years back from a merchant—it's rare, from what I'm told."

The farmer laughed, apparently satisfied. "Sure, and rarer still the man strong enough to lift the big bastard, eh?"

They talked for some time then, of small, trivial things, the weather, food, life, and it was nice. The sun sank low as they spoke, yet still no one made a move to leave the table. Certainly, Cutter did not, for the conversation seemed to be more than just talk—in some ways, it seemed to him, to be healing. A salve for the many bruises and nicks that life left a man with, and he soaked it in, all of it, the way a man, long in the cold, might stand and glory in the feel of the sun on his skin. Feledias too, he saw, made no move to cut the conversation short, but took part in it along with them, even making a few clever jokes in a way that reminded Cutter of when they had been children, back before their world, their lives had been taken from them.

Finally, Alder yawned. "Well, I guess you two must be exhausted, and here I've been yappin' my gums."

Cutter shook his head. "It's a pleasure, Alder."

"Agreed," Feledias said.

The man grinned. "Well, that's nice of you to say. Anyhow, if you want to follow me, I'll show you to the barn—it ain't much, mind, but at least it's dry."

He rose, and Cutter and Feledias followed suit, walking after the farmer as he led them to the barn.

They climbed a ladder up to the barn's loft, said goodnight to the farmer, and in time they'd lain down on two separate piles of hay. Ridiculous, maybe, but as Cutter lay there, satisfied, his heart full if not his stomach, that pile of hay seemed more comfortable than any bed he'd ever slept on.

"A good man, isn't he?" Feledias asked, and by some trick of the darkness, his voice sounded like that of a child, the way he had sounded so long ago in their father's castle.

A good man. Cutter had spent a long time in the darkness. Sometimes, it seemed that he had spent his whole life there. And how long might a man spend there, in that perpetual night, before he forgot what the light was? How long might he spend around killers, himself the worst of the lot, before he no longer even recognized a good man? "Yes," he said finally, softly, "yes, I think he is."

He slept then. Blame it on that rare feeling of peace, or on the blanket of warm hay on a chill night. Blame it, perhaps, on the Crimson Prince, for once, being human, that and no more, but for a moment, for only a brief instant in time as his eyes closed and he fell into warm slumber, Cutter forgot.

He forgot his fears, his worries and caution. He forgot, for that moment, what the world was.

And the world, seeing this, set out to remind him.

***

For the first time he could remember, Feledias did not dream. He was not, for once, reminded of the feeling of helpless betrayal which had overcome him as he was forced, in yet one nightly vision after another, to witness his brother departing from his new wife's bedchamber. Nor did he dream, as he often did, of violence, of fire and blood and death, testament to the revenge he had so long sought on the brother who had so wronged him.

He did not dream of these things.

He woke to them.

The first thing he became aware of as he slowly roused awake, was the smell of something burning. Frowning, he opened his eyes and then he became aware of a second—and considerably more pressing—thing. Namely, the man standing over him, a knife in his hand. Feledias might not have seen this had the barn remained as dark as it had been when they'd lain down, but the barn was on fire, flames slithering up the walls like serpents.

"What the fu—" Feledias began, but then the assassin began to bring the blade down, and Feledias squeaked, trying to dive out of the way and knowing, even as he did, that he would be too late.

But instead of plunging into him, the knife stopped inches from his chest as if it had struck a wall, and Feledias became aware of a second figure standing beside the first. The newcomer was so covered in blood and gore that, for a moment, Feledias didn't recognize him. Then the light of the fire shifted, revealing his brother's face, as grim as death, his eyes dancing with wild fury.

It was the assassin's turn to squeal then as Bernard lifted him up easily by where he held the man's wrist and then threw him. The man hurled through the air as if launched from a catapult, striking the barn wall and, with a ripping of boards—and no doubt flesh—went sailing through it, out of sight.

Feledias stared in shock at the hole in the wall, at the fire crawling up the sides of the barn, then turned back to Cutter. "Are...are there others?" he managed.

"Not anymore," his brother growled, his chest heaving, the terrible black axe clutched in one bloody fist as his eyes danced wildly. For a moment, Feledias was overcome with the certainty that Bernard would kill him next. He had jested, earlier that night, about the axe being good for chopping firewood. It had seemed funny enough at the time, but it did not seem funny now, not with his brother standing over him like some giant demon bent on death, the cruel weapon clutched in one tight fist.

So powerful was the image, the *feeling*, that he let out a grunt of fear and surprise when his brother's free hand shot out. Feledias winced, then took the hand and a moment later he was standing on his feet. "Sorry," he said, "I thought—"

"I know what you thought," Bernard said. "Come on." He turned back to the ladder then, and Feledias hurried after him. "Wait, Bernard, wait, damnit, are you sure there aren't anymore?"

His brother paused, halfway on the ladder and looked at him. "Not alive, at least."

Feledias swallowed at that, relieved as his brother pulled his penetrating, mad gaze away and started down the ladder. Left with nothing else to do, Feledias snatched up his meager belongings and followed.

The bottom of the barn was a scene of carnage even the world's most talented artists would have had difficulty depicting. Half a dozen men or at least what once had *been* men, lay scattered on the hay-strewn floor, their bodies broken and twisted as if struck down by the hand of some wrath-filled god. So terrible was the devastation, the *brutality*, that Feledias was forced to fight down his rising gorge.

Bernard, though, didn't so much as glance at the corpses. "Come on," he growled, and Feledias stumbled after him. The smoke was thick now, making his breath rasp in his throat and lungs, the fire rising all around him, and he would have become lost instantly had he not been following Bernard.

He studied his brother as he followed him, his body covered in blood as if he'd taken a bath in the stuff, the obsidian axe's blade shining crimson. Had he really thought to kill him? Had he really believed himself *capable* of it? To kill him the way one might a man, with sword or bow? For in that moment his brother did not seem like a man who might be so easily slain but like the avatar of destruction itself, one that could not be killed anymore than a man might kill *war* itself.

Finally, they reached the barn entrance, and he stumbled out behind his brother and into the night, gasping for air and falling to his knees. His lungs felt as if they were on fire, and he was forced to pat out one of his sleeves where the flames had caught. He glanced at his brother to see him standing, staring at something in the distance. Feledias followed his gaze, and it didn't take long to see what he looked at—the house. The house that, only hours ago, they had sheltered in, where they had eaten and talked. The house that, just then, was on fire.

"Alder," Bernard growled. "He needs help."

"Bernard, the house, it's too late," Feledias began, "it—" But he didn't finish, for his brother took off at a run toward the flaming edifice of the house. Feledias bit back a curse, climbing to his feet and shuffling after him.

He was nearly halfway there when his foot caught on something he didn't see in the darkness. He nearly fell, just managing to gain his balance. Grunting, he looked down to see what he'd struck and suddenly felt the wind knocked out of him as if he'd been punched in the stomach. "Bernard," he yelled or, at least, tried to, but the words came out in little more than a whisper.

He looked away to see his brother starting toward the flame-wreathed doorway as if he meant to step into the inferno. "Bernard!" he yelled, managing it this time.

His brother turned. *"We have to save Alder!"* he roared, thrusting his axe at the door. *"He's in there somewhere!"*

"No, Bernard," Feledias shouted back. "No, he's not."

Bernard paused then, turning to regard him, and by some trick of the light and shadow, his face looked demonic one moment then the most wretched picture of grief the next until, finally, it settled into the expressionless mask Feledias had grown so accustomed to over the years.

His brother said nothing else, but Feledias noted the way his shoulders slumped, noted, too, the way some of that great strength, that great *power* that had possessed him seemed to fade away as if it had never been. The arm holding his axe slumped to his brother's side, and Bernard started across the yard toward where Feledias stood, not hurrying now, and being right not to, for there was no need. The time for hurry, for action, had passed.

Soon, Bernard stood beside him, both of them staring at the body at their feet. For a time, they said nothing, only stood in the shadows as sporadic orange light of the burning house and barn cast them in light one moment only to shift them to the darkness in the next.

As the light fell on them again, Feledias noted something he hadn't before, a bundle of fabric lying beside the dead man. "What—"

"Blankets," his brother said, his voice low, raw. "He was bringing us blankets."

Feledias stared in shock at his brother, saying nothing, for what could a man say at such a time? What could he do when the world burned but stand there and smell it, *witness* it?

Alder was dead. The man had given them shelter without asking anything in return, had given them food when it was clear he didn't have enough. He had showed them nothing but kindness, and he had died for it. He had died, was dead, and it was the two of them who had brought that death to him. "What are we, Bernard?" Feledias asked, aware of the tears streaming down his face and not caring. "What *are* we?"

"I am fire," his brother said, "and all I touch turns to ash."

Feledias frowned. "What?"

Bernard shook his head. "Nothing. What are we, Fel? You were right—we are monsters. Mostly, though, I am just tired."

Feledias nodded slowly, unable to take his eyes off the body at his feet. "What do we do now?" he asked.

"Now?" Bernard said. "We go to the Black Wood."

Feledias nodded again at that. "Do you think...it's bad, Bernard? To be dead, I mean?"

His brother's great shoulders lifted in a shrug. "Can't be much worse than being alive."

Bernard turned then, starting away, and as he did, Feledias saw a gash in his side about a foot long, oozing blood.

"Gods, Bernard, you're wounded!" he said.

His brother glanced at his side. "It's nothing."

Feledias frowned. "I'm no healer, brother, but that doesn't look like nothing."

Bernard gave another shrug. "I was too slow," he said, his eyes turning back to the dead man. "I always am."

That was when he passed out.

Feledias rushed to his fallen brother's side, feeling for a pulse and surprising himself by the vast sigh of relief that escaped him when he found it. Not dead then, but in a bad way.

Feledias didn't know much of healing, but anyone who had fought in the Fey Wars and survived knew enough to make a makeshift bandage, and he proceeded to do so, tearing strips from his shirt and wrapping them around the wound, tying them as tightly as he could. When he was finished, he rose, wondering what to do.

Bernard showed no signs of waking, but he knew that it was as good as suicide to stay here much longer. True, his brother had dealt with the assassins—with a grim finality—but there would be more. They were like cock roaches in that way...in a lot of ways, really.

He cast his gaze about, searching for some solution, and his eyes alighted on the blankets lying beside Alder's corpse, an idea forming in his mind as they did. Had their situations been reversed, Bernard might have lifted Feledias easy enough, but he was not his brother, did not possess his strength. Still, where strength lacked, resourcefulness might do.

Feledias nodded grimly to himself then set off for the distant tree-line of the woods. When he returned, he used the branches he'd procured to form a makeshift travois. He had never done such a thing before, but he had read of it in one of the books his brother used to mock him for spending so much time with—a point he intended to remind the ridiculously large bastard of when he woke. *If* he woke.

Feledias stepped back, nodding, satisfied at the work. The finished product might not win any prizes, but he thought it would serve. With that done, he turned back to the farmer's corpse. "I'm sorry," he said to the dead man, then glanced at his unconscious brother. "We both are." He wiped a hand at the tears flowing from his eyes then. He would grieve, later. The dead, after all, would wait—they could do little else.

Just now, though, he had to focus on the living.

A finely cared for mind, he thought, was all well and good, but he couldn't *think* his brother's stupidly large form onto the stretcher, so he bent to the task, hissing and cursing. Finally, panting from exertion, he managed to drag his brother onto the travois, consoling himself with the fact that it would be easier once he got his brother's bulk on the makeshift contraption. Which it was.

Not so easy that he didn't consider strangling the unconscious man at least a dozen times within the first hour of pulling him...but easier.

CHAPTER TWENTY-THREE

A plan is a great comfort.
At least, that is, until the dying starts.
—General Ichavian, famed military strategist

"Mae, is it too late to say I don't love this plan?"

Maeve's nerves were high, and she nearly screamed at the unexpected voice, then turned to scowl at Challadius where he stood behind her in the alleyway. Priest was next, the historian Petran Quinn in the back, looking like he'd rather be just about anywhere than standing less than a hundred feet from the castle gate. Maeve couldn't blame him. After all, the castle was full of people who would no doubt be thrilled to find them—and then proceed to make a game of killing them terribly.

"Maybe it's a bit late," she hissed.

"Anyway, what part of the plan don't you like?" Petran asked, his eyes wide and terrified.

"Well," Chall said consideringly, "I won't lie to you, Petran—the whole dying horribly bit has given me a little pause."

The historian practically turned green at that, and Maeve wished, not for the first time, that she hadn't brought him along. The problem, though, was that they needed him. No one else knew the layout of the servants' quarters—their best, and likely only chance of making it even remotely close to Matt's bedchambers. Without him, they'd likely stumble around blindly until one servant or another alerted the guards to their presence and then came the whole dying horribly bit, as Chall put it.

"Maybe...maybe we had best go over the plan one more time, Lady Maeve," the historian managed in a dry croak.

"Fire and salt but I hate you," she whispered to Chall.

The mage raised an eyebrow. "What happened to all that love talk?"

"I'm complex," she said dryly. "I can do both." Then she turned back to Petran. "Anyway, Petran, once more, it's simple enough. Chall will create an illusion to get us past the gate and into the castle. From there, you'll lead us through the servant corridors and get us as close as you can to the king's bedchamber."

"And...then?"

Maeve fought back the urge to hiss in frustration. They'd gone over the plan at least half a dozen times before they'd left Ned and Emille's home, but she knew that Petran was just afraid, that was all, and the fact was, he had a right to be. After all, it wasn't often a person tried to break into a castle to kidnap a king and far less often that they succeeded.

"Then you can stay in the corridors," Maeve said. "If you're alone, it's likely the guards won't bother you. Meanwhile, we three will get to the king's chambers—"

"Far easier said than done," Chall interrupted.

She did her best to ignore him, still looking at Petran. "There, Priest and I will watch the door while Chall does...well. Whatever it is he does. Besides bitching, that is."

Priest nodded. "Simple."

"Sure," Chall said, "but then so's dying. In case anyone's forgotten, there are guards outside the king's chambers, and somehow I doubt they're likely to just let us by without a question or two."

"You just worry about figuring out what's going on with Matt," Maeve said, then met Priest's eyes. "We'll handle the rest." *For as long as we can, anyway.*

Priest gave a nod, making it clear he understood that if things went badly—which they seemed very, very likely to do—then their mission, such as it was, could only end one way.

"Alright then," Maeve said, "everyone ready?"

Chall gave a snort, Petran trembled, and Priest nodded. Not a resounding vote of confidence, maybe, but then she thought it likely the best she was going to get, so she turned to the mage. "Alright, Chall. We're good. Are you...that is, are you sure you're okay?"

He grinned. "Sure, Mae. Fit as a fiddle—one that's been trampled by horses anyway. Still..." He paused, his smile widening. "The rest helped."

Maeve felt her face flush with heat at that. "Just get on with it, you bastard," she said, trying for scolding and not quite making it.

He laughed softly. "Alright then. No one move any more than you have to, and for the gods' sake don't talk."

He closed his eyes, and Maeve suddenly felt her skin break out in gooseflesh. One moment, she was staring at Challadius, her longtime companion, and the next, she was looking directly at the features of Rolph, the man from Two Rivers and now bodyguard to the king.

She turned to check on the other two and saw that they, also, had changed. In the place of Priest and Petran stood two women, the faces of which Maeve recognized from the "advisors" that had been gathered in the audience chamber. Maeve looked at her own hands and saw that they were still a woman's hands, though ones, it had to be said, much younger than her own.

She frowned at Chall. "We're all women."

The mage cleared his throat. "They're the only ones I could remember well enough."

Maeve rolled her eyes. "Why am I not surprised?"

He winced. "Anyway, how do I look?"

"Fine," she said. "Except the nose."

He frowned at that. "What about the nose?"

"Well, it's a bit...mushy, isn't it?"

He sighed. "Always the damned nose." He closed his eye again, waving a hand in front of his face and despite the fact that Maeve had seen the mage work his magic dozens, likely hundreds of times, it was disconcerting to watch the mashed nose shift and change. "Better?" he asked.

"Good enough anyway," she said.

"Good," he said, "then let's hurry—I can't hold this for long."

Maeve glanced at the others, giving a nod. Priest returned it, and she waited for another moment until the woman that was Petran gave a shaky nod of her own. Then they started toward the gate.

It was odd, for while the mage's magic might change their appearance, she still *felt* like herself, and so it was difficult not to imagine that the guards would cut them down as soon as they neared the gate. But as they approached, none of the four men stationed there rushed forward with swords drawn and in another minute they were standing before them.

"The gate," Chall barked. "Open it."

The four guards glanced oddly at each other, likely wondering at the change in the man's voice, for though Chall had clearly made an effort to sound different, Maeve could recognize his voice just the same.

"*Well?*" Chall demanded, and while the guards might have thought it strange that he sounded differently, they apparently didn't want to risk Rolph's ire, for they hurriedly went about the task and in moments the gate was swinging open.

"Well," Maeve said as they approached the castle door, "that was easy enough."

"For you, maybe," Chall responded in a strained voice, and she glanced over to see that he was sweating. Only, the sweat looked odd, out of place, as if it was embedded in his skin, and it took her a moment to realize that what she was seeing was the skin on Chall's face, not the illusion's.

"Chall," she said softly as they neared the door, "you're sweating."

"Shit," he responded, his voice still stounding strained as if he moved under some great weight. "We have to hurry, I'm losing it."

They approached the guards at the door and thankfully these, at least, opened it without a word. Then they were through, the door closing behind them.

Maeve glanced around, making sure no one was in ear shot, then turned to the woman that was Petran. "Well? Where's the nearest entrance?"

"Just...that is, just a moment," he said.

"We don't *have* a moment, Petran," Chall hissed. "Any second now, I'm going to lose the spell and then..."

"Easy," Maeve said in a soothing tone to the historian, "just take it easy. You can do this, Petran—the entrance. Where is it?"

The historian took a slow, deep breath, visibly trying to gather himself. "This way."

He started past her at a walk, and Chall grunted. "Better move faster, Petran, unless you want to feel a headman's axe for research purposes."

The historian didn't need anymore encouragement than that, and luckily no guards or servants waited between them and the entrance to the hidden corridors, for if they had, they would have no doubt been curious why a group of four were running down the hallway, king's advisors or not.

Petran stopped in front of a statue, pulling on one of its arms, and a moment later it slid away revealing a corridor. They hurried inside, and Chall collapsed as Priest pulled the lever to close the door once more.

Maeve hurried to the mage's side where he sat propped with his back against the thin corridor's wall. "Chall," she said, unable to keep the panic from her voice, "are you okay?"

"Fine," the mage rasped through gritted teeth, though she needed only look at his face—and it was *his* again, thank the gods—to see that he was lying.

"How bad is it?" she asked, glancing worriedly at the hand he had over his stomach where he had taken the wound. She lifted his fingers and saw that they were sticky with bloody. "Oh gods, Chall, you're bleeding again."

The mage gave her a weak grin. "Just a little blood, Mae. I'll be fine."

"Are you sure?" she asked. "Are you sure you want to do this?"

"What choice do I have?" he asked. "Priest, why don't you help me up, eh?" The man stepped forward without comment and between him and Maeve they managed to get the exhausted mage to his feet.

Chall swayed for a moment then met Maeve's eyes, but she didn't like the way his pupils seemed to swim in their sockets. "Alright," he said, "let's go—if given a choice, I'd rather die in a king's chambers than a servant's corridor."

Maeve wanted to call it off then, but she knew that to do so would be to doom the kingdom, and no doubt them as well. After all, they were too far in now, so she gave a grim nod, turning to the historian. "Lead on, Petran."

The historian complied without comment, and then they were moving through the corridors. They passed several servants on their way who marked their passage with curious, nervous stares, and Maeve watched as a serving man rushed off, no doubt to tell the nearest guards. She winced, knowing there was nothing they could do to stop him, nothing, at least, short of killing the man who for all they knew was innocent. Their only choice, then, was to count on speed, and so they did, jogging through the corridors as quickly as they could while helping the dizzy mage along.

Soon they came to a wall, and Chall hissed. "A dead end. Damnit, Petran, I thought you knew—"

"If I am correct," the historian said, "this entrance should open up two halls over from the king's own chambers, near the guard station."

"Near the *guard* station?" Chall wheezed. "Fire and salt, historian, do you *want* to get us killed?"

"It is the closest exit!" the historian said defensively.

"We'll have to backtrack," Chall said, turning to Maeve.

Maeve considered for a moment then shook her head. "No. We don't have time. The guards will know we're here soon, if they don't already. We have to go—now."

"Maeve's right," Priest offered. "One of the servants will tell them."

"Fine," Chall said, waving a hand toward the door. "After you, Priest."

The man nodded, moving toward the wall and pulling the lever. A moment later, part of the stone wall slid away, revealing the hallway beyond.

Priest stepped forward, looking both ways before turning back to Maeve, nodding. "Clear."

"Sure," Chall said, "but for how long?"

"How about we don't stick around to find out?" Maeve asked, taking his arm and following Priest back out into the hallway. She turned back to the historian, standing there with a lost look on his face. "Petran...if we don't make it—"

The man swallowed, nodding. "I will find the truth if I can, Lady Maeve. It is all I have ever done."

She met his eyes. "Good luck, historian."

"To you as well."

They were moving then, hurrying through the hallway as much as Chall's exhaustion and wound would allow until Priest paused at the intersection that Maeve knew led to Matt's chambers. The man glanced around then back at Maeve. "Two guards."

"Damn," Chall said. "Suppose it was too much to hope that they decided to take the day off. What do we—"

"I'll take care of them," Priest said, and before either Maeve or Chall could say anything else the man turned and stepped into the hall, moving in the direction of the guards.

Maeve heard the guards say something, though she could not make out the words and didn't need to in any case as it was obvious to her that they would be asking after why Priest had come. Just as it was obvious by the abrupt grunts and a cry—quickly silenced—that Priest had chosen to let his fists answer for him. In another minute, the man appeared from around the corner again, looking as composed as he had before. "The door's clear."

Maeve nodded, readjusting Chall's arm on her shoulder then turning into the hallway to see the two guards lying unconscious on the ground, neither of them having managed to draw their blades.

"You know, Priest," Chall said matter-of-factly, "you really are frightening."

The man said nothing to that as they continued on, stepping over the fallen guards to reach the door. Priest tried the handle and turned back to Maeve. "Locked."

"It's alright," she said, "I've got this."

She took out a knife—the smallest she carried—and began to work it into the gap where the door met the frame, trying to catch the latch.

"Come on, Maeve," Chall said.

"I'm *trying*," she snapped. "It isn't as if I sit around practicing, is it?"

"Well, maybe you should."

Maeve chose not to respond to that—mostly because her most likely response would be to commit murder in the hallway—instead gritting her teeth and continuing her efforts.

"Maeve," Chall said again after a moment.

"*Damnit, Chall,*" she said, turning to look at him, "I'm tryi—" She cut off as she noticed that the mage wasn't staring at her but was, instead, looking down the hallway. Maeve followed his gaze and saw a woman dressed in servant's garments standing at the end of the hallway. She appeared to be middle-aged and was cradling an armful of what appeared to be candlesticks, no doubt meant for cleaning.

For a frozen moment in time, the woman stared at the unconscious guards and the three of them, the knife Maeve held still stuck in the doorway. That moment stretched and stretched, a thousand thoughts—panicked ones, mostly—running through Maeve's mind in an instant. Then, like a bubble grown too large, burst. The woman dropped the candlesticks she was holding, screamed, and ran.

"*Guards!*" she shouted.

"Well," Chall said grimly, "there's that."

Maeve didn't waste time on words, for she knew that any minute the woman's screams would summon the guards. Guards who, finding them standing over two of their unconscious comrades and trying to break into the king's bedchamber, likely wouldn't bother with any questions. Instead, she turned back to the door, hissing and cursing as she worked at the latch.

Finally, it gave with a metallic *snap*, and she heaved a heavy sigh of relief. "Quiet now," she said, turning back to the others, then she slowly pushed the door open.

The three of them stepped inside, and Maeve was surprised to find that the room was dark—apparently, Matt slept hard. He must have been, to not have been awakened by the woman's shouts or the sounds of fighting outside in the hallway. She glanced at the bed and saw that indeed the young man's form was there, underneath the blankets, his back to the door.

"Sleeps like the dead, that one," Chall whispered.

Maeve shot a scowl at the mage, holding a finger to her lips, then started toward the bed.

"Ah, Maeve the Marvelous," a voice said, freezing her in her tracks, "welcome back."

Maeve thought she knew that voice. She hoped, prayed, that she was wrong, but light bloomed in the darkness, and she turned to see the assassin, Felara, sitting reclined in a chair, her feet propped up on the table, the lantern she had just lit sitting on its surface. The woman eyed her, raising an eyebrow as she picked at her fingernails with a knife.

"What...how did—" Maeve began, but the woman waved a dismissive hand.

She sighed. "Truly, I am disappointed. The world's *best* assassin, they call you." She rolled her eyes. "It seems like in this, as in so much else, the bards have exaggerated. You see, Lady Maeve, I thought you might be back, you and your friends. And I, being a loyal citizen of the Known Lands, could not stand idly by while you killed our king."

Maeve looked over at the bed and saw Matt sitting up, a grim expression on his face, one that looked alien on his youthful features. "Matt, we didn't come to kill you," she said, "we came to help—"

Loud laughter from the woman drowned out her words. "Come now, Maeve," she said, shaking her head. "You show up in the dead of the night, holding a *knife*, and we're to believe you came for some nice chat, is that it?"

Maeve glanced at the blade in her head and winced, turning back to Matt.

"Maeve," Chall said, warning in his tone, "the guards are coming."

"Bar the door," she said, "hold them for as long as you can. Listen, Matt—"

"Your *Highness*," the assassin snapped.

"There's something wrong with you," Maeve spoke on, aware of the sound of booted feet coming down the hallway. "Back in Two Rivers, the creature, Emma, she...she possessed you, somehow and—"

The woman laughed, but Matt held up his hand, silencing her. "P-possessed me?" he asked, his eyes wide and frightened. "A-are you sure?"

"We...we're pretty certain, yes," Maeve said.

"Sire, I really don't think we should let her—"

"*Silence,*" Matt shouted, his voice shaking with fury, and the woman quieted. That done, Matt turned back to Maeve. "You...you said I'm possessed?"

"We believe so."

"Oh, gods," he breathed, then he buried his face in his hands and began to sob. There was a strange quality to those sobs, one Maeve couldn't put her finger on until a moment later, for then he wasn't sobbing any longer but laughing as he raised his head. "Oh, Maeve, but you really are a fool, aren't you?"

There was a strange, almost feminine quality to the young man's voice, and Maeve frowned, looking at him. "Matt?"

The youth gave a cunning, cruel smile then. "Not anymore." He waved his hand. "Anyway, I'm bored. You may finish with them."

It was clear he was talking to the assassin, and the woman smiled as she rose. "Thank you, Majesty."

"Matt, please," Maeve said, moving toward him, "don't do this. We care about you, your *father* cares about you. We only want to help."

He looked at her, shaking his head again. "Pathetic," he sneered, and that was alright, for Maeve was close now, falling on her knees before him, her hands grasping desperately at his trouser legs.

"Please, Matt, we need you, and you need us. Please, let us help you," she said, her head down.

"No," the king said, slapping her hands away. "I don't think so."

"Y-you're sure?" she said.

"Yes, I'm sure, damn you!"

"Very well," Maeve said, giving up the pretend sobs. "Then I'm sorry."

"Sorry for wha—"

He never got to finish the sentence, for Maeve slammed the handle of her knife into his temple in one smooth motion. Fey-possessed or not, the human body was still the human body and so this one did what they all do when struck in such a way—it promptly went unconscious.

Matt collapsed to the bed in a heap, and Maeve rose, turning to the assassin. "Priest, watch the door," she said, eyeing the woman. "Chall, do what you can. I'll take care of her."

The woman, Felara, shook her head, her small smile well in place. "Clever," she said, "but you know it makes no difference in the end. You cannot best me—that, I believe, we have already discovered."

A moment later, Maeve heard the sound of the guards banging on the door, trying to break their way in. It wouldn't take them long, but she couldn't think of it. Instead, she thought only of the woman standing before her, that and nothing else. She had been distracted before—she could not allow herself to be distracted now.

She drew a second knife, twin to the first and the woman did the same, grinning all the while. Then, slowly, she stepped away from the table and they began to circle each other. "You know," Felara said, "I'm going to enjoy this."

"That makes one of us," Maeve said. Then she charged.

***

Chall glanced at Maeve and the woman in awe, watched their blades flashing out again and again, too fast to follow. He wanted to move forward, to help her, but he knew that he would only get in the way and likely get them both killed. Besides, he had a job to do.

He turned back to where Matt lay, unconscious, on the bed, then started toward him. Seeing him there, without the cruel sneer on his face, he looked like the young, innocent boy he had first met in the Black Wood with the prince. He had been naïve, that boy, but there had been a goodness about him, and Chall thought, looking at him then, that there still was. He sat beside the boy, slowly reaching his hand toward his forehead.

Going looking then, with no idea of what he was looking *for*. He'd tried to tell the others that what they'd asked of him wasn't like a healer excising a boil, but they had not understood, had counted on *him*, the mage, to understand. He only hoped that they hadn't been wrong to do so.

As soon as his fingers touched the boy's forehead, he pulled them away with a hiss. There had been something disgusting, something *revolting* in that touch. It had given him the same feeling a man might get when preparing to take a bite of food only to find his spoon swarming with maggots.

He flexed his fingers, not wanting to touch the boy again but knowing that he had no choice. The others were counting on him, even now fighting, risking their lives so that he would have an opportunity to do this. "Lucky me," he mumbled. Then, "Sorry, lad, but I think this is probably going to hurt...for both of us."

Then Chall took a deep breath and reached out again. The feeling was as strong as it was the first time but this time he did not pull away. This time, that sickening feeling washed over him in a great wave, one that seemed to want to carry him away. And so Chall did the only thing he could think to do—he let it.

CHAPTER TWENTY-FOUR

The strongest foe a man might ever face is himself.
—Common saying of the Known Lands

The first thing Cutter became aware of was grunting, hissing curses from somewhere above him. The second was that he was moving. He opened eyes tacky with sleep and was greeted with the back of a man's head above him. It took him a confused moment to realize that the man was Feledias and that the movement he'd felt was his brother dragging him across the ground on what appeared to be some sort of makeshift stretcher. "Fel?" he asked, his voice a dry rasp.

The hissing slide of the stretcher across the ground stopped, and abruptly he was falling. Cutter grunted as he struck the ground, and Fel, his hands now free of the stretcher's handles, turned to stare at him with wide eyes.

"You're awake."

"I...I think so," he said. "If this is a dream, it's a strange one."

"You son of a bitch," his brother said, his tone somewhere between relief and annoyance. "I thought you were going to die. Being perfectly honest, there were a few moments when I almost wished you would. You have any idea how damned heavy you are?"

"Sure," Cutter said. "I lift me everyday."

His brother frowned, shaking his head. "There's your version of a joke again."

"Anyway," Cutter said. "What happened?"

Feledias snorted. "You passed out, that's what happened. Oh, you can kill six men but gods forbid you do anything so pedestrian as *walk*. I've spent the better part of a day dragging your ass through the woods, having to pause every thirty seconds to cut these damned bushes out of the way with that damned axe of yours."

Cutter frowned, his thoughts returning to the barn, to the dead man, Alder, who had done nothing but try to show a little kindness in a cruel world and had promptly been punished for it. Feledias must have seen some of his thoughts on his face, for he also frowned.

"Sorry, Bernard."

"Sorry?" Cutter asked. "What for?"

Feledias sighed, rubbing at his hands, and Cutter saw that he had bandages wrapped around them, blood staining the makeshift rags where his hands must have blistered dragging the stretcher. "You were right—you said we should stay in the forest, but I insisted and because of that...because of that Alder's dead."

"It's not your fault, Fel."

"No? Then whose fault is it?"

"The assassins come to mind."

"Assassins that wouldn't have even been there if it hadn't been for us, and *we* wouldn't have been there had it not been for me. Thanks for trying, Bernard, but I have spent some time studying philosophy and logic, and this is one argument you aren't likely to win—unless, of course, you decide to give me a couple of good hits with that axe of yours."

Cutter grunted. "Don't think I'm up for hitting anything just now."

"More's the pity," Feledias said, turning away to look at the woods around them but not before Cutter saw the anguish on his brother's face.

He grunted, working his way to his feet. It was a slow process, for he hurt all over, his exertions from the night before having not only left him with a new wound but also serving to awaken the agony of those others he'd experienced in New Daltenia, ones that had just begun to heal.

He put his hand on his brother's shoulder. He did not speak, for he did not know what to say, what he *could* say. Even the greatest bards, the greatest of the world's writers, he thought, would have struggled.

Sometimes, words failed, that was all.

His brother glanced at him, a grateful look on his face. "I'm glad we're going, Bernard. To the Black Wood, I mean."

"Glad to get your chance at dying?" Cutter asked. He meant it to be a jest, to bring some levity to the moment, but his brother did not laugh or smile, only nodded.

"Yes. You said you were tired, Bernard, and I'm tired too. Fire and salt, am I tired. Tired of the world and the Fey, but mostly, I think, tired of myself."

Cutter wanted to make his brother feel better, to offer him some comfort, but the problem was that he felt much the same, so he only nodded. "Well," he said, glancing around and up at the sky. "You'll get your wish soon enough. We should only be a day, maybe two outside of the Black Woods."

"And then..." Feledias trailed off.

Cutter shrugged. "And then we'll see. Come on, Fel. Let's go."

"Are you sure—can you walk?"

Cutter considered that for a moment then finally nodded. "I can walk far enough."

***

Chall stood in darkness. A darkness more complete than any he had ever known, darker, even, than the hidden tunnel through which he and Maeve had traveled when trying to evade the assassin, Felara.

It was as if his magical connection to the boy had somehow ripped him from the world he knew and sent him hurtling into some great nothingness, one in which there was no one, no *thing*.

He was alone, more alone than he had ever been before.

And he was afraid.

He felt the panic begin to take hold, felt it in the gooseflesh on his arms, the chill that ran up his spine. *Take it easy,* he told himself. *It isn't real. However bad it is, you are within the boy's mind now, and it isn't real.*

An easy enough thing to say, to *think*, maybe, but not so easy to believe. His breath was ragged, as if he had run a mile or, if he were being honest with himself, considering the shape he was in, a few dozen feet would have been enough to do the job.

Chall had known himself long enough to know that he was not brave. Oh, he had done plenty of brave *things*, sure, but he had never been brave himself. Instead, he had always relied on Maeve and Priest, and Cutter, him most of all, borrowing from their courage to do what needed to be done. But they were not here now, *no one* was. It was only him, and his fear. And...something else.

He could smell it in his nostrils, a foulness, the smell of corruption and decay, could *feel* it in his flesh, his bones like some feverishly warm sickness spreading through him, growing more and more virulent the longer he remained here. He wanted to run then, to flee this terrible place of darkness and despair and go back to the world of the living. It was bad there, yes, but it could be no worse than this.

Only, he did not flee, for he knew that if he did, he was dooming the boy—possibly the world—to some terrible fate at the hands of alien creatures that they did not, perhaps *could not* understand. And so, he called on what little courage he had, and he did not flee. He stood.

You are Challadius the Charmer no longer, he told himself, *haven't been for a long time, maybe, but perhaps where a man loses one name, he might find another. Challadius the Courageous, perhaps? Challadius the Chivalrous?*

He snorted at that, and the noise sounded strange in that place, wrong, somehow, and that brought the fear back.

Perhaps you are a coward, he reasoned with himself, *so then don't be you. Be someone else. You're an* illusionist *after all, you bastard.* He thought of the prince then. Cutter had his faults, the gods knew the truth of that, but the man was no coward. Why run from something, after all, when you could beat it to death without getting out of breath?

But Challadius was no Cutter.

He thought of Maeve. She, too, was brave. Brave and wise, and he had wondered, sometimes, if one came from the other. But Challadius, while he was many things, was not wise, and so the thought of trying to adopt her courage here, now, was like trying to slip into a tight dress. Ridiculous and more than a little offensive.

Desperately, he cast his thoughts out further, and his mind happened upon Priest. The man always so stoic, so damned *honorable*. Chall had chided him for it often, but the truth was, he had always respected that about the man. Respected his quiet sense of duty, speaking no more than necessary, doing no more than necessary—but never doing less. The man was not possessed of a loud, angry strength like Cutter but of a quiet strength, one that came not from anger but from something else...

Belief. That was it. Belief in his goddess, yes, but more than that, a belief that things would work out, that good would, could *only* triumph, in the end. Chall had never been much of a believer in anything save another round of drinks at the tavern, or another bed with, if he was lucky, another woman waiting beneath the covers. Yet, he tried to believe now, tried with every fiber of his being, and as he tried the waves of panic began to recede a little. Not much, maybe, but hopefully enough.

"Hello?" he asked, his voice echoing in that great, nothingness. "Are you there, lad? Is *anyone* there?"

At first, there was no answer, nothing at all, in fact, until...there was.

A whimper, no more than that, the whimper not of a man but of a child in that moment when he woke from a nightmare and his mother and father had not yet arrived to console him, to assure him that those things which he feared were not real.

"Hello?" he said again. Another whimper. It was difficult to tell from which direction it came, for it seemed to come from all around him.

Chall was afraid—could not ever remember being more afraid in his life save, perhaps, for when he and Maeve had lain together, though that, at least, had been a good kind of fear, the best kind. Still, he found himself thinking of words Priest had told him once, long ago. It was years gone now, when the four of them had come upon the devastation of a village which had been attacked by the Fey, the buildings torn down to their very foundations. Some of those who had survived the attack sat with their heads slumped in defeat, moaning in despair but others—

most, really—had already begun the task of rebuilding by the time they had arrived.

Chall remembered Priest saying that they were brave, those men and women who had begun to rebuild, and Chall himself had mocked him. If they were brave, he had said, they would have joined the army and fought. And he remembered now, remembered *deeply,* what Priest had told him—*There are many forms of courage, Challadius.*

The words echoed in his mind, again and again, an answer to that darkness, that whimper, an answer even to that feeling of sickness, of decay, that was creeping into him.

There are many forms of courage. Sometimes, most times, maybe, the bravest thing a man can do once he's been knocked down is to stand up again.

He had dismissed those words at the time, dismissed them the same way he had dismissed so many things in his life. He did not dismiss them now. Now, those words served like an anchor, the only thing, it seemed, that kept him from floating away into that great darkness that surrounded him.

And so Challadius the Courageous, Challadius the Chivalrous, walked into the darkness. First one step, then another. It was not easy, taking those steps, but then living never was. The only other option, then, was to lie down and die, and given such a choice, even a coward might choose life.

Another step, another, the darkness pressing against him with each as if seeking to impede his progress, but Chall gritted his teeth and shuffled on, his hands out before him like a blind man, hoping that he would find something soon, *scared* that he would.

Another whimper came, and he did not think it was only his imagination that made it sound closer than it had before. "I'm coming," he said, his voice sounding breathless. "Just hold on a little longer." He did not know if that last was for the unseen child or for himself, perhaps both.

He continued forward and then grunted in surprise as his fingers touched something cool. He recoiled immediately but when no monster reared out of the darkness to devour him, he reached out a tentative hand again. It took him a moment, in the darkness, to realize that what he was touching was an iron bar. He moved his hand slowly left and right, touching more of them, and then he knew what it was. *A cage. It's a cage.*

A whimper came again, this time from right in front of him, so close that Chall started at the sound. Then he knelt and, as he did, something came into focus. A small candle, it's flame pitiful against the black surrounding it. A candle, but one that had shrunken until it was little more than a nub. And in its weak light, Chall saw something else—a small boy, huddled in the corner of the cage, sitting with his back pressed against it, his arms wrapped tightly around his legs. He rocked back and forth, letting out an occasional whimper.

Chall had never met Matt as a child and yet he knew him the moment he saw him. "Thank the gods, lad, you're here. Listen, it's me, Chall, I've come to…" *Come to save you,* he'd been about to say, as if he were some knight out of a storybook. "I've…I've come to help. If I can."

The boy did not respond, only went on rocking, whimpering, and Chall frowned, another feeling coming over him then. Not fear, not this time, but anger. Anger at the cage which imprisoned the terrified boy, yes, but more than that, anger at the one who had put him there. "Matt?" he asked again. "Can you hear me?"

Still no answer. For a moment, Chall was puzzled at this but then, his anger growing, he understood. In moments of great pain or tragedy, some people recoiled from life, retreating from the world into their minds, their thoughts, seeking solace there. But when even a person's mind was turned against them, where were they left to flee?

In another moment, he knew. If they could not flee into their minds, then those poor souls would do the next best thing— they fled to memory. To a remembrance of when life was better, when the world was not so cruel or, at least, if it was, they had not known it.

He did not wonder at what he had to do now, for he knew. The boy had retreated into memory, and so he must follow him. Chall took a slow, deep breath, and reached his hand through the cell bars. The moment his hand touched the boy's forehead, the child's body went rigid.

Then Chall was in another place, not in the darkness any longer but standing in the early morning sun along with hundreds, thousands of others. Not that he seemed to stand so much as float above the scene. He saw Cutter and Feledias, Maeve, and Priest, even the historian Petran Quinn, all gathered on a stage. Matt was there too, looking frightened as he moved toward the front of the platform to stand before thousands of the people of New Daltenia.

His coronation, Chall realized. *This is his coronation.* His eyes alighted on another figure standing on the stage, this one grossly overweight, and he winced as he realized it was himself. He had little time to think of it though, for the boy seemed to be looking at someone in the crowd, and Challadius followed his gaze, the breath catching in his chest as he noted the woman from Two Rivers, Emma, moving through the people in the crowd as if they were made of vapor, a cruel grin on her face.

Fear and anger warred within him at that moment. Even then, she had plagued him, had sought to take him over, perhaps had been doing so already.

"You evil bitch," Chall growled. He hurled himself toward her, *willed* himself toward her, but he did not move, for in this place, in the boy's mind, he was a spectator, that and that only. And so he was forced to watch as the woman moved onto the platform, invisible to everyone but the lad who looked at her with an expression of barely-controlled panic as she whispered something in his ear.

Then, suddenly, Matt looked up, his eyes staring directly at Chall and, once more, the world changed, pulling Chall along with it.

***

Maeve came at the assassin with everything she had, her two blades flashing in again and again like twin steel serpents. She felt better, this time, stronger, after having found some much-needed sleep. The woman was still fast, incredibly so, still strong, but she did not seem quite so fast, so strong as she had before.

For her part, while the assassin managed to evade or parry each of Maeve's blows, she was not smiling this time; instead a frown of concentration was on her face as she ducked in and out of the attacks.

Finally, Maeve saw an opening and lunged forward. The woman spun, planting her boot in Maeve's stomach and kicking her away but not before Maeve was rewarded with the feel of one of her blades sliding across the woman's arm. Not a deep cut, but as she regained her balance and stared at the woman, noting the look of shock on her face as she gazed at the cut as if unable to believe it, she thought that it was well an important one.

"Huh," Maeve said, slightly breathless as the woman's kick had nearly knocked the wind out of her, "not invincible after all, huh?"

The assassin sneered. "It's a flesh wound, nothing more."

Maeve nodded. "True," she said as they began to circle each other again. She could hear the sounds of the guards banging on the door, trying to get in, could hear Priest's grunts as he held it, but she did not turn. Her eyes were on the woman, that only, and she forced a smile she did not feel. "Only a flesh wound, but one given to you by an old woman. I asked about you, you know, in the city. Asked people about the woman who claimed to be the greatest assassin in the world, and do you know what they did?"

The woman stared at her with fury in her eyes, but she said nothing, and that was alright. "I'll tell you," Maeve said, grinning. "They laughed."

"*Lies,*" the woman hissed. "My reputation is well-known in the city. They would not laugh, they would not *dare* to laugh."

"And yet...they did," Maeve said. "I was told that you were a nothing, a nobody. Just some street waif with delusions of grandeur and, based on that cut on your arm, I'd say they're right."

The woman wasn't angry now—she was furious. Maeve could see it in the tense set of her jaw, her rigid shoulders, and could see it better still in her eyes, dancing wildly with fury. "*I'll kill you, you old bitch,*" she said, and then she was rushing forward, the time for talking done as she came at Maeve like a storm of steel.

Maeve did not try to counter, she only retreated, weathering the storm of the woman's fury. She was angry, and that was good, for angry people made mistakes, angry people didn't pay attention to the little things. Little things like the glass Maeve "accidentally" knocked off the table as she backpedaled away from the woman's blows.

The woman did not notice this, so intent was she on attacking the object of her anger. *"Fight me!"* she growled, spittle flying from her mouth.

Maeve ignored her, continuing to back away under the onslaught, circling again. Everyone, she knew, had their weakness, if one looked close enough. The cleverest tried to hide them, but others, like the assassin, wore them in the open. And there was no great wonder at what the woman's might be. It was pride.

The woman paused for a minute, her chest heaving from the effort, and Maeve grinned. "Tired, are you?" she asked, then shook her head. "Yes, it seems they were right—just a street waif, nothing more."

The woman screamed in anger then, barreling toward her. Maeve circled, moving back toward the table, back toward where the glass lay on the floor.

"Fight me you old hag!" the woman shouted.

Maeve did not though. Instead, she continued to back up, watching the floor out of the corner of her eye, noting the glass. She moved past it, tipping it with her foot and then pretending to stumble. The woman came on in a rush, as Maeve had known she would, her foot striking the glass. She let out a grunt of surprise and then she was falling forward, into Maeve's waiting dagger that pierced her through the chest.

Maeve stood there, the woman bent over her blade. "An assassin's job," Maeve whispered in the woman's ear, "isn't to fight, lass. It's to kill. Someone should have told you." She bared her teeth, her own fury showing now. "And you shouldn't have hurt Chall." And with that, she drove the blade in deeper, jerking it up and into the woman's heart. The assassin's body went rigid and then she collapsed, Maeve following her down.

***

Chall stood on a snow-covered path outside of a small home. The house was set apart from a village that he could see in the distance. The doorway stood open and, within the house, curled against a large chest, was a child, one Chall recognized as the same one he had seen in the cage.

Matt.

Chall hurried forward, stepping through the doorway. The child was sobbing, his head buried in his arms, but he looked up as Chall stepped inside.

"Wh-who are you?"

Chall winced at that, looking around the place, but if the woman, Emma, was within, she was doing a damn fine job of hiding. "Don't you know me, lad?" he asked, moving to kneel beside the boy. "It's me—Challadius."

"Challadius?" the boy asked, blinking and running his arm across his face, wiping the tears away.

Chall smiled, relieved. "That's right, lad. It's your friend, Chall."

"Challadius the Charmer?" the boy asked. "You...you look different than I expected."

Chall frowned. "Different? What do you mean, lad? I look about the same as when we met."

"Met?" the youth asked, and Chall winced in frustration. Clearly, the boy, at least this *version* of him, didn't know him, and how could he? After all, there were many years yet before disaster came to this small village, many years before they would meet in the Black Wood.

"Where is this place?" Chall asked, choosing to try a different tact. Perhaps if he could find out where they were, he would learn *why* the boy had retreated here in the first place and maybe be able to help somehow.

"You're kidding," the kid said, giving a small, shy smile, and if Chall had not loved Matt already that smile would have been enough to seal it.

"Say I'm not," he said, giving the youth a smile of his own.

"Well, this is Brighton, of course," the boy said, still smiling but with a mixture of confusion on his face now.

"Ah, right," Chall said, nodding. "And this house?"

The boy looked at him then with what might have been defiance. "This is my father's house."

"I...see," Chall said, remembering that Cutter had told him the youth had been adopted by a family in Brighton. "Your...your father and mother?"

"No," the youth said, frowning. "Not *that* father. My *real* father."

Of course. Where else would the terrified youth flee than to Cutter's side, where safer in all the world? Except, perhaps, at the man's back, out of reach of that deadly axe. "And...your father?" he asked. "Where is he?"

Tears began to gather in the boy's eyes then. "I...I don't know. I've called for him, for help but...but he hasn't come."

"Help with what, lad?" he asked.

The kid shook his head, his face paling. "You...you shouldn't have come here. It isn't...it isn't safe. She's out there, somewhere," he said, eyeing the open doorway as if he expected a monster to appear within it at any moment. "She...leaves, sometimes, but she...she never goes far."

Such was the boy's terror that Chall felt the panic begin to rise in him again, but he fought it back down with a will. "Outside, is she?"

The boy nodded.

"Well," Chall said, rising, "then we'll just close this door, how'd that be?" He moved to it, grabbed the handle, but the door didn't budge. Frowning, he tried harder. "Damned thing must be...stuck on something." He grunted and hissed, but the door refused to budge.

"It...it won't close," the boy said. "She won't let it."

Chall frowned, finally giving it up. He looked back to the youth. "This woman, do you know who she is?"

"She's mean," the boy said, not answering the question. "She...she's scary. Now...please, you have to stop talking. She'll hear."

Chall was not a man accustomed to anger, righteous or any other kind. He had always believed that when a man got angry it was all too easy to get in a fight, and fighting often led to someone getting killed, maybe him. And since he'd never much cared for the idea of dying, he had eschewed anger altogether. Annoyance, though, that he had felt plenty.

But he was not annoyed, not now. He was angry. Furious. The child knelt there weeping, terrified and alone, waiting for help that would not, *could* not, come, for the man for whom he waited had been exiled by his command, sent to his death. Only, of course, it hadn't *been* his command.

"On your feet, lad," he growled.

"No," the boy said, shaking his head furiously, "she'll...she'll see, she'll come."

"Let her," Chall said. And then, gentler as he knelt beside the boy, putting a hand on his shoulder. "You can't hide from life, lad. Take it from a man who spent the last fifteen years—" and, truth to tell, he thought a damn sight more than that—"of his life hiding. It doesn't work. Besides, hiding isn't living, is it?"

"But...she'll hurt me. She'll hurt *you*."

Chall shrugged. "She didn't invent pain, boy. I've been hurt before. Something tells me you have too. Maybe it's time we showed her that she can feel pain as much as cause it, how'd that be?"

"But...how?" the boy asked, and though he was clearly afraid, Chall could see a small glimmer of hope dancing in his gaze as he looked up. "You'll...you can beat her?"

Chall considered that then, finally, shook his head. "This is not my place, boy. Here, I am powerless."

The youth's shoulders slumped at that, but Chall forced his gaze back up to him. "But then, so is she. She is only a visitor here, lad, only as welcome as you allow her to be, for this is *your* home. *Your* place, and here, you have all the power."

"But...she said...she said that it was too late, that—"

"She lies, lad," Chall said softly, hoping that he was right, for such a possession as the Feyling had worked was not something he'd experienced before. Still, it *felt* right. "Here, she cannot hurt you, cannot control you. Only you can."

The boy seemed to consider that, then finally he rose to his feet. Chall rose with him, offering his hand, and after a brief hesitation, the boy took it. "Ready?" he asked.

The boy gave a shaky sigh but a firm, determined look came over his face in another moment, and he nodded.

"Good," Chall said, smiling, "it's time you saw the sun again, boy. Past time."

A Warrior's Curse

He led the youth to the door, stepping over the threshold and, after a pause, the boy followed.

You DARE?

The voice seemed to reverberate from everywhere, seemed to roll off the distant Barrier Mountains, from the Black Wood, like the thundering intonation of the gods themselves, and Chall felt the youth's hand tighten in his.

"Steady, lad," he said. "Smoke and mirrors, that's all it is. Just smoke and mirrors." *I hope.*

The boy nodded, and Chall took a slow breath, steadying himself. It began to rain then, and the sky, that had been clear moments before, suddenly roiled with dark, pregnant storm clouds. The wind also picked up, whipping at Chall's clothes, his hair, making the raindrops feel like a thousand tiny needles against his exposed skin.

"Steady," he said again, and whether this was for the boy or himself he couldn't have said. "You can do this, lad," he went on. *You have to.*

One minute, the road in front of Cutter's home was empty. The next, she was there, the woman from Two Rivers, her eyes dancing with fury, her fists clenched at her sides. "*Who are you?*" she demanded as she looked at Chall. "Wait," she said before he could answer, "I know you, I *remember* you. The magi who travels with the Destroyer. Well," she went on, flashing a smile that held no humor, "know that your powers are useless here, magi."

"As are yours," Chall said, forcing more confidence into his voice than he felt.

Her smile widened then. "Is that right?" she asked, then she turned to the youth. "Is it, boy?"

Chall could feel the boy's hand trembling in his grip then. "You can end this, Matt," Chall had to shout to be heard over the roaring wind. "She is not the master here—you are."

The boy, though, didn't seem to be listening. Instead, he was looking at the woman with wide, frightened eyes. "I...I can't," he said.

She laughed then, a melodic sound that was somehow terrible, carried over the wind. "Do you see, magi? He is broken, pathetic. As are all your kind. I do not have power here, you say? Come then—let me show you."

She raised her hands and thunder boomed overhead as if in answer. Chall could feel her calling on magic, could feel the power gathering, only it was not true magic, not *real* power, but her will. A powerful will, one that seemed ancient, as old as time itself. "Get behind me, lad," he said, thrusting the boy backward. He called on his own will, his own open hands stretched out at a low angle to either side, sought for his will past his fear and worry, past his certainty—one he had carried with him all his life—that he was not enough.

Suddenly, the woman thrust her hands forward and lightning shot in his direction. Chall focused his will into a blue, translucent shield in front of him and sparks flashed as their two wills met. He hissed and cursed as the shield began to give way, doing his best to force the woman's power back, but his will was no match for her own. The shield broke. Only a tiny part of it, but enough to let some of her will, some of her power, through.

Chall screamed as he flew backward. The wind was knocked out of him as he hit the ground hard, rolling across it. He knew that the ground was not real, knew, too, that the rocks which cut at him as he rolled were equally not real, but that did nothing to protect him from the pain of those scrapes.

Finally, he came to a pause, lying on his back, gasping for air. He started to try to rise, but then she was there, standing over him, her hands on her hips, a cruel smile on her face. "My power is real, magi," she said, raising one hand to the sky. A flash of light shot out from the sky and lightning like yellow fire began to coalesce around her hand. "My power is real, and you will know it before the end."

She brought her hand down then and terrible pain shot into Challadius, roared through him, and he screamed.

"*Leave him alone!*"

The pain suddenly cut off then, and Chall panted in relief. The woman turned and Chall followed her gaze to where the boy, Matt, stood, his small hands clenched into fists at his sides.

"What did you say, boy?" she demanded.

The youth quailed for a moment but then seemed to rally. "I said, *leave him alone!*" he shouted, and a wave of power erupted from him, sending the woman staggering back.

Chall saw that the woman was not smiling now but frowning, her eyes narrowed in anger. "You *dare* defy me?" she demanded. "You think you have felt pain now, boy? You think you have felt loss? You have no idea what I can do to you."

"You can't do anything," the child said. "Not here." He glanced at Challadius who gave him a weary nod before turning back to the woman. "This is *my* place."

The woman's expression flashed with what might have been panic then, but only for a moment, for then her features twisted in rage and she started forward, raising her hands to the sky as she did. Lightning surged down from the roiling clouds, and she shot her hands forward again.

"*Lad, watch out!*" Chall screamed, but he might as well not have bothered.

The twin bolts shot toward the youth who was slowly walking forward. He did not look scared, then, he looked determined, and as the energy reached him he swiped out a hand in an almost casual gesture, and the lightning went flying off to the side. The youth grinned then, continuing forward.

The woman, Emma, hissed and cursed as she threw more and more magical tendrils at the youth, but they were no more effective than the first. After a moment, Matt didn't even bother waving his hands, allowing the energy to warp and twist to avoid him as if afraid to touch him.

Then he was standing before her, the woman panting and looking afraid. "It was my mistake," the child said. His form shifted, blurred, and when it resolved, he was no longer a child but the young man Chall had met in the Black Woods. "Killing you as I did, inviting you in." He gave her a grim smile. "I will not make the same mistake again." The youth's eyes seemed to flash a deep, emerald green, one that strangely reminded Chall of the eyes of the Fey King, Yeladrian—at least before Cutter had chopped off the creature's head.

Matt reached out, seemingly in no hurry. The Feyling screamed, clearly trying to get away, but it was as if she was held in place by some unseen force. Matt placed his finger on her forehead, the barest of touches, and she arched her back in pain, screaming as if in terrible agony. Chall watched in disbelief as she suddenly began to come apart like torn fabric, pieces of her flapping away like dandelion spores until, a moment later, they disappeared altogether.

Chall was left staring in shock and, despite himself, despite the fact that he knew Matt was his friend, he was afraid as he stared at the man standing over him. It was a fear similar to that he felt whenever he witnessed Cutter fight, but there was something else in the youth's green eyes, too, something other than his father.

Then the youth looked down at him, smiled, and his eyes reverted to their normal color as he offered Chall his hand. "Chall," he said, "are you okay?"

Chall allowed himself to be pulled to his feet, grunting as he looked around. "She's really gone? I mean...did you kill her?"

"I destroyed her," Matt said, so casually that it gave Chall pause. "There is a difference. Now, the others need us. Are you ready?"

Chall blinked, nodding. "I'm ready," he said, deciding that he couldn't get out of this place quickly enough.

Matt nodded then and the world shifted once more.

***

The next thing Chall knew, he was back in the king's bedchambers, blinking and feeling drowsy as if he'd just come awake from a very deep sleep.

Matt was there too, looking at him. The youth smiled, and while he was clearly the same young man he had been before the Feyling's possession, Chall felt that there was also something different about him, something that reminded Chall of Cutter. "Okay?" the youth asked.

Chall nodded, running a hand across his sweaty forehead. "I think so." Then he remembered Maeve, and he shot to his feet. He paused in shock as he saw Maeve standing over the woman Felara who lay on the ground, a knife sticking from her heart.

Maeve sported several cuts and scrapes where the woman's attacks had clearly scored her, but she was still alive, thank the gods. "Maeve!" Chall shouted, rushing forward and pulling her into a tight embrace. "You're alive."

"Only just," the woman said tiredly, hugging him back.

"But...I thought you said she was better than you," Chall said.

Maeve shrugged. "I was motivated. And Matt? What happe—"

"I'm fine," the youth said, walking forward with a smile. "It's good to see you, Maeve."

She grinned, pulling him into an embrace. "Ah, but it's good to have you back, lad." She leaned back, looking at him then. "You are *back*, aren't you?"

He grinned. "I am."

"A little...help, if it's not too much trouble," a voice said, and they all turned to see Priest standing on the rubble of the broken-down door, wielding a chair to keep what looked like an army full of guardsmen gathered in the hallway outside the chamber at bay.

"Stop!" Matt shouted. "These are my friends!"

The guards stopped, staring at each other uncertainly. "Majesty?" he asked. "Are...that is, are you sure?"

Matt grinned, putting a hand on Chall's shoulder, another on Maeve's. "I have never been more sure of anything in my life. Now, please, leave us."

The men did as requested after two moved into the room to retrieve Felara's corpse, and minutes later the four of them sat, exhausted, at the room's table.

"I'm sorry again, to all of you," Matt said. "For...all the trouble."

"Nothing to apologize for, lad," Chall said. "After all, it's not every day that a person gets possessed by a Feyling, is it?"

The youth gave an embarrassed smile, reminding Chall of the child he'd been in his mind. "I guess not. Anyway, I'm still sorry. To my dad, too. I'd like to tell him." He frowned then. "Where is he, anyway?"

The other three shared a glance, and Chall turned to him. "You...don't remember?"

Matt shook his head, clearly frustrated. "Only...bits and pieces of the last week. It's as if...as if I was dreaming, sort of."

Chall grunted. "Well, lad, in some ways, you were, though I think it's safe to call that one a nightmare."

The youth nodded, smiling. "Anyway. My father?"

"Right," Chall said, wincing as he glanced at Maeve and Priest, "look, lad, about your father..."

CHAPTER TWENTY-FIVE

*A man's life is like a path he walks
A path upon which he can only move forward.
He may look back at the trail behind him, but he may never again revisit it
It lies in the past, that trail, and therefore well beyond his reach.
—Rodarian Dalumis, poet, excerpt from "The Ramblings of Life from a Rambling Life"*

Cutter pulled his mount—a draft horse he'd procured in a small village they passed—to a halt. A moment later, Feledias pulled his own horse to a stop beside him and, for a time, the two brothers sat silently staring at the woods in front of them. Finally, Cutter dismounted and a few seconds later his brother followed suit.

"You sure we shouldn't take the horses?" Feledias asked.

"They won't go any farther," Cutter said, gazing at the great forest spread out before him. It was early morning and yet the woods were dark, as they always were. "Not into the Black Woods."

Feledias grunted. "Wiser than us, then."

"Yes."

Feledias gave a heavy sigh at that. "I'm sorry, you know."

Cutter glanced at him. "What for?"

His brother shrugged. "Everything, I guess."

Cutter nodded. "I'm sorry too, Fel." He thought of Matt then, at the castle, thought of the others, and of Layna, but Matt most of all. "I'm sorry too. For all of it."

Feledias gave him a small smile. "Well. Are you ready?"

Cutter shrugged. "Yes." He started forward then. Into the Black Woods, into a darkness that, it seemed, had been waiting for him all his life. He paused on the edge of the forest, standing halfway between the light of the world and the shadow of the Black Wood, and stared back at the kingdom he had left, *his* kingdom. He remained that way for a time, trying to etch it into his memory, soaking in the warmth of the sun, for he did not think that he would feel it again.

"Alright," he said to his brother, "let's go."

And then, side by side, the brothers stepped into the waiting darkness.

And now, dear reader, we have come to the conclusion of *A Warrior's Curse.*

I hope you found your most recent journey into the Known Lands to be…well, if not pleasant, at least enjoyable. The next book in the series will be coming soon.

In the meantime, if you're looking for something else to read, don't worry—I've got you covered.

Want another story of an anti-hero in a grimdark setting where a jaded sellsword is forced into a fight he doesn't want between forces he doesn't understand?
Get started on the bestselling seven book series, The Seven Virtues.

Interested in a story where the gods choose their champions in a war with the darkness that will determine the fate of the world itself?
Lose yourself in The Nightfall Wars, a complete six book, epic fantasy series.

Or how about something a little lighter? Do you like laughs with your sword slinging and magical mayhem? All the world's heroes are dead and so it is up to the antiheroes to save the day. An overweight swordsman, a mage who thinks magic is for sissies, an assassin who gets sick at the sight of the blood, and a man who can speak to animals…maybe.
The world needed heroes—it got them instead.
Start your journey with The Antiheroes!

If you enjoyed *A Warrior's Curse,* you'd make my day if you took a moment to leave an honest review. It only takes a minute but it makes a tremendous difference!

If you'd like to reach out, you can email me at Jacobpeppersauthor@gmail.com or visit my website. You can also give me a shout on Facebook or on Twitter. I'm looking forward to hearing from you!

Turn the page for a limited time free offer!

Sign up for my new releases mailing list and for a limited time get a FREE copy of *The Silent Blade,* the prequel book to the bestselling epic fantasy series *The Seven Virtues.*
Go to JacobPeppersAuthor.com to get your copy now

Note from the Author

And so we have reached the end of *A Warrior's Curse*. But for Cutter and his companions, I am afraid it is only just the beginning.

For the kingdom of the Known Lands is sick, dying, maybe. Yet still, like a patient writhing upon his sickbed under the ministrations of healers, it might yet be saved, might yet be brought back to health.

But the road back, as with the patient twisting beneath the healer's bloody knife, will no doubt be a painful one.

Cutter, the greatest warrior of his age, journeys with his brother into the Black Wood, an alien place of old magic and older feuds, a place of the Fey, a place of death.

Meanwhile, in New Daltenia, Cutter's companions have saved Matt, the king, from the Feyling Emma's possession. But that possession was only one small piece of what they face, and the work has only just begun.

All that has come before was only but a prelude. Here, then, is the true story. Now begins the Saga of the Known Lands.

I would like to take this opportunity to thank all of those who made a tremendous difference in the writing of this book or, in the case of my wife and children, my life in general. Thank you to my baseball-bat-wielding son, Gabriel, for making sure daddy was wide awake to write by the shortcut of hitting him in the knees a few times when he wasn't paying attention. Thank you to my daughter, Norah, whose refusal to sleep at night has educated me on just how long a man can go without sleep of his own. And thank you, of course, to my wife, Andrea, who has chosen—I never said wisely—to embark on this journey of life with me. Pray for her, if you can. I'm sure she could use it.

I also want to thank my beta readers who have so graciously offered their time and energy to help my books be better and have even done so with a minimal of name-calling which, no doubt, I would have largely deserved.

And lastly, thank *you*, dear reader. You who, with your support and comments and reviews always make me want to strive to do better, to be better. I can't promise I will be—but I promise I'll try. So stick around, alright? It only gets better from here...

Probably.

Until next time,
Happy Reading,
Jacob Peppers

About the Author

Jacob Peppers lives in Georgia with his wife, his son, Gabriel, newborn daughter, Norah, and three dogs. He is an avid reader and writer and when he's not exploring the worlds of others, he's creating his own. His short fiction has been published in various markets, and his short story, "The Lies of Autumn," was a finalist for the 2013 Eric Hoffer Award for Short Prose. He is the author of the bestselling epic fantasy series *The Seven Virtues* and *The Nightfall Wars*.

Printed in Great Britain
by Amazon